Mustang Valley

Sienna Judd

To becoming damn good at who we are, instead of chasing perfect.

Chapter One

MOLLY

I WAIT at the edge of a waterfall shower, hoping it doesn't blast hot, then cold, like it did at my old place. There, I had to rush in and out of the unpredictable spray in bursts to rinse, wishing my hair wasn't so long. But here, in this beautifully furnished new apartment, everything is pristine, and the temperature stays at one hundred and two degrees. The fancy dial says so.

Morning light streams in through a small, glazed window, illuminating the travertine-tiled bathroom in a soft, sandy glow. I rub suds through my hair. Life is about to change for the better. I hope it will. I need it to.

I don't want to hurry through this first shower here, but I have to, so I lather my legs with foam and quickly run a razor in long strokes over my calf. With water massaging my back, I recall the ways I hustled to get here, under this perfect spray in a bathroom fit for a Fifth Avenue spa. I got up earlier than all the other stable hands, found and corrected any mishaps and poor horse care. I even did that damn spreadsheet on cost efficiency of feed and stall bedding.

I didn't enjoy asking a high schooler working the weekend shifts at the stables to double-check my basic Excel formulas. I wasn't exactly a straight-A student in high school, and that was almost ten years ago. But to get the job, my humility was worth it.

I can still see Colton Hunter, CEO of PMR, Purple Mountain Enterprises, nodding and pulling his lips downward, his brow furrowed and impressed. After the interview he granted me, he gave me my dream job along with a shiny, unused key to this beautiful apartment. That key is the whole reason I came to Starlight Canyon in the first place. That key is compensation worth more than my paycheck.

I rinse off excess shaving foam like it's the murkier moments of my old life slipping off me down the drain. But it seems like yin and yang are true. Because apparently with every dream, there is a nightmare. There's only one catch to this aspiration of mine coming full circle. I have to live with Dashiell Hunter. My boss. The lone wolf. Man of few words. Notorious grump. And the cowboy whose hat I had to go over to get this job through his CEO brother.

When I moved to Starlight Canyon for my fourth stable-hand gig, it was because I saw the ad for manager and the apartment that came with it. I knew I'd mostly be competing with seasonal workers who would come and go, and that my three years' stable experience would give me an advantage. Thing was, Dash, wasn't interested in actually hiring anyone, including me.

So, I went to his brother, head honcho of every single business the Hunters own, and showed him why I was the best hire. Dash might not take kindly to that, but I'll figure it out when I have to. Giving up easy isn't in my DNA. Whether nature or nurture, my balled-up fists are here to stay. If Dash wants me out, he'll need more than his snake-skin boots to do it.

I close my eyes and let the warm, soothing water rain on my face. God, it feels good to be almost there. I have less than three months to get this plan over the finish line, and only one thing stands in my way. That one thing *is* my boss, but I know I can figure out a way to get the apartment to myself. Dash might be my nightmare, but I'm probably his, too.

How little time he spends around us ranch hands, or anyone for that matter, tells me he'll likely move out when he realizes I'm not going. It will only be a matter of time. Hopefully. It's not like this apartment is the only place for him to live. The Hunters have plenty of options. He used to live with his sister over on the private side of the ranch, she told me so herself. And even though it's hard to believe, given his grouchy disposition, she also said she misses living with him.

I don't want to leave this shower. I wish I could stay under it until the hot water runs out. But Colt Hunter offered me more than a job and keys. He threw me a friendly piece of advice. Dash apparently works at night and sleeps a lot of the day. I wouldn't be surprised if it's because he's a werewolf. Colt said if I'm out the door working by five-thirty, I should be able to avoid Dash in the apartment most days.

Since I usually hit the stables by then, I figure I'd better keep that schedule because avoiding his royal grumpiness while he lets Colt's undermining decision marinate is defi-nitely a good idea.

Reluctantly, I turn off the dial, and the shower stops. I sigh and remind myself I can have another one in here whenever the hell I want. This place is mine. Home. I allow myself a few more moments of satisfaction, then step out into the steamy space and onto the plush, deep-pile rug. I wriggle my toes into the soft surface, and a tight squeal escapes. This bathroom is so damn lush. I can't wait to have my sister here with me.

I look around and don't see my towel. I don't know what time it is, but I was only in the shower for seven minutes or so, maybe a little more. I'm sure there's a cushion of time before Dash gets back, so I confidently swing open the door and stride to the room where I left my suitcase this morning.

I scurry along the floor, hoping in vain I don't leave water-shaped footprints to the bedroom I claimed as my own. There are two in the apartment, both identical in decor, but one, though sparsely populated, had evidence of male belongings on a shelf and a digital alarm clock on the nightstand, so I left my suitcase on the top of the bed in the other, assuming it was vacant.

But when I turn around the oak doorjamb, ninety degrees into said room that is supposed to be empty, it isn't anymore.

Even though my heart is racing like a hummingbird, I'm completely paralyzed. Because there is Dash Hunter, staring at me and my dripping body, stained pink from hot water, naked as the day I was born, right there in front of him.

It all happens in less than a second, but every embarrassing moment unfolds as if in slow motion. Dash holds my Elsie Silver book and tosses it down quickly. Though I clearly startled him, though he has a buck-naked employee before him, though this suitcase and that romance book are total intruders, his gaze is the same as always. His piercing green eyes absorb me and my birthday suit like we're just another nuisance.

I rush back around the doorframe, heart pounding against my ribcage, crumpling at how it's shitty enough Dash doesn't want me here and now he's seen me in the buff? *Damn it.* I don't like anyone seeing me without clothes, but certainly not my boss. *Definitely* not Dash who floats around this place with judgment in his shoulders and constant disapproval in his grunts. Fucking hell. He definitely noticed the stretch marks on my upper thighs, rosy like a fresh swipe from a tiger claw after that hot shower.

I send my voice around the doorframe to the glowering face I see in my mind's eye. "I forgot my towel. Can you hand it to me, please?"

He doesn't say a word. My scorching embarrassment stops time. My heart thrashes. Every drop of water slides off my body dramatically and explodes on the floor, messing up *his* space. It seems to take forever before he extends my towel through the doorway in a large, manly, very tanned hand.

I grab it hastily. "Thank you." I wrap it around my boobs as much as I can. Now I wish I had a bigger towel. Staring at the ceiling, I shake my head as if telling the universe I can't believe she did this to me.

The last thing I want to do is turn and face Dash wearing only a terrycloth strip. And the second to last thing I want to do is tell him about me living here before his brother does. Or maybe Colt already did? But by the way he threw my book down, as if caught by surprise, he had no clue he'd be finding me and my things here this morning.

I squeeze my eyes shut and take a few cleansing breaths.

I remind myself I'm not doing this just for my own personal gain. This cause is bigger than me. And that? That gives me the strength to square myself in the doorjamb. Still, I cling to the tuck of my towel, white knuckled.

I prepare to launch into a speech about tolerating each other, but to my surprise, Dash speaks first. I haven't heard his voice many times. It's rare for him to speak. He's not much of a manager around here. And when he gives directions, he usually does it with nods, head tilts, and high eyebrows show his disappointment.

The sound comes into the space, flat but rich, masculine, and damn if this man doesn't have a panty-melting voice. "Colt hired you."

I smile innocently, because I am innocent, and also because I want to show Dash I'm harmless. I don't want to fight with him. I don't like fighting with anyone, but I will always stand my ground. "He did."

I wait to see if he will say something else. He holds his tongue, but his gaze wanders the length of my body. He considers me, staring with inquisitive eyes that have me wriggling inside. This man wears *I don't give a fuck* like a badge of honor. He's a mystery. He stands there, keeping me waiting and curious. The moment is as if quiet thunder rolls in a sky that could boil over, or could drop a torrential downpour.

I refuse to avert my eyes in this duel, and while he watches me, I have a chance to really see him, too. And boy, is he something else. One hundred percent cowboy, with broad shoulders, strong hands, and muscular thighs obvious right through his Wranglers. I bet his skin smells of earth and leather and tobacco and just like gasoline I know it's not good for me to inhale him, but I want to.

I shake off the unexpected attraction when I remember

I'm not in the most professional attire for this conversation. I straighten my spine, and since he's not talking, I launch the speech I prepared for this moment. "It's no secret you don't like me..."

He crosses his arms. Tattoos flex, and his biceps stretch the fabric of his rolled-up sleeves. He's prepared to listen, and I note he doesn't correct me.

"... but I know we can share this place harmoniously. So it works for both of us..." *At least until I figure out a way to make you move back in with your sister over on the private side.*

His arms still crossed, he listens with firm lips and shifts to his other foot.

I try to impress upon him how serious I am. I know Dash doesn't like people who aren't from the Canyon. Hell, he doesn't like anybody. The best thing I can do is to show him I'm not some freeloader. "You didn't want to hire a stable manager..."

"That's because we don't need one, Sunshine." His words are slow, deliberate, and the timbre is deceptively comforting.

I glance down at my yellow towel. *Sunshine.*

Though I don't see Dash around much, it's true that the place runs smoothly for the most part. But I've found hooves unpicked and wet shavings left in the stalls more than once since being here. And once is enough.

I ignore his comment. "I worked seriously hard to earn this position. I come in earlier than anyone every day. I've made cost-reduction spreadsheets to show I'm serious about keeping the place lucrative. I even asked your sister if she could put on a workshop to teach more of the stable hands about horse care and how to spot common ailments."

He swallows, and his throat bobs. I've never noticed

how thick and muscular his neck is until now. He points his tongue into his cheek. A cheek that tumbles into a sharp, sexy jawline visible even under a five o'clock shadow. I really hope we can avoid each other because all these sexy details are derailing.

"I'll do a good job, Dash." My voice is as tight and determined as my fingers clutching the yellow towel. I try another smile. "Listen, it's not ideal for me either to cohabitate here with you. This apartment was supposed to be sole use for the stable manager."

His lips curve upward into a cynical half-smile. "Presumptuous."

I slap my hands on my hips, but the towel falls slightly, and I yank it up along with my dignity. I am *not* presumptuous. I'm anything but. I work hard. I don't expect handouts. I've never been given one in my life.

To Dash, most seasonal workers are golden spoon-fed kids with time and money to explore the Wild Wild West before they head back to their tame lives. That's why he doesn't think any of us deserve more than one word from him. When he is around at the yard, which isn't often, the most he says is "Hoof" or "Sweep" or "Water." Giving directives with a single word and the point of a finger, like we don't all speak the same language.

Presumptuous. I didn't know his vocabulary stretched this far, but his fancy word couldn't be more wrong.

My life wasn't tame before ranch work, and it never will be. But I'm not having a get-to-know-you conversation. My only aim now is to get us on tolerant terms, so I remind him the accommodation as compensation isn't my idea, it was theirs.

"The job description and compensation are right there on the ranch website, and it clearly states a two-bedroom apartment is part of the payment for the stable manager. I only get one bedroom. I can deal with meeting halfway if you can."

I glance around the luxurious open-plan space. Only the Hunters could afford such a palace to be above horse stalls. "This place is a thousand times more beautiful than I thought it would be. I never thought I'd live somewhere like this. So if I have to live here with you, I'll make the most of it." I appeal to him. "I'm a good roommate. I'm not messy. I'll be out working a lot. I'm sure we're both grown up enough to be civil."

His eyes narrow, then open again, and his normal blank stare is gone as a flurry of thoughts flash behind his green gaze. My optimism gets the best of me because I think he's about to be reasonable.

He's not. He turns on his heel and starts packing up my suitcase. "You can't stay here, Molly. I'll figure it out, but you are not staying in this apartment."

"Colt said..."

He shoves bras and panties and all sorts of things he shouldn't have in his hands back into the overstuffed space and closes the lid. "I'll deal with Colt... we'll find you somewhere to live..."

"Dash! Stop."

He stops but doesn't look up.

"I need to get dressed." This isn't going well. I have to do something.

The cowboy wipes his hands on his dusty jeans. He nods down at the suitcase, like he's settled a score with it. This man is a tough nut to crack, but his posture is less stiff and assured than before, and I wonder if there's still a sliver of hope.

How can I convince him not to go running to Colt? The

Hunters are inseparable, and blood is thicker than water. I won't stand a chance...

Dash keeps his gaze in the distance, past me, as he heads for the door, and his cool draft wafts over my arm.

Just when he's halfway out the door, broad back and shoulders to me, a lightbulb goes on. My Hail Mary.

"I can't live anywhere else. The reason the stable manager stays here is to monitor things as many hours of the day as possible. Do you really want me living away from the horses?"

He extends an arm up the doorjamb as if he's bracing himself. I stay focused on my argument, but his muscular ass fills my peripheral vision. He pauses, and I give him time to think about my words. He might not love people, but his affection and passion for the horses is like watching the sun rise. It's the most natural thing in the world and yet somehow awe-inspiring.

His ribcage widens, he breathes in deeply, and once he lets it out, he faces me. He takes slow steps into the room, leans against the wall, and props the heel of one boot up on it. In other conditions, I'd melt at this image. Between the undone buttons of his shirt, his pecs create a deep line that plunges down the middle of a dewy bronze chest. Even though it's around quarter past five in the morning, his skin bears the sheen of a cowboy just home from a day's work. Knee bent, thumbs hooked through two belt loops, his thigh stretches a pair of well-ridden jeans, and not a single man around here rivals this view.

I shake the attraction that has no place in my well-laid plan and reach back to the contract agreement. "We both know mistakes are being made at the stables. An extra set of eyes will keep the horses healthy. And living here is a necessary part of the package."

He flares his nostrils. "You know what else is part of the package? Me being your boss."

I swallow hard. He lets me sweat. Is he going to tell me Colt had no right hiring me? Is he going to tell me to get some damn clothes on and do as I'm told?

"Let's lay down some ground rules."

Ground rules?

"One, never go in my bedroom."

Oh my God, am I staying? I shake my head. "I would never..."

"Two. No questions."

"What do you mean, no questions?" I tilt my head.

He deadpans. "No questions about anything personal. You ask me about the horses, the stables, the mountain trails, suppliers and contacts... fine. This is a professional arrangement. We'll keep it that way." He pushes off the wall, preparing to leave. "I'm not your friend."

I don't need to be his friend, but my stomach drops anyway.

He heads through the door but leans back into it, throwing his voice over his shoulder. "You might want to buy some earplugs."

I try to lighten the mood, because there definitely is one. "Do you snore? The walls seem pretty thick."

He doesn't face me. "My alarm is loud, and I get up early."

"It's okay. I do, too."

He tosses me a look over his shoulder. "You don't get up this early."

Chapter Two

DASH

I'm TRYING HARD NOT to wish I was the water trapped in the terrycloth hourglass before me. It was bad enough when I found her suitcase here this morning. Worse when she came around the corner, dripping wet and curvy as a classic pinup girl, making me temporarily forget I don't want her here.

Molly. Colt went and hired her behind my back. I knew he had his eye on her for manager since about two weeks after she moved here. He said so months ago when we were drinking at Sly's. He said she had potential.

She came to me, a couple of months ago in May, asking for the job. I threw her request to the side, and now... I'm fucked. Clearly. Because instead of swatting aside her request to stay here in the apartment, I used most of my energy keeping my jaw off the floor. I'd never noticed the way Molly looked before. Hell, I don't know what most of

12

the ranch hands look like, but I'm pretty sure after seeing her luscious, glistening skin, even passing her from a distance all I'll think about is the lush crevasse between her breasts I know are... well...

"How early do you get up?" she asks, almost cute, as if she can handle my schedule.

"That's a question..." Despite my habit to get the hell away from people as fast as possible, I find my gaze lingering again on those soft, creamy mounds pushing out of her yellow towel.

Only now that I'm staring at the voluptuous skin pouring out of her scanty attire is my head coming to. A twang of guilt runs through me, high-pitched, like nails on a chalkboard. I should have let her at least get properly dressed before we hashed this out. But I hate surprises, and this was one of the worst kind. Still, it isn't right, her defending her side in a flimsy towel.

People describe me in many ways. Broody. Grumpy. Melancholy. I see it differently. I just like to be alone. But the one quality the general public and I agree on is that I'm a gentleman. Finding Molly here in my apartment has me compromising my values. I put my hat back on to hide both the view of her curves and my eyes from hers. I nod a farewell with my gaze on the floor and take myself out of her bedroom.

I need out of here.

I have two more horses to check on before I can find Colt in his office and try like hell to get myself out of this.

———

Two hours later, my ass hits leather with a thud when I throw it down on Colt's office couch and toss my hat beside me. I want to tower over him, stand in front of him and lean down over the desk to tell it like it is. But I've been up since three a.m. and looked in on over forty horses. For once, the workers left things halfway decent, and there wasn't much to do, so there's a lot of fight left in me, but not much standing.

My brother gives the briefest of glances and continues working. He taps a key with a stiff index finger and spins the few degrees it takes to face me. "You're up late. Or should I say early?"

"Colt..." I warn, shaking my head. I'm not in the mood for antics. Hell, I'm never in the mood, but he couldn't have picked a worse time to try. "You went over my head."

He glances at his screen again, slides his mouse around, and clicks. It's clear by his lack of urgency he was expecting me. Of course he was.

He lets out one of those sighs that flaps your lips. "I gave you plenty of opportunity, Dash. I told you a million times to hire someone. I mentioned Molly as a prospect months ago. Is this really a surprise?" He tilts his head to the side like I need to think harder. "We also agreed to bring in extra horse stock a few weeks ago. Doubling our horse stock to expand changes things significantly. We need more permanent workers, and you need a manager or you'll have even less time than you do now. You don't do much living as it is."

"I like my life."

"Horses aren't humans."

"No. They're better."

My brother shakes his head and rubs his fingers in his eye sockets. Here Colt goes again. He was single for over a decade, and now that he's found his soulmate, he thinks there's one for every one of us and is constantly projecting his love of companionship on me. I don't need it. We're different.

He's wrong about me needing time to socialize but he's right about one thing. I *have* known about our expansion for a long time. No matter how hard I wish it to be untrue, I can't take care of eighty horses. I know it. Colt knows it.

Only two things matter to me in this whole damn world. My family. And the horses. Cowboy blood runs deep in the Hunters, and horses unite us. They also provide us a livelihood. All I want is to perform my duty, hang on to the only identity I know, live my quiet life with my horses... but to do that, there's a catch. In order to fulfill my duty to the creatures, and do it well, I need a partner. And that is very much *not* who I am. I'm a solo act, not a circus.

A frustrated sigh escapes, and I rake my nails through my hair. I know I need a stable manager but how on earth am I going to live with someone? And not just any someone. *Molly*. A woman who, even though I never had a good look at before today, and boy, was it a *gooood* look, has an undeniable positive presence in the stable yard. I've always known the ones that fuck up, and it's never been her. I noticed she does a good job around here but I didn't pay attention to what she does. I noticed *how* she does it. Like a warm breeze. I'm not one to say how I feel but I do respect the way she works. Coupled with the momentary but intense urge to disrespect that tight space between her glorious tits, well, she's the last roommate I'd choose.

I could move back in with Jolie. But then, I'd be too far away to keep a close eye on all the change.

Colt continues. "That's why I've been on your case for months to choose a stable manager." He sighs and shakes his head, throwing his hands up, exasperated, like he often is with me. "Or you could have trained someone up if you didn't think anyone's up to your standard."

I rub my palms against my jeans hard and fast until they're warm. Colt gave me plenty of time, and I'm not one to argue for the sake of it.

When all my siblings were in town last, we had one of our quarterly meetings for Purple Mountain Enterprises, a conglomerate of several businesses our father started. All the siblings have a stake in something, and Colton, the oldest of us four, has been CEO since Dad passed. It might piss me off from time to time that he always has the final say, but much as I like to think otherwise, nobody, not even my mom, was prepared to take the reins after my dad died.

Colt is level-headed in a way that none of the rest of us are. He can deny himself for the sake of others in a way most people can't. So I listen to the words I already know are coming. We'll both agree Molly is staying, but I'm not keen to admit I was a fool even though I know it.

I only have the same twenty-four hours in a day everyone else does. I'm pissed at myself. Maybe I could have asked my friend, Mateo, to work with me and I would have kept the apartment to myself. Maybe I could have cast a wider net throughout Starlight Canyon, asked our family friends, the Danes, for some referrals. But now, I'm stuck with my brother's decision because there isn't anybody remotely close to Molly's work ethic within hiring distance.

Colt's blows are softer than the ones I give myself. "I know how much you care about the horses, Dash, and I get that it's in your blood to micromanage something you care about so strongly. I'm like that with my daughter, so don't think for a minute I don't understand you."

Colt is always empathetic, which is annoying because it makes it even harder to be mad at him and see this as his fault. I dig deep for a way to fight him, but he's not doing this to piss me off. He plays his role. And I'll have to play mine no matter how uncomfortable this gets.

He continues to drive his point home. "I know you think you do the best job of anyone, and for the record, I agree with you. You're amazing with those animals. I've seen you save more than one or two lives on this ranch, but there are only so many hours in a day. You're like thirty going on a hundred with those dark circles under your eyes. No man alive can care for eighty-plus horses on their own."

He folds his hands together on his desk, waiting to hear my retort. I turn over all the happenings from the past couple of months, digging for just one good reason Molly shouldn't be stable manager, but I can't because she does a good job with the horses, and the other ranch workers seem to like her, too. Worse than giving up some control over the horses, though, is the necessary evil that comes along with it. The stable manager needs to live above the stables just like Molly said. It's not just a perk, it's protection.

We need eyes on those beautiful beasts, and having been up many times myself checking in hourly on a horse with colic or waiting for a foal to be born, I know you can't do that from twenty or thirty minutes away in town.

I just don't want her living in my house. I don't want to be around anybody but definitely not someone so opposite of me. I am the clouds; she is the sunshine. I've seen it more than once. She makes people smile. They're always happy around her. She touches people on the arm when she talks to them. I don't want anybody touching me on the arm.

Especially not one who smells like that delicious strawberry-mint cloud wafting out of the bathroom this morning.

I chew on all the events leading up to this while my brother waits for me to speak. He didn't exactly pull the wool over my eyes. I was an idiot not to take Colt more seriously, for not taking the future of the business that's supposed to be my responsibility more seriously. For not having the foresight that could have had me a small log cabin built by now.

And yet again, I'm the one who put myself in this crappy position. I proposed bringing in more horses. The horses bring in the high-paying tourists, not the Michelin-star restaurant in the resort. Not even the spa. Unsurprisingly, people go to dude ranches to be dudes. And dudes need horses. At our last business meeting, the budget was set.

A few weeks back, Colt showed me the plans for the new barn going up in the upcoming months, and we'll double our stock of horses over winter. This should not be as surprising as the words I read in Molly's dirty book for the few minutes I waited for her to come out of the shower. I should have seen the problem coming. Now, the problem I ignored lives in my home.

I still have to put my irritation somewhere. "So did you make the first move? Or did Molly?" I'm not sure if I'd rather blame my blood or my employee. Both are shitty options. Both I can't escape.

He chews his bottom lip. "Did she come to you mid-May asking about the job?"

"Mmm."

"Well, that was my first move. I told her to approach you. It's October now, Dash. It's not like I've been making rash decisions."

"Mmm."

I remember that conversation in May. Molly brought me a whole business plan. She probably thought I ignored it, not getting back to her, but I didn't. It's a good plan. It just wasn't one I was prepared to give her control over. And more than that, I knew the apartment was one of the perks, and so, much as she sparked my attention, I didn't follow through.

I need to be alone. I need my space.

Starlight Ranch has a few residences besides the hotel. Big Sky is the main house where Colt lives, our mom has a granny flat attached. Bird's Eye is the house my dad built for us kids to share or use as and when.

I used to live in Bird's Eye. Then, my sister, Jolie, moved back to the Canyon, and rightfully so, into one of the four bedrooms at the property equally owned by us siblings. For years, I lived there alone. My other brother, Logan, has always made the big bucks playing hockey and has his own castle. Colt took Big Sky to have space for him and his daughter.

When Jolie moved back home and in with me, I couldn't deal with her being there. She doesn't annoy me, but she wanted to know why I do what I do, and even after all these years, I don't want to talk about it. So I planted myself in the apartment intended for a stable manager, telling a hurt Jolie, who was excited to be *roomies* (her word, not mine), I should have done it a long time ago to look after the horses better.

Colt's still in lecture mode. "I've been watching the stable hands for a while, and Molly has potential. I told her to make her intentions known to you in the summer. She wants the job. She wants to stay here long-term in Starlight Canyon. She has passion for this. She really does. It's a passion I know you'll identify with."

I dig my thumbs into my eye sockets. "All right, let me get this straight. I didn't respond to Molly, and she went over my head to you." It's a statement, not a question, since the woman in the yellow towel is evidence enough.

"She did. I hope you can respect her for that. She has tenacity."

I lean back against the leather couch, stare at the ceiling, and press my fingertips together.

"Hey." Colt massages me with his voice.

I'm too tight for him to make a difference.

"She's going to be great. Did you even read her business plan? She worked hard on it. She's not just some city girl who always wanted a pony. She's serious. She has three, nearly four years' experience already. And we need that around here. She's someone you can work with or I wouldn't have done this. There aren't many personality types I would pair up with yours, believe you me."

I don't argue there aren't many matches for me because zero is the actual number. And *not many* is a solid educated guess.

I swipe my hand down my face and lean over, elbows on knees and head hung. There's no use arguing with Colt. He's not messing with me. He's never been that kind of big brother. Not like Logan who loves a practical joke or two. Colt has had to be responsible from a young age when my dad died and much as I constantly resist, he's considering the family, and just as importantly, the horses. I'll never say it out loud, but my schedule is wearing on me, and the nightmares I used to have once in a while are growing thicker because of my exhaustion.

I already came to terms with Molly having the job before I even entered his office, but I still can't stomach her living with me. I consider if I can last a winter in the Canyon in a tent. "Just tell me we can build another apartment over the second barn."

I glance up, and there's that empathy again in Colt's brown eyes, but also, they don't answer how I want them to.

I shake my head and pull my lips into a tight line. "Colt, you have to get the plan redrawn. I'm not a demanding person. You know that. I keep my head down, roll up my sleeves, and get shit done without moaning. But I need to live alone."

"That's going to tack on some time to the build." His mind immediately starts calculating the cost.

I know I'm asking a lot. Colt might run the conglomerate, but when it comes to the bottom line for the horse side of things, I've got it on lock. We aren't making much money on the resort business yet. Not really. I know that.

Shifting from a working ranch to this luxury resort with a spa and a restaurant epic enough to woo a Michelin-star chef to the Canyon was a huge investment. It's one where we have yet to rise much beyond a flatline of profit. This play for more horses will help get us off zero for the first time since opening the gates.

Me asking for the barn to take longer and cost more money doesn't make business sense. But my instincts insist on it. "How long, Colt? I'll let this Molly thing go and give her a fair chance, but that other apartment needs doing."

I hate asking him for this. Colt is busy as hell. He's already managing a new house build on the private land for Sam, his wife's, family. He has a special needs daughter with lots of hobbies... I silently promise myself to take Eve out to a rodeo and give him and Sam a date night if he agrees to this.

Colt doesn't deny me, but he does let out an exasperated sigh. "We've already broken ground, so I think we can still get this done in a couple months."

Two months.

I take my hat off the leather cushion and put it on my head. "Thank you." Pressing my knuckles into the sofa, I push up, ready to get home for some food, reading, and hopefully, some sleep.

When I get back to the apartment, Molly is gone. But her sweet scent still lingers just as much as the sexy image of those droplets of water on her shoulders and her long brown locks, wet and clinging to her chest.

When I bask under the shower myself, I can practically feel her presence in there, can imagine her rubbing the strawberry-mint shower gel she left in here all over her feminine curves. It's been a long time since I shared personal space with a stranger. And an even longer time since it's been with a woman as beautiful as Molly.

I let my hand wander down to my dick and stroke it smoothly with my eyes closed, imagining it easing in and out of the dark, deep crease between her breasts. My dick throbs at the thought of squeezing her tits tighter together, wrapping her soft skin around my shaft, thrusting deep between them. I'm hard as fuck, harder than maybe I've ever been in just a split second of thinking about her curves. And when I let my mind wander to what my fingers might feel searching up under that yellow towel, it takes all but a second before hot cum releases over the back of my hand.

That woman is trouble. And she's my trouble now.

Chapter Three

MOLLY

DASH WASN'T wrong about the earplugs. His alarm blared in the middle of the night, loud, obnoxious, beeping that persisted for a good twenty seconds before his hand came down on the snooze button. I tried to go back to sleep but my adrenaline spiked when the most annoying sound in the world entered my ears.

I listen through the wall. My mind draws a precise image of Dash drawing his shirtsleeves over those tattooed arms, sliding jeans over his muscly ass, and buckling his belt over his tight hips. Ten feet away through one measly wall is the hottest, most mysterious man I've ever met. And a cowboy at that. I have to stop reading my Western romance books immediately before I romanticize the notion of Dashiell Hunter. I'm here to do a job, and it isn't one of a stripper, no matter how much seeing him makes me want to take my clothes off. That's saying a lot because I'm not fond of being exposed and naked.

I snuggle the duvet up against my chest. Why the hell is he up at three in the morning? I know he's been micro-managing the stables, and it's understandable. Though most stable hands and ranch workers love horses and are typically attentive, one or two of them are always distracted. Maybe they're hungover. Maybe they're having trouble with their girlfriend. Maybe they're having money problems. Distracted minds leave things. Trough water left running in the pasture. Stall lights left on. A hoof wasn't picked out. Something goes wrong every day while I'm here, and that's probably why Dash is here before I arrive, before anyone else, to see what was messed up from the shift before.

But three o'clock in the morning? In my efforts to prove my value, I tried to always arrive by six. And I don't think there's been one time where he wasn't here before me. Still, I figured him living just above the stables and here at the resort, he'd be up at four-thirty at the earliest.

Three. a.m.

By the time his boots clunk intentionally across the oak floor toward the kitchen, I'm not even trying to ignore the sound of him anymore. Water rushes out of the faucet. The faint gurgle of the coffee pot sneaks under my door. I listen hard, carefully. Not much happens until the sink runs again and his boots make their way to the front door which, out of courtesy to his should-be sleeping employee, he closes with a quiet click and an almost silent turn of the key.

By now, I'm wide awake with wonder. And excitement. So I, too, get to work early. I'm down with the horses by four-thirty, and by five, I sense Dash's presence again, working with the same creatures I do, but keeping a distance and eventually, he's gone altogether.

I don't break the news to the other workers. There are seven of us employed regularly here at the resort. After our run-in yesterday morning, I had doubts that after Dash went to Colt, I wouldn't have the job after all. Or I'd be packing my suitcase, moving out and not managing anyone or anything yesterday. Sure, he made the rules, and that kind of suggests I don't have to leave, but maybe those rules are just for now? He never said I was hired. He never explicitly said I could stay.

I spend the day as normal, going about my business and not even telling a soul about my move. When I get back here from my day of work and grabbing a bite to eat in town with two of the stable hands, it's eight o'clock, and Dash is already in his bedroom. He didn't leave a note or say a word all day, so I go to bed, too, still wary as to whether I'm really staying here or not. I wish he would have just said something. Anything. Maybe I should have asked Colt today...

I settle down and manage to fall asleep easily after being up for nearly twenty-four hours, but all too soon, Dash's three a.m. buzz is hacking through my skull again. But this time, I try to get back to sleep because for the time being, this is my life, and although I've never been one to need much sleep, six or seven hours would be a preference.

I finally creep out into the open-plan space at five a.m., after two hours of tossing, turning, and reading. It's dark and magically still. Moonlight pierces through the window and along the wooden floor like a tight silver ribbon of a birthday gift. Even though my crusty lids are heavy, I shake my head with pure delight. This is not the apartment the Hunters had showing on the ad for the job.

They must have renovated it. Dash probably didn't post the new photo to keep people away from applying. All I know is this is the most gorgeous place I've ever lived. It's a far cry from my house growing up in South Shore, Chicago. We never had money to upgrade anything, and the couch I watched cartoons on was the same one I watched reruns of *Gilmore Girls* on as a teen. Maybe my mom replaced a toaster or something, but often, our things were from thrift stores anyway, so it was never new-new.

I switch on a light and stare at the living room. Everything in this place looks entirely unused; either Dash isn't here much or he's meticulous. The remotes are lined up in a row on the coffee table. The couch pillows are neatly tucked into corners at the far end. My bedroom is off the kitchen, and I make my way to the beautiful oak table with chairs, again, nice and square against the top. The only evidence of the place being used is the upside-down coffee cup in the dish strainer, washed I'm guessing by Dash this morning, and half a pot of coffee.

With a mug next to it.

And small notepad with the logo from Starlight Ranch Resort. There's messy scrawl on it:

Molly,
Make yourself at home.
Dash

A smile dances on my lips, and my heart flutters because these four words mean everything. This little note makes it official. I'm the new Starlight Ranch Stable Manager.

And I don't have to leave this place. I let out a sigh, holding the note to my chest. I'm so close. *We're* so close. I rush to my bedroom to snatch my cell from my nightstand

and text my sister, who I'm likely to wake, but hell, everyone loves starting a day with good news. I pad quick steps along the floorboards to the open-plan space and take a short video scanning the living area and send it to her, along with a text.

ME

> UPGRADING YOU FROM THE DORMS.
> BIG SIS HAS THE ROCK-STAR
> APARTMENT ON LOCK.

I head back in the kitchen, sliding my socks along the smooth floor like a happy-go-lucky ice skater and get a mug for my still-warm coffee in the pot, and when his offering steams my face, a twang of guilt passes through. Dash was here first. He chose to live here for a reason.

I shake my head. I have to believe my reason is bigger to keep on going. I need my sister with me.

By the time I'm pouring creamer in, my sister texts back.

LILS

> OMG! ARE YOU SHITTING ME?

ME

> NOT ONE BIT. I GOT THE JOB!

LILS

> I LOVE YOU, BABE. NO LIMITS. SO
> PROUD OF YOU.

ME

> CHANGE THE STORY.

LILS

> CHANGE THE STORY. NEW ONE BEGINS
> IN TWO MONTHS, GIRL.

ME

SORRY I WOKE YOU.

LILS

BEST WAY TO START A DAY. LOVE YOU.

I thought I'd feel like shit when I descend upon the stables, but my giddy energy at landing my dream job and getting so damn close to the finish line of my four-year plan provides me with enough adrenaline and elation to hum a tune. I hit my first stall this morning in a stable full of just me and my favorite animals in the world and I am bouncing with joy.

My earbuds bang out a Taylor Swift tune, and I dance around the buckskin quarter horse, singing, not loudly, but enough to get my blood flowing and to take my mind of the nip in the cold October air.

"Can't you see-ee-ee, you belong with me-ee-ee..." I point in the air, rocking out, wondering who the hell Taylor is singing about, then return to folding down the stable blanket over the flicking tail of Hound Dog. I two-step, thinking about the lyrics... I'm not waiting anymore. I'm here. Where I belong. I've finally been seen. I wrap my arm around Hound Dog, give him a little hug, and sing with my cheek against his neck, crooning the rest of the lyrics I know by heart.

I run a body brush along his thickening coat. My breath comes out in puffs as I sing and dance around the beautiful horse's body, grooming more dramatically than usual in an effort to stay warm. I finish smoothing his coat and dance out of the stall backward with his horse blanket slung over my arm... And right into someone large, solid, and smelling of earth and the familiar spice that lingers in the air in the apartment above.

With my free hand, I reach up and manage to take one earbud out. "Dash. Hi." I wiggle my earbud in my hand. "Just waking up to some tunes."

He nods. "Taylor Swift." He passes me and enters the stall, inspects Hound Dog. "At least it's country music."

I don't correct him that she sings lots of genres, because honestly? I'm impressed and very surprised a man like Dash even knows who she is. And it makes him even more attractive than the shearling coat he has flung open, revealing his broad chest. He's been working if he's already warm enough to unbutton. Which is the tiniest, and if I really think about it, inconsequential clue to what Dash gets up for in the middle of the night.

He walks around Hound Dog, lightly checking my work.

I shove my earbuds into my pocket. "You've already been out?"

"That's a question, Sunshine."

I know Dash doesn't want me around, and his little nickname isn't meant to be sweet. It's probably a reference to my bubbly nature. My yellow towel? Dash probably thinks people who are optimistic are naive. He has no clue my optimism takes true grit. He has no idea how many times I chose this hopeful road of mine over one a lot darker. He doesn't know I've even taken a few detours. But there's no use telling him that. All that matters to Dash is I do my job right, and even though I'm seriously confident in my attention to detail, the smallest part of me shrivels thinking what he'll do if he finds I've made a mistake.

It's only the first stall, though... if he came to catch me out, he should have waited until I got through all my checks and the other ranch workers have come and gone from morning jobs.

He pats Hound Dog's rump. "We'll go around together this morning. I want to see how you do your morning checks."

We? Is Dash playing nice and not just waiting for me to mess up?

"Okay," I agree, trying not to sound surprised. "Let me start by putting this stable blanket away."

"No. Put the blanket over the stall door. You have workers for blankets. *Your* morning job is to check horse health and the yard safety. Leave tack to the workers."

He says it like I've already messed up. Or maybe it's just how he talks. Direct. Unemotional. But somehow, I hang on every word; his voice is so deep, so rich. It tumbles into the space like a mellow country music song.

Dash rests his forearm on the horse's back and snags his finger in a belt loop, waiting for me to get closer and observe.

"Right." I hang the blanket over Hound Dog's stable door. I turn back to Dash, stiffen my arms, and let them drop to the sides but stay by the stable door. Being close to him and smelling him again feels... like something I should avoid doing too often.

He takes off his hat and stuffs it between the stall bars. He weaves his fingers through his hair. My Lord he is perfectly tall, dark, and handsome. "You're going to have to come closer if you intend to inspect the horse."

"Yeah, I know." I swallow, but my mouth is dry, and I tell myself it's just the autumn morning stealing my cool. I absolutely do *not* find my boss sexy.

He smooths his manly hand up along Hound Dog's spine toward me until Dash is standing next to the horse's head. "Top to tail. You need a system so you don't leave anything behind. If you don't notice the symptoms, a horse can't let you know he's unwell until it's often too late."

He gazes at me in such a way it imposes the seriousness of the matter. I already know how to inspect a horse for health issues. But right now, I feel something like a painter who went to community college and now I'm getting a lesson from Picasso. I move into Dash's space, where we can both look closely at the whites of the horse's eyes. We're close enough for his spicy, leather scent to encircle me. We're close enough for his white clouds of breath to collide with mine.

Focus, Molly. I take out the notepad and pen I keep in my pocket.

Dash's gaze falls from the horse's face to my note-taking items, and he probably thinks it's silly, but I like notes. Lists. They make me feel secure, and I need an anchor right now. Not that Dash makes me nervous. Maybe a little. I don't even know what the feeling is he gives me.

Moments later, I'm glad I brought the pen and paper for more reasons than having a way to keep my eyes off Dash. The cowboy checks for more than just boogers in eyes and signs of blankets rubbing like we did at the other ranches where I worked.

Dash basically gives me a lesson in veterinary preventative medicine. He inspects the horse's eyes, easing one open with sure but delicate fingers. Hound Dog is so comfortable with him, he doesn't even swish his tail.

"Come closer." Dash doesn't take his gaze off the pony but curves his finger with a beckoning motion, calling me to his side.

I do as I'm told and step my feet beside his. In order for us to examine the same two-inch-wide eyeball, I stand with my side flush against his. There are multiple layers of fabric, down, and synthetic fluff between us, but the pressure of his arm against mine sends unmistakable flutters underneath my skin. Even through the shearling, the weight of his muscle, the firmness of his hard-working bicep is... reassuring. And that spicy smell of his enters my nose the way a baking cake does. Mouth-watering, irresistible.

He doesn't seem to notice me salivating, thank God.

"The membrane here should be pink. Pale pink. If it's white or red, or kind of purple, the horse could be dehydrated. That's a problem as much in summer as it is in winter, so we check every day. Every season. And if it's yellow, we call Jolie over."

I wonder if Dash's vet sister taught him these things. She's super amazing with the horses, but Dash has a mastery that seems to even surpass an expert. It's horse whisperer stuff. Not only does Hound Dog allow Dash to poke and prod, he gives the cowboy a nuzzle afterward, as if to thank Dash for the attention. The sight draws up the corner of my mouth with an endearing half-smile I can't resist.

My boss runs me through the rest of the checks he wants me to do, both on the horses and observations within the stable environment like how much goes in (and out) of each horse daily. Unlike past managers, Dash is, despite probably hating it, an incredible teacher, telling me not only to do what I'm told but why it's important to do it. And for a moment, I wonder if he wants me to fail or to succeed because this lesson is teaching-a-man-to-fish kind of stuff.

I take notes, silently watching him use his capable hands on this creature. They slide along every bit of the horse's hair smoothing down in firm strokes. It's impressive he's been waking up in the middle of the night then makes the time to come here after... well, whatever it is he does, and doctors the ponies so thoroughly. Here I thought he came to the stables to catch people wasting electricity, and this... this is what he's been doing all along. Ensuring the health of these creatures, giving them TLC, treating them like the precious beasts they are.

Inside this enigmatic, off-limits grump is a soul capable of immense care and attention. If a woman could be on the receiving end of such healing attention, she'd never ache again.

He stands after inspecting his last hoof and brushes dust off his hands. He runs his eyes from my toes to the top of my head as if making up his mind about my capabilities. Our gazes meet briefly, and his eyes sear right through me. This man is a million times more confident in silence than I am. He's intimidating. I don't know if it's intentional or not, but his confidence, his self-assurance, is more alpha than I can take in one moment. I lower my gaze and stuff the notepad and pen into my large winter coat pocket.

He snatches his hat and puts it on. "Let me know if you have any problems or questions." He moves alongside me to leave.

But I still have more to prove. "Dash?"

He doesn't turn, just sticks his hand up on the stall frame, lifting his jacket and exposing a mighty fine ass.

"I wanted to talk to you about one of the items in my proposal. From May. If you ever read it?"

"I read it." He squares himself to me again, comes into the stable, and lifts that boot on the stall wall, knee bent, probably because he's tired from his night of meandering.

I'm sure he doesn't intend to look sexy. But he oozes it. I'm covered in sticky, hot cowboy lust.

I tell myself this will subside. Soon, just like all the hot guys I've met, he'll do something to go from a ten to an eight, and I'll be able to talk to him without swallowing first.

"It's about the Christmas season." I stuff my freezing hands in my pockets. "I proposed some winter activities for around here. I thought if we brought some seasonal activities to the ranch, we could increase winter income. When I first came here, I was talking with Savannah up at the hotel, and I really think having sleigh rides and some other things could make this place a year-round destination."

Dash folds his arms over his chest. He narrows his eyes, and the mere fact he's changed his stony expression must be positive. Right?

"Jolie said the Danes have eight, maybe nine Belgians they don't use for showing anymore and they'd probably be willing to sell for a good price, especially just before winter."

I remember when I first thought of this idea. Finding the horse sled was like playing Santa, and even after nearly four years of ranch work, I have yet to be around the mighty seventeen hand draft horses much. It excites me, but I think (hope) it makes good business sense, too. A lot of ranches are pretty empty in the winter, and that's a mistake. There are plenty of people who would pay for a snowy winter escape, especially when the main draw is sleigh rides behind giant horses.

It's a fantasy. It's something I would have loved to do as a child. But I also ran the numbers, and if we get started ASAP, we could pay off the investment in the horses and sleighs this season. Maybe even in a few weeks if we can get the social media exposure. Savannah at the hotel would help. My sister, too. She loves this sort of thing. He hasn't jumped in with a no, and now I'm positively glowing with the idea.

"Maybe we could even get a Santa or have a winter ball..."

Dash's nostrils flare in thought. He chews his lip, and it's the most I've ever seen his face move, so he must be thinking hard. I hope that means there's a yes somewhere inside there, even if it's fighting with a no.

I lay my hand on his arm and find the nerve to look him straight in the eye. "Honestly, sleigh rides will sell. And nobody around here is doing them."

He darts his eyes to my hand, uncrosses his arms, forcing my hold to drop. He clears his throat and shifts on his feet, almost as if uncomfortable. Shit. Maybe I shouldn't have touched him. I got too comfortable. I'm always too friendly. If he went around doing that to female employees, they'd probably call him out for it. I have to remember, I'm a boss now. I can't read his expression, but it's different from the ones I've seen before.

I hope I haven't fucked this up.

He tips his chin up. "The Belgians will live out?"

Wait? Did he actually read my proposal? Or is he merely suggesting that because it makes the most sense?

"Uh, yeah, that's the idea. We'll have some shelters built. We want them to be hardy and have nice thick coats anyway."

He turns to leave but puts a finger in the air. "Line it up."

He walks away, leaving me alone, wishing I had someone to hug and high five. I'm giddy. It's my first business project ever in my life. Pride fills me, and I swear I could just float away on this feeling. I squeeze my fists tightly and wiggle my body around, jumping and doing some sort of victory dance.

Then, my cell beeps.

JOLIE

HEY, HEARD FROM COLT OUR BEASTLY
BRO GAVE YOU THE JOB YESTERDAY!
WHY DIDN'T YOU SAY? WE NEED TO
CELEBRATE TONIGHT! INVITE EVERYONE
OUT TO SLY'S!

I love this woman. Jolie Hunter is the kick-ass, take-no-prisoners hype girl, with a tiny side of crazy that every woman needs. We met in the line at the local coffee shop when we were both fresh in town, her back from living away, me totally new. We were both ordering with different baristas at the same time, asking for the last piece of carrot cake. When we realized, we gazed at each other, and instead of tossing a coin for it, decided to share. We've been friends ever since.

ME

SOUNDS AMAZING! I DIDN'T SAY
BECAUSE HE WASN'T EXACTLY CLEAR
ABOUT THE "OFFER."

JOLIE

YOU MEAN YOU DON'T SPEAK
CAVEMAN? WELL LET ME TRANSLATE—
YOU'RE IN! SCRATCH INVITING
EVERYONE. JUST BRING GEORGIE. I'LL
SEE IF I CAN WRANGLE A FEW MORE.
CELEBRATE WITH FRIENDS WHO WON'T
TELL YOUR BOSS YOU NEEDED YOUR
HAIR HELD BACK. LOL.

ME

HAHA. GOOD POINT. CONSIDER IT
DONE. I CAN BE THERE AT SEVEN.

JOLIE

I'LL HAVE A ROUND AND A TOAST
WAITING.

Jolie and I exchange a few more texts. I tell her about the sleigh and ask her for the Danes' number to arrange it. She sends me a thousand different celebration emojis, and finally, I shove my phone back in my pocket.

Moments ago, I was super aware that I didn't have anyone to hug, and yet again, Jolie crawls out of the woodwork to tell me I'm not alone. But a faint urge to invite Dash along, too, whispers inside me, despite Jolie suggesting it be friends only. He told me we aren't friends. And she probably knows he doesn't like going out. I do, too. The one night I was at Sly's with Dash, months ago, he brought Colt along to entertain on his behalf and didn't seem like he enjoyed being out one bit.

Still, the reason I'm celebrating is because of him. He hasn't done this out of the kindness of his heart, but me having this job, being a boss myself, advancing in a career that feels so *me* is down to him giving me a shot. I earned it. But that doesn't mean I don't want to thank him with a toast of my own.

Chapter Four

DASH

She only had to go and touch me. It wasn't sexual. It was nothing more than casual, friendly human contact when she laid her hand on my forearm and sent sparks flying through me. But apart from my family, most notably my mom and my niece, Eve, who might be single-handedly responsible for not letting my heart wither away completely, I haven't made physical contact with a human in a really long time. Certainly not an attractive woman. I never stopped to calculate how long it's been until Molly... a good five years, I suspect.

After the incident with my dad at fourteen, I pulled away from people farther than I already was. I tried to have casual sex, drink-fueled one-night stands. The debauchery of my early twenties was something that carried on longer than it should have from high school. Rebellion and self-destruction was how I responded to my dad dying. Everyone has their own way with grief.

Me? I was the first guy to get a tattoo in high school, hell, nearly first in my family. My mom was furious I found someone to give me one at fifteen and even more upset I didn't try to hide it. *And* I ignored her pleas to not get more until I was old enough to understand the permanence. As if I don't understand permanence. I learned permanence in the most brutal way possible and I'll never forget it.

The girls in high school saw me as the bad boy and took chase like girls do. But those girls turned into women. Many of them are married now, and the ones that aren't, I've known them for too long. It's not a one-night stand to them. It's a hopeful evening, and I'm not in the business of breaking hearts. Not when I know full well how deep that shit hurts and how the torture lasts a lifetime.

Since I've always been the reserved type, it wasn't too hard to slip into this loner lifestyle.

But when Molly touched me this morning, something inside me woke up. Something I need to tread down on with a very firm boot.

Stepping into the barn with the sunrise behind me, I was already swatting away fluttering creatures in my gut at the thought of seeing her, she only had to be singing with that adorable, child-like voice. She only had to be dancing around cute and sweet, enjoying her work, different from how I do, but just as much. I only had to go and notice her coat was low-quality and her shabby synthetic cowboy boots would never withstand a winter here.

I try to ignore my detailed observations, but Molly's pearly smile, her tiny hand scribbling on that notepad, the way her hair fell down onto her cheek, and how she trailed it back played out in memorable slow motion. I swear I could smell her strawberry-mint shampoo, too, when she leaned in to inspect Hound Dog's eye. I don't even remember glancing at her while we examined him, but somehow, I still see her round brown eyes, all focused and motivated.

And all of these images followed me back up to the apartment. When I hopped in the shower, I could still feel her hand on my forearm, as if it reached right through all that padded leather and right to my skin.

And now I'm stuck here all alone, wanting to go to sleep, but my thoughts race. Work is the only way for me to escape my tendency to overthink. Being in the elements, caring for something other than myself, keeps me present. But all I've got to do now after this Molly encounter is make some food, and that kind of work isn't strenuous enough to take my mind off things.

I get some eggs out of the fridge and set them on the counter. Butter. When I clatter around for a frying pan, my cell bleeps. It's my sister.

JOJO

MOLLY JUST TOLD ME YOU APPROVED HER SLEIGH IDEA! THIS IS GOING TO BE SO MUCH FUN. CAN I HAVE A FREE RIDE, OR ARE YOU GOING TO MAKE ME PAY?

I know Molly and Jolie are friendly. In Molly's May proposal she mentioned setting up vet-led workshops held by my sister. I knew those two were in cahoots somehow but I didn't know they were close enough for Molly to tell my sister about her every move right after it happened.

ME

I'M SURE WE CAN FIGURE OUT A
BARTER.

JOJO

THAT'S WHY I'M TEXTING. HORSES ARE
READY AT DANES' RANCH. MAYBE I CAN
OFFER YOU A VETTING AND WE ALL GO
OVER TOGETHER? BUT YOU WILL OWE
ME A SLEIGH RIDE!

I put the eggs back in the fridge and pop a piece of bread in the toaster. This is just what I need right now. Distraction. The Danes and Hunters go way back. James Dane was my dad's best friend, and Monica Dane still hangs out with my mom on the daily. Ashton plays professional hockey on the same team as my brother, Logan, and Jolie fits in there somewhere, too. I suspect she'd like that *somewhere* to be on Ashton's lap.

Or maybe that teenage crush was squashed by time, distance and Ashton's hideous now ex-wife.

ME

COOL. I'LL BE AT BIRD'S EYE IN THIRTY
IF THAT WORKS.

JOJO

LOGAN AND I WILL PICK YOU UP OVER
THERE. I WANT TO SAY CONGRATS TO
MOLLY IN PERSON. SHE'S REALLY
EXCITED ABOUT THIS, DASH. DON'T
YOU DARE DRIVE HER INSANE. THIS
MEANS MORE TO HER THAN YOU
KNOW.

Making Molly's day was not my intention. Making money, making the right business moves, was all I wanted. All I *need* to do. Still, being told Molly is happy and I had something to do with it makes my heart flutter. I send a grumble through my chest, hoping to squash it.

But as I eat my toast, this does feel like a whole lot more than turning a profit for me, too. A sleigh. Draft horses. I don't want the tourists who come along with them, but I do love a draft horse, and the Danes have some of the most beautiful ones around.

Since helping my friend, Mateo, on the Danes' ranch years ago, I haven't been around a Clydesdale or Belgian. My dad would have loved this idea.

And Molly's the one who brought it to his ranch.

Before we load into Logan's SUV, my brother and sister take a good half hour shooting the shit with Molly in the tack room. I wait, throwing sticks for my dog, Memphis. I'm not going back near Molly just so I can fixate on another likable thing about her.

Finally, my brother and sister wave goodbye, and they crawl into the front. I take the back of Logan's car, with my Border Collie, happy to be out of the bite of the wind.

But Logan takes another kind of bite. "Molly is just a slice of apple pie, isn't she?"

I run my hand along the back of my pup.

Jolie narrows her eyes at Logan. "I hope you mean that in the *sweet as* kind of way."

He smirks. "As opposed to what?"

"You know what I mean," she deadpans.

"Just saying I like her, that's all. She seems really determined." Logan glances in the rearview mirror back at me. "You need that around here. The resort has such insane potential. She has vision. New businesses need vision."

I have vision, too, I just know my family thinks it's tunneled. It probably is. I like what I know and know what I like. I also know what I don't like, and I don't like apple pie and Molly being in the same sentence coming out of my famous, good-looking, playboy brother's mouth. It gets worse.

"We'll have a good time tonight," he says.

Jolie turns around to face me. "Oh, we're going to Sly's to celebrate Molly's new job, but I figured you wouldn't want to go. Do you? It's us, Molly, Georgie, and Ashton."

Fuck. Only went and added another shit-hot single famous man into the mix. Drunk hockey cowboys are already magnets for women. Add drinks all over that, and it's a done deal. I imagine Molly all dolled up, cleavage tumbling out of a low-cut top, and tight jeans firm around her curves. On display. A protective urge digs my nails into my palm. "You figured right. Not interested, but thanks for the invite."

I decline but have never had more interest in going to Sly's than I do right now. But I have self-control. Molly is a grown woman, and if she can't handle herself, I'm sure Jolie will unleash her Wonder Woman rage on them.

Still, horny cowboys and hockey players with their arms around Molly is all I can think about.

Thankfully, Jolie quickly changes the subject, and I listen in on her new conversation with Logan.

"I can't believe you and Ashton are already starting up the season again. The off-season felt short."

"I don't know, always feels long to me."

Logan loves hockey, and he's made a comment here and there that makes me worried he thinks it's coming to an end before he gets a chance to win a Cup.

"I wonder if Ashton will ever actually move back here.

Can't believe he kept commuting back to Los Angeles last season." She sounds salty.

"He's moving back. His divorce is final now. He's done what he had to do."

"He should have never married that gold-digger in the first place."

Logan doesn't correct her. Ashton's divorce was front-page news. His ex took him to the cleaners.

Jolie simmers. "Like she even needed the money. I have no idea what she had over him. They don't have kids or anything. And she owes her entire B-rated acting career to him anyway. She never would have made connections if he wasn't invited to Hollywood parties."

Logan lets Jolie riff. She can go on and on when it comes to defending our brother's best friend. My opinion of him has always been solid, but when it publicly released that he conceded so much of his fortune in the divorce, I did think to myself there's no smoke without fire. I couldn't help but wonder why she had him over a barrel.

When we finally pull under the laser-cut metal sign reading *Moon Ridge Ranch*, I'm hardly listening anymore. Unlike my brother and sister, I have been up for hours by this point and could use more than a piece of toast in my stomach. But getting these horses sorted sooner rather than later is the only way to secure any income from the purchase when the snow arrives.

I remember this idea from Molly's proposal and stewed on it because even though I didn't want to hire her, I was keen to put it in action. I know the resort accounting has been running on a knife's edge since the minute I urged everyone to agree to it being changed from a cattle ranch several years ago. I never told them exactly why I couldn't cope with ranching anymore, I just made the case that it would be more lucrative, and since the ranch and how it makes money is my responsibility to the family, they all followed my twenty-six-year-old lead, trusting I'd figure it out. But truth be known, I still question every day if I can lead us out of the red. My heart conflicts with my head far too much when it comes to making business moves.

Colt is more optimistic about the finances than I am, but I'm not sure this place touches him quite so deeply. I love the ranch so much I live in fear of losing it.

Logan switches off the ignition, and when we step out, tall-ass Ashton and his tiny mom, Monica, are already waiting for us by their big barn. Logan immediately fist bumps his hockey teammate. Jolie walks over, hugs Monica, shoves her hands in her back pockets, and goes quiet. It's the first time I haven't seen her give Ashton a hug, too, and even though nobody else notices, to me, it's highly suspicious.

Monica rubs her hands together. "Well, here we are. Another Hunter-Dane deal to be struck?" She hitches a thumb in the direction of the barn. "Follow me."

The Danes don't have as much land as we do, but their facilities are fantastic. We enter an enormous industrial arena with grandstands and everything. They're at the center of this town's livestock and horse showing, rodeo, you name it. They even gave my best friend, the great Mateo Domingo, roots. Looking around, it's a not so humble beginning if I think about it.

Monica and Ashton already lined up nine horses—eight Belgians and one glorious, giant Clydesdale that has to be eighteen or even nineteen hands.

Monica stands next to the tallest creature. "Molly told me eight were needed, but I had to bring out Romeo, too. Mostly because he has a real bond with Buttercup, and if he doesn't go with you, I can't keep him anyway. He doesn't have a herd anymore. He's retired..." She throws her hands in the air.

It's the name of the game here on the Danes' Ranch, and for most farming and ranching folk in the community. When the animals don't do their jobs... well... it's a sad fact, but the sadness doesn't make the practical decisions go away. She'll have to sell Romeo on to a solo owner. Nobody likes to break up a herd of horses and definitely not a pairing. Not people who have seen first-hand that animals can be heartbroken, too.

Even though my own heart broke a long time ago, a few shards still poke around in my chest, and horses always seem to steal a piece.

I wander over to Romeo's side. His withers are my height. I'm six-one, so his head has to be reaching seven foot. He's enormous, glorious. I go to inspect his eyes but struggle to do it in a way that's comfortable for him. Not without a stepladder. His ears prick in my direction, and his lids rise, opening his giant eyes with curiosity.

I'm so not leaving this guy behind.

I pat his neck. "Molly told me you had a fire sale price going for our sleigh project. You aren't showing these horses anymore?"

"It's just getting to be a lot, Dash. You know how it is." She gestures toward Ashton a few horses down the line chatting to Jojo and Logan.

Jolie is still acting funny with Ashton. But my attention is drawn back to Monica.

"My kids are all off doing their thing in the world, dancing on ice, serving the country. I don't have time for it all anymore. I'll still have my ponies, though. Love doing the lessons for the children."

I nod and rack my brain for the numbers Molly ran in

her proposal, but part of me doesn't care. The Danes never screw the Hunters and vice versa. We practically gave them most of our cattle when we opened the resort.

Monica hands me a piece of paper with a number because she hates negotiating out loud. Fifty grand. Given the price of a hotel room at the resort, the horses will more than pay for themselves this season if we can draw in the winter tourists.

Jolie is now on the far end already inspecting the first of them. I suppose I am predictable. She knew I wouldn't say no.

I lift the paper, roll my lips into a thin line, and nod. "This is for the eight. What do you want for Romeo?" He'd be more of a pet than anything, but I don't want him living without Buttercup. I can't handle thinking about a forlorn horse.

Monica lets out a sigh. "So there's one thing with Romeo, and maybe Jolie will pick up something today. He hasn't seemed quite right for a couple days. Muck is inconsistent... I'm pretty sure he needs a feed change or is getting some sort of gastrointestinal problem. I'll give him to you free, provided you understand he might not be in great health and that you promise not to separate him from Buttercup. He's an old boy, and I'll hardly get anything for him anyway."

I run my hand along his flank. Retirement horses are my vice. I hate how they're often left to rot. Owners give up their stables to the newer, shinier model, meanwhile, these veterans deserve to be revered for a lifetime of service. They can still enjoy a nice easy trail ride out if you let them. "We'll keep him and Buttercup together."

"Promise?"

"Yes, ma'am. You know my word is good." I tip my hat.

"I know, Dash. It doesn't even pain me to say goodbye knowing he's with you. And Molly. She's very caring. I'm glad you finally pulled your head out of your butt and hired someone."

I step toward the next horse in line so she doesn't see the grumble in my eyes. *I didn't hire her.*

I make my way down the line, checking out the stock, and something like enthusiasm grows warm inside. I try to push it down, not get too excited. We have no clue if this will lure in winter business. But the hell if *I* don't want to try a sleigh ride.

When all is said and done, Monica and I agree the Danes will bring the horses over tomorrow.

I drop Molly a text so she can prepare for the extra work involved and hopefully get some weekend help in on a weekday. And get the contractors out to prepare field shelters.

ME

NINE HORSES INCOMING. EIGHT FOR THE SLEIGH OPERATION AND A BONUS FELLA.

MOLLY RUSSO

OMG! I'M SO EXCITED TO MEET THEM ALL. I BOOKED HANK AND SOME EXTRA HANDS FOR THE FIELD SHELTERS THIS AFTERNOON. THEY'LL HAVE A HOME BEFORE IT'S TOO COLD.

There's a fine line between being presumptuous and prepared. Job done, I slip my cell back in my pocket, but it bleeps again, so I slide it back out.

MOLLY RUSSO

DASH, THANKS SO MUCH FOR
BELIEVING I CAN DO THIS.

I stare at the emojis she sent. Prayer hands, a celebration, a pony head, and heart eyes. I almost smile. One of those sharp shards in my chest catches on her light and flickers.

Chapter Five

MOLLY

I PICK up a mostly seasonal ranch hand, Georgie, at her house, promising to be her designated driver. The last thing I want to do in my first week as manager is need my hair holding back. Funny, and tempting as it was when Jolie suggested we rave, I have no interest in sleeping through my alarm. Not that I'd ever sleep through Dash's. But even though today in the stalls he seemed to be training me for keeps, I'm still certain he'll take any reason to let me go.

Georgie and I get out of my car at Sly Bull's. Starlight Canyon's premier bar. I have sneakers on, but Georgie is dressed to the nines. We've been working together now since I arrived in the Canyon for high season and we've gotten to know each other well. Her husband has been away on deployment ever since I've been here. I know she's lonely. I know she's always worried. It's nice for her to be able to forget that fear for just a night, so I'm more than happy to help her have a few drinks rather than me.

Jolie said she'd meet us at the bar, and when we walk in, she's already sitting with her brother and *him*. I know a lot about Ashton Dane, one of the tallest hockey players in the league, Hollywood regular and the man who changes Jolie's breath and tone when she speaks of him, even though she thinks she's acting normal.

And boy do I see what she likes. He is a tall drink of water all right and the kind of man who instantly brings on the thirst. He's six foot to Heaven, all dark, disheveled hair and hooded eyes. He has a serious face and eyes that could probably shift from the bedroom to the sin bin in two seconds flat. Goddamn. No wonder Jolie practically orgasms when she says his name. And when he sits next to his teammate and best friend, Logan? It's like a pantheon of Greek gods because her brother is so gorgeous I can see why he doesn't struggle to maintain his reputation as a woman-izer. If you're going to have a one-night stand, he's the one to do it with. He's actually extremely charming, too, and knows exactly how to make a woman feel comfortable.

Logan is more clean-cut than Ashton, with a single rogue curl tumbling down his forehead, natural and boyish but so perfectly placed it's a wonder if he put it there as bait. Though his personality is playful, he has a sophisti-cated look about him, and his white button-down shirt is opened to just the exact place that has the female gaze wandering the same way a man can't take his eye off cleavage.

It's not bad company for the night. But only reminds me how someone even hotter is missing.

Georgie clicks across the floor next to me, and just like

Jolie promised, there are five drinks waiting on a table. The three stand when we approach.

Jolie greets us with open arms. "Girls, girls!" She hugs Georgie. "Shit, babe. Sexy for a weeknight."

Georgie wears a slip dress, hanging off her tall frame like a model with her long, lean pins strutting out of the bottom. The thing would be a crop top on me, but Georgie makes it look sexy-classy. She has an elegant beauty that even a skimpy dress can't destroy. Though now that I consider her in Jolie's admiring arms, she has lost a bit of weight since spring. I sometimes wonder if she's always telling the truth about things being "okay."

Georgie tucks hair behind her ear, bashful at the compliment. "I take every opportunity I can get. It's a bit much for Sly's, but my grandma always said, never save your best."

Jolie smiles. "I'm glad you didn't. I'll get a pic of you, and we'll send it to Noah. He can jack off to it in a time of need."

Georgie shakes her head and laughs but agrees with a nod to sending her deployed husband a photo. She greets the guys, who she already knows, and Ashton approaches me, thrusting out a hand to greet me. His beastly mitt makes mine appear to be a child's.

"Hey, Molly, nice to finally meet you. Congrats on getting past the gatekeeper and making it to the inside," Ashton says.

People keep treating me like a dragon slayer for getting the stable manager position, as if Dash is a mythical creature at the gates of some cave of treasure. And now that I think of it, it's not the worst depiction. At least in how I used to see him. But the cute note he left by the coffee, the way he mentored me in the stalls this morning... he might be softer than people let on.

"Thanks... Nice to meet you. You're the second person after Logan I saw on TV before meeting in person. Who knew this would happen in Starlight Canyon of all places?"

He cocks his head sideways, with an almost shy smile, and pulls out a chair for me. Logan and Ashton might be wealthy hockey players traveling the country, but the cowboy upbringing is evident. I remember Logan rushing to open the office door for me when he and Jolie stopped by the stable yard.

Jolie takes her chair next to Ashton again, and I swear she scoots it just an inch closer to him. The scratch across the floor, hardly audible, makes its way to Logan's ears because he snaps his head toward the pair, drops his gaze to the small space between them, and clouds pass over his eyes.

Jolie's gaze darts to her brother, and instantly, she leans away from Ashton. It's all over without Ashton really noticing anything himself, but the brother-and-sister tele-pathic conversation is interesting. Why would Logan care if his sister is into his best friend? You'd think it might be nice to have a bro become a brother.

Anyway, the brother and sister turn their attention back to the table, and Jolie raises her glass in the air for a toast. We all follow suit.

"What is this?" I ask, peering into the glass.

Logan tips his drink slightly toward me. "It's a Dark and Stormy. We figured you can handle it." He winks at Jolie, and I'm sure they've been joking about Dash.

I know they're only kidding but I find myself defending my boss. "He's actually pretty nice."

"Nice?" they say in tandem. Then share a look that

makes it very clear they think I either like him or he likes me. As more than a boss-employee thing.

"Why is it such a big deal I think he's pretty nice?" I ask, bobbing from Logan to Jolie to Ashton. Finally, my gaze lands on Georgie who shrugs, drink still in the air, center table.

Jolie forces us all to clink glasses. "Here's to Molly. Who fills all things dark and stormy with sunshine."

We touch glasses, but it takes me a moment to swig because when Jolie calls me sunshine, I'm immediately thinking about the enigma back in the apartment. Dashiell Hunter. My God does his nature draw me in. All mysteries do. I hope I'm not just running around in circles lusting after the wrong kind of guy yet again.

The rum cocktail makes its way down my throat, and my hope for the alcohol being strong enough to quell my constant thinking about him is futile. It only seems to fuel the fire. I think about the last time we were here and Colt tried to make us talk. I think about how hot he is, one foot up on the wall with his fingers through those belt loops. I let my mind wander to his tattoos and his capable hands on that horse today.

I've got serious beer goggles, because in my mind's eye, Dark and Stormy has quickly become Sex on the Beach.

Thankfully, we talk more about other things, and I'm only having the one drink, so slowly, as we chat about Ashton's house search in Starlight Canyon, I'm coming down the other side of Dash Mountain.

Logan punches him in the shoulder. "So glad you're back. You'll find something."

"I better," Ashton says. "The closet in my high school bedroom is only a few sweatshirts wide."

Jolie has had two drinks now, and it's evident in her

choice of words. "Fucking bitch. She better not ever step a foot in this town or I'll cram her in that closet. She owes every fucking ounce of her career to you. User, gold-digger..."

She trails off, but I'm pretty sure she calls her a bitch again.

Logan lifts his eyebrows. "Tell us how you really feel."

"You don't agree?" she asks.

"You know I do." He nods.

Ashton shoves his fingers in his eye sockets but wears a smirk in the shadow of his hand. Clearly, Jolie has his corner as much as she does the rest of her friends. Anyway, his ex must be vile if she has Jolie talking about her like that.

I try to keep the conversation flowing without prying too much. "So, your ex is still in LA?"

"Thank God, yeah." He drinks.

Georgie asks the question I wanted to. "Why did you only just now move back for real? You played last season with the Scorpions and you and Chloe broke up like a year ago?"

Now this is a detail I know because on more than one occasion Jolie complained about how Dane was back hanging on to his old relationship with his ex. She said that was why he wouldn't move back in spite of playing hockey for the team here. Only this month did she change her tune. To a very quiet one. Though she still speaks of him some-times now, it's with discretion, and by the way they are both jittering their legs together, allowing them to occasionally touch, maybe these two are closer than Jolie lets on.

Ashton tips his empty drink to the side. "I'm going to need a lot more of these to get into that. And for the doors to stay open past closing."

Jolie instinctively rubs his arm in a caring way, like she

knows every last detail. Logan darts his eyes to her hand, and she instantly brings it around to Ashton's back and slaps it more like a guy does when a friend is down in the dumps.

Ashton is saved by the bell when we're joined at our table by Bobby and a very pretty girl on his arm. Guess it's my turn for a grilling. Bobby is the smart-ass problem child over at Starlight Ranch. He's a lot younger than me but walks around the ranch like he has a lifetime of conquests behind him. He makes more mistakes around the stables than any, but his ego yells louder than I ever could. Bobby did mention his desire for the manager position after I arrived, applied and didn't get it. Unsurprisingly, Dash didn't hire him either.

Maybe if Bobby had as much tenacity as he does audacity, he would have thought to go to Colt, too. If I've pegged Bobby's type right, he'll be less than enthusiastic to take directions from me.

"Well, if it isn't Miss Manager herself," he says like a smiling assassin.

Here we go.

"Hey, Bobby," I acknowledge him. "You know everyone at the table?"

"Course I do." He nods at Logan and Ashton then returns his snide gaze to me. "Climbing that Starlight Canyon social ladder one rung at a time." He delivers his insult with a smile.

I'm not the only one at the table stiff now. All eyes are on Bobby. He has his arm around his blonde date, and she shrivels away from him almost imperceptibly. He is one hot cowboy, but his attitude is ugly, and good for her that she knows it. I hope I don't see those two leave Sly's together.

Though he's just landed a clever insult, spouting

venom back isn't my priority, so I don't respond at all to his poke. I need to get Bobby on my side at some point. At the end of the day, even though he's sloppy, he is knowledgeable, and having a baseline of people like Georgie, Bobby, Hank, and a few other residents of the Canyon as permanent staff will help me more than ever when the crowds and inexperienced seasonal ranch hands roll in. I know. I was one of those just a few years ago and learned a lot from people like Bobby who knew how to ride before they walked.

I know it will take time for Bobby to accept me as his manager. I'm not one of *them*. But I never expected his next low blow.

He scoffs. "Shame I don't have all the *skills* you do." He trails his judgemental gaze along my body, allowing a brief stop at my breasts. "Guess Dash just doesn't think I have your assets."

Jolie stands, and her chair nearly knocks into Bobby's date. "I think it's time for you to leave, because I'm a few drinks deep and I think I'm starting to hear things." She smiles, but it's more like a sneer.

Ashton chimes in. "Man, don't make me stand up, too."

Bobby glances at Ashton and Logan, licks and bites his lip like he's had enough. I wouldn't tempt a man to stand who shreds ice and beats bodies into plexiglass for a living. Bobby tips his hat.

"Enjoy the rest of your night." He ushers his date away to the far end of the bar, but she glances over her shoulder with an apologetic look.

Jolie sits.

"Thanks, guys. Bobby is going to be... a challenge. I can stick up for myself, but I'll have to figure out how to pick my battles with that one," I say.

Georgie is tipsy. "Just fire his ass. You can find someone else. He's such a prick."

I laugh lightly. "Yeah. But he's a prick who knows what he's doing. And he does care about the horses. And even though he doesn't respect me, he does respect Dash. So what if he doesn't like me? We don't have to be friends to work together."

And there it is. My return to thoughts about *my* boss. The one who isn't my friend.

Logan pipes up. "Good attitude, Molly. Assholes are part of the territory in ranch life. Contrary to popular opinion, not all cowboys are gentlemen."

I circle a finger around the ring of my glass and wonder if Dash is gentle. I will need to erase these dirty thoughts before morning. Hopefully, he'll be in bed before I get home tonight. I wonder if he sleeps naked.

Chapter Six

MOLLY

I DIDN'T STAY OUT MUCH LONGER, and Dash was in bed when I got home. I hardly fall back to sleep after his alarm again, this time wide awake with equal parts curiosity about his whereabouts and excitement for the day to come.

When I get up at five, a little earlier to prepare for the Belgians' arrival, the day begins with another note by the coffee.

I'll be back by six.
D

It's an old married couple's kind of note, and the irony makes me laugh to myself and shake my head. I don't need to keep tabs on Dash, but he's being considerate neverthe-less, because today, all I really wanted to know when I woke up was if he'd be here with me to sort the new herd out.

But it isn't about having help.

I'm not afraid of hard work. I've been rolling up my sleeves my whole life. When other kids moped around bored on the playground over three-month summers, saying there was nothing to do, I was at home cooking, cleaning, and making dinner for three. Or lying about my age to take on a job at the corner store. Or running *errands* for my mom.

I don't remember a time when work wasn't part of my life, so it's my nature now. But I never thought I could enjoy it quite this much. And I'd like to enjoy it *with* someone. And that's why, staring at the note, knowing I'll have someone to smile with, or maybe in this case at, makes this even sweeter.

Life has been slowly changing and evolving into some-thing much more authentic. Since moving to New Mexico when my baby sister got into college in Albuquerque, I don't have to pretend so much anymore. I don't have to pretend I'm my sister's mother (as much as in many ways, I feel I am). I don't have to pretend I'm a hustler just to survive city life. I don't have to pretend I'm smarter than I am. Being a ranch worker, all people care about is that you went to the school of life and got straight A's in common sense. The past three and a half years, I've eased more and more into my own skin.

Dash doesn't get how him backing this project affects me. I know it isn't normal to gush to this level, but me getting this stable manager position, and having an opportu-nity to grow and learn after years of being nothing more than a boulder carrier, is... liberating. This must be how my sister felt when she got into college. It's like the door with the big prize has opened.

I put the note down on the counter and smooth it with my hand. Having Dash here today is like having someone around when you catch the big fish. My mind wanders to why he said yes. Did he read my proposal? Does he simply love horses and he can't say no like a collector? I deflate slightly, thinking maybe it was faith in his own ability rather than mine that got him to say yes to the new venture.

I bite my lip and scrape my teeth along it. I won't mess this up. I'll make this the best damn winter wonderland in the country, even if I work 'til my hands bleed. Though if they do, I probably won't even notice because damn do I love what I do now. When you have to do something you also want, well, that's probably what it means to find your purpose. I've finally found mine.

I drink Dash's very strong coffee, so strong I almost pull a face, when a faint beeping comes from below my kitchen window. I rush over and there in the yard is a giant horse trailer with *Moon Ridge Ranch* written on the side. *Shit.* They're early.

By the time I hit the dirt in the yard, the trailer is parked, and behind me a pair of boots scrape across the gravel and dust, quickly, jogging in my direction. When I turn, there he is, the midnight cowboy himself, rushing toward me. The cloud of cold air puffing out of his mouth precedes him like a country music star bursting through smoke screen on stage. How the hell does he manage to look so sexy doing such ordinary things?

When he reaches me, his cheeks are boyish and rosy from his morning in the cold. A smirk hides beneath his lips. "You're late."

I smile, wishing mine would coax a real one out of him. I lift my eyebrows. "Or maybe you're early."

We stare at the back of the parked trailer when two of the Danes' stable workers get out and come around back. One of them hands Dash a clipboard with paperwork on it and a pen under the clip and goes back to the trailer.

Dash shoves the clipboard into my hands. "This is yours."

I read the document. It's the sale agreement. "No... it's for you."

He watches the men open the trailer doors but cocks his head to the side. "Your stables. Your budget. Your idea... *your* signature."

My eyes track Dash and his ass wandering over to the workers to get stuck in and help unload the horses. I stare down at the clipboard. *My* stables. *My* budget. *My* idea... I've never felt so empowered. So validated. So... I fill with a warm sensation, one that consumes me whole, leaving no trace of doubt.

I'm actually doing this.

I read the sale agreement carefully, not wanting to mess anything up, when Dash's low voice steams into my space. "Whoa, boy."

I glance up. It's the Clydesdale. The extra horse Dash bought. He's a beaut; and enormous. Pitch-black all over, he's a fairy tale dream horse waiting for its knight in shining armor. Though he's a fairy tale, he's also agitated.

Dash flips the lead rope over his neck and takes the two ends of rope beneath is chin, giving him more control over the horse. What kind of giant has he brought here? Most draft horses are large in size but softies in character. Gentle giants. This one... well, he's not bucking and rearing, but his hind leg kicks up and out every so often as if wanting to send Dash off two ways to Sunday.

But my boss isn't alarmed. He just pats the creature, tries to keep him calm, then stops in front of me. "Romeo needs a stall."

Romeo's leg kicks out again, but Dash doesn't even flinch.

"He looks like he'll kick the shit out of any stall we have," I say, trying to contain my nerves at having a horse as big and feisty as this on the yard.

"Pretty sure he has colic." Dash pats Romeo's neck.

Oh shit. Colic is basically belly aches in horses, but it can become serious fast and even killed a horse at one of my old ranches. That's why Romeo is kicking. Horses with colic try to bite or kick the sides of their flanks with their hooves. Poor things can't reach very well. "The Danes sent him anyway?"

"Jolie saw to him yesterday, so we knew it might be coming. Our job is to get him better." Dash walks on past me toward the barn, disappearing into the stables, and he doesn't come back.

I don't get why we'd buy a horse that Jolie vetted yesterday and was showing signs of illness, especially illness that can kill a horse. But there isn't time for questions. There won't be time for answers either because I have a day of work ahead of me. A bigger day than others. So I leave Dash to tend to Romeo. We'll have to divide and conquer for now.

I sign the paperwork and spend the next hours situating the Belgians in their new pasture and double-checking their troughs and supplies. I stop by Hank and the other workers I brought in to get the field shelters built.

When I get back to the yard, regular staff wait for me in

the tack room where I reassign duties now that we have new horses here. Bobby stares at me with thin lips and crossed arms. If he thinks I'll be intimidated by that he'll have to try harder. I'm not one, but I do have the patience of a saint.

It's a manic day, but I hold it together. I go down my checklist and tick all the boxes... but all I can think about is Romeo.

I finally make my way back into the barn an hour later. I unzip my coat and fling it over a bridle hook outside one of the stables. It's warming up now, and I've been working my ass off. I smooth hair over my forehead and follow the low hum coming from a stall at the end of the barn.

I find Dash, shirt with one extra button undone, patting Romeo. His baritone voice offers a comforting vibration, and it almost works on me, too. I know we have some intense hours ahead. What I've learned, and from what Jolie told me, it isn't recommended to leave a horse with colic alone. It's going to be a long night.

Dash doesn't turn to face me, but sensing my presence, he stops humming.

"Does that help them?" I ask. "Humming?"

Dash still doesn't turn. "It helps *me*."

His confession softens my heart. "You have a nice voice."

"Mmm."

I enter the stall. Romeo seems calmer now, but when I touch his neck, he feels awfully hot. "Do you sing?" I ask, making conversation to help pass the time. A lot will be spent in this stable in the hours to come.

Dash doesn't answer.

"Sorry... that's a question." I join Dash on Romeo's side and stand close to the stable wall, as far away from him as I can, but personal space is limited. Staring at the back of his thick, muscular neck and the dark curls at the base of his skull, I remember the thoughts that ran through my mind last night. His neck is tan. Even in October.

Just when I think only silence will answer, he says, "I do. I sing a bit. But just for myself."

I joke, "Yeah. Don't see you hopping up on stage at Sly Bull's anytime soon."

"Hm." It comes out like a punctuated laugh.

Romeo flicks his head back suddenly to nip at his stomach, and Dash flings himself back to not be hit by the huge, hard skull. His boot slips on the heel, and he falls into me. We both slam against the back wall of the stall, but he braces a hand to the side of me, stopping shy of hurting me. Still, in this moment, we're chest to chest, crushed together so close I taste his minty breath. The extra button on his open shirt exposes his dewy golden skin. His pecs are a forceful, delicious pressure on my breasts, and it has my nipples peaking instantly. One hand braces him just over my head, and the other is wrapped around the small of my back, where he caught me before I banged my shoulder blades into the hard cement breeze-blocks.

My arms are straight down to my sides, and he holds my weight in the palm of his hand. His hips have fallen into mine. He stares down at me for what feels like an eternity. I'm sure it isn't, but time just stands still. I'm a two-inch slip from my ass being on the floor, but his grip is so firm, some-how, I know I'll never hit the ground.

Now I know why this man is the boss of even creatures ten times his size. His firm energy secures me in the most alpha way imaginable. He grips my back; eases me up to standing, and I look down at my shirt. He takes a step away.

I brush myself off, even though there isn't a speck of

dust on me, but I need my attention to be somewhere other than him.

His voice is low. "Sorry."

I'm not sorry. I'll probably feel him on me for days to come and Lord knows I'll enjoy it. Tattooed men who are totally wrong for me are my vice. And my go-to fantasy. And I haven't had one touch me in a very long time.

When he's upright, he examines his finger. "Shit..." he whispers.

He's bleeding on his finger that slammed into the cement blocks. It's dripping right down into his palm.

Instinctively, I reach out for his hand to help, but he yanks it away.

"Don't..." His brow is pinched. He's annoyed and he takes two more steps back from me.

I'm such an idiot. Two seconds ago, I was in la-la land, thinking we were perfectly poised for a romantic embrace, but this man doesn't even want me to put a bandage on him.

He pulls a handkerchief out of his pocket, shoves it around his finger, and squeezes. "I texted Jolie. She's going to give Romeo some pain meds and take the afternoon shift here so you can tend to the others."

I can't stop staring at his hand. "I can grab the first-aid kit, Dash. Is it bad?"

"You should be worrying about the horse, not me. You're here to do a job, and I'm not one of them."

His words aren't particularly harsh, but they cut through me anyway. I remind myself he doesn't want to be friends. I remind myself that's not why I'm here either. "Fine."

"I'll stay with Romeo 'til noon," he says. "Then Jo can take over. You come in at five, and I'll come down at ten until twelve. Then we swap every two hours if need be. If you can handle that?"

I nod. It's going to be a seriously long day, and night, but of course I can handle that. I'll pull an all-nighter if I have to. This black beauty isn't going down on my watch. And by the determination in Dash's eyes as he sucks on the side of his finger, he won't let it happen either.

I've been in the stall for hours, totally fine, but come nine o'clock, I discover I'm horribly afraid of the dark. There's no trace of sunlight left and the moon is covered by clouds. The horses are all back in their stalls, and the sounds they make, that are usually so comforting, are now like cracking twigs behind me in a deep, dark wood.

Worse yet, since taking over from Jolie, Romeo seems to be in more and more pain. I don't know if it's just my imagination. Maybe I'm extra emotional and worried because I've been up since three or four or whenever the hell I emerged from my in-and-out sleep after Dash's alarm went off.

Still... I have to trust my judgment. I've been working with horses for nearly four years. And lots of them. Romeo is sweating. He keeps lying down and wanting to roll which is just about the worst thing a horse with colic can do. But he's enormous, and though I'm a capable horse handler now, I struggle to get him to come with me back on his feet.

I know Dash will be here in an hour. But a lot can turn for the worse in that time... so I make the decision I've been considering for the past thirty minutes.

I heave Romeo to his feet again, hoping he'll stay that way while I'm gone, and I head up to the apartment. I don't want to get Dash. I don't want to let him know I don't know what to do. I don't want him to think I can't handle all this on my own... but this isn't about me. It's about Romeo.

Even though he'll probably bite my head off, I open the door to his bedroom, gingerly, quietly. It's stupid really, because I'm about to wake him up so I should kick it open with a foot and make some noise, but part of me wants to *see* him.

Am I perverted? A peeping Tom? Maybe. Because I really do want to glimpse him when his eyes are closed. I want to see the man without the mystery.

He's dead asleep. He doesn't even really make any sleepy breathing noises; it's still in his room apart from the lullaby of moonlight dancing in through a curtain he left half open. A gentle glow illuminates his chiseled features. I almost suck in a breath he's so... beautiful.

Dash's lips gently part. They're sensual and luscious and so... I wish I didn't have to wake him from this serene state. He never appears this calm. His eyes are always concentrating and his brow stern. It's wonderful to see him relaxed. And I'm no Prince Charming waking Sleeping Beauty. I'm the one who has to break his peace. Should I? I might feel guilty about it, but I have to.

But not before another peek. Half his chest is exposed, and a lean, muscular arm lies on top of his duvet. He's almost a silhouette in this light. I can't make out the sleeve of tattoos on his arms but I wish I could. What would a man like Dash choose to paint on his body?

All I can make out is a word in solid letters. *Billy.* I know from Jolie that was their dad's name. And I can't help the thoughts that spring into my head. Maybe Dash is hardened from grief. Maybe all he needs is some warmth to melt the ice.

I'm a nurturer. A helper. A giver. I don't know why I'm this way but I'm sure my childhood has something to do with it. My mom's chronic pain, addiction and physical absence forced me into a caretaker role at a very young age. But I don't hate it. I like doing things for people and giving them what they want. It doesn't empty my well to help people, it fills it.

And this man? I want to know what's behind his intense eyes. Is it actually an ache? He refused my touch and even a damn bandage like a wild, wounded animal.

I contain my sigh. Like most women, I'm a glutton for punishment. A mysterious guy like Dash intrigues me more than one who tells me his story openly, which is actually messed up. I'm always out to heal the bad boys. I'm always seeking the broken ones.

But it's time to fix myself, and besides the fact that Dash makes it very clear he doesn't need a friend, he isn't mine. He's my boss. My very sexy, tattooed, tortured, hot cowboy boss. I need to serve myself an immediate cease and desist fantasizing order right now.

Plus, I'm being kind of creepy staring at him.

How do I wake him? I want to slide the back of my hand over his masculine bone structure and comb my fingers through his hair but I settle on an arm shake. His inked skin is warm in my hand and a lot smoother than I thought it would be from a man who tries so hard to be a walking, talking callous.

"Dash," I whisper. I use a louder voice because the whisper doesn't work. "Dash…"

He wakes, but not the way some people might with a human sitting on the edge of their bed in the middle of the night. Dash isn't that kind of person. His head flicks in my direction, his eyes wide open momentarily before narrowing them to focus on me. He inhales a sharp breath through his nose.

"Dash, it's Romeo... I think he's getting worse."

With that, the cowboy hops up fast, completely unconcerned with the fact that he is buck naked. His powerful ass moves swiftly, and my greedy eyes work hard to memorize his every inch. All I get is his backside bent over, legs just wide enough for me to vaguely make out his balls. He opens a drawer and, taking out boxer briefs, he slides them over the best view I've had in ages. He snatches his work jeans that are slung over a chair.

He turns to me, chest bare apart from the patterns on his skin. He buckles his belt over the angles of his hip bones and what I can't see, but imagine, is a very happy trail.

He clears sleep from his throat then asks, "What's going on with him?"

I'm still sitting on the edge of Dash's bed. I stand and nervously throw the covers back into being partially made then wipe my hands on my jeans. "Um... he's sweating. Keeps lying down and wanting to roll. It's hard to keep him on his feet. I'm sorry I came to wake you but..."

Dash smooths a shirt over his head. "You did the right thing." He swipes his hands over his face, followed by fingers through his hair, and when he faces me again, he seems wide awake. "Let's go sort this guy out."

Chapter Seven

DASH

Waking up to Molly's touch was—well, I imagine, because I wouldn't know much these days—like waking up to the sunrise. I've been startled out of my slumber by the world's loudest, most annoying alarm clock for so many years.

I don't know if I was having my incredible dream before or after she arrived in my bedroom. It's remarkable all the same because I either don't dream or have bad ones. But my mind was on a secluded beach, sand perfectly warm, massaging my back as I lay in it. The sound of waves lapping on the shore had me totally relaxed. Sea birds punctuated the consistent lull of waves just enough to remind me I was on vacation.

Then, my arm got all fuzzy, like energy from another world was flowing into me. And that's when my mind began to break back into reality. A reality where someone was touching my arm. I knew right away it was Molly. I didn't know how. I hadn't even opened my eyes yet. But... I know the feeling of her now.

I was hazed, so her hand stayed on me long enough for me to like it. Long enough for me to have a split moment of desire to sweep her into the bed and under the sheets with me in a chance to offer the rest of my skin the heaven of that touch.

But when I finally woke enough to talk sense back into myself, a shameful part of me was glad there was a problem because it helped erase those reckless thoughts.

It's a concern how much I like being close to her.

Now she stands almost as near as she was sitting on the bed next to me. We work around the small stall, made even smaller by a horse two sizes too big for the stable. Molly has no choice but to invade my personal space. I tell myself a lie that I hate it, but it's a cold, cold night, and even in this shitty circumstance, the woman has a warm presence I can't deny.

I pull up Romeo's lips to get a look at his gums, and Molly is there with me, shoulder to shoulder. She wants to learn more, I know that's the only reason her side touches mine, but after her being in my room with me naked under the covers, images of her in that towel come flooding back. I get itchy. How could I be thinking about the curves she flaunts under that puffer jacket at a time like this?

It's dim. With one sole stable light holding out the darkness, she leans into me, just like that morning I showed her how to examine the horses like I do. Her sweet perfume is long gone, but I like her smell even more now. It's uniquely her. Something like the scent of rain approaching while standing in a field of strawberries and mint. And hay. But that might be the stalls.

Her side brushes against mine, and we're practically

cheek to cheek as we squint, trying to take in the shade of Romeo's gums.

I dart my eyes to the side for a glance at her beauty, and her face displays an empathy for Romeo that makes her even more attractive than she already is. She strokes his under belly with that soft, caring hand of hers, and my mind is drawn to my own forearm. I still feel her warmth on it like a phantom limb. I wonder what it would have felt like if I'd let her touch me longer tonight. It's an affection I'll never allow, but I want it just the same, even though I know that kind of closeness will never work for me.

Knowing that a decision will be made on Romeo's fate tonight makes my heart come alive in a way I'm normally very good at suppressing. That's all this is. I get emotional over the horses, and it's seeping into my other thoughts. Plus, there's nothing wrong with a little admiration for the way someone handles the horses.

Though I'd say it's a little more than admiration. I'm absolutely fixated on the way her hand soothes Romeo.

Once, when I was about nine, I stayed with my uncle and aunt up in Montana. While I was there for the summer, they had to put their dog down after a freak accident, and I had to go along to the vet since I was too young to leave back. My aunt told me to wait outside, but then, my uncle suggested it's an important experience, for a ranch boy, to be in the room.

They stroked that dog, petted and petted and petted it to the point I thought there wouldn't be any skin on their palms when we left the sterile, white room. Now, I recall the way they touched their dog. They petted him to soothe themselves. They petted him for one last touch to commit to memory. They did it for *them*.

Molly touches Romeo for *him*. Her caress isn't that of a

lamenting, worried rancher. She's deliberate. Full of hope to heal. It's more like maybe if she gives him enough of herself, he'll be okay. My throat goes dry and thick all at the same time. I give it a good, firm clear, take out my phone, and put a flashlight on his gums for a second time, just to be sure getting my sister is the right thing to do. She might be sleeping by now since I asked her to come at three for a shift.

Romeo's mouth illuminates all right, but a lot more than that shines, too. How the hell is Molly still so beautiful after being up for what has got to be a good fifteen, sixteen hours?

I pat Romeo's side. "His meds have worn off."

"He's in a lot of pain." Molly's eyebrows pinch together. She keeps on stroking.

I'm done seeing what I came to see but I don't step away from Molly's side. "I'm sure you're making him feel a lot better. It's the best you can do."

She turns her face to mine, and we're close. Real close. Nose to nose close. I can count her eyelashes she's that near. Her lips are only inches away.

She whispers with soulful eyes. "Why do you love horses so much?"

It's a question. I told her not to ask any, but something about the darkness, the methodical, lulling movement of her hand still working affectionately over Romeo's coat and the fact that I don't want to leave this space next to her has me answering. "In part it's just being a cowboy. But... my dad. I was close with my dad, and it was... our thing."

It was more than a thing. It was *the* thing. We spent all our time both with our horses and the wild ones.

I bite the inside of my cheek. "Why do *you* like horses so much?" I ask in return, because I genuinely want to know. How does a woman from inner-city Chicago love a horse the way her hand loves on Romeo?

She lowers her eyes; I marvel at how thick her lashes are.

"You'll think it's stupid. I'm just a silly pony-mad girl who romanticizes the creatures."

"Try me." Romanticize horses? That's my MO.

"Besides their beauty?" She exhales. "Just they're so strong... they could be so much more destructive but they aren't. They..."

She laughs at herself, and I know she thinks I'm judging her, but I'm genuinely interested.

"They wear their hearts on the outside and have a huge range of emotions. You know?"

Her gaze lifts again, and I want to dive right into it, because her thoughts are just like mine, and I haven't had any company for a while.

She continues. "I'd like to be brave enough to display what I'm really feeling. And even if it's sadness or fear or whatever, be perceived like a thing of strength." She's still caressing Romeo's neck. "Is that stupid?"

It was the least stupid thing I've heard anyone say in a really long time. "Maybe we have something in common after all, Sunshine."

She draws her lips into a thin line, but a bashful smile dances somewhere in the middle of them. Her mouth is luscious even pulled in tight.

"So what's the verdict?" She points to his mouth. "Did his gums tell you anything?"

I pat him gently. "Time to call Jolie."

"Shit. Does that mean it's bad?"

I don't know. My senses tell me he's going to be okay. Mostly, I trust my gut, but not when it's about something as monumental as life and death. I stopped trusting that instinct a long, long time ago.

I don't answer Molly because I don't have one. I'll leave that to Jolie who I text. I don't slip my cell back in my pocket because even if she's sleeping, she'll get back to me soon. She knew Romeo wasn't right, so her phone will definitely be on.

Molly stops rubbing Romeo and leans against the stall wall. She must be exhausted. Today has been no ordinary day, with nine new horses on-site, one of them sick, and it's not like she has much additional staff. Even though behind closed doors I made sure a lot of the background tasks were sorted, she's been up for hours. A tendril of hair falls over her crinkled forehead. She's tired. And worried sick. I can help her with one of those things.

"Why don't you go on up now and get some sleep? I'm here."

She pushes that strand of hair back. "I wouldn't sleep now. I want to wait and hear what Jolie has to say." Her sigh is long and uneasy.

We stand for a beat of silence before she says, "You can go back up."

"Mmm." I'm not leaving either.

I lean on the wall next to her and make an excuse that we rub arms because the space is tight. I don't have the usual claustrophobia I get when close with someone like this. Instead, it feels cozy.

We wait for Jolie's text in silence, but the space sings with autumn nighttime. Crickets chirp, but already less than in summer. The doves that nest in the eaves hoot, sounding a lot like owls, but their song is more relentless. The stalls let off the occasional rustle of a horse down the row nibbling at their hay net.

I prop my foot on the wall and when I take my hand up to loop a finger through my belt, it brushes against Molly's.

"Oh... sorry," she says, maybe only now realizing we're standing shoulder to shoulder.

She offers a smile, but it's not the one she usually wears. It's full of worry. Now that we've called Jolie, it's no longer a *wait it out and see* situation. I have faith Jolie can comfort Romeo but I don't like seeing Molly like this. So I try to distract her.

"How did you end up in New Mexico?"

She whips her head around to gaze at me like she's surprised I just spoke. She probably is. On some level, *I* am.

"My younger sister got into college here. So I moved, too. Well, actually it's hard to know which way around it was. I always wanted to move out west and work on a ranch. And she always wanted to go to college. It worked out for us both."

"Did *you* go to college?"

"Me?" She says it like I just asked her if pigs fly. "No. I love reading but somehow I was never good at school."

She seems to be degrading herself, and I hate that for her.

"Well, you're highly intelligent. I'm sure if you really wanted it, you could have."

She offers me a grateful smile, so beautiful it makes me greedy for another.

"That's nice of you, but I really don't think I could have." She shrugs.

"I didn't go to college either," I offer.

"Really? I thought education was a Hunter thing."

"Yeah? Suppose it is, but I was a fuck-up in high school." Or maybe I was fucked up. Either way, I was lucky to graduate.

"Is that when you started getting all those tattoos?" She bumps into my side, trying to lighten the mood.

It almost makes me smile wondering how long she was looking at them before she woke me up. "A few of them were in high school, before my mom found out who was doing them for her under-age son. That had me waiting a couple years for more."

Molly's cheeks grow round, and a ghost of her usual bubbly self is there again. "I can't even imagine being reamed by Joy Hunter. Jolie tells me she's fierce."

I blow air out of my nose. "Yeah. It's not fun. I have plenty of experience."

Molly considers me for a moment, like she's searching for a reason why I'm not like my siblings and wants to ask me. I'm not like them. Logan is a pro-hockey player. Colt is classy cowboy CEO material, and Jolie is a vet. I was born on the ranch. I work on the ranch. And I'll die on the ranch. But I'm not pursuing this life by default. Often, when the others complain about the strains of their work lives, I know this career is more me than theirs are them. This isn't a job. It's an identity.

The question in Molly's face disappears even though she never asked it. Maybe she gets me. After all, she chose this life over any other she could have had, too.

Just then, my phone beeps with a message from Jolie that she'll be here in fifteen minutes, and even though I'm relieved for Romeo, I don't really want to leave the stall.

But in what feels a lot faster than quarter of an hour, Jolie arrives with her vet van and equipment like she said she would. She listens to his gut with a stethoscope. She takes his temperature. She examines Romeo with all her expertise while Molly and I stand flush with each other, and I don't know about Molly, but I'm not really watching Jolie.

Inappropriate as it is, I'm thinking about how I might get her down in a stall another night.

When Jolie finishes with Romeo, she says, "All right guys, nothing too crazy going on here. But you two go on and rest. I'll stay."

"Nah. I'll stay," I offer.

"No. Go. You'll only have to call me again if symptoms don't subside." She pats his side gently. "I couldn't sleep either thinking of him. Something special about this one, eh?"

I agree. Monica Dane obviously thought so. Molly does. Guess Romeo lives up to his name.

"Go on. Seriously. If I can't handle it, I'll text you, Dash."

"Thanks," Molly says, walking out of the stall.

We make our way upstairs, and I open the door to the apartment for Molly. She steps inside and flicks on the dimmer lights, quickly quieting the bright light, turning it down to a place we can both handle at this time of night.

We take off our boots. I do it more slowly than I normally do. I know I could use more sleep. I know Molly needs sleep. But it's the last thing I want to do. Molly slides across the floor in her socks, and I notice one has a stain on the toe area which can only mean her boots have a hole in them.

She walks backward toward the kitchen. "Don't suppose you're hungry?"

I'm not. But almost without giving my mouth permission it answers. "Sure."

Chapter Eight

MOLLY

I'm not hungry. I'm shattered actually, having been up more or less since Dash's alarm went off almost twenty-four hours ago, but the combination of feeling nervous about Romeo and dealing with a stomach full of butterflies from talking to my hot, elusive boss has me knowing I won't sleep when my head hits the pillow anyway.

And I'm curious. Maybe it's natural for any human to explore the great unknown, but something about this quiet cowboy enraptures me. But now that we're back in the apartment, away from the heightened emotion downstairs and the safety of the darkness, maybe he'll only remind me of the rules.

I pop two pieces of bread in the toaster and press the button down. When I spin around again, he's leaning against the wall. So damn sexy.

"Sooo... *boss*," I say for my benefit more than for his, "I know you said no questions, but... how about you give me three?"

He flares his nostrils, and his eyebrows twitch like he might smile. His expression is lighter, amused. "Three questions?"

I shrug. "Yeah. You can ask me three things. I'll ask you three things. You know. Kind of like a conversation," I tease.

"Are you messing with me?" He cocks an eyebrow.

"Do you want me to?" As soon as I ask, I turn away, head down, and stare at the toaster so he can't see the pink creeping into my face. I brace myself on the counter, willing the toast to pop up, because that kind of question is laced with way too much innuendo for a professional relationship, and I need a reason to not look at him until my face cools.

His hand appears on the counter next to me where he leans on it casually. "Go on. Shoot."

Shit. It's not like I prepared anything. What do I want to know about this man besides everything? I think back to him humming in the stable. "How long have you been singing? And do you play any other instruments?"

"That's two questions."

"Fine. Singing. Go."

He points at me casually. "I'll give you a freebie. I play guitar. And I started singing in church when I was maybe six or seven. Some other people in my family sang, too and we'd jam together sometimes."

Damn it. Now I have questions about his answer. Who did he sing with? Why is it past tense? What does he like to sing? Will he serenade me, preferably naked sometime?

"So that's why you're so good at singing. Been doing it a long time." I nod.

The way he leans on his hand next to me, so... like a protective wall of muscle. How can leaning be so sexy?

Sienna Judd

"How do you know I'm good?" he asks.

"The timbre of your voice. The vibrato and richness when you hum. It's obvious you can sing and have good tone. Feel free to jam here anytime. I love live music."

The toast pops up. I bend down and take two plates from a cupboard then reach up for the peanut butter, but I can barely get to it, and my fingers push the jar back instead. Dash steps closer, into my space. His hips make contact with the small of my back, his hard torso grazes my shoulder blades, and when he stretches up and over me, his body connects with such a small touch but makes such a dynamite impact.

His tattooed hand and forearm appear before me when he sets the peanut butter on the counter. I'm practically shaking with butterflies from being so close to him that I don't know if I'll keep the knife steady.

"Thanks," I manage.

He crosses his arms, and his hands behind his biceps make them bulge and stretch the fabric of his shirt like it's two sizes too small. "My turn?"

I focus on the spread, willing myself to not let my mind wander to his naked ass from earlier. "Huh?"

"My turn for a question."

"Oh, yeah."

I finish slathering on the peanut butter, and his finger slides his plate along the counter and out of my vision. My eyes follow the finger, the veins in his forearm, and every stroke of lucky ink right up to his emerald eyes.

"Go on then."

"How big is your family?" He takes a bite of toast as if it's a casual question. It is. But I don't always like talking about my family.

"Just my sister and my mom." I take a bite, too.

He swallows. "You're as good at answering questions as I am."

"Not much more to say than that."

"Your mom must miss you. Both her daughters being gone for years?"

"Is that your second question?" I challenge, hoping he'll drop it.

He swallows and narrows his eyes coyly. "Let me rephrase because I don't want to know what your *mom* thinks. I want to know what *you* think. Do you miss your mom?"

How did I not see a question like this coming? In a family like the Hunters? One so tight-knit that they think about each other all the goddamn time? It's more complicated than that for me.

"I won't judge you if the answer is no," he says, low and inviting.

"I just don't think the answer is the kind of conversation you might expect from a late-night Q and A. And I'm on a woo-woo journey to being more authentic so I'm all about the straight shooting now."

"Woo-woo?" His eyebrows do that kind-of-smile thing again.

"Yeah, you know, new age, personal development, green smoothies, and yoga kind of thing. I'm trying to be more comfortable in my own skin so I'd rather not answer than lie."

He tilts his head to the side. "Try me, Sunshine. You think I don't want to hear what you have to say, but I'm more intrigued than ever now. Did you use this tell, don't tell with Colt to intrigue him, too?"

I narrow my eyes at his low blow but I can see he's not serious. He's teasing. And I like it. "Fine. You want to hear it?

My mom has, for however long I've known her, been addicted to painkillers, and it wasn't exactly a *normal* childhood. So, of course, I miss her. She loves me and gives me insane amounts of affection when she's lucid. She is sweet, kind, and... she's been working on recovery for over six months now."

I throw my hands in the air. *Fuck it.* Might as well let it all hang loose. It's not like Dash will be telling everyone my business. "But I don't miss lying to the pharmacist or the landlord for her. So missing her isn't really a yes-or-no answer. We'll see what she's like when she moves here. It might be like meeting her for the first time. Or like having the part of her I do miss." I take a bite of my toast, surprised by the sting that creeps to the back of my eyes at the sound of my own voice, actually confessing this feeling.

I've never really told anybody that taking care of my mom's addiction got me down. I usually kept it to myself. I didn't want to bog her or my sister or anyone I've ever met down with that shit.

I quickly chew another bite of toast and swallow. "My turn again."

Dash seems to have abandoned his late-night snack. He traces a finger along his lower lip slowly, back and forth, concentrating and staring at me with deep, thoughtful jade eyes, like he listening real good and he's not sure what to do with what I just said. But he sure as hell isn't ready to move on from it and he's trying to figure out what it means about me.

I don't want him feeling sorry for me, though that's not exactly what I see in his gaze. His eyes are intense, and the silence is making me nervous.

"So..." I want to learn more about him. And I need this buffer question to get my own head straight. I'm not sure if my question will lighten the mood, but it's meant to. "When was the last time you smiled?"

Just when I think he'll have to dig deep, like the man's face will crack when it happens, he answers immediately. "Yesterday. With my niece, Eve."

"I'd like to see that."

"Because you don't believe it or because you want to see me smile?" he deadpans.

Is he flirting, being sarcastic, or simply asking because he doesn't know? The neutral look on his face gives nothing away, but he is standing so damn close now my cheeks are heating up.

"Is that your last question?" I ask, not even knowing what I'll answer anyway.

If he's flirting, I kind of want to flirt back, even though I know it's just that stupid idiotic part of me that always chases the unattainable. If he's not flirting... he'll never exchange questions with me again. This is probably a one-off anyway. We're both emotional about Romeo and probably both deliriously tired from such a big day...

"Yes, Sunshine." He tilts his head, and damn is he cute like that. "It's my last question. Do you not believe I smile, or do you want to see me smile?"

I let out a breath and shake my head. "What can I say, Dash? I'm a nurturer. I like seeing people smile. So..." I cross my arms in hopes of slowing down my racing heart. "I want to see you smile."

He leans his hand on the counter again. This time, it's right next to where mine is. One millimeter closer and we'd be touching.

"I see. You like seeing people happy. So what makes *you* happy, Molly?"

Why does his voice ooze like honey all over my body and I want him to use those lips of his to lick it all off?

I need sleep.

But I want to answer his question. What makes me happy? Taking care of my sister. Taking care of the horses. *Freedom.* Though I've never really had much of it. I'm trying hard not to make myself small anymore, but equally, baby steps. I don't think Dash wants me to launch into all that makes me happy. He might never play three questions with me again if I dump on him twice in like, five minutes. So even though I don't want this game to end, I say, "You're out of questions, boss."

He lifts those glossy eyebrows. "Can't blame me for trying."

"Been rule-breaking since high school, hey?"

He blows a laugh out of his nose. He waits, arms crossed again for me to ask my last question. I try not to stare but want to make out the black and gray ink all over his arms, wondering again what kind of images a man like Dash feels worthy of immortalizing on his skin. His sleeves are somewhat busy, but one that catches my eye is a Day of the Dead style skull tattoo with a cowboy hat.

Dash must feel my eyes on his skin because he repositions his arms. "Is it that hard to choose another question? Or was it that easy to figure me out?"

I still desperately want to ask him where he goes at night. But this... whatever it is that's happening, is something I don't want to risk never happening again. Maybe it's the people-pleaser in me. Maybe it's the way he's just so damn off-limits and for these ten minutes he's been focused on me.

I've never been the popular girl, and this is more than just getting attention. It's connecting. I think. Maybe I shouldn't have started this game... So, I settle on an old-fashioned getting-to-know-you question I've used since moving away from home and meeting other transient souls. "What's your favorite place on earth?"

His face gives the same impression I suspect mine did when he asked if I missed my mom. It moves more than it did even when his eyebrows twitched. The question is unwittingly complicated for him just like his was for me. I feel it in my bones—I've hit a nerve.

That funny, metallic feeling I get in my belly when I think I've made someone uncomfortable tickles deep inside, and I think about giving him an out. I think about telling him mine is somewhere silly and giving him the idea it's not a serious question. But just like he was, the fact he doesn't want to answer makes me all the more intrigued. And anyway, I get the impression Dash is comfortable being serious. Just not exposed.

He raps his knuckles on the counter like we're done here. "You need to get some sleep." He turns on his heel and walks toward the door.

I watch his broad shoulders and firm, Wrangler-stamped ass walk away from me, bend over, and start putting on a boot. "I'm going to see how things are below with Jolie and Romeo."

I tell myself over and over that I didn't do anything wrong, even though it feels like it. He puts on his coat and hat, opens the door, and steps through. But before he closes it, he pokes his head back in a few inches.

Though I can't see his eyes below the felt rim, his deep, velvet voice answers. "Mustang Valley."

Chapter Nine

MOLLY

I LIE in bed for a long while, tossing and turning, with two simple words and four syllables impossible to ignore like a pebble in my shoe. I finally fall asleep out of sheer exhaustion.

I set my alarm for the usual time, knowing even I need a few hours of sleep, though there have been plenty of nights when I haven't had so much extra work, I know I need to rest my body. My alarm goes off at five, and I hop out of bed like I never slept. I want to see Romeo. Dash provided a fantastic distraction, but now, all I can think about is if I missed something important. Like saying goodbye. Things really can turn on a dime with horses. One minute they're winning a Kentucky Derby, the next minute they've had a heart attack or are being put down when they break a leg.

It's disturbing how quickly animals can be lost, and the thought gives me shivers. I shake my head, trying to jiggle out the pessimism while I finish toweling off. I throw on some clothes, grab my jacket, and smooth on a bobble hat to protect my still-wet hair from the cold morning air.

My stomach gurgles, in part from tiredness, in part from the insanely powerful motor oil cup of joe Dash left behind for me this morning. I need to stay positive. Jolie was there. Dash was there.

When I arrive in the stall, Romeo is there, too. *Thank God.* He seems a hell of a lot better. Dash is busy tying on a hay net, and Jolie is leaning against the wall like an upright tomb of a pharaoh. Black-lined eyes and all.

"Hey, girl." No matter that she looks tired, her voice is still bright.

"Wow." I wrap my arms around the Clydesdale's neck the best I can on my tiptoes. "Is it just me, or has the big boy recovered?"

"Think so. Often colic passes, but the odds aren't good enough for me to need a night of sleeping over watching it." Jolie smiles. "Why are you up so early?"

"I always get up at this time. I just don't usually hit up the stalls this fast but I had to see how he was."

Jolie pats Romeo's flank. "I gave him more pain relief, managed to get more fluids in him after that, and salts. With that, he worked it out on his own." She checks her watch. "But I'm running some blood tests to rule a few things out and see if he needs a special diet or if there are any preventative things we can do."

I give her a hug. "Thanks so much for watching him last night and coming by so quickly."

"You got it." She rubs my back.

Jolie is easy to get along with. She's warm, inclusive, and made me feel at home on Starlight Ranch right from the get-go. Now, I see another side to her I respect. Where my emotions started to get the better of me with Romeo, Jolie kept herself steady, had confidence in her ability to pull him through... maybe that's what it's like being from a family like the Hunters. Maybe when you have a safety net, you're more likely to jump.

"When is the sleigh arriving?" Jolie asks. "I'm so damn excited."

"Tomorrow."

Dash looms in the corner, listening, cross-armed. He hasn't said a word. Not even hello. Neither have I, but I will. For some reason it feels a little like it's the morning after, some sort of walk of shame, like something happened last night that didn't.

Jolie and I talk more about the winter activities, the new menu at the hotel restaurant, and her coming to hang out with me and Lily at the weekend. My sister is coming to Starlight Canyon. Something I failed to tell Dash.

Dash lets a huff out of his nose—well, it isn't audible, but I see it leave his body—just before he goes to whisk past me out the stall door.

I'm not going to let things get weird. I grab his arm lightly. "Morning." I say brightly, but also like, hey, you gonna say hi or what?

Then again, it's not like he usually says good morning to me. Maybe I'm the one being weird expecting it.

He rolls his lips. "Morning." He pauses for a moment like he might say more but then just tips his hat to me and Jolie, all ready to leave again.

"Oh, just a minute... I need to tell you something. My sister is coming at the weekend. I wanted to let you know. We aren't loud or anything so we won't keep you up. But I just wanted to make sure you keep your shorts on." It's meant to be a joke, but it's one that reminds me of his steel buns again. Goddamn, what I wouldn't have given for him to turn around and see the front view.

His jaw works, and even under his stubble, his muscles clench visibly. It's so hard to read this man sometimes. He always appears to be resisting the world around him. And usually, his answer is silence, just like this time. He simply nods and leaves. Never have I met such a quiet person who also leaves a room so much more silent when they depart.

Jolie crouches and packs up her kit bag. "Well, I better get a few winks before going on my rounds at the Danes'."

"Sure. Thanks again..." I bite my lip. "Hey, can I ask you a question?"

She stands and slings the bag over her shoulder. "Course. What's up?"

"Has Dashiell Hunter always been this grumpy?"

She laughs lightly. "Is he giving you a hard time? I'll have a discreet word with him if you want me to."

"No. Not at all. He's fine. Trust me, I've dealt with major assholes over the years."

She rolls her eyes. "I can only imagine. Some ranchers are fucking pigs."

"Yeah... Dash isn't... I was just wondering why he's, so..."

Jolie's smile goes stiff. She watches me consider my words, then finally, her smile fades slightly. Her eyebrows pinch in thought while she internally collects memories of little Dash. "My brother has never been bright and bubbly. But..." She looks like she's going to start telling me a story then thinks better of it. "He's been through a lot."

The way she says it, I know I shouldn't ask more.

But she offers another crumb. "He's the serious type. Always been a brooder. Moody. But some people carry around more than others, you know? I'm sure it's hard to see

91

it when you don't know him well, but his attitude is actually easy to forgive. He's one of those people in life who takes time to know just how much he cares. He never says it, but he cares a lot. He's not as scary as people think he is." She gives me a half hug, her bag slinging down over her arm.

I help lift it back over her shoulder.

She blows a fallen strand off her forehead. "Let me know if I need to give him a kick in the ass, though."

That's all I get? Geez. The Hunters sure know how to build up the mystery.

"Yeah. I'll be fine. We're... fine." *I was just hoping to get some girl-to-girl gossip, but thanks for nothing.* "See you at the weekend."

"Yeah, can't wait to meet your sister."

"Me, too."

When she leaves, I go to stall number one and start the morning checks Dash taught me to do. And here I am, thinking about him all over again. Was last night a one-off? Was I imagining it being awkward this morning? Why did he go funny when I asked about his favorite place? And... how can I get us in the kitchen together again?

Chapter Ten

DASH

I DIDN'T NEED to answer her last question. How did that woman get me talking? I don't owe anybody a piece of me, just like I try not to take more than my fill of anyone around me. But our twenty minutes in the kitchen might have been the closest I've felt to anyone outside my family and Mateo. Our time in the kitchen and me saying those two words, which might as well have been spilling my life story, has me aching for more of... whatever the hell it was Molly was offering.

Last night, I softened in her presence. Both physically and mentally, something about that woman came right through all those walls I've built. And she pushed through them effortlessly, like a ghost.

But as soon as I mentioned Mustang Valley, that hard, stiff feeling of being a walking, talking fortress overcame me, and by the time I found Jojo in the stable, I was back to my old self again. Or so I thought. Jolie and I kept each other up all night by shooting the shit about her nutty horse, Ted, the new farrier taking over from our old one, and about Christmas coming up and the presents we might get for Eve and our mom.

Back to normal.

Then, Molly emerges again in the morning, all smiles and wet brown hair like when I found her naked in the apartment. Her big brown eyes and the relief of her seeing Romeo okay warms me all over again. Seeing her smile melts me. I thought I was immune to this kind of emotion and now I've met my kryptonite.

She and Jojo seem to be great friends. Though Jolie takes to a lot of people, she's no fool and doesn't talk to just any old ranch hand. Jolie updates Molly to the status of Romeo's health, then they start talking about the sleigh being delivered and some other plans I hardly listen to because it's time for me to get out of here and make an attempt at reestablishing my schedule. My habits keep me sane. Occupied. And give me a sense of purpose outside myself that I need back right now. I need back in my routine. I need to go back to the predictable life I built, part useful, part busy, that stops me from thinking and wanting things I shouldn't have.

But as I head past Molly out the stall door, she touches my arm. "Morning." She says it like I've been ignoring her. Wobbling her head, she chucks me a silly smile.

This woman is some Marvel character, because her hand sends electricity up my spine. "Morning."

I roll my lips into something like a firm smile, though I'm not sure they curve upward. I don't want her to think I'm ignoring her, quite the opposite; my mind is hellbent on keeping her front and center. Which is why I tip my hat wanting to leave, but she catches me again.

"Oh, just a minute... I need to tell you something. My sister is coming at the weekend. I wanted to let you know. We aren't loud or anything so we won't keep you up. But I just wanted to make sure you keep your shorts on."

She lets out one of her little giggles, the ones I've only ever heard in the distance before, and it feels good swarming around me like bubbles in a hot tub.

Her sister? Shit. I can hardly handle one Molly, I'd never deal with two. But just as quickly as that thought enters, another, more curious one does: *There aren't two Mollys. Because this woman is one of a kind.*

Good Lord. One piece of peanut butter toast and she's got me wrapped around her finger. It's probably just all that pent-up sexual energy getting the best of me. Not a lot of men could live around a curvy, voluptuous girl next door who doesn't mind getting her hands dirty and not have some kind of attraction.

But I'm not a lot of men. Some men can handle loving and losing and making up and breaking up. I don't have a heart to give. I know better than to let us cross any lines.

———————

I haven't been to Mustang Valley in the daylight for a long, long time. I tell myself it's because at night, when the wild horses are here, they're snoozing. They spook less, and it makes my job of checking the water piped into a dried-up watering hole nearly twenty years ago easier. The real reason might be something else. Maybe I just appreciate how at night, I'm sure to be alone.

I tie on my Appaloosa, Amigo, at the very end of the

line. I spin the crank and water hisses out of the mains and into the piping. Step by step, I trace the pipe and remember how when I first started doing this with my dad, the long rubber hose sat on top of the earth. Now, so much dirt covers the pipe that in places, it's completely buried by moss.

But I don't have to see it to know where it lies or how important it is. I came here almost every day with my father when I was younger, apart from Christmas, maybe birthdays and other special celebrations where he allowed a day of rest. But otherwise, rain or shine, storms or drought, we'd ride out to the top of the ridge and do the hike on foot to make sure it was all in working order.

It's the place of all my biggest extremes. Awe, when Dad and I saw a mustang foal being born while hiding quietly, mouths hanging open behind some bushes. Anger, when we noticed one year there were less mustangs than usual after reading about a roundup in the paper. And of course, it was here I experienced the darkest agony I've ever known. *Will* ever know.

But lately, I come here, and my feelings have slowly, over time, transformed into some sort of numb.

By the time I reach the edge of the ridge giving way to the valley, I remember my dad's advice, in this very spot. *"Life isn't about being happy. It's about being useful. But what you'll find, son, is that when you're useful, you're happy."*

I hate thinking it. I hate thinking anything about my dad not being perfect because he was my hero. But that advice was his flaw. He was wrong. I make myself useful every day, but no spark of happiness ever flickered. I keep coming to this valley, day after day, serving the wild animals that live here, waiting for the happiness he said I'd find. I've been coming here every day for eighteen years and I can't remember one goddamn day I felt something like happiness.

But I come for the memories that are the closest thing to it.

I need to hike down into the valley to the watering hole to see if it's filling. Even though there's a longer trail I could take down with Amigo, you can't risk bringing a domesticated horse around here. Amigo, as his name suggests, might be my friend, we have a bond as close as any, but herd mentality in the equine world far exceeds human connection. So I amble down on foot, and it's strange to now see the obstacles my feet have been programmed to avoid in the years of darkness. Sagebrush. Agave. Even a few lone tickseed sunflowers bloom yellow in spite of autumn, aside my path.

It's a steep, nervy trail that winds down. It's mostly safe, apart from a few places where I slip. But I know exactly what branch I can grab to steady myself. It isn't a long scramble down, and I know it like the back of my hand.

It's a cool day, but I can still smell the earthy, minty smell of the mountains when I hit the bottom of the valley. The mustangs are at the far end, a wide berth from the watering hole, so I can inspect the entire length of the pipe, check for any leaks. None.

A sole whinny releases into the valley, and its echo reaches all the way to me. I squint, trying to get a glimpse of the feral, natural scene. I'd love to stay here all day and clear my thoughts. But surprisingly, even a trip to my favorite place on earth, the one that usually cleanses me of any madness occupying my brain, doesn't reset this time.

It's futile. I think of Molly every step back up the hill. I think about the surprise in her eyes when I agreed to exchange questions in the kitchen. The delight made her gaze sparkle, and I never thought I could make someone so giddy just by talking to them. I think about how she felt pressed into my chest when I fell into her in the stable, how the small of her back was soft and womanly and I worried about her hitting her head against the wall. I think about her rubbing herself with minty-strawberry suds in the shower. And by the time I reach Amigo, I'm circling through how a woman who's had to grow up so fast can still wear a playful smile every day.

I take the long, trail ride back, and when even the bitter wind can't claim my attention, I know the only thing to do is avoid her. The next few days, I manage to steer clear and relieve some of the ache to talk to her again by jacking off to the image of her dripping naked curves. Replacing one urge with another I can handle. Me wanting her physically is easier to dismiss than wanting to play three questions again.

Chapter Eleven

DASH

THE DAYS PASS, but inevitably, as I'm her boss, we cross paths, and Molly texts me that the sleigh arrived.

MOLLY RUSSO

IT'S PRETTY DAMN BEAT UP LOL. I HOPE I DIDN'T MAKE A MISTAKE WITH THIS ONE.

I'm in my bedroom and sit on the edge of my bed. The sheets are still ruffled. I never leave my bed unmade. Just like I never go to Mustang Valley in the daytime or nearly smile when I receive a text. This woman has come into my life and turned it upside down.

I swipe my hand down my face and scratch my near beard, staring at her message.

ME

FOR WHAT YOU PAID, I EXPECTED IT.

MOLLY RUSSO

YOU DID? I'M NOT SURE YOU'LL
EXPECT THIS.

ME

I'LL BE DOWN IN TWO TICKS.

MOLLY RUSSO

I'M IN THE STORAGE BARN.

By the time I get to the large hanger-like barn we have for machinery, only half of Molly is here. I'd say it's her good half, but both of them are nice. The sleigh swallows her head and torso. Her round, curvy ass and two legs dangle out. Whatever she's doing inside the sleigh has her ass wiggling side to side, and her feet dance to keep her balanced and in this position.

Good thing we don't have HR around here because I let myself stare at her for quite some time and I'm pretty sure my tongue is hanging out.

If I had my way with a backside like hers, I'd peel down those jeans, spread open that luscious ass, and bury my face into the lot of it. I'd lick until my chin was soaked then sink myself balls deep, digging my fingers into her womanly peach, slapping into her soft skin until she moans and doesn't even know her own name anymore.

Maybe I've jacked off to her one too many times.

Just then, her feet hit the ground, and the other half, the one with that effervescent smile, appears. She has a drill in her hand and if she wasn't already sexy enough, this woman with a power tool has my dick pressing eagerly against my jeans. Goddamn, I could use another wank.

Molly swipes fallen hair off her forehead with her arm.

"Hey!" She wiggles the drill. "I figured this baby is going to need to get worse before it gets better."

I find three things attractive in a woman. Curves. A nice laugh. And grit. Molly has all three.

From her text, I thought I'd find her down here, hands on hips, Hank by her side, wondering what the hell to do now that she owns a pile of wood that couldn't be further from her initial idea of winter wonderland. But no. She's ready to dismantle this snow ark and put it back together piece by piece until it's right.

I had no idea she was so handy.

"The thing is," she lifts the drill, "I borrowed this from Hank and don't know how to change the drill bit. So, I haven't gotten very far."

My lips dance. She borrowed the drill ready to embark on a huge carpentry project and doesn't know how to use it. Goddamn adorable.

"Do you have the bits?" I ask.

"Yeah." She gestures me over to a workbench on the far wall where she has the whole set open. She puts the drill down in front of me and stands close.

She must have gotten warm working because her jacket is off. She wears a thin t-shirt, and with my height, I have a clear view of the most fucking sexy, juicy cleavage I ever laid my eyes on. Two perky nipples point right at me. For the second time in just a few minutes, I want to dive into Molly's skin.

I clear my throat. "Why isn't Hank here helping?"

He should be here. He's maintenance. He knows how to use a drill. He could have kept my mind out of the gutter.

"He's still working on the shelters for the Belgians which I told him was more important. But the state of this sleigh? If we want to get bookings for the first snowfall, there's no time to waste." She pats her notebook, the little one she used to take notes when I showed her how I wanted the horses checked. "I'll make a diagram so I know how to put it back together, but I figured every piece will need sanding and painting. It will look so much better if it's done piece by piece."

It will. It's also a lot more work than giving it a gloss over, but I love that Molly doesn't shy away from it. Not only that, but her energy isn't deflated. The work, this project, seems to energize her. Or maybe it's just her default sunny self and she only has this one mode. Still, I can't help but think what a good quality it is. One I'd do well to have.

"Which bit do you think you need?" I ask.

She takes a bigger one out than the one she's got. "This."

She grips the bit between her index finger and thumb, and when I go to take it, the pads of my fingers make contact with her soft, warm skin, and I know, I fucking know, I better stop jerking off to her before this raging attraction, that can even make my dick twitch at the touch of an index finger, gets out of hand.

I've deprived myself for a good number of years. Mostly, it's been okay, because nobody really caught my eye. But Molly? She catches my eye and then some. And every time I try not to like her, she goes and does something like care for Romeo, or wield a drill, or hang her ass in my face.

I grab the drill off the workbench and show her how to replace the bit. Like usual, she watches to learn. Another thing I admire.

The pit of my stomach works hard, like I'm hungry, but I know it's not for food. I hand Molly the drill.

"Thanks for the lesson, chief. I can do that." She smiles.

I offer a closemouthed grin in return.

She receives it and smiles even brighter, and my heart

thumps, telling me to pay attention, but I want to think of something other than her pink, full lips and pearly teeth I'd like to slide my tongue between.

She glances at the sleigh. "So, you think with me, Hank, and maybe Bobby we can finish this sleigh off in time for November snow? People are in full-on Christmas mode by then a lot of times. I suppose I can always use a stock photo on the website and book for mid-November."

I consider the twelve-person sleigh. That's a hell of a lot of panels. We probably have a couple of weeks though before snow, and my capacity for work, and on no sleep, is high. And my excitement for this project is surprisingly high, too. The beat-up classic sleigh gets my blood pumping.

"Yeah. We can handle it."

"We?" she asks.

"Yeah. We." I take off my coat and roll up my sleeves. "Your bottom line is my bottom line."

I'd love our bottom halves aligned.

"Thanks, Dash. You know you don't have to help, but Hank being busy... Bobby said he'd come by in a bit."

I grab a screwdriver off the workbench. I should go out to the toolshed and get another drill. But I don't want to leave, not even for a minute. Maybe someone else will be here when I get back. And I don't like someone elses.

We head to the back of the sleigh and set to unscrewing panels. We move in silence. The faint smell of her perfume hits me when a gust blows in from the open floor-to-ceiling barn doors. Her hair is up in a messy bun, and now the nape of her neck is the third place on Molly's body I'd like to bury my face.

She catches me staring, but darts her eyes back to the next screw in the row she's undoing. She swallows, and I watch the column of her throat work.

103

She considers what to say next. "So, Colt and Jolie tell me this has only been a luxury ranch for four years?"

"Mm-hm." I ignore the cramp in my hand, there only because I was simping too hard to go to the toolshed.

"Why did you stop ranching? Your cattle is with the Danes now from what I understand?"

Why is it that Molly's small talk is actually big? I don't like talking about the one thing that makes me less of a cowboy. And that I'm a big hypocrite, too. I ranched with Dad for the longest time and never thought too much about what was happening to those cattle. But after Dad passed, I didn't want anything to do with it. I eat burgers and steak. It doesn't make sense, but neither does a vegan buying their cat tuna fish.

I rub my hand. "Couldn't look the cows in the eyes anymore," I admit.

It's the first time I ever have admitted it. Even though my family knew something was up when me, a people-hating introvert, proposed a hotel on our land, I never really explained to them why I pushed for it.

She leans against the back of the sleigh. "I like that about you."

A strangled laugh erupts from my lips. She must be joking. What's to like about a cowboy that can't ranch? But the way she's staring at me with those totally non-judg-mental eyes seeps into my chest. I thought my heart would shatter even more if I ever admitted to not being a *real man*, but Molly's gaze doesn't break me, it feels more like I'm being put back together.

"Well." I point the screwdriver at her. "It's our secret." I get back to grinding away at a screw.

Her drill whirrs, and a screw drops, clinking on the cement floor. "Well, if you're going to do this thing, I say you do it. All in. I know the bottom line is better than the past couple years but I'm all ideas for making Starlight Ranch even more lucrative."

"Oh yeah? Better than winter wonderland?"

Whirr. Clink.

"Maybe. My sister is graduating early, BA in events management. And I was telling her about the sleigh rides and the hotel. She told me we should get into weddings. Or get into being a honeymoon destination. It's all about the networking..."

I flap my lips.

She throws a hand to her hip and gives me a completely undeterred toothy grin. "What? It's a good idea!" She shakes her head then taps my arm. "You just don't want more people around, but I'm afraid you just chose the lesser of two evils." She's joking, but when she focuses on her next screw and lines up the bit, she says more sincerely, "We all have to do that sometimes."

I think about what Molly told me in the kitchen about her mom. I think about the stained sock and the hole I know is in her boot; and she never replaced them. She didn't buy herself new ones because the money probably went elsewhere. I think about her thin winter coat. I'm pretty sure this woman knows all about making choices. And she rarely chooses herself.

Chapter Twelve

MOLLY

Working side by side with this inked-up cowboy is not easy. Hard as I try, as much as I will myself to stop thinking of him sexually, this man fucking fills out a pair of Wranglers and tight white tee like a woman created him. Lo and behold. Ariana Grande was right. God is a woman.

And beyond the sex candy I want to suck on as we tuck into this ungrateful task, Dash is being really nice to me. I never expected him to teach me what he knows, support me, hang out by Romeo's bedside, or really be anything more than a grumpy boss to me.

And he. Is. My. Boss. A good one at that. Between Dash and Jolie, I've learned more in a few days here than I did in a few years at other ranches. He deserves to know this. I stare at a rusty screw in front of me and wonder how the hell I'm going to loosen it. "I really appreciate you being such a good mentor."

He hums a laugh. "Is that what I am? I just want things done my way."

I giggle. "I know that's the truth, but at my other ranches, the managers would usually just give me a list of things to do. Or tell me what to do and never take the time to explain. You telling me why we groom or what I'm looking for when I pick a hoof makes it easier to remember. I'm going to train all our staff that way. Less lists, more explanations."

He nods but stares at the screw he's loosening. My God does this man have a gorgeous, thick, golden neck.

I reach into the depths of my mind, wondering what else we might talk about. What else I could say or do to make the most of this time. I glance at my watch and know Bobby will be back here to help with the sleigh soon. I told him to come by ten-thirty. I don't want him here anymore, not only because he told a couple of the others I didn't deserve the manager's job, but also because it means Dash will probably leave.

In fact, Dash probably needs sleep at some point today. Maybe I'm selfish in not telling him Bobby's coming but I really want to know more about him. Every time Dash peels away another layer, I see something worth admiring. He might not have the time of day for just anyone, but he's loyal to his family, cares deeply about the ranch, and even though he adores his work with the horses, I get the feeling there's so much more to his story.

To my surprise, he asks a question. "Are you warm enough in the apartment?"

"I'm okay." I tap my hip. "I have plenty of insulation."

He stops what he's doing, and I have never seen Dash's face so animated since knowing him. His eyebrows are pinched tightly together, and his eyes are wide like I just said something crazy.

His nostrils flare. "What did you just say?"

I'm used to making little jokes about my weight. I started doing it as a defensive thing in high school. The funny, bubbly big girl got more friends than the sad big girl on a diet who never seemed to lose weight. But now that Dash is staring at me like he wants to slap me silly and asks me to repeat what I said, I realize these are the kind of words I've been trying hard to eliminate from my vocabulary.

I try to shrug off the pink creeping into my cheeks, but more likely it's turning to red. The tips of my ears burn now, too. "Why are you staring at me like I'm a nutjob?"

He shakes his head. "Can't believe a woman who looks like you would put herself down." Something between disbelief and a warning signal flashes across his eyes. "Thought I heard wrong."

A woman who looks like me? His words enter me and explode through my body like a prism of rainbows. I'm not used to being complimented, not even indirectly, which is all Dash did. But having a man devastatingly gorgeous as him even suggest that I'm... attractive? Is that what he was saying? I'm sure I'm overthinking this and reading into it.

But then, he leans against the last panel left on the back of the sleigh and... smiles. Again. For the second time in thirty minutes. And damn is Dashiell Hunter smiling a sight to behold. It almost takes my breath away. And best yet, I'm not sure anyone else around here has seen it but me. In this moment, it feels like his smile belongs to both of us.

We're standing there grinning at each other like goons when Bobby comes racing in, interrupting our moment, or the closest thing I'll ever have to one with Dash.

"Hey, sorry I'm late," he announces, breaking the spell I'm under.

Dash's smile fades when he sees Bobby.

Yeah. That smile was just for me. Something inside me squeaks.

"Great. You're here," I say, not meaning one word of it but working hard not to sound disappointed.

Dash immediately steps away and goes to put his screwdriver back in its place in the workbench. I know I might see him later in the apartment, maybe, or tomorrow morning, or sometime very soon because we live and work together, but it feels like he's going off on an around-the-world cruise or something.

I need to stay focused. This sleigh isn't fixing itself.

"Bobby, could you go on out to the toolshed and get another drill? Make sure you get a set of bits, too, and you can help me finish taking this thing apart until you sign off?"

"Aw, Molly. No can do..."

This is how it's going to be with Bobby? Fighting me every step of the way...

"The pastures need me..." he churns up his millionth excuse this week.

Dash turns to Bobby, leans on his arm against the workbench, posture stiff and manly. "Bobby."

Bobby turns away from me and gazes at Dash. "Yeah?"

His voice rumbles low, like thunder. "I think what you meant to say was *yes, ma'am.*"

Bobby opens his mouth, but no words come out. He searches for a reason to make Dash reel back an intention to punch him in the face; because that appears to be his next move.

Dash's body clenches, not waiting for Bobby to respond. "Go ahead..."

"Yes, ma'am." Bobby says the words but doesn't face me, he stares blankly, defeated, into thin air.

But Dash isn't finished. He steps closer to Bobby and scans him head to toe. "Hand in your resignation or treat Molly with respect. Those are your only two options at Starlight Ranch. If I hear otherwise, I'll make the decision for you."

Bobby nods.

"Now go on and get that drill."

Bobby walks off, his body probably raging with schemes of revenge, but I don't care. Dash sticking up for me is everything.

"Thanks for that."

"He gives you any more trouble and he's gone."

My heart flaps wildly. Dash just sided with me. He chose *me* over Bobby, who, by the way, I thought he liked because he's a local boy and one of the only full-time staff around here. But... Dash backed *me*. Confidence swells inside me. I can do this. No... I have *done* this. I'm bursting with more of that pride I felt when he handed me that clipboard to sign for the horses. I want to crash into him with a hug... *and rip our clothes off*... but I keep my cool.

He doesn't know just how big all of this is for me. The goal I set for myself nearly ten years ago while reading a book about the west, late at night when I couldn't sleep, is an actual reality. And the intention I set for myself almost four years ago when my sister went to college... it's real, too.

Dash hooks his thumbs through his belt loops. "I'm heading to town now. You need anything?"

"I'm good, thanks."

"All right. If you need anything, drop me a text."

The most pure, content feeling rises from my toes and

up through every cell of my body. Dash, who months ago refused to hire me, is now the best mentor I've ever had, and to top off is now offering to pick me up a loaf of bread from the Super-Mart. The pride was one thing. But I never thought such a simple gesture as asking if I need something from the grocery store could make my knees buckle.

When I get back up to the apartment after a grueling day of work, Dash's door is closed, so I assume he's sleeping. Whatever he does in the middle of the night, he skipped because of Romeo, and the next couple days, too. I guess he's eager to get back to his schedule.

He seems like a creature of habit. I've only been living here a short time but I notice his boots are always put together and aligned, either inside the door or on a tray outside to catch the mud and water if it's been wet out. His towel is always folded and hangs tidy over the drying rail. He rinses out the bathroom sink and wipes it down. He never leaves a dirty dish in sight, but then, apart from his morning coffee, maybe he doesn't eat here.

He's actually a great roommate, better than my sister will be in terms of cleanliness, but hey, it's a trade I have to make. Not that I wouldn't choose my sister over a man any day of the week, but something inside me still twangs, telling me it's a foolish exchange.

I toe off my shoes and pull off my socks. One of them is soaked because of that damn hole in my boot, but I'm resisting buying another pair. It's my third pair this year alone. The catch twenty-two is I can't really afford super high-quality boots, but the cheap ones fall apart fast, working as much as I do. I'll be getting paid better now that I have this management position, but a wet foot isn't as irritating as my sister's college loans, and I promised her, when she considered not going because she felt she should be earning not spending, I wouldn't let her stress about it. And that means college loan payments are my priority.

All I need is a plastic bag to line the insides. I've just been too busy to think about it. Too preoccupied to think of anything really. Even food. Since moving in, I haven't been to the grocery store for a while, and all I have is my peanut butter and bread here, but after thirty-five thousand steps and being up for sixteen hours, I have no interest in driving to town. Maybe I should have asked Dash to pick something up. But like most people, I don't like asking for favors.

I pad quietly to the kitchen, trying not to disturb my roommate, but when I reach up to grab a glass for water, a guitar strums behind his bedroom door. The plucking is gentle, melodic, and I wish he was on my side of his door. I adore hearing and watching people play guitar. I follow at least nine, ten guitar channels on YouTube. I never played an instrument growing up and am always taken with people who do. Maybe it's the discipline, I've always admired hard work, or maybe it's that music has a way of allowing emotion the way nothing else does. I just love it.

I stand dead still, trying to make out the tune he's playing when the sound of his deep, rich voice, even quieter than the guitar strings, hums. His humming isn't how ordinary people hum. It's more like singing, and the melody melds with the chords he plays. I strain my ears, wondering what the song is, asking myself what kind of song a man like Dash would like to play on his guitar.

I can't be sure... it sounds familiar. Something I've heard on the Oldies station back when my grandma was alive and had it going in her kitchen all the time over the long summers we spent with her when Mom actually had some work on. Those were good summers. Those were summers where an adult actually took care of me.

My ears strain, and the richness of the same voice I heard in the stables enters me. God, I love Dash's voice. Singing. Humming. Speaking. For a man who shows little emotion, his tone is packed full of it. It's one of those voices that's like a massage rubbing all over your sore muscles.

He stops strumming, and I quickly head to the kitchen, just in case he comes out of his room. I don't want him catching me staring at his door. I run the faucet and fill my glass, thinking he might emerge, but he doesn't.

Disappointing, but I should have expected it. We are not friends.

My stomach rumbles. When I open the bread box, inside, next to my half loaf, is a small white box with a note on it.

Sunshine,
Thanks for working so hard.
D
PS Eat this. Or else.

I open the box, and inside is a slice of carrot cake with fluffy cream cheese frosting and a tiny fondant carrot. He got me dessert.

I glance back at his closed door. I can't figure this man out. He's prickly. He doesn't stay in my presence longer than he has to. He never wanted to hire me or have me in his space but now... he does nice things for me? But if I try to do something nice for him, as simple as a bandage, he can't run fast enough.

And our conversations... it's clear neither one of us is used to pushing the boat out too far with our feelings. He's definitely holding something inside that steely frame of his but... then he tells me a secret.

And me? I try not to burden others so I keep a lot inside, too. But when we exchange just a few words, it doesn't make me worry the way I do when I've told others about my thoughts. I don't wonder if I'm being judged or have said too much. It's a relief when I talk to him.

I guess when you find someone who cares, or maybe doesn't care at all, it feels good to unload.

I eat my cake and suppress the moans purring in the back of my throat because this carrot cake is the most orgasmic thing I've experienced in a long, long time. It's the cake from CCs I had when I first met Jolie. She told me all about the town's favorite baker. I even follow *Sugar Shay*, the woman behind the famous cake on social media. But I went on a dessert ban after that last slice. This Shay woman is my new best friend, and she doesn't even know it.

I savor every last morsel. I stare at Dash's note, and something about it takes away what I'd usually feel right now. I don't feel the least bit bad that I ate a piece of cake for dinner. Dash said I was... well, he didn't say it, but I think he believes I'm fine just the way I am, and even though it's silly for a man's opinion to make a difference, he's not just any man. And it does make a difference whether it's right or not.

I clean off the box and chuck it in the recycling, then take a drink of water that I should have had earlier because now I'll have to pee in the middle of the night. I'm tired.

Still, I consider the TV, wondering if he hears it would he come out to see me? Nah. I hate TV and I don't want to disturb him so I head to my room, and just when I think the day couldn't get any better, sitting in front of my bedroom door is a brand-new pair of boots.

Chapter Thirteen

DASH

A CERTAIN SATISFACTION surged through me when I bought Molly those boots and that cake. I didn't even hesitate at the idea but I did tell myself it was not the way to stop fixating on her. And me buying her things wasn't exactly upholding the *we're not friends* statement I made when I first allowed her into my life. Into my space. Into my every fucking thought.

But when she put herself down today, well, I'm a show-don't-tell kind of guy and I meant what I said. I hate that the woman would even dream of starving those curves. That's what had me walking to the counter at Creme de la Cremes asking for Shay's famous cake. I tapped my foot waiting in the line, like everyone there knew the cake wasn't for me. Like I was doing something secretive and illicit by buying it. I couldn't have felt more exposed if I was buying her a goddamn ring.

But by the time I walked out of the store with a tiny white bag hanging off my fingers, I reasoned it was appropriate to reward her for a job well done, all her hard work. That's why I bought the cake. It's like leaving donuts in the break room. Sure, she's being paid to do the things she does. And even staying up all night once in a while is part of the job. But she's even more than I bargained for. It's like a bonus for her extra grit. That's all it is. Boss-to-employee gratitude.

And she needs proper equipment, too. The boots? Like buying a new hammer for Hank.

Starlight Ranch has come alive with her ideas. Her bubbly energy already infuses any space she occupies, that much is clear to see, but now, her positive outlook on growing a business I struggled to care about, actually has a bright future. Of course it does. Everything is bright around Molly.

Even me. Well, I'm less dim anyway. I don't know if I should let myself like it or not. But like my mom always says, you can't control your feelings, just what you do with them. And me? I bought boots and a slice of cake.

When I wake up to my trusty alarm at three, it's Friday. I'm pretty sure Molly said her sister arrives tonight. I'm secretly thankful I have a reason to move out for a couple days with her sister staying. I'm not quite ready to face her and what she'll say after finding the cake and boots last night. She'll glow. She'll be sweet. She might hug me. Avoiding her is the best course of action.

Molly has the horses in check, they'll be safe under her watch, and that I trust her with them speaks volumes. But what speaks more is me moving out. Where several weeks ago trading the virtual stranger I could keep at a distance for my sister seemed like a good thing, trading back is the farthest thing from what I really want. Molly is hardly a stranger now. I don't want her to be.

What the fuck is going on with me?

I pack my things quietly in just the dim of my lamplight and throw them in my car before driving to Mustang Valley. I do my job there, and after, I return my belongings to Bird's Eye, back with Jolie, and decide to not make my morning trip to the stables.

My mom texts saying she and Eve are at the big house today, my niece is off for doctor's appointments, and asks if I want to come by. Yes, I do. I love time with Eve. She always takes my mind off anything too serious because her ever-present attitude just reels you back to the ground when you find yourself floating away.

I spend time with my mom that morning, set up an obstacle course in the ring for Eve and her horse, Claude. And, probably pissing my sister off since she thinks he loves me more than her, I ride her horse, Ted, out on the trails and unleash him in a wide-open space. The boy has a gallop so fast you wonder if you'll have a face left afterward, and the wind whips and claws at me in his speed. None of it makes me think of Molly any less or the fact that I haven't told her I was leaving. Not even dinner with Sam, Colt, and the rest takes my mind off my lack of communication.

Not that I have to. Not that I usually do. But something inside me feels it was wrong not to let her know.

That evening, I step into my old home. Memories flood in when I see the special chair I left behind in exchange for more privacy. Dad's chair. I put my duffle bag down at the door and head over to the beat-up leather recliner that used to have his indent in it, but now fits my ass perfectly because I sat on it every day after he left it behind.

I glance around. Jolie has womanized the place. There

are new pillows on the couch, a fancy, city-person coffee machine, and some of those bottles with sticks in them that make a room smell nice.

Molly made our apartment smell nice with just her presence, but especially when she'd have a shower. Man, that strawberry-mint shampoo smell would fill the entire apartment, first with its scent, and when she'd open the bathroom door, along with the smell came a dewy burst of humid summer that took the bite out of the dry, autumn air. Our apartment smelled like the taste of perfectly ripe fruit.

I get up to read the label on the reed diffuser, and though *clean cotton* smells nice, I don't prefer it to Molly's summer.

Jolie is over at the stable apartment with Molly and her sister who I never even bothered to ask her name. My heart twangs like an out-of-tune guitar string because I ignored Molly today and didn't bother asking her about a woman I know is one of only two family members. I shake my head.

Why would she even care if I care anyway?

I take my duffle bag up to my room when my mobile beeps and it's a text from my brother.

MOTHER PUCKER

> HEY, MAN, IT'S MOON RIDGE FRIGHT NIGHT. FOUR OF THE GHOSTS CALLED IN SICK. WANT TO HELP OUT WITH ME AND ASHTON? YOU'RE NATURALLY SCARY. LOL

Moon Ridge Ranch holds two community fundraising events every year. One is a summer event, good old-fashioned carnival style, and the other is their Fright Night, with a full-on maize maze and a haunted house. They've been holding it every year, and given they've donated proceeds multiple times to causes near and dear, and that

they're friends, and that I desperately need a distraction, all
roads lead to a yes.

ME

AT LEAST I'M SCARY FOR REASONS
OTHER THAN MY FACE.

MOTHER PUCKER

HAHA. FUCK OFF. IS THAT A YES? WE
NEED TO GET THERE ASAP. FIRST
TICKET IS AT SIX-THIRTY.

ME

FINE. I'LL MEET YOU OVER THERE.

Scaring the pimples off teenagers will definitely take my
mind off things. Or at least that's what I thought until I was
standing in the pitch-black of the haunted house, my
nostrils flaring, swearing I smelled strawberry mint in
the air.

Half hour later, I'm there.

Ashton greets me first, shaking my hand and pulling me
in to slap me on the back. "Hey, bro. Thanks for making it.
Mom was freaking out she'd have to cancel. We're still one
ghoul short, but it will do."

I look him up and down his massive frame. "Yeah, well,
you count for two."

Behind him and my brother is the Danes' hay barn,
empty in September, hay sold off to equip people for
winter. The barn is empty one month out of the year, and
that's now. Monica and my mom come over with clipboards
in their hands.

"Boys. Thanks so much for making it." Monica's face is

tight and frazzled. "There's some bug going around the ranch hands, and I have a few who are seriously laid up. Don't want the entire town getting sick even though they offered to come, bless 'em."

My mom glances at Ashton and Logan. "Good thing you boys have a night off."

Logan rubs his hands together. "Karma, baby. I nearly wet myself in that barn when I was ten. I'm taking no prisoners tonight."

Monica puts a hand on her hip. "Don't you go making people cry now."

"Are we here to scare, or are we here to scare?" he asks.

Our moms share a glance, and both pull their lips into tight lines.

My mom puts a hand on Monica's arm. "I can still call Sam and Colt instead. Just not sure..."

Monica cuts her off. "No, no, they wanted to bring Eve and her friend around. It's fine." She turns back to us. "Just behave. You're big. You're burly. You're scary."

Logan and Ashton, even in their mid-thirties, laugh like goons at the prospect of making people jump.

Monica and my mom set about organizing us volunteers into different zones in the barn. It's amazing how far it's come since being a boy myself walking in the dark through this exact space on Halloween. With the fluorescent lights blaring above, I see the zones created by everything from pallets to ride-on lawn mowers... anything to help keep people to a path that weaves around the wide-open space. Right now, it looks mostly like a mess.

But I know how this haunted house works. The scary part is that the building has no windows. When the lights go out, you have to feel your way around. Even without the likes of me and the others making creepy noises and jumping out, walking through a pitch-black barn could make the most confident person uneasy.

We position ourselves in our zones, and I have to say, being a scarer isn't for the faint of heart either, but soon, my night vision adjusts just enough I can make out general shapes of people working their way through the path of doom one after another.

The makeshift pathways created aren't wider than allowing one or two people to come through. I make a low groaning noise or a full-on *boo*, depending how the mood strikes me. And for an hour, I don't think about what Molly is doing with Jolie and her sister. That is, until I *know* what she's doing with them.

Someone opens the barn door, letting in a sliver of light from the outside and a conversation that, because the barn is still and silent, I hear crystal clear.

It's Molly. "Let's go through together."

Another woman's voice, must be her sister, because it isn't Jolie who says, "No way. It will be so much scarier if we go on our own."

"Yeah, that's what I'm trying to avoid." Molly laughs. It's not her usual giggle. It's nervous.

Jolie says, "I started coming through this place when I was ten, Mols. We'll all go and wait by the exit at the end. Leave no woman behind lest they be taken by a cheap Pennywise costume."

"Shit, Jo... you had to go and mention clowns?" Molly sounds nervous.

"I'm sure you can handle it," Jolie reassures her.

"Who's saying I can't handle it? I just... fine, let's just go. Jolie, because she's done it before, then Lily then me."

"Still afraid of the boogeyman?" Lily, her sister I guess, teases.

"Fine, *you* go first," Molly says.

And that's when I presume all three of them step inside at once and close the door behind them.

It's still as can be, apart from the occasional bump and a scream Lily lets out when Logan quickly flashes a light over his face. She makes her way farther, and I know Jolie has started, too, because she must have bashed something and lets out a big ol' *shit*. When the first woman reaches me, Lily, I wonder if she's anything like her sister.

My dark, eerie moan fills the space between us.

Her feet jump a step back. "Fuck," she mumbles nervously, clutching her heart and I have to admit, scaring people carries its own bizarre satisfaction.

Lily continues onward past me, feeling her way through the shadows.

It's not easy getting out of my corner of the maze because it seems like the exit would carry on naturally forward, but you have to feel around a lot for a doorknob to open a door that's just a frame and a door propped up between pallets. No escape is the scariest thing of all.

But Lily is pretty calm and figures it out. The door creaks open, and I make sure to close it quickly for the next victim.

A loud noise erupts ten feet away from me, something between a roar and a *boo*, and Jolie's blood-curdling scream echoes in the barn. It's curt but loud and it's instantly followed by a nervous laugh.

"Ashton? Is that you?" she says into the darkness. "I swear that's you." Her voice fakes confidence, but the slight wobble betrays her. Even a grown woman would be scared in this place. "Ashton... I can smell your cologne. I know that's you..."

As is his job, he's silent, and she goes quiet, too, but

before too long her feet shuffle along the floor. She's being more careful now she already hit herself working her way through too fast. When she gets into my space, I whisper a line in a sinister voice I know will stand my sister's hair on end.

"I want to play a game..." I hiss.

"Oh shit... I'm fucking..." I can't see her clearly but I know this line from her all-time scariest movie, *Saw,* has her patting around for the exit frantically. "Fuck you, Dash... that oversteps the mark."

I tighten my lips holding in amusement. She knows it's me but she'll never prove it.

All that bravado, with Molly. Jolie deserved it. Jolie escapes through the final door and joins Lily. The two of them whisper and share a giggle near the exit of the barn itself.

"Guys? Are you finished now?" Molly must have heard them, too, and she's entered my tiny corner of the dark maze.

Her breathing is quiet but quick, and I can practically hear her pulse in the small space we share.

"Girls?" she calls out again, her voice wavering.

"Yeah, we're done. We'll wait," Lily calls to her.

"Okay..." Molly whispers to herself, not knowing I'm inches away. "Almost done," she says in an effort to self-soothe.

I know I'm supposed to give her one last hair-raising fright, but her fear ripples the air around me. It's palatable and too real for my liking. She feels around just inches away from me, and I wonder if her hands will land on me while I silently wait, not wanting to freak her out any more than she already is.

She mumbles to herself, "How do I get out of here?"

She releases a high-pitched sound, between a whine and a groan.

There is something seriously wrong with me. Like some sort of fucking pervert, I breathe the air in deeply, trying to capture a bit of her sweet perfume I exchanged for the smell of laundry at Bird's Eye.

She senses me. Maybe feels my heavy breathing and snaps her head around in my direction. "Is somebody there?"

I put her out of her misery. "It's me."

"Dash?" Her voice trembles.

"Yeah. You okay?"

She lets out the breath she's been holding since she realized I was behind her. "I'm fine. I hate this shit, though, not gonna lie."

"I got you, Sunshine. You need to just spin around one-eighty. Behind you is a door. Find the knob. It's right behind you."

"Okay..."

She turns, and my night vision barely makes out her hands patting along the door.

"I can't..."

She's so scared her hands are in panic mode, and I'm not sure she even made sense of my instructions.

I reach around her. The space is small, that's what I tell myself when my hips meet her peachy ass. I do it to feel around in front of her, of course. But my reasoning doesn't stop my manly reaction. Instantly, my dick fills with wanting, a need to press into her more forcefully, to rub the ache that's building in my jeans. Never has something so goddamn inappropriate felt so fucking good.

This is wrong. Really, really wrong. Molly works for me. She trusts me as her boss, she's scared shitless right now,

125

and all I want to do is reach both hands around her front and take those tits into my palms, play with her nipples between my fingers, then tear down her jeans and panties and force my throbbing cock deep inside her.

Her hair smells fucking gorgeous, nearly touching my nose. What I wouldn't give to wrap my fingers around her throat, tip up her chin, and take her from behind.

She adjusts herself; I swear she eases her body back into me.

"Thanks..." she whispers.

I know whereabouts the knob is because every time the door opens, the faint exit sign illuminates it. But I take my time, feeling around the doorjamb, and let my cheek brush against the top of her head. Her silky hair stimulates my skin with impossible lust.

"Why are you so scared?" I murmur.

She twists her head ever so slightly and the tip of her ear sweeps across my lips. My heart beats harder than it did before, so hard I'm concerned she can feel it right through her winter coat. We're so close; it feels too good to peel away... my mind wanders to places it doesn't belong. Sliding my hand up her torso, over her voluptuous tit, grasping at her throat, and forcing her mouth onto mine...

She spins toward me a little more, and her shoulder leans into my chest. "Once, when I was younger and my mom took one of her naps, the TV was left on all afternoon. *Nightmare on Elm Street* was on. I was just too young to be watching something like that, I guess."

Fuck, this woman will be haunting my dreams for sure. Why? Why do I allow myself a touch? But I do. My hand follows the length of her arm, and I take her hand in mine. "You're almost out of here." I twine our fingers together, and lead her hand to the doorknob. "Here it is..."

It is not easy to let go of her, but I do. To my surprise, she doesn't make a run for safety.

She pauses for a beat. "Dash?"

"Yeah?"

"Are you coming back to the apartment when my sister leaves?"

The way she feels right here against my body has me thinking I shouldn't. I'm too close to crossing the line. Too close to doing the wrong thing. "Just giving you some space, Molly."

"Oh, right."

It's just two words but her disappointment suffocates me, so I make it sound less emotional, more logical. "It's supposed to be your apartment."

"True."

Does she want me back? It sounds like she does. And the way she hasn't yet opened the door and still gently leans against my body sure *feels* like she does. I could stand here forever and never care about leaving the barn. But I find the self-control, reach to her hand again, and help her with the knob.

"Have fun this weekend." I guide her hand to ease the door open.

Red light from the exit sign glows on her cheek. "I already am."

Chapter Fourteen

MOLLY

I NEARLY DIDN'T MAKE it back to the apartment on my legs of jelly after the haunted house. Not only was I forced to pretend being scared was fun but... Dash. Until now, I thought the attraction was only one way, but unless he had a magic wand in his pants, he liked touching, too. I went from being terrified and not able to get out of that dark barn fast enough to wishing the floor would give way and drop us right into bed. I swear the sexual chemistry was a potion working on us both tonight.

He let his cheek fall onto my hair. His lips skimmed my ear... his breath fell over me alive and sparking with heat that made me enjoy darkness for the first time in my life. I could survive a million nights if Dash was in them. Damn, I wanted him to make a move. I imagined his hands snaking around the front of me, to tug me into him. I wanted to slide my touch inside his pants and stroke that hard dick pressing against my ass. I yearned for him to lower his lips just inches more and glide his tongue in my mouth. Halloween is a night for fantasies, and a hundred of them found me in that barn tonight.

But as usual, he controlled the interaction, not me. Even though his dick was definitely hard against my ass, he let me go. Reflecting on that moment, it was more than sexual, too. He eased my fear. He calmed me.

Dash could have given me one last fright and I would have peed my pants at that point. But he sensed how serious it was. That barn wasn't fun and games for me. I hated every moment of it until I got into his space.

But I'm afraid of the dark. And Dash? He's afraid of the light.

He's a mystery no one could ever blame me for trying to solve. All this time, all these months, I watched Dashiell Hunter move around these stables with his heavy, grumpy presence and thought he was just a dickwad who thought he was better than everyone else. But over the past weeks, the tiny peek he's let me see through those emerald-green curtains has been nothing short of someone deep and caring.

I'm probably reading into him. I'm probably doing that thing again where I pretend the bad boy is a tortured soul who just needs my healing touch. I like helping people. I like people needing me and depending on me. Like my sister. It's never been a burden to support her. Her reaching for the stars brightens my world, too.

Later that night, when we plop down on the sofas in the apartment, Jolie with a wine bottle in hand and my sister with three glasses, I know bagging this gig in Starlight Canyon was for both of us. She and Jolie get on like a house on fire; even though my sister is about ten years younger, the two have a lot in common.

They're both gregarious and super smart, and while Jolie pours the wine, they discuss the thing they have in common—Golden Sierra University.

"So, you're graduating early, Lil?" Jolie already has a nickname for my sister. Nicknames seem to be a Hunter thing.

"Yeah... worked my ass off, but it's worth it."

Jolie hands Lily a full glass. "You didn't want to stay around in Albuquerque and just take some throwaway courses and finish off the year there? Have one last semester of silly fun before joining the real world?"

My sister glances at me with a smile that's anything but disappointed, even though I know the true weight of her answer. "Who wants to pay all that money? I'm ready to *make* money. Be a boss bitch."

Jolie laughs. "I like that. So you're done in December. Any prospects for work?"

"Not just yet. But I'm definitely moving back with my sister." Lily sits next to me and wraps her arm around me. "Reunited in Starlight Canyon. Who would have thought?"

Jolie hands me a glass and sits down with hers. "Molly told me you're in hospitality. I'll keep my ear to the ground for you."

"Thanks."

We all sip. I sense Jolie isn't staying long since her glass only has an inch of liquid in it. She takes one drink, then eyes me over the goblet. "You took a while finding your way out of that haunted maze tonight."

I drink. "Nerves, I guess."

She puts her feet up on the coffee table. Her socks have pineapples on them. "Did Dash send you over the edge?"

If only she knew what a loaded question it was. Her raised eyebrow tells me maybe it is.

"No. He took pity on me."

"Did he now?" She says it suggestively.

Lily darts her eyes back and forth between us. "Is there something I don't know?"

"No." I shake my head quickly, so quickly it comes off as defensive.

Jolie swirls her wine. "I'm just saying, he was back in Bird's Eye with me for a couple hours, and I've never seen him so goddamn grumpy. He's different living here with you."

I laugh lightly. "I promise you, he isn't. Still a grump, believe you me."

"Oh, I'm sure he is." Jolie laughs. "But he *is* different with you."

My heart thumps in my ribcage, and my stomach floods with fireworks, because even though my mind doesn't believe it, my body wants it to be true.

"Well, I think we get along all right." I say it and feel a little guilty because I still need to figure out a way to get Dash to move permanently back in with Jolie.

My sister being here reminds me Dash and I aren't some fairy tale. My sister can't come live in some castle in the air. She needs a room. A bed. Stability.

My plan all along was to earn this manager position, and this apartment, and give my sister a place to live while we pay down some of the loans she had to take. I contributed to her tuition as much as I could, but a college education is damn expensive. Her having free accommodation when she graduates will help so much. And maybe when she moves out, my mom will move in. I want her here, too, because I haven't given up hope on her either.

She's been stepping down her dose for a while now. At least she says she is. And she does sound and look so much more alert and bright when I talk to her on video calls.

One day, the three of us will live a new chapter with a happy ending. Me having this apartment to use as is best for my family is the backbone of the plan.

Jolie finishes the last glug of wine and stands to take her glass to the sink. "Sorry I can't stay longer, gals."

Lily stands, and they hug goodbye like they're long-time friends. "Thank you for taking us to Fright Night. I had a fab time."

"Yeah, wait 'til you see the summer festival. It's all about the dunk tank. I'd stay longer but I have about a hundred bovine vaccinations to do tomorrow at a ranch an hour away, so it's an early start."

I hug Jolie goodbye, and Lily and I take up places on the couch again.

Lily says, "So why didn't you tell me you have a thing for your boss?"

"I don't. And even if I did, it's irrelevant."

"It's just fun girl talk," she says lightly, having no clue just how not fun having a thing for my boss is.

Dash doesn't feel like a simple crush or a hot guy we're talking about in passing on a night out. I really need to ignore the deep curiosity and... whatever else this is that is far beyond him being super gorgeous. The thing about him I want to take care of. But as usual, my sister, who was forced to grow up beyond her years, figures me out anyway.

"You like him," she deadpans.

I don't answer.

She circles her finger around the rim of the wine glass. "And that would be fine except he has two red flags. You said he has tattoos." She puts up her index finger. She puts up her middle one. "And he's a lone wolf."

"Most women don't think tattoos are a red flag. Quite the opposite."

"For you that combo is lethal..."

I know what she's thinking. "He's not like Donovan."

"I just know how much you thrive on nurturing people."

I want to argue, but she knows me better than anyone else.

She shakes her head. "You saw Don as some man in need of healing. Meanwhile, he treated you like absolute shit and cheated on you."

"Worse than that," I remember. "We were never even really together. I was just his fuck toy. He cheated on his fuck toy."

"Exactly. And that sucked. You were devastated. I just don't want you investing in another guy who's some sexy bad boy not good enough for you."

I scoff. "Dash is like, thirty or something."

"Dude... are you serious right now?" My sister is already getting tipsy. She's new-ish to drinking at only twenty-two, and I doubt, given her straight A's, she does much going out.

"Yeah. I'm serious right now," I joke and mock her. "All right. Straight shooting, I do find him intriguing. Yes, he is sexy, tattooed, and most definitely a lone wolf"—in fact, I'm not sure if he'll even come back Monday, and his lack of communication irks me—"but he is really good to his family. He's incredibly tender with the animals..."

She stares at the floor and shakes her head. "Billy the Kid... Jesse James..."

I laugh. "Dash isn't robbing banks, Lily. And actually, yes, he is really gruff with everyone, me sometimes included, but he also stuck up for me recently. He's empowered me. Trusted me to take the reins here..."

"Good pun."

"And that makes me feel very, very good. I've never been a manager before or the one in charge, and he, well, he's a great mentor and does make me feel like I can really succeed. So unlike Don, who made me feel lower than low, he's nothing like that. He's an amazing boss and helping me grow."

She shrugs. "Fine. You've swayed me for now. I just want to make sure you feel comfortable staying here long term and don't get involved in something you feel the need to run from. You've been happier these past months in Starlight Canyon than I've seen you in a long, long time. Maybe ever."

I reflect on what she's said. It's true. I love it here. "Yeah, I really am."

"And Jolie is so sweet."

"Most of the workers are great, too. And at the hotel. The Hunters have a good thing going here."

She leans back into me and puts her feet up. "I'm going to love it, too. I feel good about this, Molly." She drops her head to my shoulder. "Change the story."

"That's what we do, baby sis. Change the story."

Chapter Fifteen

DASH

I STAYED at Bird's Eye for a week, only seeing Molly from a distance once or twice. After that haunted house, I must have jerked my cock a thousand times and I still couldn't look at the woman without getting half-hard. So, I mostly kept a distance, going back to my nighttime routine in the Valley and early morning checks on the stables a little earlier than usual as to not run into her.

But now, I need to check on the shelters outside, too, so the process takes longer than usual. Our Belgians and Romeo are doing just fine this morning, rustling to my presence as the sun rises over the mountain, sending slivers of daytime into their corral.

I pop a head collar over the black draft horse and lead the big boy to the crossties so I can look him over. I fold back Romeo's horse blanket and throw it over a railing, give him a brush. His coat is already thickening, preparing him for the winter. I'm deep in the meditative state I often find myself in when brushing a horse. Just then, a voice comes from behind the horse's flank.

"Boo!"

I jerk slightly at the surprise.

It's Molly.

I drop my gaze to the ground below Romeo. She's wearing the boots I bought her. Glad they fit.

She steps around to my side and gives Romeo a pat. "He's doing so well now, isn't he?"

"Yes. he is," I continue grooming but glance up briefly at Molly. The sun is just beginning to poke up behind her. "You're here early."

"Yeah. I was hoping to catch you. We finished the sleigh."

She looks pleased with herself. She should be. They got that done a lot faster than I thought possible.

"Great. I'm impressed. How did you get that done so quickly?"

"Well, I have you to thank for that. After you talking to Bobby, he finally started moving his ass when I told him to."

I laugh because I can't help it. "Good."

"So I wanted you to see it and also maybe see if you can stick around this morning and teach me how to harness the horses? And we need to check the harnesses, too, because, like the sleigh, I'm pretty sure they won't be right."

"Sure." I finish checking over Romeo for signs of his blanket rubbing and go about my other checks.

Molly lifts a hoof and starts picking it out. "Is Romeo your last check?"

"Yup."

"You know you don't need to come out here anymore. I really do have it under control." She stands and uses her forearm to swipe some of her shiny, chocolate hair off her face. "And Jolie and I had the training session for all the staff who are still here. We taught them everything you taught me and then some."

Molly is the kind of person who needs to feel like she's needed and doing a good job. I won't deprive her of that. "I believe you do. I don't come here to check up on you. I come here because I like being useful."

"Oh. Well, in that case, I'm sure the horses love the extra fuss."

We finish the morning checks, and Molly goes to grab Romeo's super-heavy rug; her strength surprises me. It's damn sexy, but I take the blanket out of her hands anyway, like a gentleman does.

"I got this."

After letting Romeo off the ties, I open the corral for our boy and all but two Belgians to graze. Molly and I head over to the storage barn.

Our boots finally hit gravel.

She gazes at the ground as she talks. "I never thanked you for the boots. I wanted to do it in person, but you never came back to the apartment, and I haven't really seen you much in general."

"No need to thank me," I say, but a warm sensation climbs up my torso. I'm glad she likes them. It took me longer to decide on them than it does on my own.

"I sure as hell am going to thank you. I was wearing plastic bags over my feet in the other ones." She leans over and bumps into my arm. "That's our secret, though."

The corner of my mouth raises into a half-smile. I know Molly is just one of those friendly types. She's always hugging people hello, and when she walks around with my sister, they often have their arms looped through one another's. But all the times I had my dick in my hand thinking about her, and how highly I regard this woman... it feels like flirting.

And I like it.

She continues. "I hope you think we did a good job on the sleigh. We worked really hard. All the seasonal workers apart from two are gone now."

"I appreciate you making this happen..."

We turn the bend of the open, double barn doors, and there, in all its glory, is one stunning twelve-person horse sleigh. I'm speechless. It hardly seems possible this got done in a week. Maybe Molly sleeps less than I do. Or maybe she charmed the remaining seasonal workers into helping for fun. Apart from Bobby, people respond to her and always seem eager to do what she needs. And even Bobby is on board now, apparently. Good thing, too, because I meant what I told him.

I walk toward the sled slowly, like I'm inspecting the Rosetta Stone or something, and start walking a circle around it. "Well, I'll be damned. This is... something else."

"You like it?" she asks, beaming like she's staring at her newborn child. "I didn't want to go with red, it seemed too cliché and obvious. It did cost extra to get the exact shade mixed at the hardware store, but I color-matched the Starlight Ranch logo, that deep purple..."

I smooth my hand along the side. "... and the trim in gold." Yet again, Molly impresses me. Even I can't wait for a ride in this sleigh.

"I made sure we used lacquer," she corrects herself, "I mean, *varnish*, because Hetty at the hardware store taught me the difference now. Anyway, it should be really durable, so hopefully we won't have to paint it again for at least a couple years. Maybe three. Which is good because the labor and paint cost..."

"I hope you're proud of yourself," I interrupt her. "*I'm* proud of you for getting this done to such a high standard." I shake my head, still admiring the horse sled.

But Molly doesn't reply, so I turn to face her, and her eyes are glassy.

"You okay?"

"Just..." She blows out a breath and shakes her head. When she's back with me, the gloss is gone from her eyes. She steps closer, next to me, until her strawberry scent blooms into my space. "Yeah. I am proud. And I'm glad you like it, too."

I stare at her face, searching for that look again, the one that briefly exposed a completely different side to Molly, a side I've never seen. Even in the kitchen, when she shared a little about her family story, it was wrapped in positivity. Her mask might have slipped, and it tugs at my gut that she thinks she has to be perfect for everyone.

We're not friends. Not exactly. But if we were, I'd figure out a way to let her know she doesn't have to be perfect for me. That sunshine went behind a cloud for a minute, and I wish I could tell her just how much I love dancing in the rain. It's real. It's raw. Even though I could, maybe, make her feel a little better by telling her this, as usual, I keep these kinds of thoughts to myself.

But it's the first time in my life I feel selfish instead of safe for keeping my distance. And that feeling crunches in my chest like my heart is made of tinfoil.

She climbs up into the front row of the sleigh. "God, I hope it snows soon."

"Forecasted for next week," I say.

"Really? Good thing I set up the page on the site."

She pulls her phone out from her bra strap, and it's a fucking wet dream. I'm getting thick imagining my face buried where that cell was.

She pats the seat next to her. "Come on up. I'll show you."

Even though my pants are getting tight, it's easier to deal with that than my ribcage running out of space. This woman makes my heart feel too big for my chest. I grip the side of the sleigh and hop up in one swoop, then take the place where her hand said I should. Our legs smooth up against each other. Her thigh is warm, and I bet the insides of them are just the cozy place a man needs as winter settles in.

Her arm leans into mine when she shows me her phone. She swipes up. "I used a few stock photos, too..."

She's talking, but it might as well be in another language because my brain doesn't register one single word. When I tip my head in her direction to look at the screen, her hair is inches from my face. Her cheeks are round and a gentle pink while she smiles at her cell screen. I close my eyes, wish for just a second that I never learned how much loving something ruins you, because I really like being around this woman.

I have a hunch we're not so different, because now that I've seen that cloud pass over her light-brown eyes, I know she's complicated, too. I'm sure if we were to let something happen, we'd make a real good mess of each other.

She clicks off her cell and spins her head to me, and she's close enough for me to smell her lip gloss, which is more watermelon than strawberry. I'm a damn fruit connoisseur, apparently.

"What do you think?"

I didn't pay attention to a goddamn thing. "Impressive."

She tucks some hair behind her ear and flutters her lashes until she's staring either at my dick or the floor of the sleigh. "Just need that snow."

This is crazy, me sitting here sniffing this woman. Every vein in my body is sizzling with some sort of burning need to touch her again. Now that I know what it feels like, I can't get it out of my head. I get up sharply. "Let's go check out those harnesses."

She slaps her thighs and rubs them. "Yes. Better get to work."

I dart my eyes around the space, looking for the harnesses and feeling hot.

Molly jumps down. "They're just over here."

I take off my hat, scratch my head, and put it back on, but electricity is charging through me at the speed of light. I just can't be close to Molly. "On second thought, Sunshine, might be better for Georgie to help. She and her brother used to do horse pulling."

I need to get out of here. I start walking backward. "She'll be better at helping." I turn but throw my voice to Molly. "Have her call her brother, Grant... they'll be better at this than I'll be."

They damn well won't be better. But when the chill of the bitter air does nothing to stop my skin from bursting into flames, so hot for that woman, I know it's better I sit this one out.

Chapter Sixteen

MOLLY

DASH LEAVES, and though him walking away from a conversation, me, or anything he doesn't want to do shouldn't feel new, this time, it does. This time, it raises suspicion, because Dash Hunter *never* says someone else will be better than he is. Not when it comes to the horses. The man never sleeps to make sure mistakes aren't made, for God's sake.

Now why would he leave, when we're having such a celebratory moment? I can't believe I almost had hope for us spending the morning together. Instead, he makes me nearly cry saying he's proud of me (something I'm not sure anyone has told me before) then leaves in a hurry. Did I do something wrong?

The habit to think everyone else is my responsibility runs deep, but I don't have time for that shit today, and anyway, I'm trying to change that about me. I don't want to stop caring for people, I like this part of me, but I promised myself I'd stop killing myself trying. I need to be loved for who I am, not what I do, and if Dash doesn't like me or want to be around me, even though I really like being around him... well, so be it.

I'll keep telling myself that until I believe it.

I call Georgie like he suggested and hope it's not too early. Like a lot of horsey people, she's already up and answers on the second ring. I tell her she's been recommended, and her brother, Grant, too. She lets out a delighted *eek* into the phone and gets back to me a short time later to say this brother of hers is thrilled to come help harness up the Belgians today.

An hour later, I wrap my stiff, frozen fingers around a mug of hot coffee in the stable's office, waiting for Grant and Georgie to arrive. I've got a few more outdoor chores in and could use them to get back to a normal human body temperature before hitting up the barn again. I turned on the plug-in heater, but it's doing little to cut through the temperature drop today. Maybe Dash was right. Usually, New Mexico sees snow by mid-November, but maybe we'll get some early.

Just then, a Hummer pickup truck grinds to a halt on the gravel outside. Damn is that thing fancy. I've seen a lot of super vehicles around these parts, cowboys sure do like their trucks, but usually, they put them to work all day, wash them up, and show them off at night. But this truck? It's more the kind you wouldn't dare put a scratch on.

Georgie steps out of the passenger side followed by a tall, classic Hollywood, but still ruggedly handsome man out of the driver's side. He's the older, male version of Georgie who, frankly, is drop-dead gorgeous herself. It can only be her brother, Grant. He's as pretty as his truck.

143

I put down my coffee, lamenting that it's still half full, and step back out into the air. "Hey!" I immediately rush over to Georgie who I can't believe is technically my employee. Judging by the shiny wealth she just stepped out of, I'm not sure her family needs the money.

I had no idea. Georgie drives a Toyota Yaris Hybrid.

When we finish our hug, she yanks her brother closer by the sleeve of his very, very clean shearling coat to say hello, too. "This is my brother, Grant."

Grant is even more attractive up close than he was stepping out of the vehicle, and though I like the handsome contours of his face, his clothes are so clean he's more like the model for them than a cowboy who uses them.

Grant holds out his hand and smiles. A dimple joins the conversation. He has a real charm about him, even if he isn't my type, I can hardly meet his gaze; he's so damn glorious.

"Morning. Molly, right?"

"Yes. You can help today with the harnesses and our sleigh?" I try not to say it like I don't believe it. But I don't. This guy just doesn't look like he's gotten dirty a day in his life.

"I was excited when Georgie called. We haven't done horse pulling since we were what? I was nineteen and you were sixteen?" he asks his sister.

"Something like that." Georgie talks to me. "Grant left the state fairs behind to run off and be a horse trainer."

"Oh, you do that around here?" I ask.

"I spend November and December at home, the rest of the year in Kentucky. Home now for extended vacation and glad to have something fun to do, so thanks for bringing me by. Starlight Canyon gets sleepy when the tourists leave."

I shrug. "Seems that way." I usher Georgie and Grant toward the storage barn, and they follow. "I'm hoping to change that a bit. At least for this ranch. The sleigh is my winter tourism project."

"Great idea," Grant says. "I'll book it if it's up and running before I leave. Been a long time since I've sat behind a draft horse."

We arrive at the barn. "Here she is."

Georgie gasps. "Damn, Molly! This is spectacular." She walks over and smooths her hand across the shiny, purple wood. "It's gorgeous!"

Grant whistles. "That's a beaut."

"It wasn't like this when it came to me. It's been a lot of hard work, and I'm hoping the harnesses won't need as much attention as the sleigh itself did."

Grant sees the harnesses in the corner, heads over to them, and squats, taking a leather strap between his fingers, inspecting it. "Usually you find people tend to their harnesses even better than trailer or sleigh or what have you. Horses can pull all sorts of crappy shit, but they can't do it for long if their equipment fails."

He runs his fingers over more of the black leather and all the parts I have no idea how they fit together.

"What's the verdict?" I ask.

"Yeah, the equipment is in tact," he says.

Georgie crouches next to him. "Some of these straps haven't seen much work at all."

A wave of relief splashes over me. I failed to put this calculation into the cost, and when I searched online how much two new harnesses would be, I wasn't sure I'd get much change from five grand. Who knew?

Georgie asks her brother, "Are these harnesses big enough for Belgians? They look a little small."

My stomach drops. Fuck.

He stands with one in his arms. "Nah. These are fine. Grab the other one," he tells his sister.

I run to take it off her. "Let me."

After bringing two of the Belgians in, out of the wind and into the barn, Grant and Georgie reminisce on old times while I ask all the questions in the world about horse pulling. Grant lights up remembering his childhood. He said it was when horses were fun and not there just to make money.

They move through their instruction very quickly, guess it's like riding a bike, and I *think* I wrote down all the instructions for getting the horse dressed up with such a complicated piece of tack.

Once the horses are back in their pasture, I shake my head. "There are straps and buckles everywhere. I hope I can remember this."

Grant slings the tack over his suede-covered arm, and I have to admit, he wasn't at all worried about getting mud on his snakeskin boots and his fresh-from-the-shop-looking coat. It's now dirty as hell, but he doesn't seem to care and hasn't spared his fancy clothes a second glance. Guess he's a real cowboy after all.

"Molly if you need a hand at all this winter, let me know. I usually get bored by December. I'm used to working round the clock with my thoroughbreds. It would be nice to have something else going on."

"That's an amazing offer. I might need you to train all of us on this equipment. I'm not sure my other ranch hands know how to do this either." Actually, they probably do. It's likely common sense for them since most of *them* didn't grow up in the inner city and probably knew how bridles worked before they could read.

He leads me by the back toward the parking lot like a

true Southern gentleman. "We'll exchange numbers. And maybe the three of us can go out for a drink sometime? With Georgie's man gone, I think she gets bored, too."

She nods quickly. "Boredom isn't the right word. Lonely more like it, so yes, I'd be up for a drink."

We reach the Hummer, and I hug Georgie goodbye.

When I go to shake Grant's hand, he says, "What, I don't get one of those?"

I didn't think he'd want one but I'd never refuse. I'm a hugger, too, so I take his massive mound of man and suede in my arms, friendly, of course.

They get in the car, but before Georgie closes the door, she says, "I'm surprised Dash wasn't here for this. I would have thought he'd love to be a part of this whole thing. He used to watch all the pulling competitions, and Jolie told me he always wanted one of our draft horses, a big black Clydesdale we had named Zeus. Where is the boss this morning?"

So it *was* weird he took off in such a hurry. Or at all. I wasn't the only one who thought he'd want to be here. Was he giving me independence? Or did he have something more important to tend to? Maybe get back to whatever it is he does all night long?

"Something bigger going on I guess. But when it snows, we'll do a practice ride and I'll make sure to invite you."

"Amazing," she says.

Before she closes the door, Grant tips his head down and says, "Don't forget that drink."

I give him the old finger pistol then I wave them off and head back into the office returning to my now-cold cup of coffee. I check the weather forecast. No snow just yet. I resume my search for a sleigh driver on some of the local social media ranch and equestrian groups, also noting we need two more ranch hands for the winter. We need more help now that we have more horses.

But I simply stare right through my screen, because all I can think about is how everything seemed to be so friendly and comfortable this morning, and then Dash just up and left in a hurry like he did. And even more than my wondering why he left was me wishing he didn't. There's no one I wanted to harness up the horses with more than him.

That night, when I reach the top of the staircase leading to the apartment door, I'm surprised to see Dash's boots outside in the hallway.

He didn't want to hang around with me this morning but he moved back in? I laugh to myself. I'll never figure this man out. He's already in his room when I enter, and after listening closely, *very* closely, he's not strumming his guitar either. Sleep. He needs it.

I need it.

But that night I spend hours tossing and turning like a Mexican jumping bean. At three, his alarm blares, and unlike the few other times I've heard it, he turns it off on the first bleep. Maybe I'm not the only one who can't sleep.

I listen to him go about his business, and when the door to the outside clicks shut, my eyes do, too, but the sleep still isn't coming.

What's with this guy? I throw the covers off me in a huff, and the cool air wafts over my body, only making me feel more alert. *Fuck it.*

I get up to make a cup of hot cocoa and while I wait for the kettle to boil, I stare at Dash's door. Where the hell does he go in the middle of the night? I tap my foot. Chew the inside of my cheek. His door practically calls my name.

Dash had only two rules for living together, and he was fine breaking one. The other won't hurt. I tiptoe, for absolutely no reason at all, over to his door and half expect an alarm to rage when I turn the knob. It doesn't, and when I step into Dash's room, his dog, Memphis, tips his head up from his bed in the corner.

I point at him. "Don't tell on me."

He lays his head back down.

I wonder what he could possibly not want me to see in here. What could be hidden underneath that perfectly made bed or in that shiny, dust-free dresser of his?

I crouch and use my cell light to illuminate a completely barren landscape of flat wood flooring. Hm. Sliding my hands under his pillows, I come up empty. I smooth the creases I made in his cotton covers back to the military crisp I found. All else that's in here is his closet, which also reveals nothing, so I head for the drawers. It's the most obvious place of all, but I also fear the hardest one to snoop in without being detected.

But to my surprise, Dash's secret isn't hidden under a mound of socks or folded into the last pair of boxers in a pile. In the top drawer, there's nothing but maybe twelve or fifteen identical leather notebooks and a pen. I take the one from the top and open it. The first page shows Dash's writing, and it's something of a title page. He's written: *Mustang Valley January 2023*. And every page after is a date, notes, and a bunch of numbers. Measurements? One page he writes about pipe quality. On another page, he's written: *5 new foals*. On another: *stallion missing*.

Page after page is the same, until I come to yesterday's date, and he's simply scrolled: *watering hole frozen*.

I pinch my eyebrows together, flipping through these notes like it's some sort of hieroglyph or code to crack. I don't know what his notes mean, but one thing is crystal clear. Every night, apart from several skipped in the sequence, he goes to Mustang Valley.

Mustang Valley. His favorite place on earth.

The kettle whistles, and I jump so hard I drop the notebook on the floor. Shit. I hope it didn't dent. The high-pitched squeal continues as I quickly examine the cover of the notebook. It seems unscathed, and I try to put it in the exact same position as I found it, rush out of the room, and grab the kettle off the burner.

I brace myself on the counter, wondering what takes him to that place. How it can be so special that he does the graveyard shift there every day of his life? Since... gosh, it looked like there are years' worth of notebooks there.

Maybe that's the real reason he was never that good in school. Was he up in the middle of the night as a teen?

I pull up a new browser page on my cell and search for Mustang Valley, New Mexico, click through to a map and see it's actually super close to here. My short fingernails make a blunt sound when I tap them on the counter, telling myself I'm an idiot for even considering it. This is crazy. It's like, three in the morning, it's damn cold outside, and dark...

But the next thing I know, I have my coat on and Memphis on the passenger seat. And the new boots he bought for me are pressing down on my accelerator.

I've gone totally mad.

Chapter Seventeen

DASH

AIN'T GONNA LIE. I'm goddamn tired today. I'm not sure if I managed a few winks in between the tossing and turning. I worked myself delirious once I heard Molly come home. I knew I shouldn't have moved back. But I went and did it anyway. This has been happening constantly in my world since Molly has become... a *thing*.

When my alarm went off, I already looked at the red numbers enough times to have anticipated it and slapped it off within one buzz. I tried to be quiet as usual, hoping to not disturb my sleeping beauty, and crept out to the place that used to give me solace.

But when I get to the Valley tonight, I'm too unsettled for even the relaxing moonlight on the mountains to put me on the right path. I'm struggling to resist that woman and yet I found myself moving back in. I've lost control.

Control is what I need. Finding control after my dad

died is what got me through all these years. Control. Predictability. And resisting... *feelings*. Molly bites into all the basics. She constantly surprises me with her determination, her ideas, her kindness, and whatever happens when I'm in her presence is like magic. It has no place in this world. Not in my world anyway.

I work my way down the pipe with my headlamp on. I've always been a night owl, but once my dad passed, what I like most about night here is the sight deprivation. All I see when I work is a five-foot-wide portion of the world. All I can do, see, touch, and hear exists in my lamp's spotlight. Usually. But tonight, I make my way down the path, following the pipe and still, a whole world of thoughts are shining in my head.

Just then, a dog barks up on the cliff top. *My* dog. Memphis? And then... a scream followed by the distinct sound of something falling down the steep hillside.

The dog keeps barking.

"Memphis?" I shout into the wide valley, and my voice echoes a thousand times.

Woof. Woof. Woof.

Yeah, that's my dog all right... who the fuck stole my dog and came here? I run in the direction of his barking, and a distressed woman's voice sounds out.

"Dash! Is that you?" The woman makes a noise something between strain and burning tears. "Dash, hurry... I need help..."

Molly?

I race to the bottom of the steep slope, the one I knew how to get down safely but Molly didn't. My bright head light reveals the scene. She fell and slid onto the steepest bit. She has a toe perched on a rock and hangs on to a sagebrush with white knuckles.

"Shit! Molly!" My heart immediately races, and my feet carry me without even thinking to the spot underneath her.

Memphis continues to bark.

Molly calls up, "It's okay boy." She tries to reassure him, even though her shaking voice tells me she's scared shitless. Even in a moment like this, always thinking of someone else.

She's not actually that far off the ground now, maybe seven feet, but she must have had a straight fall and a massive scare before hitting the only small ledge on that portion of the slope. What the hell is she doing out at this time of night? On her own? In the dark? *The fuck?*

There's not time for thinking about that right now. I position myself under her. "Let go, I'll catch you. I need you to look where I am and come off backward right at me." I realize my headlamp is probably ruining her night vision. I place it on the ground so it lights me up and put my arms out to catch her. "See. I'm right here. I got you, Sunshine."

"It's too far." Her voice wobbles like she's about to cry.

And then, I'm pretty sure she does.

"I promise it's not. I won't let anything bad happen to you, just jump into my arms."

"I'm too... heavy."

"Even if you had a hundred more pieces of cake you wouldn't be. I got you. Now let go, because you've been very unlucky and you're in the one spot there's no other way down than to jump."

She grits her teeth and lets out a little whimper that makes me feel for her. She's more scared now than she was in that haunted house.

"You can trust me." I don't want her falling by accident and me not being able to break her fall or have her scrape down the rest of the way and gouging something open. "Molly. Look at me."

Her eyes meet mine.

"I got you. When I say I got you, I got you. Now come on. You count to three in your head and come to me."

Three beats later, she's incoming, and I have soft mounds of her flesh gripped in my hands, taking the fall. I get her feet on the ground, but she loses her balance and her grasp is so tight on my arm, she takes me down with her. When we hit the ground, she's on top of me.

She's breathing hard, sucking in ragged, strangled wind, her body taut with shock. Her fingers still dig into the sides of my arms. But then, she melts. The warm weight of her body sinks into me and she drops her head to my shoulder, chin tipped inward so her breath stutters against my neck. Molly is trying not to cry. I bet she barely ever cries.

And I don't want her to now. She's safe. We'll sort the rest later.

I cup her head, nesting her closer, hoping to infuse her with some comfort. That would have been terrifying. Falling into the darkness like that. I know I shouldn't, but it feels natural; I kiss her forehead."I told you I got you. You're safe now."

She shakes her head almost imperceptibly though the tip of her nose flicks my earlobe sending sparks through my skin I really should be trying to put out.

"Jesus... I don't fucking deserve..." She doesn't finish. Her body releases everything she's been trying to hold in and she cries quietly into my neck.

My skin is moist with her tears. Closing my eyes, I try not to enjoy the most human interaction I've had, possibly ever. Her emotion spilling onto my skin is like an explosion inside me. It's shameful. Me, basking in her tears and this closeness. It's fucking perverted. My mind knows this was nothing but an accident ending well, but my body screams this is intimacy.

I could say it to myself a thousand times but logic will never calm my rioting nerves. I concentrate to keep my hands from wandering up the sides of her coat. It takes every ounce of self-control to not tilt my head and line up our lips to see, see if when our mouths meet, if she wants mine as much as I want hers.

Her voice is muffled and puffs against my skin. "I actually thought it was fucking over, Dash. I'm so stupid. I was..." she sniffs, pulling back tears along with it but her voice is still thin. "I was creeping forward to get a look at you and didn't even notice there was a ledge, and then I just...I thought I was going to die."

"Don't say that." *I really don't want her saying that.* Not ever. But definitely not here. I stroke her head, more to soothe myself than her. "I told you I got you."

I caress her silky hair until her breathing steadies. But me? I tingle and throb fucking everywhere and at the same time am utterly paralyzed. I wish there was a way to crawl up inside this woman so I never have to disconnect from this indescribable feeling being so close to her.

The air thickens around us, pushing us closer. My body and every thought is so tightly connected to her now it's like we're the only things that exist in this world. Her luscious thighs wrap around one of my own; it's hot between her legs. She wriggles, like she's adjusting herself for a better connection down... there. I'm right where I've only ever imagined, and the real thing is a million times better than my own mind could have ever made it.

The smell of her strawberry hair has me thinking about all things pink and how close her pussy is to my body. Only two layers of blue jean between our skin. My mind races having her here in my arms like I thought of taking her many times before while pumping my thick shaft in a frenzy. I swallow hard, thick, and none of what I'm feeling or thinking goes down with it.

Her lips are featherlight on my skin. She traces the tip of her nose along the shell of my ear and everything ignites with wonder. I lay there unmoving, ready to get burned by the small fires she dots along my neck when her nose traces back down my lobe and along my stubble. I don't have the willpower to extinguish this flame, even though I know if I don't, a full-blown wildfire threatens to steal every ounce of logic, every scrap of self-control.

I fist the fabric of her coat at the small of her back. My other hand still lingers at the base of her skull.

She whispers. "Thank you. I'm sorry I followed you."

Her innocent words shatter me. I glide my hand down the back of her head and to her neck, stroking my thumb around to the column of her throat. Her pulse beats fast. "Are you hurt?" I circle my thumb. She's so soft, so cold from being out here at night. *Following me...* apparently thinking about me as much as I do her.

"Maybe a graze or two." Her hand floats up my arm, and her fingers lace through my hair. She scratches my scalp and grasps at the tufts.

I nearly let out a goddamn sigh. "I'll sort you out when we get back."

She lifts her chin, and her lips flutter on mine with her every word. "Are you mad at me?"

I can't see her face well, just the backlit shape of her, glowing like an angel in the light of my headlamp. I imagine her eyes, big brown, endless. The heat of her mouth and her warm moist breath tumbles inside my own.

My voice is gravel. "I could never be mad at you."

We're motionless for a moment, but then she tugs at my hair again. I don't know if she's just grounding herself or making a move, but all hell breaks loose. I kiss her hard and delight in the freshness of her cool lips. I kiss her like a man who's been waiting years to do it, and I don't even care if she knows. She moans into my mouth, and I lose myself in her. Wrapping my hand around her neck, rubbing my thumb along the column of her throat where the vibration of another purr ruins me, I devour her.

Her kisses are hard, as greedy as mine, and I'm desperate to break her open. In this moment, I forget myself, my rules, my need for control, and slide my tongue inside her mouth ready to own her. Ready for her to own me.

She returns every move I make just as unbridled. Just as brazen. Her heat burns away the torture of waiting, giving way to a lava flow that gushes down my torso and straight to my dick.

I grip both sides of her head now, mostly to prevent myself from putting my hands other places, places that are pressed against my chest, my thigh, places I once saw for a split second in a moment of glimpsing Heaven, naked, dripping... an angel in my house. And that's what I think of her. She's an angel. Otherworldly. Too good for me.

I keep kissing her, circling my tongue, swallowing everything she'll give me but brace my hands along the sides of her head, holding on to a reality and logic that's quickly slipping away into the wintry thin air, because the warmth of Molly's body is everything right now. The tender weight of her breasts is the only place I want to be.

Molly's body writhes feverishly on top of mine. When I explore her mouth and rub my thumb along her precious, smooth throat again, the motion sends her wild. Her core humps my thigh. I shouldn't, but I lift my leg deeper between her legs, offering her the contact she craves. God, I want to make her feel good.

She works her hand down the side of my body and slides it up and under my coat. Her fingers are gentle, like a spring breeze waking me up, reminding me how fucking good it is to be alive. My skin explodes with yearning, my nerves chase after her fingers the moment they leave, hunting her down, craving another touch.

I've never felt this way before. Never had a hunger so painful for another person's touch. Every part of me wants her, my cock forces itself against the zipper of my jeans. It screams to have the same treatment as my ribcage.

It's like she heard its call. She moans into my mouth and skims her fingertips along the waistline of my pants, inching them as far as she can into the tight space. Our chests are rising and falling faster now. And all I can think about are her fingers and how badly I want to know how to make her feel like this. How I wish my touch would enrapture this goddess the way hers does mine.

I'm hot. Searing with electricity. My dick is painfully hard knowing how close we are to crossing the line I worked to draw, over and over again because Molly has a way of sending wind across the sand between us with her every smile, her every laugh...

The tiny whimpers in her throat vibrate my thumb; she's grinding harder now on my leg. I'm ready to tear her goddamn clothes off. I'm ready to spread open her legs and lick her until she's dripping, then sink my cock into her honeypot. I fucking want her. I've never wanted a woman, maybe fucking anything, so much in my entire life.

But I keep my hands on the sides of her face, as if I'm a

gentleman when I'm really not, with all these thoughts of absolutely ravaging her going through my mind. We kiss hard. I take her tongue and knead her lips... I take everything she gives me.

But then, my jeans button opens, and her hand drives deeper down my pants. Her fingertips tingle over my hair and reach the top of my rock-hard sheath and...

I grab her hand to stop her. This can't happen. I want it to. But it just can't. I can't give Molly what she deserves. She's a good girl. There's only one way this story ends, and it isn't a fairy tale. "I need to get you home."

She pulls her hand out shamefully fast. "I'm sorry... I..."

"No. I'm... Don't be sorry, Sunshine. But..." Fuck, I can't string together one goddamn sentence. I'm dizzy with her. I swallow hard. "I just need to make sure you're okay. That you're not bleeding. And it's cold out here in that little jacket of yours."

She pushes her body up and off me, and my body throbs in the wake of her absence. Some devil on my shoulder tells me I'm a fucking idiot to lose this chance with her.

"Yeah. I'm okay." Shame clings to her words.

"Really... Molly?"

Her gaze is hollow in the lamplight.

"We're good," I reassure her. "Seriously. I'm just worried about you, that's all."

She nods, rolls to the side of me, and I hurry to my feet to give her a hand. I've never been one to feel awkward, but we stand in the dim light, both frozen by feelings we can't say. I'm not exactly sure what the feeling is running through my veins but I'm unstable.

Memphis rushes into the space between us, wagging his tail and panting.

Molly crouches but sucks her teeth, and I know she

159

bashed something. She pats him and brings him into her arms.

"I'm so sorry I brought you here, boy."

He licks her face.

I grab my headlamp. "Follow me. Fortunately, there's an easier way up than the one you took down." I offer her my hand, and her touch ignites my arm all over again.

This woman... what the hell am I going to do with her?

I lead her up the path, gripping her tightly, so when she slips, I catch her. Her hand is surprisingly warm. It's feminine, fine and soft, apart from one small callous that reminds me she loves the same things I do.

She's favoring one of her legs, hobbling. I keep my hand around her waist until we reach the cars parked in lay-by on the road, where not so long ago, Molly discovered my secret spot. I wonder how many times she thought about me before coming here. Can't be as many times as I've thought about her.

I point to my truck. "Hop in mine. We'll leave your car here and get it tomorrow." I open the passenger door and hold her hand until she's safe inside.

The ride home is silent, nothing but the odd bark from Memphis when he sees something we can't through the darkness. Something I wonder if I'll ever see.

Chapter Eighteen

MOLLY

WHEN WE GET to the apartment, I fear what will happen, what might be said, when we turn the lights back on. What will I see in Dash's face when every manly feature from his cheekbones to his strong, stubbled jawline and his green eyes are on display? With full knowledge of my betrayal?

Not only did I betray his trust, and one of only two rules, but I kissed him. Or did he kiss me? No... it was probably me. Let's face it, I've been nuts for this guy for a while now, and the moment was so... emotional. Yes, that's what I'll say. Emotions got the better of me. Of us.

But why, Molly, why did you have to go and put your hand down his pants?

"You okay?" He startles me out of my deep, spiraling thoughts.

I wonder how long I've been standing here staring at the closed door of our apartment.

"Of course. Just still a little frazzled."

He opens the door, takes off his coat, and puts it on the hook, then leans his shoulder on the wall. His tight Henley has those same buttons open, exposing the slightest bit of his chest. Whenever he has a button-down shirt on he has a couple open. Because Dash is a real man who gets hot with life. A man who gets his hands dirty... working hard. My breasts loved being in that delicate dip between his pecs. I wish I could bottle that feeling and drink it whenever I'm down. Or trying to have a really quick orgasm. But I'll have to wade through the public shame before getting to my private fantasy.

"Take off your coat." He turns and walks toward the kitchen. "And the pants..."

Oh my God. Take off my pants? Why... I look down and see my jeans are bloodstained over the knee of one leg. Between the shock of the fall and our kiss, the adrenaline kept the sting at bay, and I didn't even notice.

Dash has already found a first-aid kit and brings it into the living room, sits on a couch, and opens it on the coffee table, poking his finger around, sifting through the various bandages.

I still haven't moved.

"You got something there that needs tending to," he says, all businesslike.

Even though I was ready to give Dash a hell of a hand job in Mustang Valley and let him do absolutely anything he wanted to my body, getting naked now, here, with lights on, even if they are dim, has me crumpling in on myself.

"Lose the pants, woman. Come." He pats the cushion next to him. "Sit."

Memphis goes to his papa's side and sits obediently. Seeing as I don't have any bandages of my own in the apartment, keeping mine in the manager's office, I have no choice but to use his. So, I stand behind the couch and wiggle down my jeans, and when the fabric hits my injured knee, I know it's deep. I suck my teeth.

Dash glances up. His eyebrows are pinched together, and he almost looks... worried.

I'm not going to make him ask me again to sit down, I definitely need piecing back together, and he's just trying to help. He probably won't be inspecting my underwear, that are so not the cutest pair I own, and I really regret not having something besides cotton on.

I sit beside him, and he takes my leg, raises it onto his lap to examine me. "Mmm. I don't think you need stitches, but I'll use some Steri-Strips."

I try to think of Dash like some ER doctor instead of my sexy rescuer, but with him this close to me, my body is zinging. He leans over my hips to grab the supplies from the coffee table in front of him. When he reaches, his torso grazes my hip bone, and I wonder if there is a less compromising position we could do this. A position that doesn't feel so much like foreplay.

He has a can of anti-bacterial and shakes it. "This might sting a little."

He sprays it on, and I nearly jump out of my skin.

"Fuck. That's more than a little, Dash."

He runs his fingertips soothingly along the inside of my thigh and blows where he put the anti-bacterial, cooling my knee, sending goosebumps up my leg and right to the apex between them where my core grows heavy and my clit tingles. I don't even need him to touch me to unravel me. My cheeks flush. But he'll probably pass it off as pain.

"Sorry, I had to do that."

"I'm fine," I say, even though I don't want him to stop

running his finger along my skin the way he is. I don't want him to stop blowing. My gosh, it feels good to be touched like this.

I don't think I've ever been touched like this. I hardly ever bothered my mom when I was younger if I was bleeding. I remember being really little, scraping my knee, and there were no Band-Aids in the house, so I used toilet paper to stop the bleeding and left it overnight. I woke the next morning, a scab had partially formed around the toilet paper, and I ripped it off. It started bleeding all over again. But I still didn't ask my mom for help. If she wasn't at work, she was napping, and I didn't like to trouble her.

Still when I analyze my past, I focus on the good things that have come from it. And not wanting to bother my mom has made me very self-sufficient. I always thought of it as a superpower. A strength. It is. It really is.

Even so, watching Dash's thick fingers delicately dab some gauze around my knees to dry the remaining spray, hardly touching it each time, blowing to dry my knee ever so slowly so he won't hurt me, has my lids stinging. Everyone deserves a little tenderness sometimes. Only now am I seeing that many of the times I was being *strong*, telling myself to suck it up, I actually denied myself grace. And he's giving it to me; being so careful even though I did him wrong.

And that's all part of the enigma that is Dashiell Hunter. He exudes disapproval with his dismissive posture, but he couldn't be more caring. He encourages me at work. The cake. The boots. The bandages. Nobody's ever really taken care of me before. I was bound to fall for the first guy who did. But that's not what this is, and I need to remember that.

Dash stopped us from going farther in the Valley.

It's not the same for him as it is for me. Even though watching him dab my skin for the fiftieth time, staring at my leg like it's the most precious thing in his life right now, could make a girl think otherwise. When he's done cleaning my wound, he tosses the gauze on the table, leans over me *again*, and I so want to comb my fingers through his boyish brown waves.

I am so impossibly, bone-deep attracted to this man, and every time I deal with him he surprises me. On the outside, he's gruff, standoffish, and can be brutally direct. But on the inside... he puts sterile strips on a woman who only went and snooped on him.

Which I need to address. I had no intention of getting caught when I went off to find this Mustang Valley and watch him in the night. But I suck at lying so I should have known better. This was inevitable. My mouth goes dry. "I'm sorry, Dash. There's no good reason I should have been where I was tonight."

Shame rushes through me. I don't deserve to be stitched up when I invaded Dash's privacy, something he clearly cherishes.

He doesn't glance up from my knee. "How did you know where I was?"

Fuck. This could create serious issues between us. Maybe he'll fire me. But I won't lie to him. "I went in your room tonight."

I expect him to stop helping me, stand and fly off the handle, but he peels another strip from the clear plastic tab and applies another. "And why did you do that?" His voice is low, coming from deep within his chest. As always, not a single word betrays his emotion.

I can't tell if he's mad, but it doesn't change what I have

to say anyway. "I was curious." It's roundabout, but still the truth.

"About what?"

I reach deeper. "About you."

He stops applying the strips and stares at my knee. "Why would you be curious about me?"

Is this my punishment for breaking the rules? He's going to humiliate me into admitting the truth? Well, I deserve it. "You intrigue me."

"Mmm."

His response is an acknowledgment, yes, but puts me on total high fucking alert because now he knows. He knows I think about him even when he's not around, and that? It's a huge confession.

Dash sticks the last sterile strip into place, silently, not giving me even an inch of... well, what do I expect? Reassurance after I snooped through his things like an untrustworthy liar?

He traces a finger gently along the side of his medical handiwork, and my skin exhales at his gentle touch. "I'm impressed you told the truth."

My breath stops. Isn't he mad?

Frankly, I'm impressed I told the truth, too. Dash isn't scary exactly, but he has a very alpha and edgy dangerous thing going on that keeps you on your toes and not wanting to cross him. But he's never been anything but nice to me, not really, apart from nearly depriving me of this job.

"Are you mad at me?" I have to ask. I need to know outright or I'll wonder forever.

"I might have been." He lifts his gaze off my legs, and it sears right through me. "If it hadn't ended with that kiss."

"Oh." I laugh lightly, lower my eyes, thinking he's going to bring up the *second* thing about tonight I need to justify.

And he's making light of something that, even though it was reckless, will remain in my memory as my sweetest rebellion ever. He's joking about it. It's probably a good thing. He's going easy on me...

But to my surprise, when I dare face him again, he's not playing.

My voice comes out quietly, so muted I might as well not be talking. "It was the shock, I guess."

He finishes tending to my wound and he rests his hand casually on my thigh. "I guess."

His job is done, but he sits next to me like we're staying here all evening, me in my cotton panties just having a relaxing late-night conversation with my hot boss. Yeah, completely normal.

We sit in silence for a while, both pretending to stare at Memphis falling asleep in his bed on the other end of the room. I really don't know what else to say. It's rare for me to be at a loss for words, but I am, because my mind reels with what could have happened. I nearly risked everything tonight. If I lose this job, Lily and I won't have a place to live, not rent-free anyway, when she graduates in December. I'll never be able to give Mom her second chance, a place to start fresh with better health.

Lily's spunky eyes glimmer in my mind. I guided her here. I told her we'd change our story here. I told her a small town was where we could find the extended family we always wished for. I sold her this vision that Mom could heal here. And I nearly threw it away.

Maybe I have. Dash hasn't said much. I dart my eyes to his face briefly, and it's obvious he's still thinking. He's always thinking, and I really hope he isn't thinking about how he can't trust me anymore. I love it on this ranch. I love this job, the horses, the people I work with. I actually even love living with him even though I know I still have to figure out a way to give his room to Lily.

But there really is something about this man. If his thoughts are working toward firing me, it sure doesn't feel like it. His fingers still caress my thigh in floaty movements, putting me at ease. How does he do it? Moments ago, I was hiding behind a sofa worried about showing him my legs, and now, the way he touches me, it's just so affectionate, and everything about it says: *I'm not going to hurt you.* It's not hard to understand why he's so good with animals. He's damn good with this one.

I still want to ask him what he was doing at Mustang Valley.

But before I can, he taps my leg gently and says, "We better get you to bed."

I slide my legs off him and sit up. "I only have to get up in an hour or two anyway."

He stands. "No. You rest up today. Take the day off. I don't want you walking around on that leg."

"It's totally fine..."

"No, it isn't." He suddenly seems disheveled. "You go on and get in bed, and we'll see if those strips hold before I have you on your feet all day. I can handle the hooligans for today."

I smile and stand but I'm not grateful, even though I should be, just bummed I won't see him much today and sit around here worrying if things are going to be weird now. Or if he'll decide working at Starlight Canyon isn't my future. "Yes, sir."

He rolls his lips into a thin line and nods, more to himself than to me, because his eyes stare off in the distance. "Come on then, let's get you to bed."

I try to walk normally and not favor my leg so he knows

it's foolish to have put me on box rest, confining me to my stable. But in truth, my knee is swollen, and at the moment I can't bend it very well. He wraps his arm around my waist, like he did walking me to the car.

I can't tell what's going on inside me. It's like I have a kaleidoscope in my belly and it's turning colors and shapes so often I can't make sense of a single one. It's definitely complicated. Do I like him touching me like this because I yearned for it all my life? Do I like it because its *him,* the single most attractive man I've ever been next to in real life, including Stephen James who my sister and I swear we saw in Chicago once while window shopping on the Mag Mile?

Now that we're indoors and the owls aren't hooting, and Memphis isn't rustling through brush, and the wind isn't in my ears, and the crispness of fresh air isn't in my nose, my senses are being taken over by Dash. His smell of leather and clean. The memory of the way he hums and how his voice fills every space like a mellow cello. His hand, calloused yet gentle, scratching sweet relief over my skin.

I'm about to go in my bedroom, shut the door, and leave all these sensations behind.

We reach my doorway, and he pauses next to me against it.

"Thanks for your help tonight." I pull my lips into a thin line. "I really didn't deserve it."

"You better stop saying that…"

"Well…" I lower my eyes.

He tips up my chin, and his gaze burns right through me. "You deserve the world, Sunshine. Seems to me, you paid enough forward."

His voice is so rich and warm I can practically feel it on my skin. He stares at me, and I've never felt so seen before.

Maybe he's right. Maybe it is my turn to be cared for. And God do I wish it was by him.

I guess tonight, it was. I offer a small, grateful smile.

He keeps my chin tipped up as if he might say more but he doesn't. His gaze is so intense it's blazing a trail right through me, wrapping its fingers around my heart and tying a string around my lungs. I can't breathe with him staring at me like this. And then... he smooths his thumb in small circles on my chin, caressing me gently, while staring at me under his magnifying glass.

I can't take much more of this. My clit is tingling, my core is heavy, a storm is brewing in my belly... my heart is pounding so hard I think I'll faint soon. And when his thumb flicks over my bottom lip, I part my mouth and whisper, "If you keep looking at me like that... I'm going to catch on fire."

His jaw ticks. "Fuck it."

He grabs both sides of my face and crashes his lips into mine, and I give my mouth to him willingly. He kisses me furiously, his stubble rasping at my chin. His tongue takes a quick taste, and when his lips leave my mouth, I think it's over before it started, but he just moves his mouth to my neck and covers me with wild licks and bites. My head sighs back, opening my body up for him to take.

One of his hands threads through my hair, and the other wraps around my waist, securing me close to him. This kiss races me down a raging river of lust and emotion. I'm getting swept up, swept away by a current so powerful I know I won't be in the same place when all this is over. Nothing matters. Not that he's my boss. Not my knee. Not all the risks I'm taking. I should be fighting this, but I can't. It's like death by this man's kiss is my destiny.

He lets his hand from my head fall to my breast where

he caresses, firm but gentle, and traces a circle around my tight nipple with his thumb. He peels his lips from mine for a moment, dropping his forehead to mine. He fondles and squeezes and strokes my tit. "Fuck, Molly..."

My core throbs for him. All I have energy for is doing everything he wants so I can make him say those two words again. His hand wanders up my chest and wraps around my throat, and that thumb of his runs gentle pressure up and down the column of it, his touch takes ownership of my breath. My reason. And of course, any will to say no.

This kiss is more than what we shared in the Valley. I know it is... and by the way his tongue devours me and his manly moans tumble down my throat, he does, too.

We aren't stopping at kissing.

Dash scoops me up in his arms, steps through the threshold but before he carries me to bed, he kicks the door shut with his foot... like a gentleman.

Chapter Nineteen

DASH

I CAN'T RESIST this woman anymore. She's owned my mind from the minute I saw her dripping wet in the doorway of this very room. And even though my past put up a fight, it's almost like there's some external force controlling me, because as I take Molly in my arms to her bed ready to become one with this beautiful woman, I shut that voice out completely.

I put her down carefully on the bed, and it's the last careful thing I do. Nothing about this is careful. It's reckless. Dangerous even, because I know full well the kind of pain a woman like this could cause me. But right now, I'm willing to put my life on the line just to have her for one, sole night.

I rip my shirt up and off so hard I swear a button of my Henley pops off. She yanks her shirt overhead, too, and the pace is fast as we race to take the rest of our clothes off. But when she unclasps her bra and those exquisite tits of hers exhale all over her womanly torso, I know I'll be fucking done in two seconds flat if I don't slow us down.

I straddle her, run my hands up her sides, grazing her nipples with my thumbs along the way. I draw her arms up overhead and pin them to the bed. "No need to hurry, Sunshine." I nibble her neck. "I'm going to take..." I kiss down to her collarbone... "My..." Peppering my way to those breasts, more full and luscious than I even imagined... I suck her nipple into my mouth and bite gently. "Time."

Sucking her flesh into my mouth, I moan onto her tight, pebbled nipple, devouring her breast greedily. Her skin is every bit as smooth and powdery soft as it looks. It's skin you can get lost in. I could sustain myself for a lifetime on the taste of it.

"Fuck, Molly, you are flawless."

Her head falls back when she hears my words. I never stop running my tongue in circles around her dusky, pebbled nipples. They keep calling my name, but I reach up to wrap my hand around her exposed neck. I love the beat of her pulse pounding under my thumb, feeling her life. With my hand there, there's no hiding how she responds to me. I flatten my tongue and lick around on the soft skin of her breasts. Her groan vibrates my palm. I take her nipple between my teeth, and her throat bobs, swallowing; her jaw clenches.

Her pleasure is mine. I want to please her. I want it all.

Trailing my tongue down her breastbone, I trace her skin, kissing and nibbling her flesh and arriving near her core. Molly's stomach is perfect. I want a real woman. Curves. Skin to sink my fingers into. Abundance. Molly's body is all of these things. She's real. Every inch of her is

authentic, it's life. It's raw. And it's making my cock so damn hard my pulse pounds wildly in my shaft.

By the time I get to her hips, I'm fucking feral. My teeth scrape against the skin just next to her panties, and I breathe in that womanly fragrance my fantasies about this woman just couldn't find. Her smell is delicious, a tempting musky honey. I bite the fabric of her panties and yank it away from her pussy then let it snap back against her folds.

Pink. Fucking. Cotton. Pretty. Playful. Natural. Just like her. I hook my finger through the fabric at her hips and slide them down. She wiggles, dancing them loose to help me. I'm extra gentle over her knee, and when I finally have them in my grasp, I fucking inhale their scent because it was the sense I just couldn't conjure when I fisted my cock to the thought of her. And I'm never going to forget it.

She blinks hard, watching me with her scrunched panties in my hand, breathing them in.

"Fuck, Sunshine..." my voice rumbles, "you smell good everywhere."

She covers her eyes, hiding, embarrassed, but I don't play that game. We're both going to be here for this. I pry back one hand and put the panties in front of her nose. "Go on."

She lets out a curt, disbelieving laugh, but her gaze settles on mine. I'm dead serious. Molly breathes in her scent, and there's something about her doing that that's even better than when I did it.

"You smell that sweet pussy? If you smell like that, fuck, I can't wait to taste you."

I throw her panties to the side.

She bites her lip bashfully. "You have quite the mouth on you..." She says it nervously, but I hear what she's really saying. She wants more.

It's right there in her eyes—desire, wonder... Nobody has ever spoken to her this way.

"You want to see what kind of mouth I have on me?" I flare my nostrils. "Open those luscious legs."

She spreads them slightly. I wet my finger and slide it through her dripping folds.

"Wider, baby."

She obeys and has her nimble legs so wide open for me I wonder if she used to be a ballerina. I sink my fingers into her thighs, easing them open that little bit wider with pressure, and stare at her pretty little pussy. Prettier than I imagined. The mere sight of it is making me so hard the skin of my cock is stretched to the extreme. It almost hurts being this hard. But it's the best kind of pain ever. It's a pain us men endure because the relief is ten times sweeter than any you'd ever feel.

"You're staring..." Her voice wavers.

"A body like this is enough to make me lose my mind..."

"Dash..." Her cheeks stain from the praise.

I lower myself onto the bed, my cock rasps the sheets. I can't help but rub myself on the stretched cotton because the touch of anything right now on my tight skin is divine. I'm panting at the thought of wetting my dick between her folds, sinking into her dewy insides, having her pussy wrapped tightly around me.

But more than getting off myself, I want to satisfy her. I'm going to make this woman feel so good she sees stars. I trail kisses up from her knee to her thigh, dotting my lips right up to her center, and rub my nose over her clit.

"Mmmm...." She moans.

I want more. More mewling. More moaning. She's not the only one who likes praise, but I want it in the form of her cum dripping down my chin.

"Look at this pussy. Already soaking the bedsheets, Sunshine. Desperate for my dick."

She claws at my shoulders. "Dash..."

The sound of my name out of her mouth sends me crazy, but I hold steady. I can't just dive right into a woman like this. She deserves to be savored. Devoured slowly so I'll never forget her taste.

I lick from her entrance up her folds, lapping slowly all the way to her clit. I lick like she's a goddamn ice cream on a hot summer's day. I circle around her sensitive nub like I don't want to spill a drop. I don't. I try not to think about how I'll never have her skin on mine again after this, but I do, which slows me down even more, as if I might even be able to make time stand still and pause right here, forgetting the rest of my lonely future.

I never thought of being lonely before spending time around Molly.

I push her thighs into the mattress and pepper kisses in the crease of her hip. I run my fingers along her soft outer folds, feathering the slightest touch, making her squirm and build up to wanting this as much as I do.

As if she ever could.

As much as I'm trying to go slowly, my near to bursting cock is telling me I won't last forever. It hasn't had anything more than my palm for years now, and Molly is my personal idea of perfect. Her tits, her hips, her brown eyes, and thick thighs... ten out of fucking ten.

When her nails scratch my skin and her fingers tear at my arms, I know she's ready for more, too, and I need this. I need her, with or without words to ask for it.

With a flat tongue, I sweep from entrance to clit, feeling every ripple as I go, and it doesn't take long before I give up the slow dance and dive right in. My nose drips with her desire, my stubble is soaked, my chin is balmy with lust. I'd paint myself with her cum if I could. She writhes underneath me, and I groan into her core, grunt like a goddamn animal.

I swirl my tongue. "You are so fucking delicious."

She threads her fingers through my hair, pushing my head deeper into her core. She squirms underneath me. Her clit grows at my touch, and I know she's close. I lick two fingers and plunge them inside her. I ease them in and out, curling them at the top when they're deep inside.

"Ah..." she gasps. "Fuck..."

That's exactly what I do. I fuck her with my fingers and eat her out with more fervor than anything I've ever done. I want to bring this woman to ecstasy. I want to make her see stars...

Molly digs her nails into my shoulder blades, her legs tense, her toes curl, and I suck her rock-hard clit into my mouth as she lets out a cry.

"Oh my God..."

She pulses under my tongue. Hot, silky cum soaks my hand right down to my palm, and I clench my jaw, hold myself back from releasing right here on the bed, because the feeling of Molly coming on my face is enough to make me spill, too. Shit, before this, the mere thought of her worked.

When the wave stops crashing through her, I kiss her thigh and sit up. Her cheeks are full of blush. Her eyes are heavy and lazy.

She covers her face and hides from my admiration.

I peel her hand back off her eyes. "Don't."

"Don't what?" she asks shyly.

"Don't deny yourself pleasure. Doesn't it give you pleasure to have a man stare at you like you're the only thing in the world?" I trace a finger down her throat and over to where her heart is. It's beating hard. "You. Are. Intoxicating."

Her face softens, and she smiles without smiling. "I want to make you feel good, too."

"Oh, you will." I sit up and straddle her.

She inhales my dick with her gaze and exhales her words. "Jesus..."

I drag my shaft back and forth, sensual, slow, barely touching her womanly stomach. "You like that? You want this?" I pump my hand from root to tip and let my thumb circle my head and smooth the drip of desire right down my length.

She darts her tongue over her lower lip, eyes not leaving my cock. She sinks her teeth into her bottom lip like she wants to taste it. Her chest rises and falls more frantically and when those chocolate eyes of hers melt all over me it's the most hot-blooded I've ever been. I dive into her gaze. It's sinful, playful and holds just enough fear to make our adrenaline rise.

I don't know what the hell we've gotten ourselves into but my mind won't even go there. Every drop of blood now fills me so hard, my cock is savage. It's a goddamn weapon at this point and I know I won't last long inside her.

Fuck, hold it together, Dashiell.

I lean down to kiss her but my dick skimming down her stomach to her thigh is unbearably erotic. "Be right back, just need to grab a condom."

She grasps my arm. "No. I'm on the pill. And... I... I haven't been with anyone for a really long time. If you know what I mean."

She's clean.

"Me neither..." I run the palm of my hand gently along her throat, thumb her puffy, pink lips. "You sure?"

There's nothing more than I want to ride her raw, to feel her pussy all over my skin, to pull out and see my dick glistening with... *her*.

She reaches down and curls her delicate fingers around my dick and jerks her hand up and down the length, it's so fucking good I can't handle it and stop her hand mid-stroke. A guttural breath moans out of my lips. I concentrate to hold back releasing right into her little palm.

She licks her lips. "I'm sure. Are *you* sure?"

Only a fool would let her ask twice. Gripping her hips in my palms, I flip her over on top of me in one fell swoop, switching up positions so I can see her. I'm not being on top tonight, crushing my view of this goddess.

She's lying on top of me and widens her legs, and I take my dick in my hand and guide it in and along her slick folds. Her indulgent breasts crush into my chest. Much as I love all this skin of hers on mine, I need a visual. I lace my fingers through her chocolate strands and cup the back of her head. "You know what I want?"

"What?"

"Sit on me. I want to watch you ride me tonight, Sunshine."

I sit up against the headboard. She pushes herself up onto her knees, her legs wide across my hips. Her pussy is perfect. A smattering of womanly hair. Glistening just for me. I smooth my hands down her powdery skin and try my best to keep it slow. I could blow it all in a millisecond; my cock is at full attention, ready to dive inside. I'm dying to feel her walls clenching around me. But I know this moment is fleeting. I don't want my memories to be, too.

I twine my fingers through hers. I let my eyes trace

her every curve, impressing her beauty, this moment, and the way she makes my heart feel alive at the sight of her into the deepest most untouchable places in my mind. One day, when I'm old... I'll think back to this moment I had the most breathtaking woman in the world mounted over me, her hand in mine, her body ready to surrender to me.

I have no words, just a deep, satisfied rumble. I could stare at her until the world stops turning. I soak my fingers in her folds one last time. I savor her closing her eyes and sucking her teeth when they graze her clit. I slip a finger inside before her insides pulse on my cock.

But a man can't wait forever. My heart beats in my dick, my ears, my chest. It pounds everywhere and urges me forward.

Thank God she's ready, too, because next thing I know, Molly's in charge. I have her perfect peach in my palms while she positions the crown of my cock at her entrance and wants to sit down, but I hold her steady in my hands.

"Play with me first. Show me how you'd use me."

She tightens her grip around my cock and makes circles around her folds with my dick. I bite my lip, watching her grind my dick against her. I love it. I want to watch this show all day but I can't take it.

I ease her ass down when she has my dick at her entrance. She stills herself over me. I control her ass downward, watching my cock stretch her.

Her breath stutters. "My God, you're big."

I'm big for *her*. This body of hers, the sweetness of her spirit, the way all her little things drive me wild, has the skin of my cock practically bursting open for her. "We'll take it slow."

She eases down on me, inch by inch. When I'm halfway, she moans, and her whimpers never stop. Sinking in further, I stretch her. Fill her.

It's heaven between Molly's legs. My cock throbs, my pulse still palpable. She clenches around me. Her pussy is a molten, silky heat like no other. She slides up and down my length as my biceps and arm muscles flex, hands gripping and controlling her ass up and down. I need to be in charge. I need to set the pace or I'll release before she's ready. And I can't do that before this woman unravels all over me. I want her cum all over my lap, to hear the sound of her round ass slapping down on her own juices.

Her pussy clamps down on me; she's bucking hard now, and her body collapses onto mine. Her swollen lips find my mouth and we kiss passionately, hard, wild. She mewls into my mouth. My fingers sink into her ass as I drive her hips down on me, at the same time thrusting and rising into her. She's writhing now, her hips grinding around in circles. Her dancing on my body like this is enough to make a grown man cry. I'm fucking weak for her. I'm losing my will. My ability to hold back.

To my surprise, she takes my hands off her hips and forces them down to either side of my head, pinning me. She braces herself, using them as an anchor to take over the pace which is fast rising to a crescendo. I'm used to being in charge, but this woman rides me, setting a punishing pace, rocking her hips back and forth over me. The backs of her thighs and her ass smacks my skin, and dirty, wet slapping noises fill the room.

She pulls herself off then drives me deep, over and over again. I try to hold back, but she's set to ruin me.

Not just now. For good. I'll never want anyone but Molly after this.

I sink in deeper with every thrust. She's growing slicker.

She's riding me like she's close again. I want her insides to drip all over me. I don't want her to wet the sheets. I want her to soak the mattress. "Come for me, Sunshine."

She sits up with her eyes closed. Her breasts bounce as she grinds herself back and forth, up and down on my cock. I have to sink my teeth into my lip to stop myself from letting go before she does. I've never seen a woman like this. She's glorious. A fucking goddess...

I reach up and with one hand grab her breast, and with the other I give her clit one last stroke...

"Oh God..." she pants.

Her walls squeeze me tight, and she gasps for air while a gush of her ecstasy wets me everywhere. I want to come with her. I brace her hips down hard against me, plunging in deep and forceful. My balls tighten, my cock spurts. Searing heat spasms out of me. I squeeze my eyes shut, trying to hold myself together because I don't think I've ever felt this level of ecstasy in my whole damn life. Every muscle in my body clenches and holds on so I don't fucking float away.

I try to enjoy the moment, but my mind races immediately to how I'll never ever feel that way again. When we stop panting, I brush hair off her face, admiring the beauty of her pink cheeks, the lazy, heavy eyelids of satisfaction, and somehow, I forget about tomorrow all over again.

She lifts herself off me. I wipe myself off a bit with the bedsheet and pull her back into my body, kissing her neck a million times before delivering her back onto the bed beside me. I want to stay with Molly. I *need* to lie with her. If I leave, I might die from the separation. It feels like she's the only reason I'm still breathing.

We're quiet. My cheek rests on one of her miraculous breasts, softer and more comfortable than the two-hundred-dollar pillow I splurged on in hopes of helping me sleep better. I could sleep but at the same time, I'm alert. Seems I've entered a world of opposites. I have never in my life felt so calm and so alive at the same time.

Molly strokes my arm with her fingertips. "Can I ask you a question?"

"Mmm."

"Why is Mustang Valley your favorite place on earth?"

It was only a matter of time before she asked this. And even though I've been kidding myself about locking her out of my fortress, the moment I uttered those two words, I issued an invitation. Maybe being alone has gotten to me more than I think. Maybe it's *her*. It is her. I never even noticed I was alone before she walked into my life.

I've kept everything inside for years. I held in tears at my dad's funeral and have been gripping them ever since. "Well, that's a bit misleading. It's my favorite place on earth but at the same time, my least favorite."

She stops stroking for a moment, considering my statement. "Will you tell me about it?"

I want to. Everyone knows the story because, well, it was obvious what happened without me ever saying a word. But me? I've never actually said what happened out loud. Not to my mom. Not to the therapist she forced me to see after I started skipping school sometimes and got my first tattoo. Not to my siblings. Not even to Memphis, though there were days when he and I sat together and I wondered if I told him, I could get this out of me and move on.

Molly has been through a lot. Her mom isn't dead, but I'm sure she understands loss just the same. I know what people on drugs are like. Shells. Shells you wish were still filled with the people you love.

I don't know what will happen when I tell her, but it

doesn't matter anymore because my mouth starts moving. "Dad and I used to go to Mustang Valley." I pause for a moment, thinking I might be able to stop it all right there.

But my mouth keeps moving. Molly definitely has a way of chipping away at my self-control. Maybe I want to. Maybe I want to talk to her about it because my throat doesn't harden the way it usually does when my dad enters a conversation.

Her touch is soothing. Encouraging.

And the words keep spilling out. "It won't come as a surprise, but I was always a moody child and I've always been different from my siblings. They're extroverted. All high achievers. If you haven't noticed hanging out with Jolie and Colt, they're... even Logan... I'm not like them."

Molly's fingers keep me relaxed.

"Anyway, Dad spent a lot of time with me because he used to say he and I were alike. We were practical, he said. Creative. Intuitive. Around the ranch, he'd teach me how to listen to the animals. He taught me how to play Elvis on the guitar, and eventually, he brought me under his wing on his most important project of all... looking after the wild horses. The mustangs."

This is the part I've never said to anyone, and the words start forming that tell-tale stone in my throat I've felt a million times before. The one that stops me from saying out loud what happened. I clear it the best I can. But it's not my courage that makes me say them, it's Molly's warmth. Her touch. The thing she makes me feel I can only describe as safety.

"Some of my best times have been in that place with my dad... He started taking me to Mustang Valley when I was twelve. For two years, we'd count and observe the herd, and we watched the watering hole grow smaller and smaller, so we put in a pipe and he showed me how to inspect it every day..." That goddamn stone is growing in my throat as I talk *Fuck...*

I press on. I press on because I'm here with this woman I know in my heart will understand, and the silence hasn't served me peace. Maybe it's the post-sex high, maybe it's some sort of building trust, either way... tonight, I'm talking.

"I was fourteen." Those words sink in. *Fourteen.* I was only one year older than Eve when the worst day of my life happened. I'd never want for this pain to reach my niece at such a young age. The thought of her experiencing anything like I did, when she's so vulnerable, pricks at my eyes. I never thought of myself that way. Like just a young boy. An innocent kid.

My throat swells so hard I can't continue.

Molly hasn't stopped caressing her fingers along my arm. "You okay?"

I focus on her touch and just know I have to finish the story. I have to get it out of me. "We rode the horses over to the clearing, the one where I was parked tonight, but by the time we got to the Valley, the weather had turned to shit. We usually checked the forecast but we didn't that day. It was downright ominous. We weaved the horses through to the ridge, and Dad told me to wait under a tree at the top of the Valley with the horses. He said he'd just run on off ahead and check the rest of the water pipe himself down in the valley and be right back."

But he never came back. I remember how the moment turned from worrying about the rain to worrying about the pipe being broken to worrying about my dad. I remember tapping my foot, going to the edge of the ridge and not seeing him, and then, the sick, sick feeling that overwhelmed me when I called his name and he didn't call back.

"So, when he didn't come back for longer than it should have been, I went down in the valley and found him." I rub my fingers over my tight forehead. "He was gone when I got there. Heart attack."

Molly's gasp isn't audible, but her chest stops rising and falling underneath my chin. She hugs me tightly into her, and I let her warm affection seep into me. It's the embrace I refused from everyone who offered over the years and yet the one I wanted and needed so damn much.

"You were fourteen?" she asks.

"Mmm. Thankfully, I was already tall and filling out by then. My brothers and I used to mess around doing fireman's carries. I guess I was running on adrenaline because I made it up the slope somehow with him over my shoulders. With the storm and being in the mountains, my cell didn't work. I got Dad over his horse, tied the horses together and..." My throat constricts in such a way it's like someone other than me strangles it to hold down the tears.

I remember crying back then. I was fucking sobbing when I led that funeral procession with my best friend, my dad, slung over the back of the horse, gone. Forever. In the blink of an eye. Never saying goodbye. "Maybe it was a sick thought, but even though he already passed and couldn't feel anything, I didn't want him falling off the horse...I just remember thinking, please, please don't fall off." My eyes fill with wetness, and the bridge of my nose stings. "I didn't get a signal for thirty minutes."

I've held these words in for sixteen years. They were words buried and etched so deep they became gospel, not only a story but some sort of guiding force in my life. Molly didn't just know how my dad died, she now knew what made me who I am.

Broken.

My muscles strain and tense under her fingers.

Molly kisses the top of my head and says sweetly, "Hey, I got you."

I let out a light laugh at her echo of my own words when she was scared, hurting and vulnerable. And when I release that laugh, a tear releases, too, sliding down my cheek and onto Molly's breast. Her heart beats right into my ear. I turn my head and kiss the blob off her soft skin, licking the saltiness, a drop of the ocean of messed-up emotions I'm never able to make sense of.

She combs her fingers through my hair and pulls my head closer to her chest, and her heart sings like a lullaby into my ear. I don't remember much else but waking up only hours later, in the exact same position, but feeling different from any other day in my life. Something has shifted.

I feel a sense of freedom.

But I know myself. It won't take long for me to build those walls again. You don't change a man overnight. Even with a night like that.

Chapter Twenty

MOLLY

DASH FELL asleep on my chest, and once I was sure he had, I couldn't help myself: a few tears streamed silently from my eyes. It makes so much sense now. What happened to Dash breaks my heart just to hear it, let alone experience something like that. It's natural for trauma to result in self-protection. And in Dash's case, this was extreme, and so were the results.

It's a painful story to hear. As only a teen he found his father dead. He had to carry his body for what must have felt like hours. He did it alone. Images of a younger Dash flash through my mind and I can't seem to stop myself looking at them. I'm drawn to his heartache. I'm always drawn to it, always believing there's something I can do to make a difference.

I never stopped caressing Dash's arm, even when I knew he'd fallen asleep. Eventually, the motion became hypnotic, and I, too, drifted off, but I'm pretty sure my fingers kept moving up and down his skin, hoping to relieve his pain. It's hard to relive memories.

When I wake up, Dash is gone, but the smell of bacon and eggs float in under the crack of my bedroom door. I lean over the bedside, my knee aching with a bruise, and grab my jeans off the floor to get my cell.

Nine a.m.

Shit, I needed the sleep, but the workers will all be here... and Dash... is in the kitchen?

It's not like him to leave the workers to their own devices. He likes to loom in the background like a strict teacher waiting to slap down a ruler behind kids taking a test. Maybe he's already been there...

I push myself up in bed and throw the covers off to see the damage on my knee. Dash did a great job putting my skin back together in a nice straight line, and I think the bruising will be worse than the cut. But my knee isn't the only thing battered. Dash and I crushed our professional relationship last night.

My body slumps, and my head falls back to the pillow. I take the one next to me and slap it over my face. *The fuck?* I just slept with my boss. We weren't drunk, so there's not even a shit excuse for us. Jesus, Mary, and Joseph can't help me now.

It's too hot and suffocating under the pillow as my cheeks heat from the thought of it, but when I shove the pillow away again, it occurs to me that Dash told me this story, *after* sex.

And *before* we did it, he was... intimate. Tender... This doesn't really feel like the accident I'm preparing to apologize for and pretend never happened. As if I'd ever be able to pretend this never happened. What happened between us, his perfect body, his naughty mouth, the ecstasy... that was a once-in-a-lifetime experience.

Shit. Here I go, falling for the tortured hero. *Again.*

I pull on some sweatpants, put my puppies back in a bra, and throw a sweatshirt over me. I brush my hair while staring at my reflection in the mirror, considering waiting for Dash to finish eating and leave, but know it's better if not too much time passes between all of this.

I'm trying to find a new Molly.

I will not suppress myself for the sake of others.

I will not let shame guide me.

I repeat two of my favorite mantras, take a deep breath, and step into the hallway. I round the bend to the kitchen, and Dash glances up while pushing egg out of a pan onto a plate to join some bacon and bagels. There are two plates.

"I was just about to wake you. You need to eat. Made us breakfast."

Guess he isn't planning on dodging the conversation either. How grown-up of us.

He pulls a chair out for me. "How's the knee?"

"I'll be fine. Nothing a little arnica won't sort. I can work today."

He sits opposite. "You won't be working today."

"I can and I should," I protest.

"They can manage."

I go stiff. What in the hell kind of spiritual possession happened between now and the Dash from yesterday? Some ghost crawled into this man and has taken over, because he's basically just suggested we both take a day off?

"I mean..." I slowly pick up my fork, not taking my gaze off him. "I think they can handle things. The sleigh is done, and we have enough hands."

"Hank, Bobby, Georgie, Rhett, and Dylan are all here."

While I was sleeping, Dash took care of business.

He takes a piece of bacon between his fingers, the same ones that brought me to places I've never been, and bites it. "I'll go down there again after we eat."

Oh. *He's not taking the day off.*

I lower my eyes and pick up the buttered, toasted bagel. "Thanks for breakfast."

His low voice practically vibrates through me. "So... about last night..."

I throw down my fork and cover my face with my hands. I don't want him to see the flames burning on my cheeks. I should have known Dash wasn't the type to go easy or understand the art of the segue. We could have eaten first, but no. Dash is a man who goes in for the kill. I swallow my food down into my churning belly then let out a groan.

"Hey..." He takes one of my hands off my face and laces our fingers. "Don't be like that."

I peek out from between my other hand's fingers. "Yeah?"

"Neither of us should be embarrassed. That was..." He pauses to think. "Unforgettable."

He stares at me with that completely impossible-to-read face, but his words...make me nervous, and I laugh, go to that awkward place where you make a joke because you aren't ready for the truth yet. "So this means we won't be pretending it never happened?"

He raises an eyebrow and gives me a half-smile. "Are you serious right now?"

I let out my breath. "No."

He's still holding my hand in his. Our elbows are propped on the table, fingers laced together, and he rubs his thumb along the back of my hand. "I don't want to put it behind us but I'm not sure I can move forward like this either."

His words go down my neck like curdled milk, and my stomach spasms. I knew Dash wasn't one to get close to people. Now I even know why. But...

He scratches his eyebrow. Scrunches his face, perplexed. "I don't really know what to do with this thing we got going on." Something between confusion and torment takes over his face. "I'm broken, Sunshine. You don't deserve broken."

This conversation is giving me whiplash. It's like he's into me and breaking up at the same time, but we're not even together.

Somehow, I muster up sensible words even though my belly churns. "Maybe we just take it one day at a time?"

His lips form a thin, hard line. "I don't really want to... you know... fall."

"Fall?"

"You know what I mean."

"Do you think you could...fall?" I say, more shocked than hopeful. I was only talking about whether we should make out again, and he's...

He shakes his head. "I don't think you could possibly understand what happens inside me when the smallest amount of joy creeps in. You're different from me. You look for chances to care for people, and I stay away from it. I shut it out. Slam the door hard. I know you've already been through a lot just like me. We both have shit but we ended up dealing in completely opposite ways. You don't deserve me doing that to you."

I squeeze his hand in mine. His words might be pushing me away, but I know he cares. And that makes me brave. "Maybe you should let *me* take care of me."

A silent laugh blows out of his nose. He shakes his head and looks at me like he doesn't believe a word I just said. "I've been thinking all morning. I don't want to hurt you. And I know how women are. There are a very small number who have sex with a man and feel nothing the next day. And I don't think you're one of them."

He's right, but it annoys me. And hurts. "What are you saying?"

"I'm saying... *asking* actually..." His eyes lower. "Can we be friends? Trust me, I'd love to have sex again because you were there, too, that shit was magical. But I know myself. And I'd rather have your friendship than nothing at all." His gaze meets mine again. "I like being around you." He offers a genuine smile, and my God is it a breathtaking sight. "That's saying a lot."

Well, this conversation is a hell of a lot more mature and open than I ever took Dash for. The quiet ones are always the wisest. Even though I crinkle inside just a little because like a silly girl I have fallen just a teensy bit. And only now is that ray of hope I had for us surfacing, but Dash is right. A lifetime of hard habits don't die overnight.

I've tried changing people before. It's impossible.

I already know he's capable of hurting me. I can tell by the deflated feeling in my chest that it's not exactly what my body wants, but my mind tells me it's the right thing. And I can always use a friend, especially one like Dash. I've never had anyone looking out for my best interests the way he did when he wasn't my friend. I have to be grateful for what he will offer me.

I squeeze our hands together tighter, as if making a pact. "Friends."

He nods.

"But on one condition," I add.

"Yeah?"

I let go of his hand before I get too comfortable holding it. "You start sleeping through the night. That goddamn alarm is killing me."

His eyebrows quirk, and his nostrils flare. He doesn't smile again, but it's something like one. "You're a very demanding friend."

"Demanding things that are good for you, too," I say, picking up my fork again.

"Fair." His eyelashes flutter downward, and he stares at his plate. A beat of silence passes between us. His thoughts are heavy and palpable. "I appreciate you."

───

Dash leaves me behind for the stables, with some arnica and feeling more confused than ever. I sit in the apartment with my leg up, icing it so I can be better for tomorrow, and I'm bored as shit. It's the first day in as long as I can remember that I'm sitting down for most of it. I tried to put on the TV, but apparently Dash doesn't watch it either because it only has basic channels, and soaps are the worst. They remind me of my mom calling in sick during summer break, saying she'd take us to the pool or something, then falling asleep on the couch instead with dramas playing in the background.

I've never really thought about why I don't like sitting watching TV before now. My feet are itchy, and I want to move around, but I promised Dash I'd rest just for today. Ugh. And to top it off, all I can think about is last night. In bed with Dash. The intimacy. The closeness. The depth of what happened is impossible to bury. Like he said, it's unforgettable.

I need to tell someone and get it out of me. Maybe my

sister is around.

I grab my cell and dial. She picks up just when I was about to give up.

"Hey," she says. "Perfect timing, I just left my class. You taking a break?"

"Yeah. All day actually..."

"What's going on?" Concern instantly hops into her voice.

"I hurt my leg last night. Not serious, but Dash ordered me to take a day off."

"Shit, Moll, is it bad? Are you okay?"

"It's fine. A cut, but I didn't need stitches, and a bruise that I'll barely feel tomorrow."

"You sure?"

"Yeah. I'm good. I'm bored. I hate sitting around doing nothing."

"Well, I have news for you," she says, cheerfully.

"I have news for you, too." I need to tell my sister about last night. I'm dying to tell someone and I don't have any other someones to tell. "But you go first."

"I contacted the hotel at Starlight Ranch. The general manager..."

"Savannah?"

"Yeah, Savannah. I told her I'm your sister, and she responded to my email. She said they don't work with a wedding planner. She told me to see her as soon as I move in!"

"That's amazing, Lil!" A wave of happiness and relief wash over me. I'm so proud to call this woman my sister. She has all the determination in the world, and I love that about her. "That would be awesome if we both work on-site."

"I know! I've missed not being around you more. Who

would have ever thought the Russo sisters would be small-town girls? Anyway, how did you hurt your leg?"

I laugh.

"Um, Mols, that's not your funny haha laugh, that's your nervous laugh. What happened?"

My words come out fast and somewhat unclear, like I'm an auctioneer. "I went to see what Dash does at night, fell down a cliff, he rescued me, and then we had sex."

"You what?" She shouts so loudly into the cell I have to pull mine away from my ear. "What the hell?"

I bite my lip.

"You had sex with your boss?"

"Well, actually he's my *friend* now. Well, and my boss, but we're friends, too."

"Oh, that makes it better? Fuck, Molly..."

"I know..." I let out a heavy breath, and it flaps my lips. "But we actually had a great talk this morning. I think things will be even better now between us. We're on the same page."

My sister lets out a big, howling laugh. "Better?"

"Stop. I know a lot more about him now. Before there was just me thinking there was a bomb of sexual tension waiting to explode, and at least now I know it was two-sided which made me feel better, and I also know he's not grumpy. He told me his story, Lil, and... boy do I get why he is the way he is."

I recount Dash's story in detail, because I tell my sister everything, but I make her promise never to tell a soul because I know how private it is to Dash.

"That's honestly heartbreaking, babe." Her voice is full of genuine sympathy. "I hate that for him. I hate he's been hurt like that. And... I don't want to sound harsh but I don't think you two should be friends."

"What? That's a bit mean," I say sourly.

"I just know how you are. You like to try and fix people. This kind of baggage needs a professional."

I know Dash's old habits will die hard, and mine probably will, too. Maybe my sister is right, but I'm not going to avoid Dash. I don't want to. "He's pushing people away because he's terrified of caring about someone again after the pain of his dad. And what will it do to him if I won't be his friend? It will just reinforce that cycle."

"Okay, Dr. Molly," she teases.

I shoot my eyes to the ceiling. My sister isn't as sensitive as I am. Or maybe she is. Maybe her coping mechanism isn't all that far from Dash's. Maybe that's how she saw it so easily. Is she brave, or is it all bravado? Only just now have I ever wondered.

She eases up. "You're okay with everything?"

"Yeah. Even though we had sex and it should be awkward, I actually feel better about where we're at than before. It was all tense but not, and sort of... I don't know. It was like there were lots of unspoken words before, and now he's opened up."

"Well, I'm not going to be pedantic about it. Sex can just be sex, and people have complicated relationships more often than not these days."

"It's not complicated. We're friends."

"Whatever you say."

I change the subject, and we talk about her moving date and when and how I'll move her in about a month's time.

One month. In one month, I need to ask my *friend* to move out. Maybe it would have been easier when he was just my boss.

Shit. Lily is right. This is complicated.

Chapter Twenty-One

DASH

I WAS proud of myself for growing like I did yesterday morning. I can't let myself fall in love with someone, but if I'm ever going to be human again, I need to try on some more relationships. Get myself out there. Or in there. I did both with Molly.

It won't be easy ignoring the ache to touch her, but I'm sure it will subside at some point, moving into a friendship. Before long, she'll be just like Mateo to me. A buddy. A pal... I hope.

The only person I ever really hang out with besides my family is Mateo. I was happy when my man moved back to Starlight Canyon permanently, though the moment he did, something else happened, too, so we didn't see much of each other.

I knock on the door, and there's Stella, all freckles and

fire, with her baby bump on full display. "Hey, Dash. I didn't know you were coming."

"Just hoping Mateo's here."

She pushes the door open farther to let me in. "You want a coffee or something?"

"No. I won't be staying long. Just a quick question for Matty. And I wanted to ask in person."

"He's out back working on the fencing for the new training ring."

Stella opens the back door, and just as she does, Matty is making his way back to the house, rubbing his hands together.

He smiles when he sees me. "Look what the cat dragged in."

Stella pushes a fallen strand of hair off her exhausted forehead. "I'm heading upstairs for a nap. See you later, Dash. And..." She pauses, narrows her eyes. "Did you do something different to your..." She circles her face with her index finger.

It's probably the sex glow. "Nah. Same ol'."

She shrugs, waves, and waddles off with her hands on her back.

"Wow, getting close to little Maximo coming," I say, already knowing it's a boy and that Matty *will* get his way with the name.

Matty comes into the kitchen. "I can't wait. I already know I'm going to want a million of them running around. Maybe I was a rabbit in a former life."

I laugh gruffly. "Imagine Hero Condoms seeing you now."

"Yeah. They dropped the sponsorship the minute I got engaged. Not that I care. I'm more happy now than I've ever been."

Mateo Domingo used to dominate the bronc riding circuit nationally, but even with all the fame and glory and women dripping off him, he's never wanted anything more than a simple bungalow here in Starlight Canyon with a wife and kids. He craved that. Security was all he needed, the yearning for it was woven through every story he ever told. In fact, he's shed just about all his shiny past now and seems so much more relaxed for it.

"Coffee?" he offers.

"No thanks. Just a quick question. It's about the mustangs."

Mateo's known me a long, long time. Though he doesn't know exactly why, he's known that no matter how much we ever got to drinking the night before, I always ended up in the Valley for the wild horses.

I lean against the wall. "I wondered if you'd be able to visit the Valley for me a couple times a week and check the pipe. I can't have those horses suffering but I really could use a day or two off duty every week."

He nods, lips in a thin line. "No problem. Just text me what to do, and I've got it covered."

"You sure? I know you've got your new school and training up your broncs. And a kid on the way..." Suddenly I feel like me, a bachelor with fuck all in my world, shouldn't have asked my friend such a thing.

But as usual, Mateo slaps my back and makes me feel like I just did him a favor. That's his energy. Total light. He's the kind of guy a woman like Molly deserves. "I'll look forward to it. I haven't been around wild horses for ages. But what brought this on? Everything okay at the ranch?"

"Yeah. Great... I just... my alarm clock is bothering my new roommate."

"You could, and I'm not saying this because I don't want

to help, just saying you could go to the Valley during the day like a normal person."

But then I wouldn't see Molly.

I don't answer.

He narrows his eyes. "No problem, man. Like I said, just drop me a text or email with instructions. Or we can meet up sometime and go out there together."

"Thanks." I tip my hat. "I'll leave you to enjoy the peace and quiet of nap time with your wife." I lift my eyebrows.

He walks me to the door and stares at me from under his own. "Trust me. I will."

Over the next few days, I don't set my alarm, intending to get to the Valley at some point in the day, but out of habit, get up at the same time without it and hurry off, hoping I'll get back quickly enough to make breakfast for Molly. Mateo will take over some Valley runs from tomorrow.

For a week straight, we've eaten together, and I swear I've never looked forward to a day beginning like I do now. In fact, I'm not sure I even really understood where one day ended and one began until I started having breakfast with Molly.

She's all messy bun and giant pajama t-shirt off the shoulder this morning. She's hugging her knees to her chest and drinking her coffee, giggling. She tells me about how down at the yard they discovered Romeo is even smarter than I thought. "So all of us are just beside ourselves yesterday. Like, how on earth are these damn horses getting out of the corral in the morning and into pasture? We put the Belgians back in twice yesterday. Then Georgie saw this..." She grabs her cell. "Come see this."

I get up, brace my hands on either side of the table where she sits, and lean over her to see what she has to show me on her cell. She searches through her gallery, and in the meantime, strawberries call to me. Her messy bun smells like all that desire I pent up before we decided to be friends and reminds me all over again how beautiful this woman is. Even more beautiful now I'm getting to know her.

I find it hard to breathe her in, harder not to kiss her bare shoulder. I'm sure these feelings will pass. But wanting to touch Molly will probably be one of those things that gets worse before it gets better.

"Oh, here it is..." She plays a video, and there, caught on camera, is Romeo, with his mouth, undoing the corral latch. "Look at him." She laughs. "What a rascal."

Some people would find this a nuisance, Molly finds it funny. It is pretty cute when horses get into mischief, most of the time.

She turns her head to talk to me, her face close enough to mine for me to see she has a few freckles on her nose I never noticed before. Maybe she covers them up with makeup most days, but in the morning, her face is raw, natural, dewy, and has a smattering of, well, sunshine.

She asks, "Are there any latches we could get he couldn't undo?"

"Probably not. Horses like Romeo can be relentless. We'll need to padlock that corral but we can keep the key there for convenience. *That* he won't be able to do without fingers."

She glances back at her phone. "I'm glad he made it through. He's my favorite horse here now. He has so much personality."

"Why don't you have him?"

Her eyes are all wide when she whips her gaze around to meet mine. "What do you mean?"

"Have him as your own. As in he belongs to you. Anyway, how are you going to learn to ride if you don't have a horse?" I lean in closer. "You do want to learn to ride, right?"

Her face brightens, and I fucking love her glow. I bask in every contour of her delight.

"Isn't he too big for me?"

"Nah. He's probably perfect. He's older, too, so he might not do too much dumb shit, and it can actually be easier to learn on a big horse. They're not so hard to stay on." I wink. *Oh Lord, I winked. What the hell is getting into me?* "What do you say?"

"I don't even know what to say..." She's beaming then lowers her eyes back to her screen, shakes her head as if in disbelief. "Thank you."

A feeling of satisfaction overwhelms me. Making Molly happy and seeing her smile is just about the best feeling in the world. It's hard not to keep chasing this feeling down, and I have been, about fifty times a day. Bringing her a hot chocolate in the day. I bought her a new coat as if I go in the ladies' section of Carhartt every day and just randomly picked it up for her...

I push myself off the table and clear our plates when Molly lets out a gasp behind me.

"Holy shit..." She gets up and goes to the window. "It's snowing!"

I join her at the window, and we stare out at the sky filling with a flurry of white flakes.

"It's coming down hard," I say.

"Think we can...?"

"Absolutely," I say, reading her mind.

We stare out in silence, but the fact that I was able to know her thoughts without her finishing her sentence doesn't escape me. She wants to take the sleigh out, and so do I.

Her bright eyes stare out at the beautiful wintry confetti falling from the sky, and I wonder what her eyelashes will look like with snowflakes on them. I wonder what it would be like to kiss her warm lips with the cold snow whipping around us... and I wonder when I'll stop wondering.

I go back to my chores in the kitchen. "You see if the driver is around, and I'll buzz my family. I'd love to take Eve out especially. Maybe everyone can come over after school. There should be enough snow by then."

"Sounds perfect."

Chapter Twenty-Two

MOLLY

TODAY, I look at the ranch differently than ever before. I'm more settled in my role. I have my own horse here now. I have a friend, and even though it's complicated, he's the best one I've ever had. I have a secure place to live. Starlight Canyon is feeling more like home than any other place I've been.

The mountains around me are winter bliss and the purest beauty. It's the purest beauty maybe I've ever seen. Maybe. Because Dash's face and soulful eyes, and the way he's starting to express himself and open up, rival all of this. Watching him unfurl fills me with awe just as mighty as the mountains.

And the way we've been getting along the past few days has filled me with total wonder at where this will all lead. Will we someday forget our physical connection? It really doesn't feel like it whenever he brushes up against me and I come alive like a volcanic explosion. And when lava rushes through my body, it doesn't burn me, it's more like I was always meant to erupt. The way I am around him is different. I'm confident and I don't quieten anything about myself anymore. I guess I'm unfurling, too.

We did our work separately this morning after breakfast, knowing we had to rush to get everything done before everyone we invited for a ride arrives this afternoon. Dash did the jobs I'd normally do outside, and I made all the phone calls and dropped texts to ensure everything was ticked off before the entirety of Starlight Ranch gets distracted by the sleigh. I like being a team with Dash. We're a pretty damn good one.

Reconvening at the storage barn, less than seven hours after separating, I'm giddy to be with him again... I watch him in the barn, heaving the horse sled along makeshift rollers to get it out into the snowy yard. I didn't think that through.

It's the men who help because the sleigh is solid and heavy. They defer to Dash. His quiet, manly way is like the truest alpha I've ever seen. All it takes is a nod, one word, and the other guys trust he knows how to get a job done.

Dash moves with composure and a charming ruggedness. And boy is he sexy doing every little thing. No matter how hard I try, I just keep tumbling... *falling*. I've told myself a bunch of times over the week it's the admiration of friendship. I told myself it's just a womanly thing to need some time to shake off desire after having sex. But being *friends* is only raising the tension. At least for me. Sharing every waking moment with him is my only wish; I'm like an obsessed teenager.

But I'm still determined to get over it the best I can. I agree wholeheartedly with what he said in the kitchen the morning after. I'd rather be friends than nothing.

He leaves to get two Belgians from the corral and comes back leading two enormous beasts by their bridles. Like the men, they obey his every whim. He's a wet dream of a cowboy.

I. Am. Fucked.

He ties them on near the side of the barn, and I follow him in to fetch the harnesses.

"Hey, don't make fun of me when you watch me try and do the harness for the first time," I say when he comes out of the barn with the equipment.

He hands me the leathery straps. "When have I ever made fun of you?"

He hasn't. Not once. Even when I did things wrong before all of this... this complicated thing we have going on, he didn't. He was blunt. And maybe a little judgmental but never made fun.

We work in tandem, fluently, and for a moment it's like I've been doing this forever until I realize that's not true and take out my notebook to check everything. He's patient with me, doesn't intervene to hurry me along but let's me learn at my own pace. I need to double-check everything on the notes I made with Grant and Georgie.

I close the notebook and glance up, he lifts his eyebrows. "You got it."

I pat Fred, the chestnut horse beside me. "I got it," I say with both pride and a hint of surprise I actually remembered how to put the contraption on right.

Our Belgians, Fred and Wilma, are finally tacked up, and just when we finish, a young voice calls out behind me.

"Uncle Dash!"

A girl of about thirteen or fourteen comes running over. Dash opens his arms, she reaches him and he scoops her into his embrace.

"Hey, Evie Bean." He faces the sleigh. "Good as you thought it would be?"

She puts her hands up to either side of her face. "Oh my gosh. It's better!"

Dash nudges her around to face me. "You've got Molly here to thank." He smiles. *Smiles.* Like beaming, sincerely happy, gorgeous smiling. Guess he wasn't lying when he said his niece brings it out of him. "Molly, this is Eve. Eve, Molly."

"Nice to meet you," she says.

I hold out my hand. "Nice to meet you, too."

"Can I hug you?" Eve asks.

Dash has told me lots about his niece with Down syndrome. He talks about her with the greatest warmth and affection. Apart from one friend, Mateo, as far as I know, she's the only other person who can ask him to hang out with her and he says yes.

He also told me she's really big on hugs but is still learning about personal space. So, I guess she wants my permission, which is fine by me because I love hugs.

I open my arms to Eve. "I'd love that."

A smile tugs my cheeks in her embrace. She squeezes me pretty damn hard, and I just love that even though this is our first hug, it's a proper one. Now I know why even Dash can't resist grinning when he's with this sweet ball of energy.

Behind her, Colt approaches the barn with his arm around a beautiful blonde who can only be the infamous Sam. In fact, I think I recognize her from that first night out at Sly's back when I arrived in the Canyon. Colt seemed to lose his shit with some cowboy and led a flaxen-haired bobbed woman out of the bar, never coming back to say goodbye. It must have been some night for him to forget his manners. Colt is so charming, it makes you ache to be on the receiving end of a yes ma'am.

Sam's hair isn't in a bob now, but it must be her. Dash and Jolie have both told me about Sam. They describe her as fair but fierce, and not somebody to mess with.

But Sam wastes no time offering me a hug, too, not quite as tight as Eve's but sincere nonetheless. "Molly! Jojo has told me so much about you." She peels back with both arms on my sides. "Thanks for letting us break in your sleigh."

My sleigh. Since coming to Starlight Ranch, I've had ownership of things. I've never been a needy or greedy person, but it's the responsibility I love. It's the faith placed in me that gets me glowing. It's amazing what happens inside when someone believes in you. I glance at Dash and can still remember the exact feeling when he gave me that clipboard to sign for the Belgians, and I hardly contain the sigh escaping my chest.

Sam, Colt, and I get to talking, and Dash is by the horses with Eve. I dart my eyes over periodically. He teaches her how the harness works. They stroke and pat the creatures she hasn't had a chance to meet yet. With her, he's so different. His energy completely shifted from guarded to open... he softens. He makes eye contact. And he makes my core go wild wondering how he'd be as a dad.

Goddamn it, I just let my mind wander on warp speed to a place it doesn't belong.

I resume my conversation, away from him, when he laughs out loud, and I can't help but twist around again. Sam and Colt do as well, so I feel less obvious looking this time. Eve clearly just said something that set him off, and his laugh is so rich and full and fucking delightful.

When my gaze is back on Sam and Colt, Sam raises an eyebrow.

"Not used to hearing Dash laugh, eh?"

Damn. This woman is switched on.

"Yeah, just thought I'd record that in my memory for times to come."

"I hope he's being nice to you," Colt says.

Nice? He's treating me like a queen actually. Making me breakfast. Buying me boots. A new winter coat. Having coffee ready in the morning and a fridge constantly stocked with carrot cake. "He's hard on the outside but soft on the inside."

Colt narrows his eyes. "You figured that out already in like, a month? He must like you."

My mind goes straight back to how much he was liking on my pussy just a week ago. Just then, a truck and a car turn up, saving the day so I don't need to continue this conversation. With my thoughts wrestling under the sheets of Dash's bed, I'm sure I'll go bright red at the next comment, and they'll see right through how much I want to bang their brother.

Jolie and a woman wearing a fur hat and turquoise earrings, who must be Dash's mom, Joy, step out of one vehicle. Dash told me a little about his mom, and I never expected her to be such a gorgeous older woman. She's the kind who oozes cool and confidence. The kind who makes you think growing older is something to look forward to.

Dash told me she was an artist, and she certainly dresses like one. Joy introduces herself, and almost at the same time, out step Georgie and Grant from his Hummer truck. Joy leaves me to welcome them, too, and Jolie and Joy join all

210

the others by the sleigh. It's like I'm throwing a party and standing at the door.

It was only fair I invited Grant as well, since Georgie was coming for the worker's ride, and he took his time to help me with the harnesses.

Grant gives me a hug hello. "Thanks for inviting me."

"Yeah, didn't want you to have FOMO since Georgie is here. Plus, you helped out a lot by coming to inspect the harnesses."

Grant glances over my shoulder and walks toward the Belgians to check out how we've put the harnesses on. Dash is discreet but darts his eyes over at the two of us. His enchanting Eve smile is gone.

Grant smooths a finger over a leather strap, inspecting. "Everything is perfect."

"Dash and I did it together. You were a good teacher."

Grant stretches his arm up on the back of Fred and creates a wall of man in front of me. "You never called me about that drink."

Call *him* about a drink? I thought it was more casual than that. He's being very... flirty. All of a sudden. And Dash is here to see it. Maybe he heard what Grant just said. I hope not. It gives the wrong impression. Like we'd planned some date or something.

I try to correct the course. I know Dash and I are just friends but I would disintegrate into a heap of ash if he flirted with a woman in front of me. "Just get Georgie to let me know when and we'll all three hit up Sly's. Maybe get some of the other guys to come, too, and make it a proper night out?"

He makes a face at me like I'm being coy or playing hard to get. *Oh shit.* I never picked up on this the first time around. He did text me once or twice to ask how the sleigh was coming along, but it all seemed natural, and I never read into it as him making moves.

Grant is seriously hot by any woman's standards, but unfortunately, I still haven't taken my eyes off Dash. And in this moment, I haven't waded through my *complicated* status. I know I'll get over it eventually, but I'm not yet.

I see everyone is loaded up into the sled. "I better go get the driver. He's in the office."

Grant grabs my arm as I'm walking away. "Mind if I come with you for a quick drink of water before we leave?"

"Course not." I smile, sure I'll be able to evade any more attention once we get on the sleigh.

Grant follows me toward the office, but we don't get far because almost out of nowhere, Dash comes in our path.

He says to me, "I'll get Jameson. Go on back to the sled."

"No probs," I insist. "I'll get him. Grant needs a drink first anyway..."

But Dash doesn't budge. He gazes at me deeply. "I don't like the way he's looking at you."

My jaw goes slack. I'm still as a statue and absolutely floored that my *boss*, because that's all he's supposed to be, especially in front of all these people, is being, well... possessive.

Grant scoffs. "Are you talking about me? I'm right here. You can talk straight to me."

Dash's gaze is glued to mine. We stare at each other, questions flashing across our pupils, and it's the first time I realize how well we've learned to read each other.

He tilts his head, asking silently if I'm interested in Grant.

I lower my head and peep at him from under my eyebrows. *Of course not.*

But that's not good enough. I'm not going to be the person who shows Dash that he shouldn't trust anybody, I want to be the person who gives him all the reasons to let me in more. Saving Grant's pride takes a back seat to helping Dash count on me.

"Grant?" I say.

"Yeah, sweetheart?" My gosh, is Grant turning on the cowboy charm just to piss Dash off?

Dash flares his nostrils, but he's an expert at the silent treatment.

"I don't know if you were looking at me the way Dash here is suggesting but I'm not the kind of girl who leads people on. This might be awkward if you have no interest in me, but just so you know, I'm..."

His eyes dart from me to Dash, who's still staring at me, and back again. "...you're interested in someone else?"

"Something like that."

Grant nods slowly, understanding exactly what's happening between me and Dash, and I hope like hell he doesn't tell Georgie.

He puts his hands up. "I'm not gonna lie, I would have happily taken a pretty girl like you out for a candlelit dinner but... I respect that."

"Thanks." I gesture for him to follow me. "Let's find Jameson and that water."

Grant laughs and turns on his heel. "Molly. I didn't need a water."

He walks back off toward the sleigh, leaving me and Dash.

Dash hooks his thumbs through his belt loops, his forehead tightens. "I shouldn't have intruded..."

I stop him. "Better to nip things in the bud. He's not my type."

Sienna Judd

Our gaze connects deeply. It's just like every other time before. Full of magnetism. Red-hot attraction and wanting. Nothing has gone away. I'm not sure it should. Whether Dash was being jealous or protective or both, I liked it.

Just then, Jameson comes out from the office. "Ready to go?"

I'm ready to go all right. Straight back into bed with Dash.

Dashing through the snow is a real thing. And in my life, it has double meaning. The sled was smooth, quiet, and a serene calming way to spend time in this beautiful environment. I thought it would add to the calm to sit between Dash's mom and Jolie, but they only kept saying what a good job he and I did. What a great team we were and how surprised they were he wasn't back up at Bird's Eye now that I'm doing such a great job and he's not needed so much.

They thanked me for pulling him out of his shell and said they noticed he's been less grumpy since I've been around. Each comment distributes one more butterfly into my belly, flitting around, gaga for him. I watch him sitting in front of me the entire time, burly arm wrapped around his niece to keep her warm, as he listens to her talk in his ear the whole way around with his undivided attention.

When we finish, hop off, and empty the sleigh for the rest of the ranch workers, Sam issues an invitation. "I have Irish coffees and cocoa at the house for any takers?"

Every Hunter there accepts, and I take a step back toward the crew going on the sled next, just thinking if I want another ride with them or to get to other jobs.

Dash grabs my arm. "You're coming, right?"

Jolie notices her brother's hand wrapped around me and smirks. "Yeah, Mols, you have to come, too. But Sam's drinks are strong. You have enough help here today? I'm not sure you'll be back."

I'm invited for drinks in the Hunter inner circle? Dash raises his dark, thick eyebrows and tilts his head, a second sort of invitation. How could I ever say no to those tempting green eyes?

But I need to make sure everyone is settled. I shuffle over to my crew. "You guys okay getting the horses back in the corral? And the lock?"

Hank salutes me. "We got it. Go have some fun. First snow of the year is cause to celebrate."

"I'm in." I beam. "You sure, Sam?"

Eve answers for her. "Leave no woman behind."

Sam wraps an arm around Eve. "That's our mantra. Of course we don't mind. Just the opposite."

Jolie drives me and Dash over to what we Starlight Ranch workers refer to as 'the other side of the road.' There's a fork after driving in the main entrance off the main road, where a sign leads either to Starlight Ranch or down a road labelled *Private*. Here is the Hunters' land they keep to themselves. Their private trails and homes...

We pull up in front of a sprawling house. Jolie lives at Bird's Eye, so this must be Big Sky. And big it is. I'm sure there are bigger houses but none quite so beautiful. It's ranch style, with a wraparound porch to provide three-sixty views of the mountains. The staircase covered in snow, and I don't know how a building could be so substantial and so cute at the same time.

The inside is even better than the out. It's a huge open-plan space, with wooden beams of warm oak. Modern in decor but with so many homey touches. It's spacious yet cozy.

Sam draws us all into the kitchen where she flickers the gas alight on the stove to heat some liquid she has stewing in pots. Colt scoops her into him from behind. She leans her head back to rest on his chest slightly while she takes the pot lid off. He kisses her hair. He takes a spoon that's sitting to the side and stirs, his body flush with hers, embracing her while they work. Man, they're cute. It's impossible to not wish something like that could be under the tree for me at Christmas.

In the meantime, two more people come, Sam's parents, and with just one family, it's a nine-person party. The only one missing is Logan, who has an away game.

It doesn't take long for the alcohol to work its way into our systems. Laughter is everywhere around me. And so are dogs.

Eve comes over to me with a dachshund in her arms. "This is Belle."

I scratch the pup. "Hey, Belle."

"How are things going with Memphis?" she asks.

Eve is the first person to ask me if I've been getting along with the dog instead of her uncle, but it reminds me of him all the same. "I think the only thing I don't like about Memphis..."

Her grin droops slightly.

"... is that Uncle Dash won't let me sleep with him in my bed. I mean, come on, Border Collies are natural-born teddy bears."

Eve laughs. "The perfect amount of fluff."

"Yeah. But mostly I appreciate just having a dog. I wanted one growing up. And ponies. And a sabertooth tiger. Until I learned they were extinct."

Her giggle fills the space between us. "My dad says all city girls want animals, just like my Sam. Want to hold Belle?"

"Of course I do..." I scoop the little wiener dog into my arms.

As soon as I do, Jolie slides into me, bumps and almost knocks me over, pretty tipsy now, and puts her arm around me. "You and Belle up for a game of Twister?"

I lift one of Belle's short legs and do the voice I think a tiny dog would have. "I'm at a serious disadvantage."

Eve explodes with laughter. "That's funny, Molly!" She scratches the top of her pup's head. "I'll play fetchies with you later." She raises her hand to Jolie for a high five and the girls smack them together.

"I'm in," Eve says then turns to me. "You have to play. Have you ever played Twister?"

I haven't. But I know the gist of it.

Jolie takes Belle from my arms, kisses the top of the dog's head, and puts her down on the couch I'm standing next to. "Come on, Mols. We have three rounds. Instant elimination."

She leads me by the hand into the living room where someone has moved the coffee table and laid out the plastic, spotted Twister mat on the floor.

Everyone sits around on the couches or on the arms of them. My first opponent is Joy Hunter. I thought it would be unfair, and my youth would be an advantage, until she shows me a pair of near splits that makes my eyes water.

"Yoga," she says when she places one foot on the complete opposite end of the board from the other.

But ultimately, the strength in my arms from years of mucking out stalls and pushing wheelbarrows wins out, and I move to round two. I watch Colt take on Sam; they are rivals to the end, but I swear Colt loses only because when his face gets close to Sam's boob, his concentration slips along with his right hand.

Dash plays his sister. He takes no mercy, and she crumbles and sticks her tongue out in response to his boastful smirk.

Which means in the next round... it's the two of us.

Dash and I stand on either end of the board. Three Irish coffees deep, he's looking more edible than ever. The alcohol only magnifies what I already know... this man is fucking gorgeous. And moments later, I have his ass in my face. For the love of all that is holy, I have to close my eyes for a moment not to want to take a bite out of his rock-hard glutes.

"Nice view, Molly?" Jolie jokes.

I swear, laced in her voice is less sisterly teasing and more innuendo. Did she set this whole thing up for us?

Dash spins again and makes a deft move to flip himself over. He's now positioned over me in a bear-like stance, and we're face to face. And man, do I love that face. Those lips. That ever-present perfect stubble of his, and I can't help but recall the way it felt between my legs. I won't last long with him over me like this, with these thoughts in my head. This wanting. I just want to give up and wrap my arms around him as I let go of these damn red and yellow dots and yank him down on top of me.

The side of his mouth quirks into a devilish half-smile, and delicious whiskey breath falls over my lips. "I'm taking you down, Russo."

If only he would. I'd let go right now. But his family is staring at us as a million indecent thoughts flash across my mind.

I purse my lips then lift my eyebrows. "What you don't know about me, *Hunter,* is I don't give up easy."

I reach over to twist the spinner, but it's just out of reach.

Colt uses his toe to push it closer. "Come on, Mols, take him down."

Dash still stares me in the eyes, but he says to his brother, "Hey. Whose side are you on?"

We make five more moves, and my arms are like jelly. His forearms and tattoos hold him up, firm, secure, so strong, and they'll never give up. All his muscles flex around me, and I want him to take me, force me deeply into his chest, and use those biceps to hold me up against a wall and take me no holds barred.

The whiskey in my system is not making it easy... in the end, I don't know if Dash is just the better man, but when trying to put my foot in an inconvenient location, I fall on top of him, my legs are wide and straddle one of his, and I have to work hard not to think about how goddamn lustful his thigh feels on my core. I fill instantly with a desire to grind myself against his leg and bring myself to the blinding orgasm only Dash's body can give me.

I push myself off fast; the alcohol is making me lose my mind. It's making me want to break this friendship agreement that I shook on in the kitchen and do naughty things to this man. It's making me want to risk it all for another night in bed with him.

I get up and look around at the eyes on us. Something like shame for all my dirty thoughts sends a shiver through me, and I wonder if anyone can see it. See how I really feel about their loving grump.

Dash is in the final with Sam, and I try not to be jealous. I try not to wish it's me back in the cage of his stiff arms, my ass in the air with his face inches away. I try not to want it to be me with my hand reaching through his legs, inches from that big, pussy pleasing cock of his. I'm a pervert. A drunk-ass pervert, and I need to get home.

So when Sam wins, and people finally stop hooting and hollering that there's a new champion on the podium, I wait until Dash is away from the group again and say, "I think I should head back now. I want to do a last stable check before going to bed and I'm... going to be honest, I'm not sure I'll even notice everything at this point. Can't be having another one of Sam's coffees."

His chest puffs in something like a laugh. "No problem. I'll drive us back now."

"You okay to drive?"

"I've had a couple, but the roads are pretty much our own personal driveways." He checks his watch. "Our plows will have been by now, but if you'll feel better about not being in a car with me we can stay here. There's a guest room and a couch."

I remember the time Donovan had a few too many drinks and wanted to drive us home. When I told him my concerns, he told me what a baby I was and how I was over-reacting. Dash... he never makes me feel that way. He justifies my every emotion.

But I'm not worried. He seems pretty sober, definitely compared to me. "Let's go back."

We say our goodbyes, and I take one last look around the warm nest of love this family has created, appreciating more deeply than they could know just how much it meant to me to have a family game night. Along with a sabertooth tiger, I would have given a lot for even just a game of Monopoly.

The Hunters have everything I ever wished for growing up.

They have each other. *This.* This is what my sister and I will have one day. When she and I have kids and our mom is better. I close my eyes and picture it. *This.*

I have to shove down the wish to want it right here, on this very ranch, because the Hunters have more than just each other. They have mountains, and horses, and sleigh rides, and... Dash.

Chapter Twenty-Three

DASH

Jolie had a shit-eating grin on her face when she pulled that Twister game out. Up to no good, and now I know... she can see right through me. Jojo knows. I might be faking it 'til I make it with Molly as a friend, but right now, I think of her as a million times more than that, and that Twister game didn't shore up my self-control.

Molly looked right in Big Sky. She fit right in with her joyous laughter and bubbly energy. She was damn cute asking Sam what's in an Irish coffee and vibing with Eve. Sam's dad brightened up when she asked him about San Francisco, and my mom let Molly try on her turquoise earrings after telling Mom how much she loves the blue-green stone. Everyone loves Molly. *Everyone.*

Molly talks the whole way home, and normally, I don't like hearing people babble on, not this late in the day, when typically, I've been up for too many hours. But Molly's voice is balm for my soul. I listen to some of what she says, but sometimes, her voice just soothes me in the background when I have to concentrate a bit harder around a bend that has already filled back up with snow after the plows. She keeps me company, and this feeling of not being alone anymore is addictive.

We park up safely outside the stables, and I get out quickly to run around and open the door for her. I take Molly's hand and help her out of the truck. A real truck. Not like the douchey one that fuckbag Grant has.

"Thanks," she says, her boots hitting the ground. She hiccups, and it's cute as hell.

She puts her hand up in front of her mouth. "Shit. I think I drank too much. It was only three drinks but..."

"Yeah. Me, too..."

I can feel the alcohol, too, but I swear I'm still in control. That is, until I realize that I haven't let go of Molly's hand all the way from the truck to the stables. When I do let go, she doesn't face me, but she reaches around in the air for my hand, so I reach back out for her. She holds it all the while she goes from stall to stall, poking her head around and making sure my horses are okay.

Her horses are okay.

Our horses are okay.

By the time we get upstairs and to the apartment, I've been holding her hand long enough my body doesn't want to let go. But I do.

Messing with someone's head is one thing, messing with their heart is another. Right now, it's like I'm galloping toward doing both, for both of us, and one of us needs to walk the straight and narrow.

That person certainly won't be Molly tonight. She's

staring at me with sultry, bedroom eyes, walking backward toward the kitchen. "You want a bagel?"

I scratch my head. "No thanks. I'm just going to hit the hay."

"Aw..." She's still walking backward and bumps into a pillar. "Oops." She laughs at herself.

She's drunk. But not too drunk for me to worry. It's reluctant. I want to sit with her and shoot the breeze and watch her laugh about the silly shit that gets people going when they've drunk too much.

But I turn my doorknob. "Night, Sunshine."

I'm naked, lying in bed, waiting for Molly to finish clattering around in the kitchen so I can go brush my teeth. I know better. I know better than to let myself run into her with her cat eyes calling to me to give her pussy a stroke.

Just when I hear things go quiet, I push myself up but to my surprise, my door inches open.

"Are you awake?" Molly whispers.

"Yeah. Are you okay?" Maybe she's even more tipsy than I thought. Maybe she needs me...

"Great..." She pushes the door open farther, and there she is. Buck-ass naked.

My God, she's beautiful. Everything about Molly screams woman; her full breasts, her juicy hips and thighs I could sink my teeth into. My heart drops seeing her like this for so many reasons.

"Molly..."

She rushes in quickly and crawls under the covers with me, throwing herself into my side. Her skin is soft and warm against me, and I can practically feel my torso sigh into her.

"Molly..." I say with less resolve than the first time.

She puts her finger to my lips to stop me talking. "Shh. Just kiss me." She traces my lips with her finger and then eases it inside my mouth.

Instinctively, I suck it, and my cock thickens. It's so fucking sensual, and I shouldn't play along.

She pushes herself into me more. "I think we both want this. Tell me I'm wrong and I'll go away."

Her words mean nothing because she hooks her leg over mine, and the hot wetness between her legs slathering across my thigh is *everything* I want.

"You're drunk, Sunshine..." I murmur.

"Oh..." She's so innocent when she jumps up and goes to my top dresser drawer, no shame in heading into there, blasting away at my privacy for the second time, and grabs the top leather notebook.

Her inhibitions are totally gone. I don't know if I should thank Sam or curse her.

Molly rummages around for the pen I leave in there, too, and writes in the notebook. My head falls back. *The fuck am I going to do with this woman?*

She jumps back into bed, her breasts bouncing brightly, just waiting for someone to press them together and fuck that space in between. My dick is painfully hard when Molly joins me again, shoving the notebook in my face, giggling sweetly.

This is far from innocent, but Molly makes it feel that way.

"Here." She's written something in my notebook.

I, Molly Russo, officially declare I am sober enough to know I want nothing more than to be with you, Dashiell Hunter.

Shit. Her bubbly cursive is as adorable as her nuzzling into my neck, nibbling it...

I close the notebook and drop it to the side of the bed. "We're supposed to be friends..."

"We are," she purrs into my neck. "Really, really good ones."

I slide my hand over her throat and use my thumb to tilt her chin up so I can look her in the eye. None of it is there. None of my darkness. None of the hesitation to love somebody. She's goddamn pure of heart.

The devil reasons inside me. He makes all the excuses every weak man with a goddess in his arms would. He tells me I'm already broken so she can't break me.

But something far worse than a broken heart is going to happen because staring into those round, brown, loving eyes of hers, I see something that will hurt me more than falling in love. I long for change when I stare into her eyes. My path has been set. I am who I am... the fall will kill me.

But why do I fucking care?

What did I have before her anyway?

She drops her tits toward me, but I'm holding her still, so only a nipple grazes some of my bare chest. Lust blindsides me. I'm weak for her. A fucking goner...

Even though I'm holding her like a man who is about to eat her alive, even though we're naked next to each other and my lips a millimeter from hers, my silence lasts too long.

Insecurity creeps into her eyes. "I'm an idiot... you don't want to..."

I take her mouth in mine, breathe in her words to swallow her doubt. I'll never let her feel that way. Like I don't want her. I fucking bleed for her.

My lips connect to the source of everything that matters to me right now. The playfulness melts out of her and passion takes over. She breathes harder, her cheeks are pink, her eyes are closed, but hints of her smile remain in round, lifted cheeks. My heart races thinking there's anything about me that can make this woman happy.

I want to do it time and time and time again. She drapes her thigh over my hip, her pussy soaks the top of my thigh. I smooth my hands all over her until they're wrapped around her curvy ass and slipping up and down her core from behind.

She moans, and I devour the sound, exploring her mouth while stroking her silky folds. She dances herself against my fingers, and every inch of me craves her. My cock is rock-solid, digging into her belly, begging me to spread her legs open and bury it inside her, but I keep my fingers moving, gliding in circles around her clit so she makes those sexy fucking noises I love.

Suddenly, she eases away, and her sweet gaze melts into something more naughty. "It's my turn to taste you."

She flattens my shoulders into the mattress, laying me down.

She peppers kisses down my neck. I take her chin. "You don't have to..."

"I *want* to..." Her words are breathy, and her eyes flicker. "So bad. You have no idea how much I want to feel your cock on my tongue. Taste you. Feel you in the back of my throat..."

I take her nipple between my fingers and roll it. It's hard, and I think mine are, too, now. "Pretty thing like you talking like a greedy little girl..."

She smiles and continues her journey of kisses down my abs. I sink my teeth into my lip when she massages my balls, grips my cock, and runs her hand root to tip before circling her tongue over the crown, wetting me with her mouth. She blows over the top of it, and the new sensation of cold has my toes curling.

My head falls back to the pillow, and when I close my eyes, all I feel is the wet heat of her mouth and the occasional graze of her teeth along my shaft, a near pain so sweet I can only call it pleasure. She works her mouth over my shaft like there's a time limit. There probably is. Her little sucking noises build the telltale tingle in my balls. I need to focus, hold back, I want this to last forever... but it can't. None of it can.

I almost let the reality of that ruin this but it's laughable I have any control over what happens here and now. Her head rises up and down the length of me and I know I'm tumbling into some gravity-free place where I have no sense of direction. I need centering.

But instead of stopping this, I weave my fingers through her chestnut strands then tug at them. "Eyes on me, baby."

It was a mistake to think connecting to her gaze might buy me more time in her perfect mouth and swollen lips. Because when her eyes water every time my cock hits the back of her throat, it's so fucking hot I slip deeper into this oblivion. One more dip in and I'll explode all over her face. And there's only one place I'm letting go tonight.

I grip her under her arm to pull her up. "Sit on my face..."

She props herself up, elbows on either side of my hips. "What?" Her mouth glistens with saliva, and it's hard not to ask to be back in her mouth, but I want mine on her even more.

"Sit. On. My. Face." I repeat, more directly, because she isn't following orders fast enough. I settle into the pillow and tug at her again. Goddamn, I need her pussy on my mouth. I missed the scent between her legs.

"I can't..." She suddenly finds one thing to protest about, and it's me licking her pussy?

"You can. And will." I urge her upward again, but she hesitates.

I'm going mad as she contemplates what I asked, taking her time... I know what she tastes like now, what she smells like, what it feels like to watch her release. Her face hovers over my stomach. Her breasts are on either side of my dick. I take this opportunity to squeeze the flesh together around my shaft, massaging myself with her body.

"Jesus, woman, I just want to fuck every part of you..." I raise and lower my cock between her tits.

She bites her lip. "You like that?"

"Not as much as I'll like ravaging your pussy with my tongue. You going to come and sit on my mouth like I told you to, or what?"

"I'll suffocate you..."

"Shit, baby, I hope you do. I'll die a happy man." I release her breasts and yank her up gently from under her arm, and this time, she follows.

Her ivory skin slides along my torso, my wet dick presses against her belly. She considers my offer one last time before sitting herself up and shuffling her straddled legs up the sides of me until, legs spread nice and wide, I have the best view in town.

She's glossy. I run my tongue from her entrance to her clit and taste that cream of hers, sweet, sweet girl that she is. I slip a finger inside.

"You go on and grab that headboard, Sunshine. Sit down and enjoy the ride."

With my free hand, I urge one of her hips down on me, and her folds sink onto my mouth. I kiss her pussy, flat tongue lapping up her velvet seam, a flick of her clit... I take her into my mouth every way possible and keep a thumb smoothing over her entrance and a finger teasing her backside. I want to stimulate every inch of this woman, electrify her, make her fucking dizzy with the best orgasm she's ever had.

"Mmmm." The hum of my satisfaction vibrates against her folds.

"Oh God..." she moans as she rocks into me, her soaked pussy sliding all over my mouth, my chin...

I push my thumb into her and circle her clit, knowing she's close. "Come for me. That's it. I want you dripping all over my face." I rub my nose in circles, suck, lick... fucking devour this pussy when finally, her thighs tremble on either side of me, her breath quickens, and her nub is swollen and hard.

"Dash..." she moans.

I love how she says my name. I love everything she does and how she does it. Fuck, I'm done. Done forever.

Her hands grip the headboard, and she rocks herself back and forth. The bed hits the wall, pounding in rhythm with the way her pussy dances over my lips. I peek up at her tits bouncing and I'm so fucking here for her wild abandon. I suck her clit into my mouth, never stopping my fingers from filling her...

"Ah... that feels so good..." Her voice is grainy.

I encourage her, invite her to let her desire pour all over my face. "Keep going..."

Finally, she lets that velvety pussy of hers fall deeper onto my mouth, and I suck. Her clit goes blindingly hard. I flick it in circles, and then her core melts while everything else hangs on for dear life, quivering everywhere. Her release is powerful. It's molten and fucking alive between her thighs.

I keep my fingers moving gently in and out of her; her breath steadies and her soul, pounded up somewhere into the clouds, comes back into her body. She finally trickles down the headboard and into my arms.

She kisses me, the scent of whiskey still there between our lips. "I want to do that to you, Dash."

"What's that, Sunshine?"

"Make you see stars."

God, this woman has no idea how lovely she is. How distracting. How I watch her from afar and dream about her when she's not there.

I roll her onto her back and run my fingers along her seam, being gentle but not ignoring that nub of hers that's still firm under my touch. I ease a finger inside her. "This is where you want me?" I slip a second finger in. "You want me inside this sweet, hot cunt?"

She closes her eyes and nods, a smirk tugs at her cheeks, sure she's turned on by my word choice.

I use my knees to pry her legs apart and gain better access to her core. I stabilize myself over her, bury my face in her neck for one last time before I watch her take me. Her neck is dewy.

"Dash..." she moans my name and it's my undoing.

I devour her lips, hasty, ravenous and no matter how much of her tongue is in my mouth I'm fucking insatiable. She arches her back, her breasts rise into me like an invitation and I say yes. I say yes to everything. I say yes to her nipple between my teeth. I say yes to her strawberry scented strands falling against my cheek. I say yes to her butterfly giggle and her good humor in the mornings. I say yes to it all.

I don't know what this means. But I know I want her to say yes to me, too. Scary as that is, not a single nerve in my body denies it or stops me from letting her seize my dick and play with it on her folds like it's her own personal dildo.

She's an eager girl. She handles my cock in her hand like it's not even attached to me, rubbing it firmly along her wet folds. She circles my crown around her clit; her nub gives back to me.

When she stops jacking herself off with me, I rest the crown of my cock at her entrance. Sensations overwhelm me. The heat. The pressure of her opening around my tip. The sight of her angelic body cushioned by my white sheets like she's resting in clouds. Fuck... I wish just one thing about Molly wasn't perfect. But she is. She's *my* perfect.

Easing my cock in just an inch, wanting to savor every minute, she's not so patient. When her hips come toward me, my cock disappears inside her pink folds and I don't think I've watched any other show with more anticipation. I enter her in slow motion feeling every contraction inside her. Every ripple. Every sopping wet pulse of her walls. She sighs in pleasure; I wish I could capture that sound because it's fucking mine.

Mine.

At that thought, I unhinge. Mine. She's only mine right now.

I bottom out, deep inside her, and my bones reach the cradle of her hips. I drop my forehead to hers. "How the fuck are you this tight, Molly?"

She answers by tensing her insides around me and I'm spurred on and sink into her deeper, faster and goddamn it, rougher, until the bed is banging against the wall again.

I hurtle into her like a steam train without brakes. My need to be inside her is so unrelenting, even the split second pulling out just to dive right back in is too long. I stay in her, deep, deep inside, taking her ass in my hands. I grind my cock to the end of her and glimpse her face. She jerks up and down to my motion, pinching her own nipples. Her skin shimmers; her hungry eyes pierce right through me like a wild goddess.

It's almost over. I fight with myself not to think about it. Not to be the Dash that always lets the end ruin the journey. I stop barreling toward my release and slip out of her just to have a look at my dick lined up to her most precious space again. Ecstasy sears through my body at the sight, spiking my heart rate and I can't reconcile the need for instant gratification and the desire to drag this out.

But it's not all up to me. She quietly begs. "I need you back inside me. Don't stop." She takes my slick cock in her hand and guides me back in.

"You feel so damn good..." I groan, pumping slowly, methodically.

Her voice is raspy. So fucking sexy. "More, Dash. I want you in deep. Harder. Let go inside me... *Baby*."

Fuuuck.

I drive in faster now, firmer like she asked, dragging my cock in and out. I hold her throat, take a handful of her breast and anchor myself as I sink into her. Her eyes are on me, full of something I probably don't deserve, but I take it like a fucking thief right now. I'm buried balls-deep. I circle my hips, and her eyes flutter shut.

"You like that?" I growl.

"I like everything about you..."

Her words break me. My chest flutters crazy with feral emotion. I thrust harder. "You do? Tell me again."

"I like your body."

Thrust.

"I like the way you talk dirty."

Thrust.

"I like you filling me with that Big. Steely. Cock..."

Fuck, those dirty words coming out of her swollen lips... I slide in and out, trying not to go too fast, but I'm losing control at this feeling of her clenching around my sheath, squeezing the fucking shit out of me, talking to me dirty with her breathy, whiskey rasp.

Her pussy is like a goddamn vise, holding on to me, gripping me as I drive in. I'm losing it. I'm light-headed. I grip her throat with more force than I intend.

"Fuck..." she whimpers. She reaches her hands around and grabs my ass, urging me into her more.

"Rub your clit for me," I demand. "Make a mess on me."

She brushes her fingers furiously over that nub of hers and I remember how it felt on my tongue. Just the thought of her arousal gushing all over my cock has me sucking in soul-shaking breaths to stay steady and wait for her.

"Ah! Fuck... Dash..."

I keep my hand on her throat and drive into her one last time and spill into her, trying not to grunt like an animal, trying not to fucking scream from the uncontrollable desire to have her forever, be inside her always... and never leave this glorious space between her legs.

I drop onto her, panting. Her chest is balmy. I kiss her neck and the taste of salty sex that's there as much as anywhere else on her body. The taste of her skin makes me want to start all over. It makes me want to run the two of us in circles. With no beginning... and no end.

Chapter Twenty-Four

MOLLY

Dash and I catch our breath, but sleep isn't in the cards. We stroke each other silently, until his dick goes thick again, and before I know it, he's drawing himself in and out of me, plunging in to the depths of me, teasing my entrance with his thick crown, filling my insides with deep, soul-wrenching pleasure.

After my two more blinding orgasms, I'm a lot more sober than I was when I opened his door naked. I think Sam must have snuck something more than whiskey in those Irish coffees, because when Dash held my hand at the stables, when he stepped away from me into his bedroom... something daring surged through me. Something more than alcohol.

And my liquid courage coupled with the threat of missed opportunity had me dropping my drawers just outside his room thinking... you only live once.

Now, lying in his arms, feeling more sober, logic tells me it was careless. It was. Nothing has changed about that. But my soul doesn't have that concern. Dash envelops my heart with his tender, firm embrace and puts me into complete peace. I should be worried about tomorrow. But I'm not. I should be anxious about what this means. But I'm not.

Because one thing I've learned about this man is he doesn't do anything he doesn't want to. No is firmly in his vocabulary. He wanted me just as much as I wanted him, and the swollen feeling between my legs proves it.

Dash runs his fingernails along the arm I have wrapped around his chest. "You okay?"

"Yeah. I'm okay."

"You're going to sleep with me tonight." His voice is heavy with exhaustion.

"Are you telling me or asking me?"

A beat. "I guess both."

"You want me here?" My heart flutters.

His fingers glide more and more slowly along my skin, and I know he's drifting off.

"Mm-hm," he murmurs.

I kiss his neck and nest my head into the coziest pillow I've ever had. Somehow, the two very different shapes of us fit together perfectly. I know I'm irrationally attached. But his firm hold never changes, even when I feel his breathing slow under my chin and I listen to his heartbeat thrum so slowly, I know he's in a deep sleep. Still, somehow, his muscles envelop me with the same flex, the same steely embrace as when he was wide awake.

He's attached, too. I'm just not sure it's the same way that I am.

I startle awake in the middle of the night. Dash's body is jolting, flinching. His eyebrows flicker up and down and pinch together. His head swipes side to side. On the inside of his eyelids is some sort of dramatic dream. He's distressed. His lips part, and he lets out a soft, almost inaudible groan. Should I wake him?

His hands shake, then jerk, more and more violently. I don't know what to do, but when another desperate murmur leaves his lips, I rip him out of this... I don't think this is a dream, it's a nightmare.

"Dash..." I rock his shoulder gently. "Babe..."

He sits up so fast, it knocks me to the side. Dash's alert, vigilant eyes dart around the room. He's panting. But when his gaze locks on mine, he releases a breath, his body relaxing along with the exhale. He presses his fingers into his eye sockets and rubs them.

"Are you okay?"

He doesn't seem okay, but it was only a dream, and now he knows it.

"Sorry..." He lets his head sink into the pillow again. "I woke you."

I stroke waves off his sticky, balmy forehead and kiss it. "You want to tell me about it?"

He shakes his head. But then sinks deep into his pillow, and after a beat, speaks, matter of fact, like this isn't the first time he's had this dream and almost as if he's accepted it will always be there.

"It's me, riding a horse away from something... I don't know what it is but I know in the dream it's something so important my heart races and I'm..." He concentrates on some image in his mind he can still see. "And I'm needing to get away... there's... urgency. And I'm galloping like fucking crazy when..." He stares into space, shaking his head. "I just run out of ground. The horse's hooves stop pounding, and we start to fall, and then..." He runs his fingers through his hair. "I wake up."

He wraps his arm around me, pulling me against his chest again. That he wants to snuggle me makes me feel like a safety blanket. And I want to be just that. He's been there for me even when he didn't know how much it meant.

His arms envelop me. "I've been having the dream for years now."

Years? "What do you think it means?"

"Don't know." His chest rises and falls under my cheek. "I really don't know. I don't know what I'm running from. Or maybe I'm running toward something. All I know is I never get there." He jiggles me under his arm. "I bet you're one of those girls who's got a dream dictionary or something."

I giggle. "No. But my sister does."

Hm. *My sister.* She's coming in just a few weeks, and I haven't spoken to Dash about it. I fold in on myself, wondering how I'm going to bring it up. I don't want him to feel kicked out. I don't even want him to leave because I'm already used to this rhythm we have. It feels like home.

But equally, am I going to share a double bed with my sister in the room next door to my boss? And is Dash, who's basically grumpy with everyone but me and Eve, seriously going to want to have my sister here? My original plan was to have him meet her when she came and see if it sparked a next course of action, but he took off like a bat out of hell.

I've gotten myself into a pickle. Worse than a pickle. Pickles are tasty.

"How do you do it?" he asks out of the blue.

"What do you mean?" I ask, hoping he can't read my

mind the way he has so many other times since we became "friends."

He kisses the top of my head and breathes in my hair. "You've been through... I mean... I hate to say it, but if I'm being direct, I'd call it neglect."

Something pinches inside when he says it. I don't like to think of myself as a neglected child, even if at times all that was in the house to eat for breakfast were pizza crusts from the day before. Even if I did do people's homework for them sometimes in exchange for some of their packed lunch. Until I wasn't smart enough anymore to offer that service.

"My mom loves me," I defend her.

I defend *myself*.

"I'm sure she does. I'm sure she loves you deeply, but that doesn't mean she was taking care of you."

My eyes sting. "Yeah..." I mutter. Even though some days it doesn't feel like it, I say, "But that was a long time ago."

I don't like people feeling sorry for me. I'm a grown woman now.

"So how is it that you can still be so..." Fatigue weighs down his voice, but he keeps on talking. "I would have thought a person like you would end up feeling less..." He almost drifts away. "It's just..."

I can't tell if he's struggling because he's about to say something bad or something good. Or if he's just falling back asleep.

He traces his fingers along my bicep. His voice is low and almost distant. "You shine like someone who's never been hurt. How do you keep smiling like that?"

It's a compliment, likely meant to make me feel good, because Dash wouldn't insult me. I know that now. Still, his words don't have the intended effect because it's the first time the sad realization hits me. "I kept smiling because someone had to."

"Mmm..." His hum drifts farther away from me.

I lie there in the darkness, trying not to let the ache of my lonely memories find a place in my bones again. I've come a long way and need to focus on the future, not the past.

Dash's heart beats into my ear, and it's a sound as deep and comforting as his smooth voice. The sound of it rumbles against my cheek.

"I like that we aren't perfect."

He says these words in a near delirium, but when I hear them, I come alive. Most women want a man who thinks they're perfect. As a lifelong people-pleaser, I'd rather have a man not looking for perfection because I am so damn sick of chasing people for gratitude. I want a man who likes me broken, messy, and even when I don't smile. Dash hasn't really seen me that way, but his words have me dropping any guard left, even if at this point, it's just a sheet hanging in the wind.

"Dash?" I whisper, wondering if he's dropped back off completely.

"Mmm?"

"I'm trying to change my story." I paint a swirl in his chest hair, right over that gorgeous heart of his.

"I like the sound of that, Molly. And I know you will."

Tears prick at my eyes. Here, in Starlight Canyon, I've already turned the page.

He's breathing deeply again now. I kiss his chest. "Maybe you can change yours, too."

Chapter Twenty-Five

DASH

I'M FALLING SO EASILY it doesn't even feel like it's happening. I should have said no and I said yes instead. Because that's what catching feelings does. It has you acting all out of character and doing things that are a far cry from common sense.

But that's just it. Being with Molly doesn't feel like I'm still searching, like I do at the Valley. When I'm with her, it feels like I've already found what I'm looking for.

Bacon sizzles in the frying pan, and I think about me having that damn dream again. I think about Molly's last croaky words. I was too tired, and scared, to let her know I heard her. Molly will change her story... but I'm not so sure about me.

The only page I want to turn is the one where Molly's in the next chapter, and she's too good for me. One day, she'll need to move on from my moody ass. She'll want someone more spirited, like Mateo. Or someone smarter with more direction like Colt. She'd probably even be better off with Logan, who, one day, when he settles down, will use his swashbuckling energy to put a smile on his wife's face to go with a sparkling Cartier ring on her finger.

I'm just a melancholy country boy living over some stables. I'm too simple for her. I'm too grumpy for her. I'm too damn fucked up for her. She needs someone who has their shit together, not someone who's been having recurring dreams about running out of ground for a decade.

Molly has been through so much. She had to face her fate day after day and have the courage to heal herself a million times. And I can't even do it once. When Molly and I first started getting closer, and I knew she was a kindred spirit, the thought of her being my soulmate crossed my mind. But it wasn't enough. There's more than one soulmate for each soul in the world. No. Molly is my North Star guiding me toward a better life. Being a better man.

I knew I was fucking smitten when she, drunk with her inhibitions down, went straight to my private drawer and wrote in my leather notebook, and instead of being mad she went through my things, I thought about how I'll forever have her handwriting etched in my book. In my mind... in my heart.

I shake my head. *You can't have that girl, Dashiell.*

Finishing off two eggs in the pan, I scrape the bottom to make sure they don't stick. My bedroom door handle clicks and Molly pads out onto the oak floorboards, all sex hair and wearing Logan's Scorpions ice hockey jersey going right down onto that voluptuous part of her thighs. She must have taken it from my drawer since her clothes are out here in a sensual pile on the floor outside my door.

I drink her in from head to toe, and she is fucking

gorgeous. But now I know why the boys go mad when their girl is wearing another man's jersey. I kind of feel like that right now. I'd rather she be in my plain black tee than a shirt that represents my brother.

"Morning," she rasps. She tucks hair behind her ear and holds her shoulders up high.

"Breakfast? Just a short walk of shame to the table." I joke to try and make her comfortable.

She rolls her eyes. "Funny."

I put the plates on the table. She sits with one knee up and tucks the jersey down over her pussy so I can't see if she put underwear on. My God, I'd give anything to be buried down there again.

I pour Molly a cup of coffee and add some creamer, as much as I think she likes, then sit opposite her, occasionally letting my eyes drop, hoping for a slip of the fabric.

She takes a bite of food. "You're almost as good at frying eggs as you are at scrambling them."

I let out a one-syllable laugh and I'm glad she's seeing humor in all this because I don't want her feeling like I do. Falling. Wanting. Already seeing the hurricane coming before the weather even turns. This woman can hurt me. She can hurt me bad.

Yet here I am, gobbling up every morsel she'll give me.

She stares at her plate and snaps a piece of crispy bacon in half. "Yesterday was... maybe the best day of my life."

I try not to say it the way it comes out, like I don't believe it. "Really?" She's the best I've ever had, too, no contest.

"Yeah." Her gaze hides somewhere on the plate. "I always wanted to have family game nights and laughing and just... all that."

Well, I guess she didn't mean *me* then.

243

She peeps up under her eyebrows, her brown eyes sparking. "And then to come home with the handsomest man at the party?" Her cheeks grow round.

Her warm smile ropes me back in again. "The pickings were slim. You only had me and two married guys to choose from."

"Even if the entire cast of *Ocean's Eleven* was there I would have chosen you." She flutters her eyelashes.

A stupid, involuntary grin spreads across my face, and my heart flickers. "Yeah? Well, even if I wasn't related to all those women, I still would have chosen you."

"Is that the best you can do?" she fishes, tilting her head.

"Sunshine, there's not even a second place if every woman in the world was lined up next to you." I mean it. Maybe I'm letting on too much and leading her on, but, I'm not a good liar and it's the goddamn truth.

I can tell by the way her heart creeps into her eyes, making them wide and bright, that telling her the truth was the right thing, even though it's what makes that wind whip harder, the future storm more destructive to admit how I see her. Like she's everything.

She eats and glows across the table from me. "So, Dash... boss... *friend*... what are we going to do with this thing?"

"Thing?" I mumble.

"There's a thing here between us. Even if it's only just the sex, there's a thing."

I nod. There is definitely a thing.

Trying to be mature about it, even though my cock is shouting like a horny teenager not to say the words, I do. "We probably shouldn't do that again."

My words make her pull a face, but she shrugs me off. "Well, what if I disagree?"

My damn heart nearly explodes. It's everything to be wanted by a good-hearted woman like Molly. But I don't know what to say. I know I'm not the one for her. And I know the longer I'm around her, the more we connect like that, all warm, and sensual, and melting into each other, the worse this will be for me when she realizes she can't fix me and finds someone who isn't broken.

She waits for my answer, but my mouth is all cotton when her cell beeps.

She gets up and finds her cell still on the counter, left there after her midnight snack. Her long, silky hair cascades down over her face, and I think about what she just said. She wants to do this again. She wants *me* again. And I sure as hell want her.

What if for once in my life, I see what happens? Loosen the reins?

The jersey stuck to her ass cheeks, the ones without underwear, convince me letting go one more time, hell, maybe even a few more times... If she can handle it. I can.

The devil on my shoulder is back. He tells me I won't get a second morning like this. This goddess in my kitchen, with her pussy open to me, wanting me... calling me to fill her up and take her again.

She bends over to prop her elbows on the counter and text someone back. She shifts her weight from foot to foot, and her ass cheeks take turns dancing for me when she does.

Molly is so. Damn. Tempting. My cock twitches and fills with red, hot-blooded man lust. I'm only a man after all...

I get up quietly, stalking her, bent over and typing something back to whoever interrupted our... *thing*.

One more time.

I paint my body along her curves, my boxers already

full, and ease my steely dick into the delicious gap between her juicy cheeks. I lean myself into her very position, my body flush with hers. The scent of her hair intoxicates me even though it's not strawberry now. Her natural, comforting pheromones fly up my nose and drive me toward self-indulgence.

Something about how our bodies align like they were made for each other makes this all seem inevitable but it isn't. I'm just a weak man; weak for this person who is as strong as she is gentle. Hard-working as she is playful. Angelic as she is human. I find myself craving opposites. Only gluttony and trouble will follow.

A thin slice of boxer brief fabric stands between me and being inside again. I'm right up on that bare ass of hers. The jersey is bunched up, sitting on top of her heavenly hips. I guide my hands along her hip bones and down to the front of her, teasing along that sensitive crease between her hip and pussy lips.

"Mmm," she purrs. "Now this is breakfast."

I swipe my finger along her smooth outer fold and small amount of prickly hair growing there. She's so fucking real. "You're still hungry, Sunshine?"

She giggles, but it sounds a little nervous. "Starving."

I shove the rest of the jersey up and over her hips and shove her ass into my hips, hard.

I lick my fingers and glide them up and down the seams of her already slick core. She's so wet even the creases at the tops of her thighs are damp. "Is this all for me? Like some kind of signal for me to come and get you all dirty again?"

She reaches her hand around and strokes my length through my boxers. She tries to push them down, but without facing me, it isn't easy. "Life is too short to be clean all the time."

I ease my boxers to the floor and kick them off to the side. My fingers are soaked with my saliva and all that arousal dripping out of her. I tug at her hair, and she arches her back, taunting me with those full hips of hers. I twist the length of her hair around my hand to get a better grip.

"Mmm. Are you hanging on to your reins, cowboy?"

I jerk myself from root to tip and stroke her entrance with my crown, admiring the view, getting hot as fuck seeing how every time I slide over her seams, my dick gets soaked. "Your ass is fucking dreamy, woman." I bend over to take a bite out of her peach and to give her one long, wet lick before I ravage her. When I stand back up, I can't help but give her ass a slap.

She starts. "Fuck..." She rubs her cheek where I slapped her. "Branded for real this time."

I watch my cock disappear inside her, slowly, letting her body adjust to my length.

"Mmmm..." she moans. "I'm still sore from yesterday."

I drag my cock in and out, carefully. "We can stop..."

Stopping isn't her agenda. "Show me how hard you can fuck me."

Her words fuel my glutes, powering them with more thrust. "I'm not sure you mean that..." but I'm already shoving myself inside with more force, her request goes straight to my cock, bypassing my head altogether.

"I mean it." She bends over deeper, allowing me better access. "Damn you feel good riding me bareback."

Fuck. I never thought I'd meet a girl that could out dirty talk a man.

I bend her over farther so I can reach around and circle my finger over her clit. She releases tiny moans into the kitchen, encouraging my pace.

I draw my cock in and out of her entrance; faster, with

more speed. More intensity. She grips the counter, bracing herself to take it. "More."

Her ass cheeks bounce every time my hips smack into her. Molly provokes me with more and more mewling, humming with delight, desire... her little sex sounds charge me. I burrow down into her relentlessly, pounding into her back side, my balls swinging.

Shooting stars sizzle across my vision. I'm holding my breath. Clenching every fucking muscle in my body and careening into her with zero restraint. Not an ounce of willpower. I'm like a man possessed.

That's the problem here. I can't seem to stop myself when I'm with Molly. I can't stop thinking about her wants and needs. And much as riding her immaculate ass raw is enough to send me to fucking paradise, never wanting to come back, even in this undone moment, my mind wanders to the other parts of her I adore—her heart. Her grit. Her empathy for everyone and everything around her.

Her tits sway every time my hips thrust forward. She turns her head, and her eyebrows pinch together. Her lips are parted, sensual and swollen. The look of her pleasure courses hot through my veins.

She grabs one of her ass cheeks, prying herself open wider for me. Her thighs tremble, and she calls my name when her pussy walls ripple around my cock.

"Dash..." Her voice is steamy. "More..."

I'm spurred on by her commands, the invitation of her nails digging into her skin to break herself open for me. I pump harder, and she gasps and lets go of her ass to hold on to the counter with two hands. Her hot release spills between us. I slam between her clenching folds, wild, hurtling...

Every nerve in my body spirals. My balls tighten and

when I explode inside her, hot cum filling the space, lewd noises fill the kitchen. Something between a growl and a grunt suppresses behind every taut muscle in my body. My abs are tight, and my body pulses with pleasure, jerking like it's my last breath on Earth.

I bend over her, panting, her back rises and falls under my chest. I dot slow kisses on the small of her back, enjoying her salty sheen of perspiration on my lips. When we both calm, I help her up to standing and twist her around to press my lips into hers. It's a kiss far more gentle than what we just experienced. A kiss something like gratitude. Because I am thankful. Thankful for what, I don't know but whatever it is fate designed, fighting it isn't working so I take what I'm given.

Molly tugs me into her hard and buries herself in my neck. "I thought you said we shouldn't do that again," she whispers. "I guess I have the power of persuasion."

"Sunshine, you have *all* the power over me." I lace my fingers through her hair, grab it, and bring her head in firmly to my chest. I wonder if she can hear what my heart is saying. I can't, but it's desperate to talk.

I lift her, hold on under her ass cheeks, and she wraps her legs around my middle. I carry us over to the bathroom.

"Better clean you up."

She holds on to me tightly all the way to the bathroom where, her still plastered against my body, I reach in for the handle and blast the shower.

I take my time with her in there. It's been over a month since I very first smelled that strawberry-mint shampoo in this apartment and couldn't get the scent out of my mind. I run suds through her long brown strands and use the same lather to smooth every inch of her curves. I press her against the wall; I can't help myself. I kiss her sweet lips and push her arms overhead, and we're back at it all over again.

When we finish, that's when I'm not sure, but maybe something changes. I watch Molly wrap that yellow towel of hers around her boobs and tuck it into her cleavage. Somewhere in the midst of the satisfied, contented smile she gives me, a spark of something new alights inside me.

If I didn't know better, that spark is something like happiness.

Chapter Twenty-Six

MOLLY

A WEEK LATER, after abandoning my own bedroom altogether, I still haven't told Dash about my sister. And I haven't told my sister about Dash—well, not that so far, he's still going to be living here when she arrives.

How the hell am I going to make this happen? I want two very conflicting things with two people I care about. On the one hand, I want to keep going and see where this takes me with Dash. I feel it in my bones. It just feels right. I don't want to put any space between our intimate moments. By the soul-deep look in his eyes every time he takes me, neither does he.

But will he want to live here with us? Hell no. At the thought of even the slightest distance between us, the old Molly returns—the insecure one who worries if I don't keep pulling at the growing connection, he'll retreat with it. No matter how many times we've laughed together, eaten together, cuddled, kissed, and God knows whatever else, we still haven't clicked our status over from friends to something new.

Even in all the euphoric times we're sharing, I still see glimpses of a cool, protective fourteen-year-old boy. Every once in a while, he withdraws and gives ground. He never flees, but I see him working to draw a line. And it's me who reaches across the invisible barrier and reminds him its safe on the other side. I've completely fallen for him and the idea of rescuing him. This is a lethal combination, but somehow, I spend every waking minute wanting to die trying. I'm like some insane crusader, fully convinced Dash is a worthy cause.

Equally, the other cause since as long as I can remember is just weeks from arriving in our territory. I can't wait for Lily and me to start this new life here in the Canyon together, hopefully with our mom. The city is no good for her. It's too hectic. It's too loud. Nature heals.

Maybe Lily and I can fit two twin beds in the room? Maybe Mom and Lil can stay in there, and I live with Dash in his room? Maybe I'm totally nuts thinking like this. Yes, I truly am. There is no fucking way Dash will want in on that scenario.

A heavy sigh leaves my body. Dashiell Hunter will never agree to that plan. *I* don't like that plan. It's ridiculous.

I need to talk to him, and I need to do it soon, before he thinks I'm deliberately keeping it from him, which I'm not. It's just... when we're together, everything else seems to fade into the background.

I'm finishing up my morning tasks on the ranch, which today, involves breaking up a lot of ice. It's November, but it already feels like deep winter. Snow sticks to the mountaintops. Pine trees are dusted like they're cake toppers with powdered sugar. It's breathtaking here. This has to be the most beautiful place on the planet. If fate thought I deserved to land here, I must have done something right.

I'm walking back from the pastures and check my watch. Shit. Picking up the pace to a jog, I hurry to my car because Jolie invited me out with her and Logan. They're having lunch at I de la Cremes in town and invited me.

I pop Dash a quick text.

ME

I'M HAVING LUNCH WITH JOLIE AND LOGAN. ARE YOU GOING? WE CAN DRIVE TOGETHER?

DASHIELL HUNTER- STARLIGHT RANCH

I SAID NO, BUT YOU CHANGED MY MIND. SEE HOW PERSUASIVE YOU ARE?

I gush.

DASHIELL HUNTER- STARLIGHT RANCH

JUST LOOKING AT SOMETHING WITH HANK. WAIT BY MY TRUCK. BE THERE IN 5.

I wait by Dash's truck, and for a minute, it's like I'm his gi

---

Logan is so different from the other Hunter brothers. Dash is mysterious, sexy, and brooding. Colt is warm, thoughtful, and decisive. And Logan, besides being just as gorgeous as his brothers, he's his own man. He's charismatic, friendly, but aloof all the same and has a flirty dimple that I bet gets him his way quite a lot.

In fact, with confidence like his, I'm very sure he's often served what he wants with a side of puck bunny whipped cream. Though he gives off player vibes, it's impossible not to like him. A lot like Jolie, he tries hard to put me at ease and acts like our short-lived celebration drinks wasn't the first time we met.

We're finished eating and he asks about my sandwich.

"Did you like your tuna melt, *Chicago*?" Logan, like all Hunters, just had to give me a nickname. "If you do, honestly, at the ranch restaurant, at bar time, the chef, Hux, does a fancy one, with celery and chilis and these little ball things..."

"Capers," Jolie adds.

"Yeah, you know he puts his Michelin-star thing to the ordinary and makes it..." he kisses his fingers, "chef's kiss, man." He tips his chin up at Dash. "You should take her there."

Dash and I glance at each other like maybe the other one has been talking to Logan about our little trysts. We gaze back at Logan whose eyes are narrowed.

"Aren't you two dating?" His eyes question Jolie. "I thought you said they were dating?"

Jolie laughs, not nervously, but like she's been caught gossiping, which is exactly the case. "No. I said they *should* date."

But she has no interest in covering it up.

I'm not sure why I expect Dash to get all awkward. I've never seen him awkward. But I have seen him go quiet, and that's exactly what he does. I might have rather him confirm or deny... but that's just not his style. He's a private guy. I respect that so I change the subject.

"Logan, Colt mentioned at family drinks the other night you might retire soon. Is that true? Must be a weird thing to decide when you've given your whole life to something." I figure talking about hockey will take the attention off... *us*. Whatever we are.

"Why does that old man always have to make out like *I'm* old, too? Colt *wants* me to retire."

"Why would he want that?"

Jolie answers for him. And Colt by the sound of it. "Because a life of hockey takes its toll. ESPN rates it the toughest sport after only boxing. Lo, you've had a broken nose, jaw, separated shoulders..."

He interrupts. "*You* broke your wrist riding that devil horse of yours." Logan laughs, not taking her seriously at all or coming across as defensive. "To be fair, Ted damn near broke my wrist, too. That horse is *loco*."

She scoffs. "You're lucky he didn't break you, too, because you're not supposed to be riding," she says. Then, she also gazes at me. "Keep that to yourself because this dumbass was in breach of contract at the time."

"Whatever. Ashton does it, too. We all have our vices."

"Too bad being a cowboy isn't your only one," she teases him

Logan shrugs with an innocent expression and that sexy-cute dimple of his, and I know exactly what she's on about.

"But unlike you, Ashton is sensible and goes on the predictable ones. You have a death wish or something."

He leans back and laces his arms behind his head. "I do like living on the edge. Adrenaline is my only addiction, Molly."

I can see why he's in the headline as an NHL playboy. He's scrumptious, so naughty he's nice, and his playful nature makes it impossible not to smile around him. Even Jolie is shaking her head, grinning at how ridiculous her brother is, like he's some lovable scamp.

Now that we've officially moved far enough away from the me-and-Dash-dating comment, I allow a glance over at my boss, roommate, and the complicated status blaring in my face like a blinking red light. I'm not sure what kind of expression I'll get back, but he cocks the corner of his mouth in a half-smile, and I figure, we're all right.

Just then, the tinkling bell goes on the door to CCs, and in walks an absolutely stunning woman with a big, square, white pastry box. She sets her eyes on Logan. "Logan?"

He swivels in his seat toward the sound of his name. "Shay! Hey, girl. Come on over..."

She bounces over, her beautiful long hair sweeping along with her and sets the cake box on the table. She gives Logan a big hug.

Shay rubs the sides of Logan's arms, and boy, am I sure she's enjoying it. I wonder how these two are so comfortable.

Jolie interrupts the moment. She's forward like that. "Hey, Shana!"

Oh my gosh... wait... is this the celebrated carrot cake connoisseur, Shana? *And please tell me there's more cake in that box because when we ordered at the counter, I noticed they were all out.*

"Jojo, my girl..." Shana bends down, wrapping an arm around Jolie. "We haven't caught up in years. Can't believe I haven't made time to see you since you've been back in town."

"Gosh, don't worry about it. I know you have a kid." She says it with enough volume for Logan to maybe hear it, in case he doesn't already know, because when they hugged, well, it wasn't an ordinary hug. "You must be super busy with the catering business."

Shana picks the box back up. "Yeah. It's going pretty well. I could probably do without the daily order from here, but I think the town would disown me if I stopped bringing my carrot cake to CCs. It's the only one I bring here now."

I put the tip of my finger on the box as if to stop her picking it all the way up. "You can just leave that with me."

She laughs and has a beaming, broad smile like a movie star. "I wish I could, but you have to share."

Dash introduces me. "This is Molly. She's manager at the stables now."

"Nice to meet you, Molly. Been in Starlight Canyon long? I don't think I've seen you before?"

"Yeah, I don't get away from the horses too much. Been here since the beginning of last high season. I love it and don't plan on leaving."

"I couldn't leave either. Though I tried."

She darts her eyes over to Logan again but so briefly I hardly notice before her gaze is back on me again.

She picks up her cake box. "Gotta drop this off and run."

But before Shana leaves, Dash catches her. "Shay. Just wondering. Do you do wedding cakes? Molly's trying to get weddings going on the ranch."

"Absolutely. They're my favorite," she says with a faraway look.

"Great, you two need to stay in touch," he says to me.

I admit, "I already follow you on social, Shana. Stalk you, actually."

"Aw. Seriously?"

"I'm cake obsessed."

Her wide eyes are kind. "You're in good company. I'd

love to be the go-to wedding cake gal at Starlight Ranch if you ever get weddings going. Just hit me up. Bye y'all." She skips over to the counter, leaves the box and rushes out leaving us with another tinkle.

Jolie punches Logan in the leg.

"Ah... what?" He rubs his thigh as if it hurt.

"Is that why you wanted to eat here instead of have chicken wings at Sly Bull's this afternoon? So you could see Shay?"

"Don't be stupid."

"I don't usually worry about sounding like an asshole, but you know she has a kid now, right? Like..." She's exhausted with him.

"Fuck, Jo, what kind of guy do you think I am?" He's not defensive, just wears that coy, boyish smile of his. "We've never been more than friends, and that's probably a stretch. I only know her because of you."

"Shana's a nice girl," Jolie warns.

"I know she is," he says, his voice laced with defensiveness this time.

Jolie throws her hands up. "None of my business, bro. None of my business." She finishes off her milkshake with a slurp. "Speaking of nice girls, how's Lil? She getting all packed up and excited for her move here?"

Dash puts his glass of half-drunk Coke down softly on the table, listening, for sure.

Jolie sure knows how to accidentally bring up subjects that don't want to be talked about. But obviously I can't ignore her, so I hope to steer her down a path. I don't want it coming out like this... here, in public. "Yeah. I'm really proud of her graduating early like this, too. And she's done it with honors."

"I wish I had her drive at that age."

"You went on and became a doctor!" I will not stand for Jolie suggesting she's not kick-ass.

"I know. But I barely scraped in. I was too worried about other stupid stuff. Things that didn't matter and never would." She stirs her straw around in a glass full of nothing. "Anyway, nice to graduate early for two reasons. One, a little less money for you two to pay, and two... you'll finally be living together again. I bet you're excited, too."

I don't think it's my imagination when Dash stops breathing next to me. He is totally stiff. Shit... this is coming across exactly how I didn't mean it to. Like I'm keeping things from him. Like I'm not being honest. Like I was trying to pull a fast one. I'm sure, under those beautiful dark waves and behind those piercing eyes, he's thinking about me going through his room now, too. I can't be trusted. *Fuck.*

Heat creeps up my neck. I'm such a dick. I really didn't keep Lily from him on purpose, it's just... maybe I did. Maybe I subconsciously avoided it and now... I don't want to talk to Jolie about this anymore. The person I need to talk to is right here next to me. And we need to talk alone.

I rub balmy hands on my jeans. "Yeah. Of course. Guys, I need to scoot. Need to get over to the tack shop and buy some salt for the troughs."

Logan says, "Nice meeting you, Chicago. You coming to a game or two this season? Dash, you going to bring her to the box?"

He responds with a simple nod, and we say our goodbyes.

Moments later, Dash and I are in his truck, and the mood is not the same as on the way here. If he was pensive before, his thoughts are now out there in another world. He's far away. Distant.

And it's up to me to bring him back. "Hey, sorry I haven't talked to you about my sister."

He doesn't answer.

"It's just... the original plan for us was for me to get the manager's job and have a place for us to live after she finishes college. So we can pay down the college debt..."

"I get it." His voice is cool and even.

"And I really should have brought it up again." I really should have. Damn it. What was I thinking not making this conversation a priority? "Anyway, I love living with you. I don't want you to move out."

"Well, I am, so there's no need to worry about it." His voice is flat. Flatter than usual. "The apartment was always supposed to belong to you, so I wasn't planning on staying permanently."

His words sting, even though there's nothing inherently mean about them. "You're leaving?"

He stares at the road. "As soon as you got the job, I went and asked Colt to build another apartment above the new stables being built. I'll take that one. It's only one bedroom, so with your sister coming, you can stay put."

Why, when he's giving me what I want, no, what I *need*, does this cut so deep? He doesn't sound angry. His words are matter of fact. And they're settling the conundrum I've been trying to work out for weeks. I should be relieved now; he knows, the room will be ready for my sister, he doesn't seem annoyed... but his body language has changed. It might be my imagination, but I don't feel like I can just reach over and hold his hand anymore.

He flips on the indicator, and the *tick-tock* noise it makes fills the truck like a time bomb, one I don't know how to defuse.

I didn't bring Lily up, but why didn't *he* mention

moving out? He never told me there was another apartment being built and that he never planned on staying with me. He was going to leave all along? When was he going to mention *that*?

My gut aches and churns with heartache. I feel like I've just been dumped out of the blue. *My* situation is totally different. I wasn't even saying Dash had to leave, just that my sister needs a place to live.

He parks up at the tack shop which is only around the corner from CCs. "What do we need? Just salt?" He asks the empty space instead of me.

We're back right where we started, and I don't mean when I started working as stable manager. I mean when I first arrived at Starlight Ranch and he probably couldn't have told you what hair color I had for the first month.

My eyes sting. "Yeah. Just salt," I say, face glued to the window so he can't see my expression. Not that he's looking at me anyway. "Thanks."

As soon as his car door shuts, my nose fizzles and my eyes gloss over. It's obvious by how much this hurts, that a part of me thought we might carry on living together forever. I thought if I sat on it long enough, I'd come up with some way for Dash and me to stay together, keep going until we rode off into the sunset.

But we're not.

And he never, ever planned on it.

I clear my throat. I'm being silly. I'm imagining the worst for no reason. Just because we're not going to keep living together doesn't mean we can't keep doing... whatever it is we're doing. But for once I want him to chase me. I want him to make the first move and tell me he wants to keep... fucking? What exactly are we doing? It's definitely more than that, right?

When Dash gets back into the truck with the supplies, we still don't talk. It's the first time I realize that whether we forge something or we don't, it will be painful to be with a man like this. I want the flowers. But I don't want to have to ask him to buy them.

Chapter Twenty-Seven

DASH

LATER THAT AFTERNOON, I go into Colt's office without knocking and throw myself on the couch opposite his desk.

He closes his laptop. "I was just about to leave... Eve and Sam want to see the *Barbie* movie tonight, and they need time to transform me into Ken."

Now would be a great time to heckle Colt, but I'm not in the mood.

"All I want to know was when that apartment is done?"

Colt narrows his eyes and watches me as he bends down to switch the power to his monitor off. "You're still moving out?"

"Yeah."

He swipes a hand down his stubble. "It seemed like things were going well with Molly, that's all."

They were. Too well. I've always known we'd need to

detach from each other. I just didn't know the time would come quite so soon. "So when is it done?"

"Wait. You and Molly haven't been hooking up?" he asks.

Leave it to Colt to be in your face. All that fucking therapy has made him so direct. He's so well adjusted. *Asshole*. At least Jolie left wiggle room *implying* Molly and I were dating. Colt puts me on the spot so there's no escape.

I try not answering, which usually works, but Colt folds his hands on the desk and stares at me like he's holding the answer to the apartment timeline as ransom. Like this conversation needs to be a quid pro quo.

"We've been together a couple times." It's a massive understatement. But so is calling it hooking up. I'd never call what we did hooking up. Hooking up isn't in the same league as what happened between us.

"Why don't you just stay put and see how things go? You two seem to get along great..."

"I'm not staying in the apartment." I raise my voice, and it's as ominous as thunder.

And now... now Colt knows this meeting is about more than the apartment because I rarely raise my voice. Even when I'm pissed I don't use volume to get my point across. *Shit*. Molly has me crawling outside my skin. She's got me totally out of control.

"Dash..." he looks to be considering his words, "... it's not like I'm keeping tabs on your love life or anything, but I can't help but notice she's the first person you've taken to, well, maybe ever."

Now is not the time for Colt to bring up my feelings for Molly. He's resurrecting things I'm trying to shove down. I'm not the man for Molly, and now we have a chance for an amiable, logical cut to the tie that binds.

And boy, am I bound. I feel it like a string around my lungs.

"You're different around her," Colt continues. "She brings out a side of you I've never even seen, and I've been around you all but four years of your thirty. Why not just give it a go?"

"We don't need to live together to give things a go." It's lying by omission because today is the day we stop doing that.

I wanted to *give it a go*. I've grown to like making breakfast for two and her sunrise smile in the morning. I actually like not getting up at three a.m. and feeling more alive in the daylight where she says I belong. She made me feel like being together was the right thing. But it isn't. I needed this slap in the face to remember that.

She didn't do anything wrong. I get why she found it hard to tell me about her sister. It's the same reason I find it hard to walk away even though she deserves a better man. The end fucking hurts. It's time. Time for us to stop. Molly's sister coming to Starlight Canyon is the perfect, easy out for both of us.

But it's like a wrench trying to turn a rusty bolt inside my chest.

I just need the timeline and to get the hell out of here. I placate Colt. "There's nothing going on that you need to worry about. Just... her sister is done with college soon and she's moving to the Canyon. She needs a place to live. Bird's Eye is too crowded for my liking."

"Oh..." Colt's shoulders relax, and the worry for me falls to the floor. "I think it needs another week or maybe two. I told them to have it sorted before Christmas."

After lunch, I couldn't bring myself to ask exactly when Lily is moving in, but remembering my siblings coming

265

back from college, it was usually early December their semester ended. That's in two, three weeks. Well, before Christmas.

In any case, it isn't tomorrow.

I get up. "Thanks. Have a good time at the *Barbie* movie." I wish it came out as a prod, but nothing is funny right now. Not even my brother dolled up in pink.

Molten lava has been simmering in my chest all day, and when I get back to the apartment, seeing Molly only dials up the temperature. She's standing in the kitchen right where I last had her. Right where she had my heart cracked wide open for her that very first night while playing three questions.

She's stirring something in a pan on the stove and twists around to greet me. "Hey! I'm making us some stir-fry."

As usual, her positivity is undeterred, which makes me think two things. Either I'm not as important to her as she is to me. Or, she doesn't realize we need to go back to the original meaning of friends.

"I've already eaten," I say. I haven't. But I don't want to go in that kitchen right now. Not when all I can think about is how beautiful she looked bent over naked and how the insides of her feel like home.

But I don't want to hurt her, even though I am, so I mutter, "Thanks, though. It'll be good for leftovers." I toe off my boots and start heading to my room, but she stops me.

"Dash." She blows a tendril of hair off her forehead and puts a hand on her hip. "We need to talk. I know you're probably upset about Lily, and honestly? I'm actually a little upset about you not saying you were moving out. So... let's do this." She turns off the gas on the stove and leans against the counter.

Shit, man, between her and Colt, this is just about all the *let's talk* I can deal with for one day. And something about her posture, all relaxed against the counter; meanwhile, I'm cascading into darkness inside, trying to scoop back up the part of me that was falling for her, and it kind of pisses me off.

This is easier for her than it is for me. That much is evident.

I take a couple of steps toward the kitchen but don't want to be too near her. I might lose my nerve. This is over. It has to be. Right here and now. "You had plenty of chances to tell me about your sister coming." And then I do it. I transform into an asshole so she can be mad at me instead of sad about me. "I thought we were being honest with each other. Guess I was wrong."

"You weren't wrong..."

A strangled laugh erupts from my lips.

"Dash. Seriously. I... should have told you, but the only reason I didn't was because I didn't want you to move out. I like living with you."

I laugh again, and it's almost like I'm possessed by some demon determined to exorcise this woman from my life. "It's fine, Molly. We had a fling..."

She raises her voice in such a way I didn't know she was capable. "It wasn't just a fling, was it?" She doesn't say it like a question. She says it like we both fully know our connection was more than just sex.

Her vulnerability brings me to a halt. The silence between us is thick and breathing with the reality of her confession. *Our confession.* Because she's totally right.

I don't want to be cruel. But venom gathers on my

tongue because I'm hurt. Hurt because this momentum is coming to an end. Hurt because she's now going to start telling me she actually likes me... and we can't be together. And that means I'm going to bruise her, too, and that wasn't the plan.

It's so much easier to float on anger than it is to drown in sadness, and the only words I find are ones to push her away. It's so fucked. I'm so fucked up. She stares at me, waiting, but I have to hold my tongue because she doesn't deserve me to end it with a fight. I still want to be her friend...

Pain creeps into her eyes. "Dash? Was it... Was it just sex for you?"

I can't answer that. Not when I need to end this. "Molly, why didn't you tell me about your sister?"

"Why didn't you tell me you were moving out?"

"Your sister coming is a sure thing. Me moving into the apartment was an *option*."

My confession catches us both off guard, and silence floats between us while we stare into each other's eyes with more questions than we have answers.

But she asks again, "Was it just sex for you?"

My God, if she only knew. Being with Molly was a spiritual experience. When I told her it was unforgettable, I meant it. But I also know, I know from the sick feeling piling up in my throat, that I've already gone too far with her. I *knew* this woman would hurt me and all I can do is try to dampen the blow by getting out now.

"No. I care about you." But I can't keep going down this road leading to nowhere. "I told you I wanted to be friends."

She nods, flutters her lashes down, and rolls her lips. "Yeah. You said that. I guess I ignored it. *Friends*." She stares at the floor, her body slumps in rejection. "You did say that."

Seeing Molly like this shreds my heart, and panic bites at all the edges. "Sunshine. Come on..."

"Don't." She raises her hand to stop me. "It's fine. You were straight with me about where you stood right from the start. You have nothing to apologize for. And..." She turns back to the kitchen and lights the burner. "It's what needs to happen."

Staring at her back and sagging shoulders, I want to reach out and gather her up into my arms and hold her. But I can't. I can't, even though something desperate inside me, something I never knew was even there, pounds in anguish against my ribcage, trying to get to her.

If only the last time we were together, I knew. For the second time in my life, I'm leaving something behind without saying goodbye the way I would have wanted.

She clears her throat, throws one last comment over her shoulder, her voice small and brittle. "I'm sorry I didn't mention Lily coming sooner."

"It's fine. Don't worry about it. The other apartment isn't ready just yet, but I'll move in with Jo, and you can get my room ready for your sister."

She nods, still staring at the contents of the pan; she's stirring ever so slowly. "Okay."

I stay for another beat, gazing at her swan-like neck under a nest of pulled-up hair. I used to kiss that neck. Now I leave it for some other man? The thought sickens me. It's less like me releasing Molly into a life better suited to her and more like I'm being a fucking coward.

When I close the door behind me, I've never felt so lonely in my life.

I spend the next five hours staring across my bed at

Molly's wall, wishing things didn't have to be this way. Wishing I could change. Wishing I could make my numb, paralyzed body open the door and burst into her room, take her as mine, and ignore all the consequences.

What the hell is wrong with me? I've put her through pain to avoid my own? What kind of sadist have I become? What was once a young boy coping with grief has turned into full-blown torture, and I always reasoned it was only me getting hurt so it didn't matter.

I try hard to fall asleep, but Molly telling me it's okay is on repeat in my head. Her voice in my mind is like the static crackle of a record at the end of its loop. Round and round, I play her grainy words, telling me it's all right when I know full well it isn't.

I want to fight for her. But it's fucking hard when the person I'm trying to defeat is myself. I can't shake the raw, painful feeling that one day, I'll look back and regret every single thing I did to let this end.

Chapter Twenty-Eight

MOLLY

I SPEND HOURS LYING AWAKE, thinking about how just on the other side of the wall is so much more than I made it out to be. I try not to cry but don't succeed. Droplets roll down my cheeks in devastated trickles. It crushes me to know I'll never feel his dewy skin against mine in a moment of wild abandon behind hay bales. The thought that I'll never touch Dash again and he'll never touch me is excruciating. I'll never smell him because we won't get that close, and he'll stop calling me Sunshine.

I know we said we'd be friends, but it will never be the same. I'm struggling to accept it. I'm struggling to accept he can discard what was happening between us so easily... because I can't. He was right. We are different. Peeling away from each other isn't right for me. I'm not afraid of being hurt if we go down the road and see it turns into two separate paths. But I hate that we didn't even try.

I stopped trusting men a long time ago. But I thought I was learning to trust *me*. And despite him telling me he's broken, despite him making it clear he wanted to be my friend, my gut told me there was something once-in-a-life-time happening between us. My intuition said it would be worth any road bumps along the way. But right now, the way a lump grows larger and larger in my throat, threatening to suffocate me if I don't just let out the tears I'm trying to hold in... it's unbearable.

I think about when he said he loved we aren't perfect. I'm not. Neither is he. I'm not looking for perfect. The moon is beautiful but covered in craters. The sky holds the sun but can be covered in clouds. I know people aren't perfect. Life is far from perfect, and I didn't idealize Dash. He isn't perfect.

But he is *special*.

Even now, heartbroken, I know this is true. I'll never meet someone like him in all my life. He. Is. Special. But I guess I wasn't special enough for him to take the same risk I was prepared to.

He warned me.

He was right.

I should have listened.

I'm not on the way to becoming a badass bitch. I'm the same sappy pushover I've always been.

I nestle my head into my pillow, and when I do, a tear slides out again. I wipe it off and text my sister. I need to feel less alone before I fall into a dark abyss.

ME

WELL, DASH IS MOVING OUT.

LILS

MY SISTER SPIDEY-SENSES TELL ME TO
ASK YOU IF YOU'RE OK WITH THAT?

ME

YEAH. IT NEEDED TO HAPPEN. I JUST
WANT YOU HERE NOW.

When I put down the phone, another tear escapes. What the hell is wrong with me that I can't stop crying over this man?

It was just sex. We were never together. But it's not that.

It's that we'll never *be* together.

———

We have weekend help at the ranch, and although I don't truly ever take a day off, I can do what I want. What I've always wanted all these years of working on ranches is to have my own horse to take care of. My own to ride off on the trails like all the tourists with their goofy grins and selfies. I failed to wish for someone to ride with.

I brush Romeo's dark coat and can't help but sigh. I barely stop myself from saying out loud to this black beauty that he's the only Romeo I'll ever have. My picker is broken. I slowly brush through Romeo's tail, working on some crusty brown thistles, when Bobby rocks up to put a horse rug away.

"Mornin', Molly."

"Hey..." I try not to be distant, but my thoughts are definitely elsewhere. I was hoping Romeo would bring me back down to earth.

"You all right?" Bobby asks, rather than rush off home like I expect him to on a Saturday.

"Of course." I try a smile but don't look him in the eye.

"You riding today? Heard Romeo's yours now." Bobby rubs Romeo's neck.

"Not today..." I continue brushing the tail but give Bobby the courtesy of eye contact; it's not his fault I'm melancholy. And truthfully, since Dash gave him the evil eye, he's been super cooperative, a team player, and actually, a decent guy. "I don't have any tack yet."

"Sure you do. Dash left it in the tack room next to his stuff this morning."

I stop grooming with the brush caught mid-stroke. What the hell kind of whiplash is Dashiell Hunter trying to give me? I shake it off and keep at a stubborn thistle. "I don't think that's for me."

"It's gotta be. The Belgians don't have tack. It was too big a saddle for any of the other horses round here. Plus, he put it in the private area. It's definitely for Romeo. And... come see for yourself."

I let Romeo off the crossties into the corral and amble with Bobby to the tack room. He points to a new saddle stand I never noticed, and sure enough, there rests a large saddle and a hook with a bridle and reins hanging above it.

Bobby stops next to the stand. "See?" He points to the saddle pad under the saddle and reads, "*Romeo*. It's even personalized."

I'm trying to be happy over any other emotion. After all, I wouldn't have been able to afford tack for ages, and this has to be the sweetest present... no, all of Dash's presents are sweet. Caring. Thoughtful. But totally out of place. One minute the guy is giving me gifts, and the next, he's cold,

274

standoffish, moving out, and stamping my heart under his boot.

Bobby runs a finger over the leather. "You know how to ride?"

"Kind of. I mean, I've been doing this for four years, so I've been on trail rides but never out on my own."

"Well, I'm done for the day. I'll join you if you want company?" he offers kindly.

I drink in the cool, handsome cowboy and think to myself that I could be taking up worse offers on a sunny Saturday. "Thanks, Bobby, honestly, I'd really love that." Any distraction from my incessant focus on Dash is welcome. "Hound Dog was last out today, so his belly is probably least full. He'll be up for it if he works for you?"

When Bobby runs off to fetch Hound Dog from the pasture, I drop Dash a text. It's the right thing to do. And much as I'd like to avoid him forever, he's still my boss, and moreover, we said we'd be friends.

ME

THANKS FOR THE TACK. FIRST RIDE ON MY HORSE TODAY. I REALLY DO APPRECIATE IT.

He doesn't text back.

I bring Romeo in from the corral, and ten minutes later, Bobby and I are tacking up together and having a conversation about ice hockey. He's going to the game tonight and tells me about how he used to watch Logan and Ashton Dane, when he was younger. Bobby is surprisingly humble when you get to know him, and I warm to him in a way I haven't before.

The more we talk, the more I realize his bravado and

ladies' man facade is just that... a facade. He tells me about his high school sweetheart who never came back when she went off to college and how it broke his heart. He confesses she was the one who got away. He tells me he's saving for his own herd of cattle because his grandpa just died and left him some land. I'm grateful for Bobby's words because I don't feel much like talking myself today and I could have much worse company.

While we're off on the trails, Bobby asks if I have a boyfriend or anybody I'm waiting on. Before I answer no, I laugh softly to myself and think... I'll be waiting a long, long time for the one I want.

And when I finally come back to the apartment, fingers frozen, nose red as a cherry, Dash's bedroom is all packed up into a couple suitcases by the door, and that's when it hits me. I won't be waiting a long time. I'll be waiting forever.

A profound, deep sadness overwhelms me, and only now, as my back hits the wall and I slide down, falling into a heap on the floor, do I realize just how much hope I had for us going somewhere. I stare at his suitcase and wonder how he can buy me tack and boots and make love to me the way he did, because yes, it was fucking, but it was fucking deeper than that, too... How can he do all of that one day and just walk out the next?

He's left his hat on the hook, and it makes me think about his gorgeous wavy hair and how it felt between my fingers. It makes me think about how when he slept next to me, I inhaled his scent and it fucking smelled like home. It makes me think about him tipping it off his head briefly, flashing me a dimple and calling me Sunshine. He told me otherwise, but my heart didn't believe we weren't falling because it *was* falling.

I stare at his suitcases and think about how we won't be having bacon and eggs anymore and carrot cake won't appear with threatening notes to eat it. It will all be different now because even though we aren't breaking up... that's exactly what it is to me, and my heart feels like it's being clawed by a wolverine. My nose stings, and I really don't want to, but I start crying.

Why can't I just pick a normal guy? Am I broken, too? Am I so messed up from my childhood that I have some weird complex, destined to choose people who I try to fix but will never love me back? And now I have to work with Dash every goddamn daaa...

"Sunshine?" His deep voice rolls down on me like fog.

Quickly, I wipe my eyes and turn my face away. "Oh, hey."

"Are you crying?"

"No."

He sits beside me against the wall. "Don't lie to me, Mols. I can't stand seeing you cry. What's going on? I promise I'll fix it. Whatever it is."

"Yeah?" Something like anger creeps up my neck. "Be careful what you promise."

"Is it Bobby?"

Of course he'd know we were out together. Dash knows all.

"No. Bobby's nice now."

He leans over and wipes some wetness from under my eye. "What is it then?"

I crack. "Stop being nice to me, Dash. Just stop."

He pulls his hand back. "Okay."

I push myself up off the floor and start off to the kitchen. I need a drink of water to wash this all away.

He follows me but doesn't say anything, and it pisses me

off. That's him in a nutshell. Mr. Silent. Just like his moving out. He could have explained. We could have talked about it more. But no. Tight Lips over here just can't...

I slam my plastic cup down on the counter when I finish.

"Molly..." he says my name like he's trying to calm me down.

But it only winds me up. I spin around fast. "Don't *Molly* me. Dash, honestly, you're really, really..." The anger swirls around with the other energy that's always between us, and I get confused again. I point to his suitcases. "I didn't want you to leave!"

"I'm just making room for your sister..."

"No, you're not! You're making a statement. And that statement is we're not together and we never ever will be. And I'm sorry... yes, Dash, I'm just another silly girl thinking I'd be the one to change you. Bet I'm probably just the most recent one in a long line of women chasing the bad boy..." My words trail off. They're venomous and uncalled for.

His eyebrows pinch together. He rolls his lips, and I know he isn't going to fight with me. Just like he didn't fight his inner demons *for* me. I inhale deeply and ball my fists, clenching the urge to lash out at him tightly into them. This is not his fault. Did he lead me on? No. Well, maybe? I don't know.

But we can't fight. We can't be friends either, but this man is what he's always been. My boss. I should have kept it that way all along and now I need to get it back to where we started.

"I'm just... we shouldn't have slept together. It did things to me and..." I cleanse some of the anger and hurt away with a deep breath. "Now, I... just need some space to get over it."

I head out the door with absolutely nowhere to be. I hang on to the doorjamb for one last word, but I don't know if it's one for him or for me. "It's going to be fine."

Chapter Twenty-Nine

DASH

A WEEK PASSES, and I manage to stay away from Molly pretty easily. I'm used to operating in the shadows, so I go back to my usual way of doing things, but it feels darker than before. I didn't realize just how much her sunshine crept into my everyday existence and made it better.

Instead of bacon and eggs with the most beautiful girl in the world, I'm back to toast and nasty-ass margarine because Jolie is lactose intolerant.

And because of Molly, I got myself in another jam, too. Mateo has been taking over the checks in the Valley, and he loves it. Today, we're having that outing here together I promised him a while back.

Doing the checks in Mustang Valley with Mateo is the last thing I want to do today. I love my best friend, and usually his company lifts me, but the mood I'm in is the kind of misery a person clings to. It's a misery I feel

280

I deserve and need as some sort of penance or self-flagellation for being such a fuck-up. It's a misery I don't want his charisma to brighten, not even for a moment. I want to hang on to this to remind me what I knew all along.

Love fucking hurts.

The thing is, I kept my distance emotionally because I thought she'd hurt *me*. I never thought I could hurt her. Not like this. Not the way I saw her soul drain from her eyes and her light replaced by something dreary.

Mateo and I walk silently down the pipeline. He already knows how to shuffle down the slope after several times coming without me, and we land on the bottom of the valley, staring out at a sea of manes and swishing tails in the distance.

He puts his hands on his hips. "It's a beautiful sight. Seeing horses in the wild."

I agree but don't even hum in return. I'm paralyzed.

"Isn't it funny? We males think we're the leaders of the animal kingdom, but goddamn do we need a woman." He smiles in the direction of the mustangs. "Stella makes it all happen."

I clear my throat. "She's good for you."

"Yeah, when people don't know horses, they always assume the stallion is in charge of the herd. You know? I suppose he's strong and protects the herd but he's nothing without a lead mare."

"Mmm." His tone has changed, and I'm not sure he's talking about Stella anymore.

"He keeps them safe, but without her, the herd starves. *He* starves."

This is the point where most people in a conversation ask what the hell the other is on about, but I'm not most people. That's probably why I need a friend like Matty who keeps talking at me as if I asked.

"So... you going to tell me or what? What's up with your grumpy ass?" He takes off his hat, swipes his forehead, and replaces it. "I wondered why you asked me to take over some shifts here, and when Jolie stopped by at mine to give the horses some vet checks, she told me you had a woman you're interested in. I put two and two together and figured you *almost* smiling at my house the other day had something to do with her, but now, you're so dark I think it might start raining." He laughs in his infectious way.

But I'm immune.

A rock tumbles down on the far end of the valley, echoing through its sharp sound, and two of the herd pull up from trying to graze in the snow and prick their ears.

I stare out into the distance. "Jolie is wrong."

"Wrong? Really? Because you look like a guy who's just been dumped."

A sharp wind whips from one end of the valley to the other, cutting right through my shearling coat. It's not a wind I run from. It's a wind, just like everything else here, I keep coming back for more. I think about my dad. I think about how right here he told me I'd find happiness one day. I think about how I thought my dad dying here ruined me forever, but when Molly fell into my arms that night, I wondered if he's the one who dropped her there.

"You know when a car won't start?" I ask.

"Uh... yeah." Matty shimmies his shoulders to keep warm.

"It's like that. I keep turning the key, keep pressing the ignition, and the engine will turn over, make some sound, but the car just never starts. I'm broken, Matty. I told her that. She didn't believe me. And now both of us are." I breathe in deeply; the frigid air burns my lungs. "I fucked up. I let it all happen because I thought maybe I could handle me being hurt, and it would be worth it because I could float on the memory of a woman like her for the rest of my life. But I never thought I'd hurt her."

"Molly?" Jolie must have told him more than he let on.

"Yeah... Molly." Just saying her name into this cold space warms it up. Even her name carries electricity.

I stare out at the herd. "We better get out of here so they can get this water before it freezes over."

Mateo nods but doesn't budge. "He wouldn't want you to be like this."

"Who?"

"Your dad."

My heart drops.

Matty's long sigh is visible in the frigid air. "Since I found out I'm going to be one, I think about what I want to teach my kids. I can tell you with certainty, he'd want you to find love. The last thing he'd want you to be left with when he's gone is loneliness. No father wants that for their kid. Just... go get her back. Tell her you'll keep trying 'til you're both driving that old jalopy with a shitty motor wherever it is the two of you want to go."

Mateo starts scrambling up the slope. "Love isn't easy, Dash. Trust me. It isn't easy even if you're good at it."

When I get back to my room, balls frozen to my thigh, I throw myself down on my bed. It's been a week without Molly, and I've been an empty shell in her absence. She breathed life into my hollow chest, and now... it's just black in there. I want her light back.

I had some idea in my head that if I don't fall in love, I won't experience pain like my dad dying again. But I was wrong. My chest is a fucking abyss. In there is an emptiness so deep there's no beginning, no end, and it threatens to take everything down with it. I could dive right in there and swim down for miles and never reach the bottom of how I'm hurting.

And the rest of my body hurts, too. Molly couldn't break my heart because it was already broken. But the thing that's sending heart-shard shrapnel through every cell in my body, making me feel like I'm bleeding all over my insides, is worse than all that.

In Molly's round, caring brown eyes, I saw more than love. In her eyes, there was a chance to change the story, just like she said that night when I pretended not to hear her. Denying that change feels like I'm murdering everything worth living for.

I think about what Mateo said about my dad. I think about my father's wise words... *Keep useful.* That's what he told me to do and what I need to focus on. It's the only possible remedy to this situation. That and time. Apparently, that works, too, but it didn't do much for me in sixteen years.

I push myself up to grab my leather notebook from the top drawer of my dresser. This drawer squeaks when it pulls out, not like the one at the stable apartment which is brand-new, smooth. I haven't made any notes about the Valley since the evening Molly crept into my room. I thumb through the pages and come to the last one, where Molly scribbled when she slinked into my room naked after we got back from Colt and Sam's.

I, Molly Russo, officially declare I am sober enough to know I want nothing more than to be with you, Dashiell Hunter.

My lungs harden in my chest. Damn, I love that woman. I do. I love her even though I tried not to. I love her even though I haven't told her. I love her even if she doesn't love me back.

I flip the page, and somehow, with the whiskey in my veins, too, that night, and not needing more than that one-page instruction to ravage her body, I never noticed she wrote on the next page, too. There, scrawled in her loopy, feminine script it says:

PS You might be broken, but I like every piece of you.

My chest cracks open; my eyes mist over. And I guess I was wrong about it being empty, because raw emotion pours out of it like there's no end to it. I suck in a stuttered breath and clear my throat three times, staring at the note, rereading it.

Damn this woman. She's turned everything I've ever known, the entire world I built for myself to survive and prevent heartache, upside down. Molly cares about me. *Me.* She's never once asked me to be something I'm not. And she's never even slapped on rose-tinted specs to like me more or pretend I'm some prince charming. She knows I'm flawed. I said I was broken. But even in this message where she acknowledges it, her liking every piece of me somehow makes me whole again. It means those pieces belong together. And they belong with Molly.

I choke on the lump and have to press my fingers into my eye sockets to stop it all from trickling out. But just as quickly as I realize I need to chase her down, a new alarm bell rings.

The way I acted? Why should she give me a chance? I only went and proved to her that I wasn't worth her effort. I only showed her hope was fruitless and I'm a fucking Neanderthal with a one-word vocabulary and survival on the brain. Frustration burns hot in my gut and forges into a steel boulder. I'm sick. Nauseated, and the room is practically spinning with dread that I ruined things between us.

But I can't let Molly go. Maybe I'm not good enough for her, but there's nothing more worth my energy than trying. Mateo is right. My dad wouldn't want me avoiding love all my life. And he especially wouldn't have wanted me avoiding Molly—a good-hearted woman with unending compassion and a soul that promises me the sunrise.

I text Colt.

ME

> I'LL TAKE OVER MANAGING THE BUILDERS NOW. I HAVE MORE TIME ON MY HANDS WITH MOLLY DOING MY JOB. JUST WANT TO GET THAT APARTMENT DONE ASAP.

BIG CHEESE

> KNOCK YOURSELF OUT. WELCOME TO THE DESK LIFE.

The next text he sends is the details for the builders, and I give them a call, offering overtime to finish the kitchen and bathroom off in the next day or two. In the meantime, I order a bed and mattress, but when I start calling to arrange other furniture and the rest, I decide to save it for Molly.

If she says yes, I want to let her make it a home. She deserves one.

And maybe I do, too.

Chapter Thirty

MOLLY

SEVERAL DAYS HAVE GONE BY, but I don't feel any better about telling Dash I need space. His presence evaporating from my life has left me feeling all dry and crackly. I miss him. I do. But I also know I need to stick to my resolve.

I'm sure soon enough, I'll get over him. No. I'm not sure of that at all.

At least my sister will be here in Starlight Canyon, and her effervescence will fill my time with a hectic business that will help me through what feels like the grief process. I was in denial. I didn't want to believe we couldn't end up together. When it all became clear, my bottled-up emotions bubbled out as anger, and now I'm oscillating between bargaining with myself and accepting the inevitable.

How can a man make me feel so secure even though I'm absolutely not?

How could I have been so wrong?

How could we have shared intimacy like that if there weren't feelings there?

The first two nights without Dash, I wanted to text him that I didn't need space and tell him I was totally fine. I wanted to squash down one feeling just to let another one run free. But one day, I'll be proud of myself for this growth. I'll be proud of myself for being honest with him about my feelings, even though I sacrificed his friendship and everything else for it. We said we'd be friends, but I'll never feel just friendship for him. This much I know.

But today is not the day. Today, I just want him back. So fucking badly.

Worse yet, I've noticed twice as many builders in and out above the newly built stables the past couple of days, so I suspect he'll be back, living on-site very, very soon. And that will make it even harder to stop thinking about him, knowing how close he is and yet just how far away that dream of *us* is.

I called a meeting with all regular staff, our new sled driver, Jolie, and even Colt turned up—I suspect just because he's that kind of guy who wants to make a person feel supported, not because he normally concerns himself with trivial things like the goings-on at the stables. I don't have to even glance around to know Dash isn't here. I feel his absence as strongly as his presence.

But I suppose he doesn't really need to be here for this either. He can read about it in the overview email I'll send and write back to me if something is wrong. I'm not sure if I'm happy or not that he's skipped the meeting. Maybe it's better this way. Every time that man is around me, I lose my head.

It's time to talk with the staff about the process of having sleigh rides and the hospitality that goes along with having guests in the winter.

"So for now," I try to muster up excitement, to not sound as flat as the beat of my heart, "the hotel doesn't have dedicated staff to welcome guests for the sleigh rides. We're working on that. But, Georgie? You've said you're happy to do hours as and when this winter? To serve the hot drinks, ensure blankets and hand warmers are ready?"

"Yeah." She lifts a finger. "Maybe we should get extra hats and scarves, too? Can we get ones with the Starlight Ranch logo on them? And get housekeeping involved in washing them daily? Because I'm all about the meet and greet but I'm not interested in laundry. As a polite request, of course."

I write down her suggestion. "You're right. We need more than blankets..."

She adds, "It does get really freezing in some parts of the Canyon. And if the guests are too cold they won't have fun."

I finish my note. "Got it. I'll ask housekeeping if they can do an extra daily load for us and get an estimate for hats and scarves... So let's talk about the rotation schedule for the horses themselves..."

I wish I could hold it together, but my words trail off when Dash appears in the doorway to the office, accompanied by a gust of wintry wind.

Everyone glances over at him, tipping a chin or hat. But soon, all eyes are on me again because he doesn't affect them the way he does me. They don't have the first clue how he crawled under my skin and inside my body, nesting in my soul like something I could hatch into true love. My eyes rest on him a little too long, and I blink him out of my vision, but it doesn't get him out of my mind.

I glance at my clipboard, trying to recall the last thing I talked about. I run my finger over the agenda, but Dash is the one intending to do the talking.

"Before you carry on, I just have a few words to say..."

Heads turn again. I don't want to make eye contact, but it's rude not to. He doesn't seem to take notice of the twenty other eyeballs on him. His gaze is on me like I'm the only thing that matters. Emotion pools deep in my belly. And just as hot as my gut are my burning cheeks, blooming already... just sensing he's about to do something mad.

His green eyes are dancing around, wild in thought, like I've never seen them before. "Molly... I... it's about every-thing that's happened between us..."

Heads turn from his direction to mine.

That sting in my cheeks creeps down my neck. *What on earth?* This isn't stable business. This is *private* business. I dart my eyes to Colt, and something like shame overwhelms me. What will he think of me? Seducing his brother... my *boss*. It's so unprofessional... My gaze flits around the room searching for signs of disapproval all around me.

All I see are mouths gaping open and amused curiosity. I'm so hot my underarms are damp. I open my mouth to stop him, but he keeps talking, and thank God ten gazes turn back on him.

He's in the zone, and it's like we're the only two people in the world. "I told you I'm broken. But I'm trying hard to change that." His eyes burn with meaning. "I get what you said. It's time to change my story." He stops for my reaction.

He heard me that night? Dash repeating the meaningful words my sister and I constantly share is... unraveling.

291

Heartwarming. It draws me right back to the hope I've clung to.

But when he stops talking, it's like some tennis match, because all the heads in the room flip with an almost audible whoosh, and all eyes are on me again.

I blurt, "Dash, we're cool. I'll come talk to you later." My nerves are on fire.

He ignores me. "I've always been a grumpy mother-fucker. All these people can attest to that. And when I was younger, people were always trying to cheer me up, but nothing really worked, I just sort of..." He takes off his hat and puts it on a nearby desk, staring at me now with his intense, thoughtful gaze. He lets out a quick, sharp breath, like something hit him in the chest and he needs a moment.

I glance around at the expressions. The faces of people who had no clue we were much more than colleagues. Georgie, Hank, and Bobby all display o-shaped mouths and what-the-fucks in their eyes. The others cross their arms like they're watching some circus. But Jolie and Colt... there's something different there. *They both know.* They wait for my response almost as breathless as their brother.

Dash stands tall, but I know how hard it is for him to express his emotions and I don't want him to feel like this is the only place he can talk to me. Maybe my silent treatment went too far? "Dash, honestly, we can chat after..."

It's like my words never made it out of my mouth.

The gorgeous cowboy's eyebrows draw together, deep in thought, holding on to something purposeful underneath his forehead. He shakes his head like he hasn't achieved what he's come here to do and he isn't leaving until he's done.

And that's when I know change is possible, because his

next words are a transformation more beautiful than cater-
pillar to butterfly.

"Molly, my dad told me that if I just keep being useful,
happiness will find me." His gaze is intense and searching.
"My dad was right. Being useful brought me that feeling for
the first time in my life. Because there's nothing more useful
than loving a person."

Jolie gasps and puts her hand over her mouth. Her eyes
are instantly glassy.

My lungs stop moving along with my heart. *Did he just
say he loves me?* In front of all these people?

He shoves a hand in his pocket and pulls out a set of
keys, throwing them over Hank's head, and I barely catch
them my hands are shaking so much. A key dangles off a
laser-cut silver keychain that says *Dash and Molly*.

I am speechless. I glance back up at him with my jaw
slack. The room is silent. My heartbeat thunders, and my
ears are whooshing. I'm dizzy because I realize I haven't
been breathing for the past couple of seconds.

Dash takes his hat off the desk, and the way his throat
bobs is slow and unsure. "All right. Sorry to interrupt, folks.
That's all I needed to say." He places his hat on top of his
head, nods a farewell, and leaves.

My mouth still hangs open just like everyone else's. All
eyes are on me. My heart races a million miles an hour. The
metal key in my hand is warm from sitting in the pocket of
the man I love, too. He's just made a confession.

But I'm supposed to be professionally running a
meeting.

Oh my God, I can hardly even breathe enough to get
my vocal cords working. Does Dash love me? And want to
live with me?

I stare down at my clipboard. "Uh... where were we?"

Jolie pipes up. "We were at the part where you run out there after my brother and tell him you love him, too."

I dart my eyes around the room. What will everyone think of their supposed manager playing love games at work? When my gaze reaches Colt's, he tips his head in the direction of the door and says, "Leave the clipboard."

I stand. My next movements are something of a stutter. I start to leave. Glance around at everyone again. Put the clipboard down. "I'll... uh... be right back."

Bursting through the office door, I scan every direction. And there he is, not too far in the distance, but already leading down the path to where the new apartment is.

"Dash!" I call. I run toward him. "Dash! Wait!"

When he turns, my God there's something new in his eyes. "I didn't want to interrupt, but equally... I fucked up so badly, Molly. I felt a public statement was called for."

"You didn't do anything wrong." But it's damn amazing he put my opinion above all the others. That he cared more about what I thought than them. That I'm a *priority*.

He shakes his head. "I hurt you. In no world is that okay. But... I meant what I said." He tilts his head. "In there."

I've never had anyone make a proclamation for me, especially not someone as private as Dash. This is a very big deal. But I'm still not exactly sure what it means.

I hold up the keys. "What is this about?"

His eyebrows dance like they do when I think he's about to smile but doesn't. "It means when you're ready, you're mine."

"Yours?" I try to smirk coyly but I'm probably grinning ear to ear.

He nods.

"Your... roommate?" Now I goad him a little.

"And then some."

"Are you saying you like me, boss?"

He laces his fingers through mine. "I'm saying I love you, Sunshine."

He yanks me into his arms and presses his lips onto mine. He wraps half of his open coat around me, protecting me from the cold. Pulling me hard into his chest where just on the other side of his sweater is the heart I managed to help put back together.

At first his kiss is gentle and searching, his comforting scent swirls around me, and all the possibility between us has me gripping his shirt and turning it all a bit desperate. When he slides his tongue between my lips, I let out a breathy moan that he devours with one of his own. He holds me tightly in his arms with passion, warmth, and something that feels like forever.

We kiss and kiss until his cock pokes my thigh and I think his fingers will be forever entangled in my hair. Just when I'm thinking if we should excuse ourselves and make up for lost time, all of a sudden, I hear a loud whoop!

"Yeeeeehaw! Giddy up, you two!" Jolie's voice calls out into the air.

We stop kissing to turn in the direction of the office. There she is, and everyone else for that matter, fingers in her mouth letting off a wolf whistle. Have they been watching the entire time? Whistles, hooting, and hollering fill the yard.

I guess it's not too early in the year for a feel-good Christmas romance.

Dash lowers his lips to the top of my head and murmurs, "Does this mean you like me, too? Because I didn't come all this way to let you go. I'll get you one way or another but I'd rather you come willingly."

I laugh in the middle space between his pecs where both the feeling and the scent are soft and sensual. My voice is muffled. "I'm coming, Dash."

I look up at him, and he kisses my nose.

"I'm coming but I can't say I wouldn't mind seeing you go all caveman on me. I might kind of like being thrown over your shoulder."

"Baby... be careful what you wish for."

Chapter Thirty-One

DASH

WE BOTH MANAGE to get a few more hours of work done today. I headed back to the apartment to push the building workers that little bit harder and help them out myself.

When they leave, I glance around the apartment I just asked Molly to live in with me and think I could have done a better job. The kitchen and bathroom have only just been plumbed. Pipes stick out because the cabinets haven't arrived, and apart from the open-plan living room and the bedroom, the place is most definitely incomplete.

Knuckles rap against the door, and Molly pushes it open. "Knock, knock."

I finish wiping my hands on a towel, having just been tackling painting around the fireplace. Slinging the towel over the rung of a folded ladder, I saunter toward my girl. *My woman.* Two words I never thought I'd be able to say.

"I'd ask you what you think but... it's still being put

together." I take her hand and walk her into the middle of the living room.

Her hand gives mine a cozy squeeze. "Kind of an analogy for this thing we have going."

I laugh lightly. I might know the tide is turning, but it hasn't come in yet. I'm not unbroken just like that. Though saying the words to Molly knitted together something essential in my chest, something that makes me feel more complete than ever, I still have years of habits to overcome.

Insecurity like I've never felt before flushes through me. "I just have to ask. Are you sure about... me? I know I'm not a perfect man but..."

Her eyelashes flutter, and she stares at the floor. "I'm here for this, Dash. I'm here for you... and you are good at *showing* me how much you care about me." She drags her toe in an arc across the floor. "But I'm worried the voice in my head might be louder than the one coming out of your mouth. And that's what will hurt about loving you. The silence."

Her gaze reaches mine again, and the fact that it's still a little uncertain scares me.

I lead her to the bedroom to sit on the only furniture we have. I gaze into her big brown eyes, and the words aren't even hard to find. I guess love unlocks all sorts of things. Even my voice.

"You want words?" I stare deeply into her eyes. "I look at you, Molly, and all the answers to my questions are right there in your eyes. I see the only person I ever want touching me ever again. I see everything in you, Sunshine. *Everything.*"

I interlace our fingers and stare at her pretty, dainty hand. "Molly, when I met you, my heart was in a million pieces, and you stitched it back together no matter how hard I tried to resist. You're magic, woman."

She tucks hair behind her ear; her smile is crooked. "Well, now I'm speechless." She pauses, looking for words of praise for me. "Dash... I wish I could tell you how safe I fee..."

I place a finger over her lips, stopping her. "*I* don't need your words... All I need is you right here next to me." I kiss her lips. "Your body speaks to me."

She lowers her gaze, bashful, but a playful desire radiates.

A wry smile tugs at my lips, and I raise her gaze to stare straight into mine. "I love you."

The delicate backs of her fingers smooth down my cheekbones, along my neck... she trails her touch along my body until she finds my dick, already swelling in my jeans. "Are you going to come here and feel how much I love you, too?"

I cup her full breast and knead it, rolling my thumb over her nipple, so hard I can already feel it through her shirt, and my cock stands up to match its enthusiasm.

She lets her head fall, exposing her neck, and I slide my hand from her breast up to wrap my hand around the column of her throat. I caress my index finger along her jawline and want to fucking devour her right now.

Her voice is grainy. "What does my body say to you, Dash?"

I trail my eyes from her long glossy hair cascading down to that throat I want to taste, those breasts I want to suck, those hips I want to secure in my hands while I ride slow and hard in that place right below the zipper of her blue jeans. "Your body tells me I don't have this situation under control..."

"Does that still scare you?"

"Not anymore, Sunshine. I decided there isn't a tomorrow worth waking up to if you're not part of it. Running out of ground doesn't matter once you're already falling. I just have to see where we land."

She wraps her arms around my neck and tugs me into her so fast we both fall into the bed. "This mattress is a soft landing." Her voice is playful and effortlessly sexy.

I can't get enough of it. She's fearless. She told me she admires horses because they're brave enough to wear their emotions on the outside. Brave doesn't begin to describe this woman. *My* woman. I'll never get sick of thinking of her that way.

My dick fills being this close to her. She folds firm arms around me, her breasts smother my chest, and she must be able to feel my heart against my ribcage. I can't believe I'm here. With her.

I rub my aching cock on her thigh and press my lips onto her puffy mouth, slipping my tongue inside to explore the taste of her, to steal her breath and at the same time give her mine. It's the best kiss of my life, and my heart shards glimmer as she pours her glow down into me with little whimpers.

This woman burst into my life uninvited, but I knew from the start I never wanted her to leave. That's the thing with love. You can't ignore it. It conquers everything with its light. Even the darkness I felt. That yellow towel and her bubbly nature was how she earned the name Sunshine, but now I know, my whole world really does revolve around her.

We melt into each other, and I fuse my lips to hers, drink her beautiful soul from her mouth. Her hands slide up the sides of my torso, pushing up my Henley. She fiddles with my zipper, and my dick is borderline painful, so I help her out, undoing my button and slipping my jeans down. While I'm undressing, she throws her shirt overhead and starts to wiggle out of her jeans, but the harder and faster she tries to do it, the less progress she makes.

I laugh. "You're so damn cute."

Her cheeks stain. "I have to jump to put them on. It's something like that to take them off, too."

I lick my lips and sink my teeth into the lower one. "We got forever, baby. I'm in no hurry."

I slowly work her jeans down and off. Followed by the panties with a Hawaiian flower pattern and think about how they're the perfect clothing to cover paradise. That place between her legs is my heaven. While I spread her legs apart, maybe I admire her a bit too long.

"You're making me nervous, cowboy."

"Why?"

She covers her eyes. "Staring at me like that. Like you can see... everything."

"Didn't you hear me? You *are* everything."

We spend the rest of the day and night making love. Being in love.

I'm never letting this go.

Chapter Thirty-Two

MOLLY

THE NEXT TWO weeks pass like a dream come true. Dash and I go to the hardware store and bring home all those little swatch stick colors and tons of tiny paint pots. We stay up late into the night, painting our new home together with his beer and my wine. We road trip to Albuquerque to furniture showrooms where we pick out our sofas and end tables. He trails me through shops while I surely bore him, asking if he prefers stripes on couch pillows or bird patterns.

And... we make a home. A real home. The kind that has a bit of each of us in it. The kind that has our souls in it.

But now, college is out, which means today is the first day Lily is officially a resident of Starlight Canyon.

Nerves sizzle through my body. Lily knows the whole story. She knows everything. And she's happy for me. She is. But today, she meets Dash, in the flesh, and I just don't know how it's all going to go down. Lily doesn't hold back.

She'll probably poke the bear. She'll definitely judge him. *Hard.* Because even though I'm the big sister, she's protective of what she has, too. And for many years, all we felt we had was each other.

Dash wants to meet up at the hotel. With the additional business of sleigh rides and residents actually filling up the rooms in what used to be the off season, the hotel manager, Savannah, had the place decorated to the nines.

We enter the double-height lobby. Lily stamps snow off her feet as her eyes trace the arc of the oak beams and twinkling Christmas lights. Her mouth hangs open. "Wow. They need a picture of *this* on the website."

She's in awe as anyone would be. There are fake boughs of holly all over the elegant woodwork, and a twenty-foot-tall Christmas tree decorated so beautifully. She's right. This lobby should be on the front page of the December *Architectural Digest.*

I've gotten to know Savannah, or Sav as she goes by, better over the past month since sorting out how the sleigh rides will work logistically with the yard. I tried to drop hints the hotel needs weddings here and more events on-site with an ulterior motive to my sister being offered an Events Manager position eventually. She'll be okay being a wedding planner to start but she didn't go into events and hotel management for nothing. I'd love for her to have a more secure position.

Security. Security like I feel now. I know I can offer it to her temporarily, obviously Dash already said she should stay in the other apartment, and there have been talks about my mom moving there, too. But Lily is a woman with her own mind, goals, and a shitload more ambition than I have.

I know she won't stop until she's a boss lady. I just hope she can find a place for her ambition here.

Dash appears from behind the manager's office near the reception desk, which is only slightly odd. I guess he might want to just make sure everything is going well, too, though almost since I got the manager's position, he's trusted me to steer the ship.

He comes on over with a hand out and a thin-lipped, boyish smile. It's a nervous smile, and I glow inside thinking how important it is for him to make a good impression with my sister. I remember how nervous I was with his mom.

"Lily." He offers a hand. "It's a pleasure to finally meet you."

She doesn't take his hand but shoves hers on her hip. "You're going to shake my hand? Seriously? Come here."

She opens her arms wide, and he puts half his body in them for her to hug him.

"Dash, I couldn't very well shake your hand. You hooked me up. Thanks for letting me use the apartment until I get on my feet." She lets go of him.

"I'm not counting the days. Stay long as you like." His eyebrows dance the way I've come to understand is his way of smiling without his lips.

He gestures an arm out toward some comfy chairs in the corner of the lobby. "I ordered some hot cocoas. Hope you like marshmallows? And extra whipped cream?" He throws me a knowing glance because him knowing me, I don't skimp on the extras anymore.

But I do wonder why we needed to come up to the hotel for that. We could have made cocoa at the apartment.

Lily drapes her coat across the back of a spare chair. "You don't have to ask me twice. Hand me the can. Love me a bit of Reddi-whip." She eyes Dash and dives right in. "So... you're the man who swept my sister off her feet."

He laughs softly. "I'm not sure it exactly went like that."

"She did tell me you saved her life."

He grabs my hand and gazes at me with a display of warmth. "More like the other way around."

She stares at us, at him adoring me openly, like he has done since the day he burst into that office with our Dash and Molly keychain.

Lily shakes her head. "Well, it's nice to see Molly finally got a guy who'll worship her like she deserves. This woman is a saint and a goddess."

I blush. "Okay, between the two of you..."

Just then, Savannah comes over with a tray of hot cocoas. Four of them. "Hey, y'all. Time to take the chill off." She puts the drinks on the table in front of each of us, one for herself, and perches on the small space left on the spare chair with our coats. "So, you must be Lily."

"Uh... yes, I am."

"I'm Savannah. The general manager here at Starlight Ranch Resort."

"Oh!" Lily takes Sav's hand and shakes it, a little too wildly, her nerves showing, knowing this woman could open the door to her new life. "Wow. Nice to finally meet you! It's such a beautiful hotel."

"Well, thanks to your sister, we have a reason to decorate it in winter. Trust me. Normally it's... well, a ghost town once the dude ranch visitors leave. Molly's breathed life, and money, into this joint."

"My sister is a tour de force." Lily never stops building me up.

"And Dash here tells me you are, too. Just graduated early with honors in hotel management? Giving me a run for my money." Sav laughs lightly. "I learned the old-fashioned way from the ground up. It's hard work, you know. I've been doing it for, gosh... thirty years?"

Lily holds a steaming mug. "I've been told it's not for the faint of heart. And I have to trust your experience. But I just love hospitality. Being around all the people having their vacations and thinking I'm the puppeteer moving around all that dancing and smiling."

It's hard not to think about how our childhood curated Lily's personality with that comment.

"I get that," Savannah answers without a beat. "It's a great feeling thinking about all the people making memories on the back of what we do."

"Exactly. And the teamwork. I look forward to being part of a team."

Sigh. We're always on the hunt for family. Neither Lily nor myself were destined to be loners.

"Well," Sav sips her hot chocolate, leaving red lips on the mug, "Dash and I were talking this morning. His mom, Joy, and I have been friends for a long while, and she leaked my secret. I've been thinking of retiring."

Lily is genuinely surprised. "Yeah? You seem so young..."

"Oh shush." She flaps a hand in my sister's direction. "You really are going to be good in hospitality. Flattery is a prerequisite for this industry." She winks.

I glance over at Dash, listening intently, but he feels my gaze and shifts his to mine. And there, in those mischievous green eyes, I know he's the one who invited Savannah over with the hot chocolates. He's the one responsible for what's said next.

"Lily. You wrote me an email saying you're interested in doing events here. Maybe weddings, you said?"

"Yes. That was me." She sits up straight.

"Well, I was speaking with Dash this morning, and what if you come on board as my number two? And, when

306

you're ready to run a place of this size, you wave me off to my retirement?"

Holy shit. Dash convinced Sav to give Lily a full-time job? Lil and I were thinking she could work her way up. Do events. Weddings... then maybe, maybe get a management position. Savannah just went and put her in the succession plan. This means so much. It means health insurance. It means paid vacation. 401K. It means... she's staying here.

I reach for Dash's hand and squeeze it. I am going to thank him later. A nice deep-down thanks, all the way to the back of my throat.

Lily is shocked. "I... I would love that. I mean, I've never... it's a lot to take on but..." She's overwhelmed, shocked and grateful all at the same time.

"... I'll show you the ropes. I'll take you under my wing and teach you all the tricks of the trade without you having to learn them the hard way."

"I'm..." For a beat, my sister is totally stunned. She shakes her head. "Yes! Thank you, Savannah. The best Christmas present I could have asked for."

"Great. Take the month to settle in. I have to figure out how to get through this first winter season anyway and don't want you getting tangled in the tinsel." She laughs at her own joke. "We'll start in the New Year." Sav stands, taking her mug with her. "Enjoy your Christmas, folks. If I don't see you before then."

Lily turns back to the table, her jaw slack. "Did you do this, Molly? Oh my God, I never thought I'd get a job straight out of college!"

Dash says nothing, so I say it for him. I bump into his side. "Pretty sure this Hunter had something to do with it."

Lily lifts her mug like she's cheersing. "Man, do I owe you favors. I won't make you regret it."

He nods, silently, humble as he always has been and probably always will be, but he earned his way out of a Russo grilling. And then some. I'm floored. Dash has been caring for me since the first day I entered that apartment, buck-naked, unsure but determined. Every day that passes I see more and more of this tender, attentive nature he keeps locked up under his gruff exterior.

My man hasn't changed who he is. He still avoids most of the people around the yard. He still needs time to himself to contemplate and refresh. His highly introverted nature didn't, and will never, disappear. But now I see, he must use a lot of this time thinking about others and not himself. Dash often points out how we're opposites attracted; he says we're magnets. But when it comes to family, we're the same. It's everything.

He squirms as my sister continues to gush with gratitude, so I change the subject before he gets too uncomfortable being the center of attention.

"So, Lil, Mom will be here a couple days before Christmas, staying with you in the apartment."

"Yeah." Lily doesn't seem as apprehensive as I am.

For me, it's a biggie. Dash will be meeting my mom. She'll be spending Christmas with all of us at Big Sky. Sam's parents are so noble. And *normal*. Our mom is... she's wonderful. A total sweetheart. But she could also fall asleep while someone is talking to her.

"I keep telling you not to worry about it," Dash says, my rigid hand in his.

Lily shrugs. "Mom is doing so well. She's been stepping down her meds for a long while and is just..." She points at Dash. "I assume he knows..."

I nod.

Lily continues. "She's so motivated to get back on her

feet and be out here with us. We've had some awesome chats."

"Me, too. That's saying something," I say.

Lily nods knowingly. We've both loved watching our mom slowly recover. It's not just about Mom being there to hear our news and enjoy her proud smiles we missed for years as we both set out to build our lives. Seeing Mom proud of herself is something the two of us have often discussed. We both Googled it enough to know that the recovery process of coming off years of opioid use is a miracle.

Often, I felt guilty being here instead of there with her, holding her hand through the excruciating dark nights and days of withdrawal. And being so far away, neither Lily nor myself really know for sure where she's at. All we can do is believe her.

But no matter where she's at, I want her here. I want to integrate Mom into this joyful existence and give her a positive focus. A light at the end of the tunnel. Even though I want this, and the three of us have been apart for too long, I'm still not sure my mom will slot right in to a Twister night.

Dash senses my apprehension. It's not the first time I've felt it. He bumps into my arm. "My mom will take yours under her wing in no time," he offers. "That's how she is."

I say to Lily, "His mom is a perfectly put-together bohemian queen."

"Perfect?" Dash hums. "Trust me, the woman has lived a life or two. I wasn't the only one who started drinking after Dad died. She'll get your mom. And they'll talk mom shit and be perfectly fine. But she will probably try and *help* her."

Lily's broad smile appreciates his words. I'm grateful,

too, not only because it's comforting to hear, in some strange way, obviously not happy Joy used to have problems, but that maybe the Hunters aren't so perfect. That we can fit in.

At the same time, I'm stunned. I had no idea Joy Hunter used to be a drinker. She's so switched on. Gorgeous. She radiates wise, earth goddess. Only now has it crossed my mind she had the hot chocolate with Eve that night, rather than an Irish coffee, even though she didn't have to drive.

Dash continues. "Hopefully my mom won't be annoying trying to drag her into what helped her in the end."

"AA?" Lily asks.

"Nah. She hated AA. She went back to be with her people. She took more regular visits to the reservation to see her auntie. Started making jewelry and doing art again, getting obsessed by her craft. She traded one addiction for another... Her house is head to toe jewels and beads."

Lily thinks nothing of Dash's candid story, but I see it. He's not exactly a sharer. I see this as him reaching out to connect with me, my family... to fuse us together the best he can.

As usual, my steady, strong man reassures me. I can't wait for the Russo girl reunion. And changing our story. Here, in Starlight Canyon.

Epilogue

DASH

Come Easter, I realized I've officially known Molly for almost a year, but it feels like a lifetime.

Molly and I have truly settled in our apartment. Lily has already had a run-in with Bobby. She punches me in the arm when we're talking, like Jolie does, and she charmed Hank into helping her put up shelves at her apartment. It brings me no end of joy seeing Molly's sister settled.

And her mom is settled, too. At Christmastime, Francesca Russo, or Frankie, as my mom and the rest of the family soon dubbed her, came to celebrate with the Hunters and never left. My own mother took Frankie on in a way I somehow knew she would but didn't realize just how deeply they would click.

Both those women needed each other. Frankie bene-fitted from having my no-bullshit mom pay for her to get some proper medical help. Frankie is one strong woman.

She'd been stepping down her meds without any medical help or therapy. My mom insisted on getting her professional help.

And my mom? Well, she found a new companion. One she probably needed. And one who likes turquoise as much as she does. Lately, the two women have been spending a lot of time at the Navajo Nation reservation where my mom's aunt still lives. They always come home with more precious stones and ideas about opening a jewelry shop on the main street.

Having a purpose has helped heal Molly's mom and my own, from a pain she seemed to have been holding on to since my dad died.

Molly and I are out on an early morning trail ride before going over to Sam and Colt's for Easter lunch. We have been on countless rides with Amigo and Romeo, and she's becoming a confident rider. Then again, Romeo adores her. Looks after her. Those two have quite the bond.

Hooves crunch through brush, and we land at the edge of Mustang Valley. I stare out at the Valley. We won't go down today because Sam and my mom have been stressing about the twenty-pound ham they got to serve all the people coming today. Sam stressed about Christmas, too. I guess catering is her weak spot. She and my mom have been talking about it for two weeks.

Molly offered to help. It was cute because I'm pretty sure she's never cooked a twenty-pound ham before but she has the composure of someone who has. Very little makes my woman flap. I admire so much about her, discover new things every day, but even a year after first meeting this beautiful woman, there's nothing I love more than her determination.

I glance over at my woman. The cowboy hat I gave her

for Christmas sits proudly on her head. Turquoise earrings dangle off her cute ears, accompanied by a matching pendant around her neck. She's straddled all sexy, and her long, chocolate strands cascade down her shoulders and blow in the breeze. Her ass stretches her jeans, jeans I can't wait to peel off later.

The tip of her nose is pink from a chill in the air that still hasn't left, even in April. She stares out at the beauty before her, the mountains, the gift of sunshine spilling over them, and searches the best she can for the mustangs down below. "You sure we shouldn't just scramble down and check the pipe?"

"Nah. Mateo said he did it this morning."

I stare out one last time at the place where, until I told Molly I loved her, was the only place on earth I ever felt any calm. With Molly, I'm a changed man. Or maybe I'm just more me than I ever was. Maybe now I'm the man I was always meant to become because I don't exactly feel different.

I feel whole.

This is the place where my heart first shattered into a million pieces. It's where I renounced love for good and where I let it back in again. I can't help but laugh to myself. Love fell from the goddamn sky right into my arms here in Mustang Valley. And I still think my dad had something to do with it.

Sam and Colt's house is hot as hell. I had to strip off the *Prepare to Dye* Easter sweatshirt Eve got me because with the fire going and an oven on all day, it's goddamn summer in here. Plus, almost a dozen bodies mill about in the space.

Hungry bellies keep stopping by to peek in the kitchen, and it's starting to stress Colt out.

I've never seen him like this before. Not Mr. Cool Calm Collected Suave Hunter.

Colt carves the ham in the kitchen, and I assemble it the best I can to look nice, per Sam's instructions, on a platter she put in front of me.

Colt mumbles, "Logan better get here in time for this ham. Sam's been stressing about this goddamn hunk of meat forever..."

Logan is typically late. In part, it's because he's the type of guy to keep talking after the conversation should be over, has to say the final goodbye, and will always be the last man standing at a party.

But another part of me thinks he's late because he likes to make an entrance. He likes to let people worry just a little bit that he won't come so they're extra grateful when he arrives. He thrives under attention and has gotten into a scandal or two because of his relentless pursuit chasing it.

Chasing tail more like it. I make an excuse that this time it was due to his away game.

Finally, the front door opens, and in bursts Logan, with Ashton in tow. Thank God those two reconciled. Though having a common enemy can do that.

Sam ushers them in, and Jolie rushes over to kiss Ashton. Logan does only half an eye roll this time. I might have rolled mine, too, seeing our sister loved up with someone, and my brother's best friend at that. But I suppose because I have Molly now, I look at Jolie having love differently than I used to. One day, Logan will catch up.

When we finally sit down to dinner, the table is beautiful, and hats off to Sam, my mom, and to Eve, who folded some of the napkins into swans.

I eat with my family, sit back and enjoy the full, rich feeling that consumes me along with one of Sam's mint tulip cocktails. I'll have it to thank for the courage I'll need in a minute.

It's hard for me to interrupt all the conversations and laughter around me to bring attention on myself.

Sam's parents dote on Eve, who can't stop showing everyone the fancy gel nails she got done with daisies and hatching chicks on them. Colt and Sam are loved-up as Sam has finally relaxed now the meal has been served. She's probably a few mint tulips deep. Logan and Ashton are in a deep discussion, a game debrief most likely, and Lily and Jolie laugh together.

And Joy and Frankie haven't stopped talking. Molly's mom has a soft smile and a gentle way about her, but I have mixed feelings. I know her addiction caused a lot of pain for my woman. And Molly never had a childhood because of it. But I also know family is all you've got, you can't leave it behind, you have to heal it. My mom got settled on that very purpose the day Frankie arrived and the pair have only ever moved forward.

My time has come, too. Time to consider the future. I clink my knife against my water glass, which feels funny, because calling the room to look my way isn't my style. But I'm working on being more open and the one thing that comes easy is praising Molly in front of others. It's like watching a diamond glitter in a spotlight. I do it as much as I can, just to see her shine.

I clear my throat. "I wanted to make a toast..." Even though I'm a lot more vocal than I used to be, a few of the faces around the table still look surprised. "It's for Molly."

I gaze down at her. She's confused by the sudden attention. I carry on with the words I have planned. Ones I hope we'll both remember forever.

"A man can love a lot of things. But, Molly, it's not the first time I've said it and it won't be my last. You are my everything."

Molly's smile fades into wide-eyed wonder. Oh, this girl knows what's coming.

I get down on one knee and pull out a ring box. "Sunshine, I want to ride through this life with you." I open the box and expose the diamond ring I had designed just for her. "Will you marry me?"

A few gasps surround me, but I don't dare take my eyes off Molly's beautiful brown eyes and lips parted in surprise. I never want to forget her face right now. I want to etch in my mind for all eternity every contour of her beauty when she says yes to forever with me. I want to be able to close my eyes when we're old and gray and think back to her pretty round cheeks and glossy eyelashes right in this very moment. The beginning of a whole new lifetime.

She covers her mouth, speechless, but I take her delicate hand and slip on the ring. I hold her hand in mine and squeeze it. "I won't let go until the end, baby. I'm hoping you won't either."

She nods quickly. "Yes, Dash."

She throws her hug around my neck, and even though we're just getting started, I wouldn't mind this ending right here.

"I'll marry every single piece of you."

How would you like a BONUS SCENE? Sign up to my newsletter to read! https://dl.bookfunnel.com/mv876atgex

OR use the QR code below. And don't forget to read on below for a sneak peek of Jolie and Ashton in *Bourbon Breakaway* below. This is a brother's best friend, forced proximity, hockey romance with sizzling *us against the world* vibes. Hope you love the sneak peak!

**Mustang Valley
Bonus Scene**

Up next in the Starlight Canyon Series is *BOURBON BREAKAWAY*.

Preorder here—> https://geni.us/bourbonbreakaway

Here's a SNEAK PEEK at the first two chapters!

PROLOGUE
ASHTON

I narrow my eyes at the teenaged guy eyeing the small of Jolie's bare ivory back, exposed by her low-cut prom dress. We slow dance, if you can call it that. It's more me holding her at arm's length and at a perfect distance to see perverted guys like the one behind her, letting their eyes roam where they don't belong.

"You need something?" I growl.

The kid attempts to look brave. It's a stiff, uncertain stare down, or stare up in this case because he's only about as tall as Jolie herself. His eye contact slips quickly when I flare my nostrils. He thinks he can look at this girl? *Wrong.*

Like a dance twirl, I swing Jolie's body around one-eighty in my arms. I make an opaque human wall with the cheap polyester of my blazer as a barrier between Joey and this loser.

My surrogate little sister lets out a long, exasperated sigh that blows curly tendrils off the side of her forehead. "I thought you'd be more... fun."

Her eyes are round and lined lightly with eyeliner, not a severe black like a lot of the other girls have going but the color of eggplant. She has glittery shadow of a similar shade on her eyelids and the makeup makes her green eyes pop. She's pretty tonight. Logan was right to send me as her date. That pimply twat was the first of many that would have her, I'm sure.

Jolie deserves better, which means she'll end up alone, because after going to college I realize all men are fuckwits. Or maybe it's being in the hockey world. Since discovering puck bunnies in college and the way my teammates treat them, I've become pretty disgusted by how we're led around by our cocks.

Sadly, I'm not immune to these male genes. I count myself among the fuckwits, but Logan knows I'd never be one with Jolie.

I hold my hands steady, floating just above putting any pressure on her hips. I balance being polite enough to perform my duty as a stand-in big brother, and touching her enough so she doesn't feel ugly. It's a fine line I walk, tough as keeping the steps to this slow dance. I have no rhythm.

She tips her head sideways, long blonde curls drip down

her bare shoulder and she casts flirty eyes upward. "Come on," she reaches up and fists my shirt. "Loosen up."

I gaze down at her. Even in heels, she's a good five, six inches below. She's a tall girl. Even just this last year of me being away in college she sprouted up a few more inches.

Inches. The flutter of her eyelashes that tease and urge me to be more fun reminds me of the shameless sass of her invitation. She sure is getting a mouth on her. Jolie texted me when the prom invitations hit email inboxes...

Hey- the hall of fame quarterback asked me to prom, but I was hoping you and your extra five inches would come with me. 😏

I'm taller. Taller than most men I meet and apparently five inches taller than that guy. But I knew what she was alluding to. And her past vocal advances have made their way to her hands tonight. She fists my shirt again like its bedsheets and she yanks me hard enough to pull me one breath closer.

I said no to being her prom date when she asked. Her innuendo has snuck into nearly every conversation and brush of a shoulder since she turned fifteen. The last thing I wanted to do was to lead her on. Besides her basically being my little sister, losing my best friend is not something I can handle. Especially after what I found out tonight- the universe-shifting lie tucked in the most obvious hiding spot, under my dad's ties.

If I said no to Joey, I would have never found that piece of paper.

I would have never fucked my entire sense of reality.

But here I am. Logan urged me to say yes to coming back to Starlight Canyon tonight, to escorting his sister to prom. He said rather a fucker he knows than a douchebag he doesn't. I came back for the weekend from college to do him a favor. That's it. And I'll be damned sure not to enjoy it the way she's suggesting and allow my best friend to demote me from fucker to douchebag.

I came back, but if I didn't, I would still be blissfully ignorant.

Jolie sways her body, dancing herself through the last bit of personal space holding us apart. "Earth to Ashton. You're... faraway... again. You've been a total space cadet tonight. What's up with you? You have something to talk about? I'm not Lo but I'll listen."

"Nothing to talk about, Joey. I'm just being your brother's soldier. Keeping an eye out for trouble. What I came here to do."

She tuts then releases a scoff. "What? You actually think any of these losers would try something with me while you're here? You could fall asleep and they wouldn't dare. Or maybe you already know that because you've been hazed half the night."

I have a lot on my mind, but I won't be a downer. It's my shit to handle and I'm won't stink up her evening. "You want entertainment? How about I do the running man next song?"

She giggles and pulls my shirt's fabric back and forth playfully. Her strength isn't enough to jostle me, but I move under her spirited touch anyway and roll my eyes, playing along to lighten the mood best I can. She's a good girl. I want her to have fun tonight. I am being pretty crap at giving her a night to remember.

But it seems her idea of a good time and mine are very different.

She releases the fabric from her grip. It's crinkled now. She smooths it and stares at the spot where her hand was. As she strokes my chest, her playfulness washes away, and it's replaced by pure mischief. "I have an idea that could spice up the night." She presses herself up and into me as if she wants to drop a secret in my ear. Meanwhile, the top of her hip skims my dick.

Pretty sure Logan wouldn't like this.

"Yeah? What's the idea?" I hope it has more to do with finding some spiked punch than the suggestion her bony pelvis is making against my cock. "Shoot."

She rocks herself back and forth over the sensitive area of my zipper. These aren't jeans. The fabric is thin, and her movement offers dangerous pleasure. I have a bad feeling about this... and it only gets worse.

"I'm ready to lose my virginity..." Her voice is almost husky, but nerves interlace her words. "...to you."

I can't help but let out a laugh. "Did you have a drink when you went to the bathroom?"

She rolls her eyes. "I wish." Her purple-lined emerald eyes glimmer. "Even if I did, I've been thinking about this for the past three years."

A strangled laugh escapes, sounding a little too flattered, and it falls down between us.

Joey slaps my chest, frisky as ever. It's hard to tell if she's serious or trying to get a rise out of me. She does that sometimes. The girl is going to be top-notch banter for a man some day. "Ashton, I'm leaving for college. I'm eighteen. You'll have graduated Golden Sierra when I get there in the fall, and I can't think of a better dick to open my legs for."

Holy hell... "You've definitely been drinking..."

She presses her tits into me. They're small but fiercely sharp. "You know I tried with you before tonight. You blew me off. And over the years, it became painfully clear, because I tried, and tried... that you won't date me. That

321

your bond with Logan is too important to risk. Or maybe you just aren't attracted to me?"

She pauses, waits for me to correct her, fishing like an angler.

She's attractive. Still all gangly limbs like a baby giraffe, but the high school boys are all over her. She knows she's pretty without me saying it. And I don't want to because the words would be taking part in this charade. This is absolutely absurd. Beyond it. How the hell did she sneak a drink without me knowing? I eye the crowd behind her suspiciously.

"Fine," she breaks the silence. "You don't like me. But I like you. And I know when I go off to college I'll start drinking and probably fuck some guy and do a walk of shame home and lose my virginity in a way that matters to nobody."

What the hell kind of statement is that? "Are you trying to guilt me into having sex with you? A one night-stand isn't your style, is it? You're not that stupid."

"One-night stands aren't stupid."

"No, but with drunk college boys, they're reckless." I think about her at Golden Sierra next semester without me and Logan to watch out for her. The frat boys, the jocks. I shudder imagining their greasy palms and drool all over this girl. She's hardly a delicate flower, but she deserves... more.

"I am reckless. Veeeery reckless. Don't underestimate what it's been like for me, especially since dad died. I've been under the thumb of my watchful mom and three protective brothers. Damn right if I'm going to get a fake ID and blow off some steam."

She wraps her hands around my back and even through my shirt; her fingernails scratch my skin. She digs in with them, strong and sensual. Aggressive. Assertive. Quite the tiger for a virgin.

This is ridiculous and has already gone too far. This is not going down well if Logan hears about it.

I put my hands on her arms to ease her away, then slide my palms down her skin to take her hands in mine. I don't even know if she's serious, but the conversation is off-limits. Even if she's kidding. Which she must be. "No. I'm flattered. But no."

"No?"

I bring my head down in one swift nod, like a gavel.

Her jaw goes slack. "You're playing hard to get? Are you seriously going to make me beg? You know I won't say anything to Logan. I wouldn't want him knowing either..."

Wait. Is she for real? "No. Not just for Lo. I'm saying no for me. You're like... family. I promised myself I'd look out for the Hunters like I look out for the Danes..."

Rejection smears down her face, leaving her normally round, sunny cheeks crestfallen. "Wow. You really don't like me." She says it more to herself than to me.

"Joey, I'm saying no because I *do* like you. You should find a guy that commits to you. An actual boyfriend. And..."

"You don't like me..." she repeats it, confronting some reality she never knew existed. Like she was holding on to a hope for us I never saw before. Her shoulders slump and her hands slide out of my palms.

"Joey..." I plead. I hurt her. Not that there was another option apart from no, but... I hate this. In all the years of knowing Jolie Hunter, I've never seen her this way. Eyes glassed over, glistening with the threat of tears.

The tip of her nose blushes. "This is... embarrassing. I thought you'd say yes." One of those hysterical laughs leaves her lips, but she sucks it back with a sharp breath. "I actually thought you'd say yes."

"Really?" As soon as the disbelief leaves my mouth, I regret it. She doesn't need to hear I haven't spent the past three years dreaming of this the way she has. It's a cruel reality I should have held back.

And it's the reality that finally releases a tear down her cheek. "Yes, Ashton. I thought you'd say yes."

My chest is tight. Flames crawl up my neck. I can't let her hurt like this. Over me? Convincing her this isn't real seems like the only thing that will help. "It's not right though... you don't mean it, Jo... you liking me is like, some... game..."

"Game?" She says it like it's the most offensive word in the English language.

But it's true. Her liking me is an age-old cliché. "Yeah, like, I'm the first guy you trusted in your life besides your dad and brothers and it's just natural to think you have feelings for me, but it's not real..."

Her gaze is equal parts fire and pain. She grits her teeth. "I know the different between fantasy and reality, Ashton."

"Hey..." I pull her head into my chest. I won't fight with her, but besides a hug, I don't know how else to fix this.

"Just..." she plants her hand on my chest and presses herself out of my embrace. "Just take me home. I don't want to be here anymore."

***

Jolie said little in the car on the way home. Her head rested against the glass of her window, her once strong, sure posture deflated in her dress. By the time I got her home, she slipped out of the car like a puddle. When her mom, Joy opened the door, she had open arms and a smile on her face. Jolie poured into her embrace. Her mom's expression quickly morphed. Her gaze shot down at me over Jolie's vulnerable, bare back, like something worse happened than did.

Then again, can anything worse happen than a broken heart?

I lie in bed for hours with her lively, sassy expression on my mind. The cute arch of her eyebrow when she said we didn't have to tell anyone. The brazen innocence in her crooked smile not having the first clue how losing her virginity to me would have caused bigger heartache than me saying no.

Though no is the final and only answer, but an ache to make her feel better rattles my bones. I've known Jolie Hunter since I was in elementary school. Joey followed me and Lo around like a shadow. Colt was always too mature for her. Dash, too aloof. So the little tomboy had us. Even knowing her all those years of skinned knees, a broken arm, bruised from puck after puck under goalie gear and layers of pillows... I never once saw her cry.

This is the worst fucking night of my life on so many levels.

After hours awake, I decide I can change the course of at least one thing.

I rush to get dressed and leave a note for my mom before sneaking out of the house. Half an hour later, I tread quietly up the Hunters' driveway, having left my car at the end and hoping like hell I don't wake their Shepards. Joy is alone now, and I don't want to scare her.

Jolie's cell was off, so throwing pebbles at her window is my only option. I throw, and throw, and wonder why my aim isn't better when I'm so good at putting a biscuit in the back of the net.

Tink.

Tink.

Tink.

Finally, the curtain peels aside, and a flash of long, golden hair mimics its motion.

"Joey!" I whisper shout. Thankfully, the bedroom next to hers is Logan's, and he's gone.

The sash slides up and Jolie's head pops out, her hair tumbles down like Rapunzel's into the cool mountain air. Her body is halfway out the window and she holds a dumbbell in her hand. "Ashton? What the hell?"

I can't help but ask. "Why are you holding a dumbbell?"

"In case you were an intruder or something."

I press my fingers into my eye sockets. *This girl.* "Come down."

She glances down at her pajamas. "Wait. Did you change your mind?"

It's a question full of hope which might have made me laugh, except I have to say, "No."

"Why are you here, then?"

"I can't leave you like this. I care about you. Come down. I leave tomorrow and I'm not going knowing I made you cry."

A sigh leaves her lips. "It's fine."

"Shut up with that. It's not fine. You were crying. Come down before your mom wakes up. Meet me on the bench."

She shakes her head and her hair dances in the midnight breeze. "Fine."

I snake myself around the house in the shadows to their backyard. It's a garden I know like my own. I spent as many hours here as Logan has at mine over the years, and there's only one bench. It sits in the middle of Joy's flower garden, a place that even I can appreciate.

I pad my feet along the stepping stones from the grass to

its middle where the bench is. Honeysuckle fills the air. Crickets sing and the trees blow with a rustling breeze that almost relaxes me. But then, the crunch of gravel rounds the bend of the house and there is Jolie, in her pajama pants and a winter coat wrapped around her body. It might be near summer, but the temperature drops here in the mountains.

She approaches with her arms wrapped protectively around herself. I tap the wood next to me and she sits. Words aren't my forte, but the best ones are typically simple. "I'm sorry. I can't do what you asked. It's not because you aren't pretty. You're the coolest girl I've ever met. I don't want you thinking you're not... worthy. You mean a lot to me, Joey. We're family."

"Stop saying that. We're not related." She hugs herself more tightly.

"No. But... I want to be your friend. Now and always. Doesn't that mean more than a fucked up night that confuses everything we know about each other?"

She considers my words while staring at the ground in front of her. She hasn't looked me in the face yet. A beat passes, but she's not ready to let it go. "It wouldn't confuse anything. It's just sex."

"You don't mean that. And it isn't just sex. What I do with girls at college is just sex."

She bumps into my side. "Ew. Dude. Come on. Are you here to make me feel better or worse?"

"See?"

"See what?" She finally raises her chin to gaze at me.

I tuck fallen hair behind her ear and caress my finger along her jaw. "You're jealous."

She rolls her eyes. "I'm not jealous."

"You are. And that's why it won't be just sex. It's more

than sex when two people care about each other. And I care about you."

She flops her head to the side and purses her lips. She's unsure.

"Hold out your pinky."

She narrows her eyes. "Why?"

"Just do it."

She holds out her tiny feminine finger, and I curl my own around hers. "I promise I'll always be your friend. You can count on me to help you. To protect you." I lean my forehead against hers. "Even though I know you don't need it."

She blows a laugh out of her nose and takes her forehead off mine, her round eyes haunting in the moonlight. God, I hope I make her feel better.

"Joey, I want to be your friend. I know it isn't what you asked tonight, but I promise it to you, anyway."

A smile tugs at the corner of her mouth. "I guess it's better than nothing."

I yank on her pinky. "Friendship isn't better than nothing. It's better than most things. Trust me. It's the basis for all things good in life. I'm offering you my best."

She lowers her eyes, but we still hold hands. Though I can't see her face well, her cheeks round the way I'm used to. "I bet you're not that good in bed, anyway."

I laugh. "Exactly. I'm terrible." I let go of her hand and wrap my arm around her, pulling her into me because it's cold out here and I don't want the chill reaching her.

She puts her head on my shoulder. "I'm still a little sad."

"Me, too," I say, thinking about my dad's tie drawer again. I squeeze her tight. "But when I pinky promise, it's ironclad. You need me, I'll come running. All you have to do is ask."

"Same."

I kiss the top of her head. "And I can't think of a better crazy ass woman to have on my side."

CHAPTER ONE
ASHTON

THIRTEEN YEARS LATER

I never thought it would be possible to consider moving back in to my childhood room at thirty-six a success story. But today, when I rolled my things into the biggest room with the smallest closet at Moon Ridge Ranch, it felt like a goddamn victory. And the first thing I wanted to do when officially back in Starlight Canyon was get some comfort food.

I walk through the door at CCs. Some things never change because the tinkle of the bell is just as welcoming and friendly as it's ever been. I missed that sound. And I missed what will follow. The simple pleasure of dessert and a strong brew to wash it down with.

And it doesn't even cost a fucking fortune either like it did in LA. Eyeing the drinks board, I remark on everything being normal people prices. And that's what I missed about home. Salt of the earth folks with nothing to prove. Just loving what they have. Being who they are.

Here, I can melt into the backdrop again. Sure, the women at the bars won't treat me like your average cowboy, even though in my mind, I still very much am. But there are enough Tom, Dick and Harrys that think I'm nothing special. To them, I'm just the Danes' kid. And that's plenty good enough for me. I sampled fame. I chewed on Hollywood attention. It doesn't taste as good as home.

Sitting down at a two top table, I take the laminated

menu with today's soup and sandwich specials in my hand, look at it but don't read it. I tap it on the counter.

The doorbell tinkles again, and I twist. *Not Logan yet.* I check my watch and it's five minutes past the time we agreed to meet, so he'll be another ten. I pull out my cell to check the news of my brother's pro-football team.

Sometimes it sucks our sports are on during the same season. But he's a star. A fucking superstar. He's getting good press as usual. I swipe over to a new screen to see how my fantasy football team is doing. Ah, crap. Can't start with Schafer this week, he's injured.

The restaurant door tinkles in the background.

Hansen has a bye week.

Tinkle.

Damn... my players are dropping like flies...

Tinkle.

I'm deep in thought over how to rearrange my team this week when a gust of cold autumn air puffs at me along with the scent of a woman. An earthy, natural perfume. Roses and... patchouli? What's that shit the hippie chicks wear? I've always hated heavy perfumes. All that artificial stuff isn't for me but this? It's an invasive, provocative breeze going past me and it perks my interest...

Keeping my head down, I dart my eyes up to see who the scent belongs to. I only catch her from the backside, and what a back side she has. Long, blonde hair reaches nearly the small of her back. Her spine curves in sensually and her round ass fills stretches her back pockets and Wrangler stamp. She's such a sinful sight. It feels like looking should be against the law. She has her long, lean pins stuffed into a pair of cowboy boots. This tasty combination of a horse riding cowgirl and the apple bottom of a pin-up model has my cock swelling in my jeans.

Who. Is. She? Seems I've been away from this small town long enough for some serious eye candy to move in. I keep my head low, with my gaze fastened to her ass so tightly it's going to hurt to pull it off.

Moving back to Starlight Canyon will not be good for my dating game. Not that I want it to be. Since splitting with my ex, I'm not ready for any level of commitment. And there won't be a lot of women in this town I don't already know. But maybe this peachy vixen is one of them... I shouldn't be thinking this. Getting involved with someone in Starlight Canyon right now, when I'm quite frankly still bitter, is probably a bad idea. The rumor mill will grind hard on it, and I've had enough of being featured on the front of tabloids.

The blonde bends down when she gets to the counter, leans on her elbows and chats with the barista. It's an innocent hello between two women that obviously know each other, but to me, it's like she's bent over to enhance my view. Her hips hitch upward invitingly, her ass spreads ever so slightly, every curve on full display. I imagine my hands hooking under in the cradle of those immaculate hips and hitching them upward...

"Can I help you?" A man's voice pinches me.

I nearly flinch. If I was a flincher, I would have. My eyes drag upward from a pair of well-used leather boots, trace dusty jeans and a henley up all the way to Dashiell Hunter's face. His expression is unmoving, but his eyes are expressive, darting from me to the ass I've been perving on and back again.

Shit. Has Dash actually gone and got a girlfriend? I've been ogling his woman?

I stand. "Fancy seeing you here."

"I was thinking the same," he offers his hand.

331

Maybe he didn't catch me staring.

He takes it in his grip, grasps me with the appropriate level of firm, nothing threatening in the pressure. But he shakes my hand slowly and stares at me bone deep, and I swallow hard, considering maybe he noticed my shady activity after all. That's the thing about Dash. He's hard to read and his gaze makes you feel very, very exposed.

Damn. Of all women to get my blood racing. Only had to fantasize about the ass that belongs to my brother from another mother.

"You're back for good now?" His voice is low and tempered.

"Yeah, I moved back in with the folks this morning until I find something. Divorce final. I'm nearly broke as I was the day I left this town."

"Mmm," Dash nods. He spins his head. "Hey Jolie. Look what the cat dragged in."

Joey is here? I glance around the tables. How did I miss her?

That's when, as if I'm watching a shampoo commercial, the long blonde locks fold over on themselves like golden satin. Like honey, it melts over a shoulder and the back I've been admiring...

I glance quickly at Dash to see if he's looking at the same woman I am.

He is.

My perfect peach stands, turns fully, and there, all grown up like a goddamn signet to a swan, is Jolie Hunter. I haven't been peeping at Dash's woman. I've been devouring his sister. It's been a mighty long time. Long enough for her to grow full, luscious breasts and a round ass that can fill out a pair of jeans like... well... a woman.

She's smiles and pushes some of that glossy hair behind her ear. "Ashton!"

She steps toward me, her hips sway and switch. Her swollen breasts, so full they must have taken every day of all these years to get like that, lead the way. "Sorry. I didn't notice you when I came in."

She holds out her arms for a hug. We've hugged before. Few times, but we have. Whenever it was my birthday and she came to the family party. When I graduated from high school. Prom night when I promised her I'd always be her friend.

I haven't been much of one of those over the years, and my body rages with a heat that tells me I don't want to be one now. Fuck. I'll cool down. I will. But when she smashes her tits into me, arms wrapped around me, giving me her signature bear hug, her breasts do not convince me this is the girl I left behind. And now, the sensual scent that had me groping her with my eyes in the first place, encircles me like some sort of spell. The fairy godmother has definitely paid her a visit.

I peel myself away from her breasts as soon as I can without being rude. "Joey..."

We stare at each other. Or maybe I stare at her. Smiles are plastered across our faces and I wonder if her toothy grin is full of as much surprise as mine is. Probably not. She follows hockey. And probably the odd tabloid or two. A sour taste lines my tongue, thinking of Jolie seeing me with Chloe in the news. I don't know why, but it does.

When did she become so goddamn beautiful? I saw pictures of her, too, over the years. The occasional tabloid quarter page of Jolie with her fuckwit ex. Josh Larose from the New York Vipers. Chloe would occasionally share tabloid news with me when Jolie and her ex were mentioned. But truth be told, Jolie always looked miserable in those photos. I figured the paps caught her on a bad day. Or in between smiles. There was nothing in those photos like the glow I see in front of me. And I certainly never noticed her hourglass figure.

I had no fucking clue.

The sound of her voice is as delighted and youthful as I remembered. It's full of warm energy. I anchor myself to that to stop my eyes from floating back down her body.

"Logan told me you only moved back to the Canyon in May." I say.

"Yeah," she punches my arm. "Thanks for never coming to see me."

"Sorry. I was busy having a stiletto shoved up my ass in LA."

"Sounds kinky," she says out of puffy, full lips. Were her lips like that before?

"I wish."

"It's been a long time," she shoves her hands in her back pockets and her tits push out into the space between us, stealing a bit of the oxygen.

I keep my eyes where they belong, but I have to work hard to avoid her tight nipples pebbled and highly alert under a thin, long-sleeved, scoop neck top. The chill in the air. That's all that is. Or maybe she's happy to see me, too. Goddamn, her cleavage taunts me.

"So," she rocks on her heels and her tits sway enticingly. "Is it good to be back in the Canyon? Or is it going to be too slow here for Hollywood's hockey boy?" She bats her eyelashes because she just made a cute little dig, but it feels like she's flirting with me.

She's not. I know she isn't. Thirteen years ago we agreed to being friends. This is just Jolie being, well, Jolie. Sassy.

Says whatever comes into her head. And why should she be friendly? We're... friends. Well, if that's what you can call two people who haven't seen each other in over a decade. Maybe more like family. Yes. Long-lost family.

Family. Cold showers. Chicken fertilizer. I think of all the things that have the opposite effect on my dick that her luscious frame does.

"Hollywood's hockey boy?" I chuckle lightly at her comment. If she only knew how much I craved for the simple life of the Canyon. So many times while out in California. "I know you are not accusing me of being a city boy, are you?"

"You've been called worse things," she teases.

"Not possible." I tilt my head. "Though some have been close."

Just then, a burly arm wraps around me, and Logan slides into the picture. "It's like a reunion in here." He points back and forth between Dash and Jolie. "You guys want to grab a table with us?"

"Too busy," Dash says. "Just grabbing a drink to take back to the stables."

"Me, too," Jolie says. "Leave you guys to it."

Logan and I take the table I bagged and sit. He grabs the menu to have a look at the specials. "Man, it feels good for us to all be back here." He reads and doesn't look at me when he asks, "Have you gone through the plays coach sent yet?"

I wouldn't remember a play right now if someone etched it onto my brain with a tattoo gun. All I can think about is how different Jolie looks. Different doesn't begin to describe it. "Nope. Not yet. I literally took in my shit from the movers at the ranch this morning and came here."

Logan puts the menu down. "Cool, we'll check out

plays over grub." He stands. "You having anything? I'll order for us."

"I was just waiting for you. Get me some of that carrot cake. And a black coffee."

"Got it. Be right back." Logan shuffles up to the counter and catches up on a word with Dash and Jolie. Well, Jolie really, since Dash doesn't talk much. I lower my eyes because I need to adjust before looking again. Reconciling Jolie's ass in my mind as one to firmly not think of sexually is going to take a second.

She's a stunner. I should have known she'd become one. Her mom was the MILF in high school.

I stare at my phone. When suddenly, crouched next to me, is a set of tits and a crease deep enough to suffocate a man. Jolie stares up at me, her green eyes sparkle. How did I never notice they were so damn alluring? How they're hooded and sexual and make her invitation seem like it's just for me?

"Hey, do you and Logan want to come out to Sly's sometime?" She loses her balance and puts her hand on my thigh to catch herself, but when she regains composure, she doesn't move it.

Logan sits back down across from me. I have to fight the red creeping into my neck at his sister's face being so close to my crotch. Especially with me thinking her lips are so damn pretty.

Logan repeats the offer. "You up for it, bro?"

"What?" My mind is numb with Jolie's hand still on my thigh, inches from my cock. You'd think I've never been touched before.

"Sly's."

"Oh, yeah. Course. Count me in."

Jolie taps my leg, this time feeling more friendly. She

336

stands and wiggles her pants back fully up over her curves. "See you later." She puts her hand on my shoulder. "It's really great to have you back."

She saunters away, hair shining like liquid gold, dripping right above that glorious ass of hers.

I put my attention back on Logan, and he has an eyebrow quirked. "You okay? You look all... I dunno... out of it."

There are a million easy excuses to use besides his sister. "Just been a lot getting everything here this morning. The storage company dropped everything at like five-thirty this morning. Guess they did an overnight drive from Cali."

"Ah, yeah, early starts are tough."

I change the subject. "Tougher when you drink too much."

"What? Coach is overreacting." Logan flaps his hand in the air and sits back, lacing his fingers behind his head. Life always looks so easy on him.

"Your drink ban officially ends in a month," I remind him.

"You wouldn't tell on little ol' me, will you? What harm could I do at Sly's?"

Logan finds mayhem wherever he goes. Usually, it's the harmless variety. Puck bunnies. Last call at clubs... But lately, he's been in Vegas more than usual and coach thinks he's getting tired on the ice. At our age, playing a good game means we can either be tired or hungover. Not both.

"You know I have your back," I reassure him. "But we don't have much time to win you a cup." I've already been part of a Stanley cup win in my years on the LA Cougars. But Logan hasn't.

My friend started his career off strong playing for some solid teams, but the Scorpions, being such a new team in

New Mexico, have struggled to get the talent. Logan and I were hopeful last season that the dream team being back together would send us to the finals, but we only reached the semis. And much as I hate to say it, I think my best friend could use a few more nights of sleep.

But it won't be starting at Sly's.

And if I can't erase Jolie Hunter's curves from my mind's eye, I won't be getting any either.

Acknowledgments

As usual I have an enormous amount of people to thank. More than I have room to put here. I'm a firm believer that a self-made person is rare.

To the one who helps me with EVERYTHING!

Char, you are a total rock as much as you are the dynamite that lights a fire underneath me. Your constant support and input has quickly become invaluable. Your PA skills are next to none and your friendship is irreplaceable! Thank you from the bottom of my heart.

For those who helped with this manuscript-

Thank you so much yet again to my work wife, Joanna. You re-assured me yet again that I basically get how to tell a story! And to Caroline Palmier, you have been epic to work with. Thanks for being so encouraging, reliable and a wonderful hype girl!

To my readers and all the incredible Bookstagrammers and Tiktokers-

Honestly, I'd never be able to have so many people read my stories if it weren't for you. You all shout from the rooftops and make me so grateful to be part of such a supportive community! I take every single DM, edit and email to heart and it keeps getting me up at five no matter how tired I am. I hope I can continue to give you the feels with my stories. You give me the feels with yours! There aren't enough heart hand emojis in the world.

About the Author

Sienna Judd is a small town, contemporary romance author who lives for all the spice. She thinks kitchens are for dancing, is a self-professed hype girl and might be known for talking too loudly.

Like every respectable woman she also loves drinking champagne and eating half of every chocolate in a truffles box.

Her spirit animal is a butterfly.